# TOMAHAWK

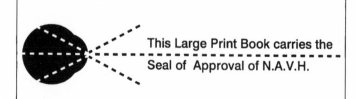

This Large Print Book carries the
Seal of Approval of N.A.V.H.

# TOMAHAWK

## DAVID POYER

**Thorndike Press • Thorndike, Maine**

Published in 1998 by arrangement with St. Martin's Press, Inc.

Thorndike Large Print® Americana Series.

The tree indicium is a trademark of Thorndike Press.

The text of this Large Print edition is unabridged.
Other aspects of the book may vary from the original edition.

Set in 16 pt. Plantin by Al Chase.

Printed in the United States on permanent paper.

**Library of Congress Cataloging in Publication Data**

Poyer, David.
  Tomahawk / David Poyer.
    p. cm.
    ISBN 0-7862-1457-0  (lg. print : hc : alk. paper)
    1. Large type books.  I. Title.
  PS3566.O978T66  1998b
  813'.54—DC21                                    98-14024

*Let this be dedicated to them both.*
*To those who forge the weapon,*
*Trusting in strength,*
*And those who renounce it,*
*Trusting in faith.*
*Those who lived through the time of trial*
   *warn us:*
*Better to have and not require*
*Than to grasp and find the scabbard empty.*
*But let us never cease to ask*
*If the time has come*
*When we no longer need the sword at all.*

# ACKNOWLEDGMENTS

*Ex nihilo nihil fit.* For this book, I owe thanks to James Allen, Roddie Alvar, Robert K. Anderson, Steve Baggarly, Lorrie and Tom Belke, Eric and Bobbie Berryman, Stan Bialas, Kenny Bryson, Randy Carrier, Horace Chamber, David C. Clink, T. Ray Colemon, Y. P. Cooper, Dave Daigle, Doug Geddes, Herb Gilliland, Vince Goodrich, Frank Green, Kay Hart, Scott and Kate Hedderich, Richard Hobbs, Robert Holsapple, Thomas Hudak, Tim Jenkins, Joshua Kendall, Robert W. Klementz, Walter M. Locke, Gary Moretti, Gail Nicula, Caroline Orr, Dave Peterson, Joseph Platt, Lenore Hart Poyer, Sally Richardson, Linda Roberts, Ken Roffler, Rich Romano, Rose Ann Shelton, Mardi Snow, Edward Speck, Robert Spiker, Paul Stillwell, K. J. Thomson, George F. A. Wagner, George Witte, Don Young, and others in the defense and peace communities who preferred anonymity. As always, all errors and deficiencies are my own.

A portion of this book that originally lay between what is now chapters 14 and 15, but that I cut from the final draft, was published in *Kalliope: A Journal of Women's Art*, Vol. XX, Number 1, as "A Stopover in Utah."

Rain, rain, and sun! a rainbow in the sky!
A young man will be wiser by and by
And old man's wit may wander ere he die.
    Rain, rain, and sun! a rainbow on the lea!
And truth is this to me, and that to thee,
And truth or clothed or naked let it be.
    Rain, sun, and rain! and the free blossom
        blows;
Sun, rain, and sun! and where is he who
        knows?
From the great deep to the great deep he goes.

— *The Coming of Arthur*, Tennyson

# Prologue
# Griffiss Air Force Base, Rome, New York

The perimeter fence was wire, veneered that morning, after weeks of subzero weather, with slick, clear ice that smoothed everything but the steel barbs.

The station wagon stopped not long after 3:00 A.M. When it pulled back onto the road again, taillights bleeding into the roaring darkness, it left two shadows crouched against that first barrier.

The wind buffeted them as they stood motionless in the knee-deep snow, peering around. The storm obliterated the hills. It wrapped a gauzy curtain around the perimeter floodlights. When they were satisfied they were alone, they lowered their heads. All around them, writhing and howling, the darkness seethed.

When they finished saying the prayer of abandonment, they hooked the figurines on the fence. The copper cutouts clattered as the wind caught their wings, rattling against the steel.

Then they pulled out the cutters.

The second fence, a few meters inside the

first, was higher and stouter, of hardened chain link. They bent again over the tool. One held the section to be cut. The other pumped the handles. The howl of the wind obliterated the clack as the jaws closed.

Beyond them, that same wind was stripping up long veils from the powder snow that blanketed the airfield. Red lights occulted above the tower. White and blue glowed deep in the storm. Occasionally, headlights wheeled near what might be terminal buildings, or hangars.

They didn't look up. They knew the layout of the base. They'd watched it for hours through binoculars. They'd eavesdropped with scanners till they knew the patrol schedule and the habits of each security team — when they stopped for coffee, how often they got out to check the fence, even some of their names. They had time, but not much. So they kept working, puffing out white clouds into the wind. It mixed their warm breath with icy snow and flung it all away into the night.

A three-foot-square section of the second fence fell away.

They dropped to the snow and wriggled through, the larger shadow first, then the smaller.

The third fence was chain link, too, but this time with an insulated wire knitted into it. There was no way to get through without breaking the white wire. The lead figure hesitated, fingering it in the darkness. A flashlight probed, shielded with a mitten. Then the cutters went to work again.

When they stood again on the far side, flat open space stretched away. The tarmac had been plowed the day before, but inches of drift had covered it again. Above that to a height of three or four feet, the snow seethed restlessly. They plodded forward, heads bent.

Slowly, the great shapes grew, until they could make out the immense down-slanted dihedral of wings, the underslung pods of engines, the long, straight lines of fuselages.

Headlights dawned on the far side, sending snow-blurred shadows fleeing across polished aluminum. They hurried their steps, reaching into their coats. A moment later, they were beneath the wings.

The slam and clatter of metal on metal was faint at first, muffled by the storm. But it kept on, now growing louder.

The headlights swept past, dwindling down the runway. Then they dipped as the vehicle carrying them braked suddenly.

They swung back, probing toward the undercarriage of the bomber.

When the security force's truck slid to a halt in a flurry of snow and its doors flew open, the two intruders dropped their arms from a pyloned cylinder. Guards tumbled out of the vehicle. Their mouths made black *O*'s in the white howl of the storm. Cartridges

11

snicked into rifle chambers.

The headlights showed a dark red patch on the snow. They pinned the man and woman under the plane like animals on a highway. The two backed away, letting go of their hammers, which vanished instantly under the driven whiteness.

"Raise your hands. Now!" a sergeant shouted.

Instead, the intruders reached into a tote bag. The guards' rifles leveled.

A banner unrolled from gloved hands, whipping out into the wind. In the glare of the headlights, it read NOT BY MIGHT, NOR BY POWER, BUT BY MY SPIRIT.

The sergeant of the guard hesitated, then lowered his pistol. The Jeep's radio crackled. He reached in and seized the handset.

"They're peace activists," he said. "Yeah . . . call the ready maintenance people. They've been hammering on one of the fuel tanks."

A question. "No. Not armed. . . . Yes, sir, threw some blood or something. . . . Right. Search 'em, cuff 'em, and bring 'em in. You got it. Better call the officer of the day. And scramble the on-call squad. Might be more of them out there."

A few hours later, in the cold white light of dawn, a security policeman approached the first break in the wire. He stopped several feet

12

off, lifted a camera, and began taking photographs: the tire marks leading off the perimeter road; the scuffle of tracks, still faintly visible, the bent-back, snipped-off steel barbs. Then blinked at what hung above the gap in the fence, swaying and dancing in the cold raw wind.

"What the hell's that?" said another, behind him. "Don't touch it. Don't take a risk, man."

"I don't think we need to worry," said the photographer. He aimed the camera again, framing them carefully in the viewfinder, and snapped off three shots from different angles as they hung there. Then he stood back as another man flipped open an evidence bag.

Carefully, holding them by the tips of their wings, they detached the handmade copper angels from the wire and dropped them into the black nylon sack.

# I

# THE PROGRAM

# 1

Slowing for the exit off 395, Lcdr. Daniel V. Lenson, U.S. Navy, squinted into a sparkle like the sunlit sea. It came from ten thousand parked cars, surrounding the five-sided building like breaking surf around a high island.

Lenson had gray eyes and sandy hair. The top ribbon on his short-sleeved whites was the blue and red on a white field of the Silver Star. Above that was the ship and wave insignia which meant Surface Line. The oldest, the proudest, but in some ways the least forgiving community in the Navy.

When a horn blared behind him, he snapped his attention back to the off-ramp. Eight A.M., and the summer air was already hot. He cranked his window shut and turned the air conditioning on full.

Today, he was starting his first tour of shore duty. No more six-month deployments. No more in-port duty sections. Time to relax, start postgraduate work, have his daughter visit — in short, get a life after four stressful at-sea tours.

Parking was horrendous. He searched for half an hour before he found a space out in the wasteland. At the south entrance, lines of buses idled, waiting to discharge passengers. A jet roared overhead, taking off from National Airport. A handful of demonstrators stood holding signs, the arriving mass dividing to stream in around them.

He remembered all at once, as if he'd blocked it out till now, the last time he'd been here. The court of inquiry. He'd been so doped up, he didn't recall it well. Just hour after hour sitting in the anteroom, waiting to testify. Seeing a man in the cafeteria he'd known was dead. He still didn't have an explanation for that. Then those iron minutes facing four admirals across a green baize table, while he spoke the words that had cauterized his pain but crippled his career.

A lot had changed since then. Susan was gone, and their daughter, Nan, with her. Bringing *Barrett* back from Cuba outweighed the fitness report Ike Sundstrom had nailed him with after the Syrian incursion. But with nine years in, he had to decide soon whether he was going to get out, try something else, or go for a full twenty. Before it was too late to start over.

He took a deep breath. Turning from the rising sun, he joined the throng of uniforms and suits and dresses heading up a long stairway. A moment later, he was lost in the hurrying crowd.

Off the main corridors, the Pentagon became narrow 1940s-tacky passageways ceilinged with rusty air ducts and dripping pipes

18

and sagging cable runs. He wiped sweat off his forehead as he compared room numbers with his orders. When a second knock brought no response, he let himself in.

A tiny front-desk area held an enlisted man and a computer. A daisy-wheel printer clattered. Dividers of frosted glass hived minuscule offices.

"Lenson, Lenson," the petty officer muttered. He stared at the orders, then turned them over, as if they might have something on the back.

"Actually, I'm not due for a couple days yet, but I thought I'd start getting checked in."

"Been to Navy Annex yet? Up on the Hill. They're gonna want to see you about your medical records, service records." The second-class looked at the front of the orders again.

"Something wrong?" Dan asked him. "This is Deputy Chief of Naval Operations, Surface, right?"

"Oh yeah. But I didn't get any — let me make a call, all right? You want to sit over there, there's a paper you can look at."

He lost himself in *Navy Times*, a discussion of the bloody stalemate in the Iran-Iraq war. Then flipped to an article about the six-hundred-ship fleet. Congress was wavering in their support of the buildup, now that they'd seen the price tag.

"Commander?"

He looked up, then rose. The other officer didn't introduce himself. Instead, he said, fanning himself with Dan's orders, "There's some kind of glitch here, uh, Lenson. I remember talking to the detailer about you, but my confused and vague impression was that you dropped out early in the selection process. Trouble is, we got a body already reported in to this billet."

"Gee," said Dan. He honestly couldn't think of anything else to say.

"Look, you're early. May be a perturbation in the system — it just hasn't caught up to you yet. You can hang your hat here till you get things straightened out. Or you could check this all out with your detailer."

Dan grabbed his hat. "That sounds like the best thing to do, sir. I'll run up and see him, then get back to you."

An hour later, he stuck his head into Alan Sonders's cubicle at the Navy Annex. Sonders was bald, and old for his rank. Scribbled-on printouts hung from the wall by dull silvery duct tape. Charlie Brown scowled down from a cartoon that had been photocopied too many times. The caption read "God put me on earth to accomplish a certain number of things. Right now, I am so far behind, I will never die." The detailer greeted him with a millisecond handshake and pushed more printouts off a chair. "Nice to meet you in person," Dan said.

"Yeah, see? We don't really have forked tongues and gill slits." The phone rang; Sonders said, "Excuse me," and started talking. When he hung up, it rang again. He looked around. "Hat," he said, pointing. Dan handed it to him. "Lunch?"

"Sure." He wasn't hungry, but it looked like the only way they were going to get to talk.

They ate "lunch" standing up at machines in the basement. Sonders got a cherry pie sealed under a solid white rime of sugar. Dan settled for coffee.

"Okay, what can I do for you today?"

He refreshed Sonders's memory: that he was coming off a *Kidd*-class destroyer out of Charleston. That he'd sold Dan on the job over the phone. Eight to five, he could see how the Pentagon worked, then go to school in the evenings. And there were three women to every single guy in D.C. "The orders came through. They look kosher. But when I go over there, there's somebody else in the billet."

"Yeah, one of our new female-type ship drivers. Off *White Plains*."

"So where am I going?"

"Well, you're still gonna be in D.C. So your personal arrangements are not going to be any different." Sonders sharked half the pie. He mumbled around it, "Ever hear of an outfit

21

called JPM-Three?"

"No."

"Know an Evans? Scott Evans?"

"I don't think so."

"How about Barry Niles?"

Dan said slowly, "I knew a Commodore Niles."

"Rear admiral now. Here's what happened. You were headed for OP-Oh three, like we discussed. Then I got a call from this Evans. Colonel, Air Force, apparently the number two over there. Niles just got tapped to take over as director. He wants bodies, line types strong in engineering and engineering duty officers. I read them a list and you got the nod. They have a Brickbat, so there wasn't a lot I could do. I tried to call you in Charleston, but —"

"Okay, I got most of that, but what's a Brickbat?"

"Systems acquisition talk for highest national priority. Sure you don't want one of these pies? They got apple, peach, cherry —"

"No thanks. What's JPM stand for?"

"Joint Project Management Office."

"What exactly does that mean?"

"I'm getting blank tape on the specifics, but I know it's something with missiles. You an 'up round' on missiles?"

"I was weapons officer on Barrett. We had Standard and Harpoon. And a lot of bugs, too."

"Then maybe it's a good match. It's in Crystal City, south of the Pentagon. I'll call over, find out where they want you to report in."

"So you're saying I'm shanghaied."

"A strong word, but not inappropriate."

Dan didn't have a good feeling. The few times he'd seen Niles — Commander, Destroyer Squadron Six then — he hadn't come away with the warm fuzzies. "Does this happen often? Getting jerked around like this?"

"Not *often*, but it happens."

"Good sign? Bad sign?"

Sonders looked back toward the elevator and swallowed the last bit of pastry. "Can't say for sure; I don't sit on the boards. But truth be told, it could be stellar, getting handpicked by a flag officer." He licked his fingers. "Give you one piece of advice. It's nice to be early, but once you show your face, you don't want to disappear again. Where you staying?"

"I just got in. Figured I'd go over to Anacostia, stay at the Q tonight."

"I'd get myself a place first, get settled. That way, you can hit the ground running." Sonders crumpled the wrapping and sighed. "Gotta get back. Want that point of contact?"

"Yeah, thanks, then I'll get off your desk."

He followed Sonders back to his office, fighting a growing anger and apprehension.

# 2

The detailer's advice about getting a place to live before he reported in sounded reasonable. He got a *Post* at the BOQ and spread it and his map out on the bed. He'd be working at Crystal City, north of Alexandria, and going to George Washington University. A place near the subway would mean he wouldn't have to drive to work.

He found an apartment in a six-story brick tower — a ten-minute walk from the Courthouse Metro stop — then drove across the river into Georgetown for dinner. He couldn't take his eyes off the women. Some carried briefcases, others shoulder totes; a few younger ones, students probably, wore backpacks. There were blondes and redheads, Asians who reminded him of Susan, Ethiopians, Koreans, poised New Englanders with good bone structure. Their glances slid past as if he were invisible.

He spent his first night in the apartment in his sleeping bag, drinking himself to sleep with a bottle of scotch.

The next morning, he stood holding an empty briefcase as the escalator sped him rapidly down into the earth.

Above him, the new buildings of Arlington

rose till they were eclipsed by curved concrete. The sky contracted to a blue oval. And still steel hummed underfoot, bearing him and hundreds of others steadily into the depths. He remembered the London Underground, pictures of people huddled in it during the Blitz.

This one was new, pristine concrete, shining terra-cotta tile. A knot of foreigners and tourists stood baffled before the electronic ticket machines. He had to take an orange train, then transfer at Rosslyn to the blue line; past Arlington Cemetery, Pentagon, Pentagon City, and off at the Crystal City exit. He paced back and forth along the platform until brightening and dimming lights signaled him to stand back.

The car was white, the color of the future. It accelerated in near silence. Lights whipped past, occulting subterranean black. The other passengers read or stared into space. A woman knitted. Not one paid any attention to this wonder. He'd ridden subways in Paris, Rome, and Boston, but this felt futuristic. Then he realized: This *was* the future. He'd wondered, when he was a kid, what it would be like.

The escalator extruded him not into daylight but into another slice of the future: a subterranean shopping mall. He navigated through spotless tiled hallways, like the pas-

25

sageways of sunken ships, flooded not with water but with fluorescent light.

When he emerged at last, the sky was eclipsed by fog. He wondered where Rickover's office was. He had to be around here somewhere, the gnomelike legend who had built this place from nothing.

National Center One was twelve stories high, with a gray concrete-slab exterior and vertical slits for windows. He showed his ID to a sentry and joined a line of uniforms and sport jackets in front of the elevators.

When the doors hissed open, he followed the tide to a gray metal security door. Two Air Force officers stepped around him. One inserted a card into a slot. The lock thought it over, then clicked open. The other man looked at Dan. "Forget your card?"

"Don't have one yet. Reporting in. Is this JPM-Three?"

"Yeah — better known as Joint Cruise Missiles." The major waved him through. "I'll take him to Shirley," he told his companion. To Dan, he said, "This way."

He followed, down a narrow corridor carpeted with orange so bright, he squinted involuntarily. Walls and carpet were new, but boxes of cans and trash, cable assemblies, and stacks of used computer paper lined the hallway. The effect was odd, as if the future didn't have anybody to pick up the trash or vacuum the carpets.

★ ★ ★

He was relieved to have the security officer say she was expecting him. Ms. Shirley Toya sat him against the wall, took his picture, and told him the ground rules while they waited for it to develop. He had to wear his pass at all times, and turn anyone in he met without one. Window blinds stayed closed. No cameras or tape recorders were allowed into the building. Any suspicious contacts from outsiders had to be reported. No gifts over a value of five dollars could be accepted from contractors. She handed him the badge. His face stared back from under wavy plastic.

"You'll be working for Captain Westerhouse, on the eleventh floor. Here's your key card. We change the combination the tenth of each month. Any questions? . . . Then I'll take you down. Maybe stop a couple of places on the way, get you introduced."

He glanced into offices as they passed. Men at desks, civilians, Air Force, Navy. Not many women, except for secretaries. Pictures of jet aircraft and missiles lined the walls. Soft music played. Aside from that, the hushed hum of the air conditioning, and the ripping tap of an electric typewriter, the place was quiet. The Venetian blinds were down, and tilted so you couldn't see the buildings opposite.

"Just a minute. Let me tell Carol you're here," she said, and ducked into a door marked DIRECTOR. A moment later, she

27

popped out again. "Admiral Kristofferson's free at the moment. You can go right in."

Kristofferson? He'd expected Niles. He straightened, sucking in a breath.

The director's office was sparely furnished. Dan was about to sound off, but the other was already standing, extending his hand. Kristofferson was stocky and graying, with a touch of bulldog about the face. Looking at Dan somewhere about the level of his chest, he said in a surprisingly soft voice, "Lieutenant Commander Nelson?"

"Lenson, sir. Dan Lenson."

"Lenson, nice to see you. I was just heading out the door, but let me welcome you aboard."

"Glad to be here, sir."

"I understand this assignment's a surprise for you."

"Yes, sir, thought I was going over to OP-NAV."

"You might find this more challenging technically. More risky career wise, too." Kristofferson smiled, but it didn't last more than a quarter second.

Dan mumbled something, not sure how he should respond to that. The admiral snagged his cap off a stand. "Sorry. Things on my mind. . . . Anyway, we're a joint office, about thirty percent Air Force at the moment, the rest Navy and civilian. You'll work for Dale Westerhouse, PMA for surface ship systems,

28

replacing one of the surface IOs."

He was making a mental note to ask somebody later what PMAs and IOs were when Kristofferson added, in a musing tone, "Every once in awhile, everything has to change. But every revolution devours its fathers."

"Sir?"

The admiral snapped back into focus. "Sorry . . . Have you met Colonel Evans yet? Shirley, you might want to take him in to see Bucky." Kristofferson shook his hand again, grip firm and dry. He bent over his secretary's shoulder for a moment, then headed down the corridor.

The deputy's office was next to the director's. Dan didn't know how formal he was supposed to be, so he took three steps in and came to attention. "Lieutenant Commander Lenson, sir."

"Oh, yeah. Our new hire. Come on in, have a seat."

Col. Scott Evans was slim and sharp-looking, and the slate blue Air Force uniform matched his eyes. He had an easy grin, a firm grip from a small, strong hand, and a faint western twang. A pipe sent up a contrail from a silver tray. He pointed Dan to a leather settee, where he looked up at pictures of F-105s.

"Flew Thuds in Vietnam," said the colonel, following his gaze. He clamped the pipe between his teeth and leaned back again, adding to the haze below the ceiling. "Not the best of times, but I miss 'em sometimes. This job's the farthest from a cockpit I've ever gotten."

"Is that so, sir?"

"Uh-huh. I'm an Air Force brat. My dad flew the B-twenty-nine, B-thirty-six. He was the first guy to get a thousand hours in the B-forty-seven. I grew up on the tour. Carswell, Fort Worth, Little Rock, Omaha. Well, tell me about yourself. That an Academy ring?"

"Yes, sir. Spent most of my time in destroyers. This is my first shore tour."

"Navy family?"

"No, sir."

"You're one of Admiral Niles's boys, aren't you? He doesn't say much, but he said something about knowing you, when we went over the list of available personnel. Must have been favorable if he wanted you in here."

"I served under him before, sir, but I don't really know him."

"Don't be apologetic about it. That's one of the paths to the top in our business. Find a boss who rewards loyalty and competence, stay on his wing and match his climb rate." Evans relit the pipe from a silver lighter shaped like a MiG. "Well, you know basically what we do here, right?"

"I've read about cruise missiles, sir. But I can't say I know a lot about them."

"This is the place to learn. Captain Wester-house will brief you in on the specifics of your job. Anything I can help you with, my door's always open. And thanks for stopping in."

The eleventh floor was even more unkempt and littered. Coke cans built an unstable pyramid in a steel wastebasket. The carpet was the same orange as on the floor above, only dingier. Progress charts and photographs of explosions hung slightly askew on the walls. But there were pictures of ships, too. He felt a little more at home.

A dark-haired captain with a crew cut, wearing rumpled, well-traveled whites, sat in a corner office with the blinds wide open, listening to a cassette recorder. He shut it off when Dan knocked at the open door. When Dan introduced himself, he said, "Lenson? Good, good. Expecting you."

When he stood slowly to shake hands, Westerhouse was nearly as tall as Dan, but much more heavily built. He looked tired. He seemed pleased to hear Dan already had an apartment. "You want to check in with the personnel support activity with your records. Need a physical, go to Navy Annex. There's a uniform shop there, too. Navy wears salt-and-pepper in the summer and service dress blue in the winter. No khakis except on travel. Let's see, we had a summary of your record here someplace. Small boys, right?"

"Right, sir. Destroyers and frigates. Department head tour on *Barrett*, DDG-nine ninety-eight. A *Kidd*, what they call the *Khomeini*-class."

"Engineering duty, myself. What's your degree?"

"Naval engineering. Annapolis."

"I meant postgrad. System engineering? Aero? Ops analysis?"

"I'm going to get that while I'm here."

Westerhouse looked doubtful. "You're going to be traveling a lot, so that won't be easy. This is a demanding billet, Dan. But it's vital to the Navy's future. I'll level with you — I'm enthusiastic about this thing."

"What exactly will I be doing, sir? The admiral — Kristofferson — said I was going to be an IO."

"Yeah, integration officer. You'd better get familiar with these."

Westerhouse handed him a folder of directives from the Secretary of Defense, the Undersecretary of Defense for Research and Engineering, and the Chief of Naval Material. Then he segued into what he expected to happen over the next year. Dan was trying to get some of it down in his wheelbook when Westerhouse said, "The arms-control folks, of course, aren't as gung ho about this as we are. Especially the TLAM-N version."

"That's which missile, sir?"

"Tomahawk land attack missile, nuclear."

32

Dan stopped writing. "Nuclear, sir? I thought this had a high-explosive warhead."

"You need to read yourself in. There are several versions of the missile being developed. . . . Is something wrong?"

Dan sat silent. He hadn't realized he was expected to work on a nuclear system. But did it make a difference? They just made a bigger bang — that and the radioactivity, but it blew away over water. . . . But Westerhouse had said *land* attack, not antiship. . . .

"Something the matter?"

He tried to shake it off, avoiding his boss's eye while he tried to figure out what was bothering him. He cleared his throat and recrossed his legs. The longer he stalled, the worse it got.

He was remembering a morning aboard USS *Independence*, during his midshipman cruise. A white oval being pyloned to the belly of an A-4. The carrier had been steaming downwind, making everything hot and airless and totally still, carrying swirls of stack gas along with her that made your eyes run like tear gas. The marines in a silent ring, weapons aimed outward. He'd come out of the island and stopped, staring, feeling it like every other man on deck. That here was the focus of some awesome power —

"Mister *Lenson*. I said do you have a problem with that?"

Dan shook his head, and just like that, it

33

was over; the moment was past. Westerhouse rattled the blinds down and swung open a wall cabinet. Inside was a dry-erase white board covered with progress schedules and financial charts. "Okay, like I said, you'll be the IO for the surface ship program. You'll bird-dog equipment development and observe flight tests. You'll go to progress conferences, honcho troubleshooting, do liaison — whatever the job takes."

He talked a bit more about the test phase and flight schedule, then looked directly at Dan. "I know this is a little overwhelming at first, so I'll stop there. At least till you can get through that reading material. One word of warning, though.

"There are those who'll tell you this program's in trouble. Take what they say with a grain of salt. A positive angle of attack is what keeps you in the air. You've picked that up in the fleet, right? Or you wouldn't be here with us now."

He didn't bother to think that one over. "Yes, sir."

"*O*-kay," said Westerhouse. "Come on, I'll take you down to your space."

They passed another combo-locked door, a vault within an area secured for secret. He guessed crypto, or secure pubs. The captain stopped at 11W50. The partitions were translucent plastic and beige steel anchored to the by-now-familiar orange carpet.

Inside one of the eight-by-eight cubes, a commander sat with his face in his hands. In an open briefcase were a lunch bag, a paperback novel, and a collection of the flotsam that accumulates on desks: a clock, photographs, a ceramic pencil holder in the shape of a Labrador retriever. Several cigar boxes were closed with masking tape.

"Newt," said Westerhouse. "Your relief's here. Want to lay a couple groups on Mr. Lenson before you depart?"

The officer uncovered his face. A second later, they were shaking hands. "Grab a chair from around the corner," he said. "I'm Newt Munford."

"You gonna make it to the lunch?" Westerhouse asked. Munford shook his head. The captain stood by the partition for a moment. Then he left.

"Sit down, sit down. Dale said your name, but I forgot it."

"Lenson. Dan Lenson."

"Okay, here's the short squirt. You're now at Joint Cruise Missiles, JPM-Three. And unless I'm way off base, you thought till half an hour ago you were assigned someplace else. What do you know about cruise missiles?"

"Read about them. Like a plane without a pilot."

Munford told him the first practical cruise had been German. He opened one of the cigar boxes. A meticulously assembled and painted miniature aircraft nestled in cotton wool. Dan picked it up gingerly, a tapered green fuselage with a stovepipe on its back.

"They didn't work that great, as I recall."

"Well, they were totally inaccurate. The only thing the V-one could hit was a city, and even then, not always. Since they had to fly straight and high, fighters and ack-ack knocked a lot of them down en route. But we still had to put out three bucks in counter-measures for every dollar Hitler spent building them."

Munford put the model back into the box and opened another. He told Dan both the Army and Navy had copied the V-1. After the war, the Air Force developed Snark, Navaho, and Matador; the Navy worked on Gorgon, Pollux, Regulus, Rigel, and Triton. But costs kept escalating, and schedules slipped. "The only one we actually deployed was Regulus. But the air boys fought it all the way, and when we got Polaris, Kennedy finally can-celed all cruise work. Elmo Zumwalt called it the worst technical decision the Navy ever made."

"Because the Russians were still developing them."

"Right. Then the *Elath* got sunk in the Arab-Israeli war and we suddenly realized the goddamn things worked. Plus, think about land attack a minute. We do that mission with planes and pilots now. But what if you could fight a war without worrying about POWs? Or if instead of having to fight at all, you just locate your dictator, pop off a couple missiles at his palace, end of problem?"

"How about the nuclear bird?"

"That's a different kettle. I think Kissinger figured it as a bargaining chip for the arms-limitation talks. But then somebody realized it wasn't that expensive, as strategic weapons go. Maybe twenty-five million a pop, including the warhead." Munford took the last model out, a slim cigar tube with straight-razor wings. "We call it Tomahawk, but the Air Force prefers to call it the AGM-one oh nine. They hate to admit they're gonna get another Navy missile rammed up their bomb bays, like Sidewinder and Sparrow. That's just a small part of the tension around here."

Dan hitched his chair up, sensing the presence of straight skinny.

"Anyway, Colin Kristofferson —"

"Admiral Kristofferson? I just met him."

"He started it, as a flying torpedo called STAWS. That's why it's so small, had to fit in a torpedo tube. He got it going with leftover funds from Harpoon, a submariner who lost his sub, and a pork-chop lieutenant commander. Along the way, the concept's grown."

"How'd the Air Force get involved?"

"A long story, but the short answer's James

37

Earl Carter. They had their own cruise program, but they really wanted a new bomber. But Jimmy scrubbed the B-one and ordered cruises for B-fifty-twos instead. The Boeing missile started crashing, and finally Congress told them to join our program instead.

"See, right now there're actually five missiles being developed here. Four are versions of Tomahawk. The Navy owns the basic airframe and all three versions of the sea-launched missiles. The Air Force has the GLCM and the ALCM." He pronounced them *glick-em* and *al-cum*. "The GLCM's a nuclear Tomahawk on a truck, for ground launch. That's the one the Greens are protesting in Germany. The ALCM's the Boeing missile again; Reagan brought it back from the dead."

"What's our part of the pie?"

For answer, Munford pointed to the bulkhead. Dan examined a photo of a huge gray mass, guns blazing out smoke and fire. "A battleship?"

"*New Jersey*. We're putting the four Iowa-class battlewagons back into commission as cruise-missile carriers. That'll be your bailiwick. Vic Burdette, around the corner, works the destroyers and cruisers, and there's another office does the subs and so forth. You guys oversee the contractors, make sure everything works, make sure it's supportable — repair parts, training, documentation. But the battleships are what everybody's hair's on fire about. I hear Niles is getting briefed in now by SecNav's people."

"Why's the battleship such high priority?"

"Because the Secretary of the Navy went on record, saying he was going to get it done in fifteen months for under three hundred and twenty-six million dollars. Clear?"

"Yeah, I guess that answers that question."

"You're gonna be spending a lot of time in airplanes. Long Beach, St. Louis, San Diego, Point Mugu, Dayton. Know anything about software development?"

"Some. Did some troubleshooting on *Barrett*."

"I heard of it. The robot ship. Ever get it working?"

"Actually, we did. Uh, am I getting a message this program's hitting rough seas?"

Munford handed him a copy of *Aviation Week and Space Technology*, opened to the headline FLAWS RESURFACE IN JOINT CRUISE PROGRAM. "I don't know how they do it, but you can't let a stinky fart around this building and not read about it in the trade press the next day."

The article, by a Martin W. Tallinger, said that the latest flight-test failures showed serious shortcomings in Tomahawk. Its guidance was behind schedule. The radar altimeter was so electronically noisy, an enemy could hear it coming thirty miles away. The booster didn't separate after launch, making the missile crash, and the program was millions of dollars over budget.

"Holy smoke."

"Yeah, it keeps digging holes in Southern California. We're not sure if it's a design fluke or sloppy manufacturing. But the bird's not your main focus. What you need to get smart on fast are three things: the launcher, the launch control system, and the ship integration.

"On the launcher, Lehman wants initial operational capability by next June, and we don't even have a contractor picked to build the thing. We haven't been able to run the LCS software for more than four minutes. On the ship-to-launcher interface, we've got power-supply problems, voltage fluctuations, and topside weight's twenty percent over spec." Munford smiled grimly. "Aside from that, you got a terrific system."

"How about this schedule slippage?"

"You'll hear certain sources say that's why Kristofferson got fired. But I don't think that's the whole story. We were actually pretty close to our timetable before they dumped the battlewagon job on us. Eleven years with the program — and he got one day's notice before they released it to the press. A certain three-star changed two of our hits into failures, then passed the word to the new CNO that the program was in the tank and he better get the coop cleaned out before all the chickens died."

"An admiral?"

"Not a fucking admiral, a fucking *vice* fucking admiral. Another piece of hot scuttlebutt is, Kristofferson wanted to second-source the missile, get two companies building it, but instead, he got a contract put out on *him*. The official reason is that we're transitioning from design into production, but it looks more like bureaucratic assassination to me."

Dan nodded slowly. Different explanations from different quarters, but the bottom line was the same. "And now it's Niles's turn."

"Yeah. Anyway, back to the battleships. We telescoped the development and operational testing to speed things up, but it isn't working out. So maybe it's just as good I'm leaving, 'cause I figure all hell's gonna break around here."

"Exactly how sick is this program? Could it be canceled?"

"It's happened before. All I have to say is, watch out for the Air Force. And the naval aviators — they'd love to see us screw the pooch." Munford grinned unpleasantly. "There's a lot going on behind the scenes. This missile scares certain people. Most of the guys were pretty motivated. But watching them nail Kristy to the cross hasn't helped morale."

Dan thought that over while Munford fin-

41

ished cleaning out his desk. "Here's the combo to the safe," he said, writing it down on a "While You Were Out" form.

"So, where are you headed?"

"Material Command. Special projects."

"Sounds impressive."

"Does it? I wasn't due to rotate till next year." Munford put the last model into his briefcase and snapped it closed. "Niles paid us a surprise visit last week. Interviewed everybody, one at a time. I didn't make the cut." He hoisted the case, and the handle broke. "This *is* my day," he muttered. "So. I'll give you a call when I get over there, give you my number. In case you need advice from a failure."

"Look, I'm sorry —"

"Not your fault. The moving finger fucks, and, having fucked, moves on." Munford looked around the cubicle. His lips tightened to a bitter line. "Good luck," he said. And then he was gone.

Dan looked at Munford's empty seat. After a moment, he moved over to it. The hard plastic was still warm.

Now he understood the hush in the offices, the distracted looks, Kristofferson's strange behavior. Munford could kiss his career goodbye, being relieved in midtour.

And it could happen to him.

# 3

He sat hunched in a second-floor room above I Street, flipping through his books as other students drifted in, settling like wary seagulls equidistant from one another.

The first night of class. Against his desk, a bag bulged with publications from the Congressional Research Service, as well as the Secretary of Defense's annual budget report, textbooks, a programmable calculator. He leafed through the reading list. Then, instead of starting on some of it, sat worrying about his new assignment.

He'd thought of shore duty as a chance to relax. Instead, he'd have to flat-out sprint just to catch up. His part of the project was behind schedule, with glitches in everything from software to where the bolts went through the deck.

A model-thin blonde in a mint green blouse, pretty and aware of it, came in, scanned the room, then left. He watched the door till she returned. When he caught her eye, she half-smiled, then took a seat in the front row.

On the other hand, Niles had picked him from the list. Did that mean his career was breaking out of the doldrums? Out of the slide induced by the disaster on *Reynolds Ryan* and his clash with Ike Sundstrom in the Med?

Several geeky guys came in wearing loose shirts and torn jeans. They sat together in back, talking and laughing. A carrot-topped woman arrived with a Lake Placid backpack over her shoulder.

But did he want another balls-to-the-wall assignment? He'd looked forward to shore duty to make some kind of rational decision about his career. So far, only the shortage of midgrade officers staying in after Vietnam had kept him promotable. But that wouldn't be true forever. He was coming up on his executive officer boards. The cut was rough, almost half —

"Is this seat taken?"

He glanced up. "No."

"I'm Zhou Xumei. They call me Mei."

He told her his name. She nodded soberly, laying her books out across her desktop.

At twenty to eight, a darkly handsome ponytailed man in a long black leather coat swung through the door and threw his briefcase onto the desk. The blonde immediately got up and began showing him some sort of thesis or report. Dan watched her lean toward the professor, watched him examining her instead of the pages.

The stripped-off coat revealed a tweed jacket and knit tie. A quick roll call, and Dr. Edward Szerenci took command of the classroom. His voice was clipped, the accent faintly

Eastern European.

"This is a course on methodology. Methodology is how we analyze a problem. Graduates from this course have a habit of ending up in one of three places: the Pentagon, the Beltway, or the Hill. Like Miss Cottrell." Szerenci nodded toward the blonde. "We don't push any policy line here. What you have to do is think systematically, master the details, and work hard."

Szerenci told them he'd been born in Hungary and had come to the United States when he was twelve. He worked for "a department of the government," and did "consulting and policy." He told them how to get an appointment with him if they wanted to discuss their work.

Dan glanced around. The others were hanging on Szerenci's words, faces lifted like sunflowers at noon. The professor reviewed the reading list, fielded a question about the schedule, then began his lecture. He paced as he talked, seizing chalk to sketch in a diagram. From time to time, he swept back a dark forelock.

"Analysis is more than operations research, although that is where many of our techniques originate. Military operations, weapons systems, economics, statistics, operations research — in approximately that order — impact our approach to a problem."

Dan recollected himself and scribbled rapidly: "Problem → model → analytical tech-

45

niques → elucidation → presentation."

After the introduction, Szerenci plunged into the current defense budget and what capabilities it bought. The chalk darted and scraped. Dan didn't have time to think. Concepts, insights, illuminating asides tumbled out faster than he could get them down. He sweated, abbreviating his words till they degenerated into scrawls.

Szerenci talked about choices in force structure. He sneered at the idea the United States should match its enemies man for man, tank for tank, plane for plane. He sneered, too, at the idea some mystical quality of generalship could upset quantitative and logistical factors. "If it's not quantifiable, it doesn't exist," he said. "Reality is all there is. Zero out your preconceptions. Let the numbers speak. That's the only way to the truth. Or what passes for it inside the Beltway."

At five to nine, Szerenci's watch beeped. He rounded off his sentence, underlined the last word on the board, and slammed his lesson plan closed. "Till Monday," he said. Dan sighed, fingering his hand as if it were made of blown glass.

As he went past toward the door, the blonde, Sandy Cottrell, said, "You there. Want to grab a beer? Our after-class bunch gets together at Mr. Henry's. Sometimes *he* comes, too."

"Sure," he said. "Mr. Henry's is —"

"Right around the corner. Mei, you coming tonight?"

Mei came, along with a silent black girl, the carrot-top, and a Korean. The trio of guys were marine buddies who had decided to go to school together. They shoved tables together in the smoky old-fashioned bar and ordered beer and white wine.

Cottrell hand-rolled a cigarette from rough-cut Douwe Egberts and leaned back, rouged cheeks hollowing as she sucked in smoke. "He's totally brilliant," she explained to the black woman. "He's always at the White House, or at JCS. He advised the Undersecretary of State in the Strategic Arms Limitation Talks. This is the second time I've taken this class."

"Are you still dating him?" the redhead asked her.

"On and off. Are you still out at PRC?"

"SAIC. Breen's out there, too."

"I thought he was at DARPA."

"Did Dr. Szerenci say you worked at the Capitol?" Dan asked her. The cloud of smoke around her put him off, as did the indecipherable acronyms, but she was obviously the axis around which the group revolved.

"That's right. Legislative correspondent for Representative Zoelcke."

"Oh yeah? That's great."

"Actually, it's not. Just junior staff for a

junior member. Eddie's going to find me a better slot, on the executive side."

"Eddie?"

"Dr. Szerenci. . . . There he is. Over here!"

Szerenci threw his coat over a chair. The barman brought two double schnappses in tiny stemmed glasses. The professor tossed them both down. He sighed, slapped the table, and held out his hand to Dan. "We don't get much Navy presence. Where are you working?"

Dan told him about the project office. Szerenci nodded, then turned to the black girl. "Frances, did you call Schroeder out at GRC? Did he have the position?"

Cottrell leaned toward him to explain, sotto voce. "Eddie considers it his personal mission to place his students. He's got to have two, three hundred people around the Hill and inside the Beltway that he's gotten jobs for."

"That's great," said Dan. He caught the Chinese woman's eye across the table. She dropped her gaze instantly. "Mei, what do you do during the day?"

"Oh, just a translating position. I am hoping to do something more interesting when I go home."

As they talked, he half-listened to Cottrell and Szerenci joking about somebody who worked at Brookings. Everyone sounded brilliant and happy and successful. He didn't feel exactly out of it, but a shadow hovered. He had two martinis, then cut himself off and got up. The ex-marines were still hammering down beers.

Outside the bar, he stopped, congratulating himself on holding down his alcohol consumption. Then suddenly, he lifted his head, checking the shadows around him.

The bar had been lively, noisy, but Pennsylvania Avenue's shabby storefronts were dark. The sidewalks were empty, and traffic had ebbed to an occasional lone taxi. He walked west, remembering a Metro stop in that direction. He was turning down Twenty-third when a siren began to wail. Strobes licked the faces of the buildings. He glanced across the street, where he saw the entrance to George Washington University Hospital.

As the ambulance turned in, someone emerged from the shadows not far behind him. If he hadn't been looking back, he wouldn't have seen him at all. For a moment, he thought it was someone from the bar, one of the other students. Then he realized it wasn't.

The heavyset man had on a stocking cap, some sort of fatigue jacket. But his matted beard indicated he hadn't seen an inspection, or a razor, for a long time.

"Hey, mister. Got a match?"

"Sorry. Don't smoke."

"Spare a buck?"

The night was late, the street still deserted

49

save for the two of them. The man stood so close, Dan could smell him. He kept one hand inside the tattered jacket. Dan hesitated. Finally, he held out the change from his drinks.

"That all you got?"

"All you're getting." He kept staring him in the eye, and at last the other looked down. As soon as the coins met his hand, he turned and limped away.

Dan breathed out and went on. Once more on the way back to the subway, he thought he heard footsteps behind him. He looked back, heart accelerating again, but saw no one. He felt relieved when the lit M sign came into view ahead, and then the hole in the earth, leading downward and back to Arlington, and eventually to bed.

# 4

He went in to work Saturday and part of Sunday, getting read in to the directives and going over minutes and technical pubs. Monday, he was at NC-1 at 0600. Niles was due in and he wanted to be ready.

When he unlocked the eleventh-floor door, the boxes and trash were gone. The carpet had been shampooed and a scent of lemons hung in the air. It made him nervous, and after a moment he realized why. It was the same scent he'd inhaled for hours in the holding room outside the court of inquiry.

Shaking it off, he strolled around the cubicles, checking out the art. A series of color photos showed a tubular blur approaching, then disappearing into a concrete wall. In the last frame, an orange opium blossom of fire bloomed on the far side. A Naval Institute poster silhouetted the U.S. fleet. Another, in red, illustrated the Soviet navy. The centerfolds and crotch shots that would have decorated a shipboard office were restrained here to a cheesecake of Morgan Fairchild in clingy red lingerie.

Next to Morgan was a sectional diagram of the missile. He leaned in. It *did* look like a torpedo. Straight-sided as a frozen foot-long frankfurter, with stubby, thin wings poking out. The tail was composed of four stiff little airfoils. A garbage can-shaped booster hung off the rear.

Pursuing his circle back to Munford's desk — no, *his* desk now — he stopped again in front of a diagram of the prototype launcher.

"Hey, Dan." He turned, to see Vic Burdette hanging up his hat. The black officer's smoothly shaven skull gleamed in the light. "New oh-seven's due in today. D'I hear something about you knowing him?"

Dan said he didn't exactly know Barry Niles but that he'd met him a couple of times.

"He was what, your commodore down in Charleston?"

"Right. He's a surface nuke. Had *Barney* and *California* before he went to DesRon Six."

Burdette moved in, checking out Dan's ribbons. "Where'd you pick up the Silver Star?"

"In the Caribbean. Look, I need to pump your brains about what you and Munford were doing. Can we get together this morning?"

From the doorway, Captain Westerhouse said, "Dan, Vic. We're going in to see the new director at eight."

"Yes, sir. We'll stand by."

Westerhouse disappeared. Burdette took off his glasses and polished them with a tissue. "How about now?"

"Sure."

Burdette briefed him for an hour, starting

with the ABL. Each armored box launcher stored four Tomahawks. For launch, it clamshelled open, pointing the tubes up at about a thirty-degree angle. "We got turned on originally to put it on three classes of surface ship: *Spru*-boats, DLGs and CGNs. Then we got the surprise tasker to put them on the battleships first."

"Munford mentioned some problems."

"There are a few." As Burdette leaned back, Dan saw a tiny golden fish on a necklace at the edge of his T-shirt. "Software's one. We're dealing with three outfits. One writes the launch control code, the other has the track control system, and the third is the system integrator."

"What's the production status on the launcher?"

"We got prototypes. Convair put 'em together by hand."

"Can they make more?"

"Not in time. They built one for *Merrill*, see, and one for shore tests. Took them two years to hand-weld 'em together. . . . Shoot, I got to go down to SPAWAR."

"You can't leave now. You heard the captain."

Burdette went to his cubicle to make a call. Dan sat looking over the timetable. No doubt about it, the delivery date was going to be tough.

At 0830, Carol phoned and said the meeting with the admiral had been postponed for an hour. Hard on the heels of that, a Filipina in thick glasses and a pink pants suit tapped at the entrance to his cubicle. She carried a six-inch-thick block of files and memoranda.

"Lucy's our secretary," Burdette called. "Yours, mine, and the captain's, but mainly the captain's."

"You boys be ready to go up to the twelfth floor around ten. I'll give you a ring, so stick close."

Dan spent the rest of the morning reading through the flight-test reports. The missile had already gone through an extensive teething period. Numerous glitches had come to light. The engine flooded out during submarine launches. The wings didn't deploy properly. They flexed and flapped when they *were* deployed. The booster-thrust vector tabs had been wired backward. Each failure had been investigated and corrected, and for about a year, as the long-range flight portion of the development program commenced, things had seemed to smooth out.

Then, right after the Air Force had restarted work on their own cruise, success percentages had taken a nosedive. One shot had launched textbook-perfect, heading inland for the Tonopah, but started behaving erratically and crashed in Los Padres National Forest. Another just missed a group of horseback riders. Inspectors had gone through what wreckage

54

remained, but no one really knew what had gone wrong. Finally, Kristofferson had filed a Method D action against Convair, holding payments until results improved. The next step was to cancel the contract.

Dan stared at the wall. The trouble with that was that the only other cruise missile the United States had going was the Boeing design. It was triangular in cross section, to fit in a rotary launcher on a bomber. It wouldn't go out of a torpedo tube, or a shipboard launcher.

A thought shuffled about in the basement of his brain. If the problems hadn't started till the Air Force had revived their missile, if a General Dynamics failure meant a Boeing success — could something other than technical bugs be responsible? He wanted to reject it as paranoia, but hadn't Munford said something like that — about watching out for the Air Force?

Finally, he got up and stretched. The time was 1050, and still no one had called about the meet with Niles. "What do we do for lunch?" he asked Vic over the partition.

"Call down to Roy Rogers, usually. Or if you're in a hurry, there's a hot dog guy down in front of the Buchanan House. He's got a propane-fired cart."

"A hot dog cart. You serious?"

"Hey, you want glamour, we'll call the Cedar Deli for a sub. The contractors try to get us to go over to Stouffer's, or to Restaurant Row. You can go if you want, but don't let them buy."

Dan got up and prowled. He wasn't used to working at a desk. Aboard ship, you were always running up ladders, checking with the chiefs, watching systems tests and maintenance, being interrupted with a call to see the executive officer or by the electrifying bong of the general quarters alarm. Finally, he said, "Cedar Deli, huh? Anything I can bring you?"

When he got back, the office was empty. He left the food and ran up the echoing concrete stairwell. Carol put her finger to her lips outside the director's office. "They're already in there," she whispered.

"I'd better go in."

"Well, all right." She cracked the door and he slipped through.

"The late Mr. Lenson," said a deep, familiar voice.

"Sorry, sir," he muttered, catching Westerhouse's eye before turning to face the man at the desk.

There were others now, but Barry Niles had been the first black senior officer Dan had ever seen. Bellicose little eyes perused him from beneath freckled lids. The mustache was downturned over grim lips. The chest in the trop whites was massive, the arms well muscled, hands big as hams. The shoulder boards of a rear admiral gleamed like cast slabs of gold. A store-size candy dispenser sat on the desk. Colonel Evans leaned against the wall by the door, one hand in his trouser pocket, the other holding his pipe. Dan noticed it wasn't lit, though.

"Nice of you to make our meeting. Atomic Fireball?" Niles pointed at the dispenser.

"No thank you, sir. I was down at —"

"Captain Westerhouse." Niles cut him off in midsentence as he reared back in his chair. "This your entire outfit? Not many for such an important part of the program. Can you use more horsepower?"

"I don't need more rank, Admiral, but I could use more bodies."

"Give me a memo this afternoon. Also any ramp-up in your budget you can justify. Travel, computers, equipment. I've been handed a sick program. What I ask for, I'm going to get. Let's take advantage of that."

"Yes, sir." Westerhouse looked pleased. Niles's next words wiped his smile off.

"Gentlemen, I'm not happy with you. The people I let go last week are not the last. That threat I just uttered includes managers, deputies, everybody down to the clerk typists. If we don't get this program back into gear, there are people one Metro stop up who will zero out the Joint Cruise Missile Project Office."

Niles swiveled to face a window. He had

two in the corner office, giving him a view down on the side ramp that went up toward National Airport, railroad tracks, and, to the east, more new buildings going up. The other looked down on Jeff Davis Highway, and, past it, the ridge of Arlington, with the pillars of Robert E. Lee's home just visible through the trees.

"I've just come from a discussion with Secretary Weinberger, the Chief of Naval Operations, the Air Force Chief of Staff, Dr. William Perry, and key members of their staffs. A grand total of twenty-six stars around that table, gentlemen. We are very high visibility right now. That means we'll be getting the resources the services have been holding up. But that also means no more excuses. If we screw this up, we'll have only ourselves to blame.

"The Secretary made it clear the ground-launched program's got first priority. If GLCM folds, Britain, Germany, Italy, Belgium, and the Netherlands — those countries that agreed to host them — won't be pleased. If we pull the rug out from under them, there will be consequences for the alliance. So that comes first, but the other versions are a close second.

"Now, your part of the program. The fleet commanders can't wait any longer for a long-range antiship missile. If Tomahawk fails, we'll probably license Exocet from the French, mated with a U.S. guidance package.

I'm not going to let that happen, because neither Exocet nor improved Harpoon are stretchable for the land-attack mission.

"I'm ready to break my pike on this one. Because that's the part of this project they're going to remember us for. Conventional land attack. Those fools in the Pentagon don't know it, but they need this capability.

"So if there's anybody here who's not ready to put his personal life on hold for the next year, speak up." Niles glared around at each of them in turn, including the deputy director. Evans straightened, tucking his pipe out of sight. "Is there anything else I should know? Tell me *now*, people!"

Silence. Till Dan, knowing how little patience Niles had with anything other than full disclosure, cleared his throat and said, "Uh, sir, I believe we're looking at a real problem with the battleships."

Westerhouse stepped in then, outlining the status of the launcher design, and the near impossibility of making the delivery date. Niles listened, but his eyes grew smaller. Finally, he growled, "Captain. Why didn't you bring this up when we spoke before?"

"It was going to be in the turnover memo, Admiral."

"Meanwhile, we've wasted a week. When I ask for something, give it to me straight! I don't want people crawling around trying to pacify me!"

Dan hoped he'd stop there, but Niles was just warming up. While they stood rigid, he subjected Westerhouse to the kind of verbal keelhauling Dan hadn't heard in years. You weren't supposed to reprimand men in front of their juniors. But Niles kept roasting till the captain grew ashen. Then he shifted his fire to Evans. He accused the deputy director of covering up problems, of not serving Kristofferson well. The colonel defended himself in a surprised voice.

Niles fell into an ominous silence. He reached for a candy and popped it into his mouth. At last, he rumbled, "So basically we need to get somebody hot making these right away. Okay, Mr. Lenson. Tell me how."

"Uh . . . we have redlines, preliminaries." He tried to force confidence into his voice, wondering just how deep into serious doo-doo he was digging himself. "But I looked them over. They might do. If we can find the right contractor."

"Make that contractors. I'm going to dual-source the missile. Might as well do it on the launcher. But I want to do it faster than anyone's ever run a competitive bid before. I might even go to three sources. If they all come up to spec, we'll have enough to equip the destroyer force, too. What'll we need to do that?"

Dan's mind pinwheeled. Then he noticed Vic doing something behind his back. He was holding up three fingers. What the hell?

Westerhouse said, "Sir, we'd need at least three million dollars to start out with." Meanwhile, Burdette was folding his fingers, held out two. He inserted one finger of the opposite hand and slid it in and out. Like . . . a slide rule. "And another engineer," the captain added hastily.

Niles said, "All right. Now, the tests coming up in Canada. When I briefed this morning, Admiral Willis said the White House staff's asking about them. He wanted my guess at a success rate. I told him I don't operate that way. I'm not going to pamper this thing. If it doesn't fail, we'll make it fail. Till we can't make it fail anymore. Then it's ready for sea.

"I guess that's about all, so —"

"That's risky, Admiral," said Evans. "That's how Admiral Kristofferson got . . . transferred. If we don't get those percentages up —"

"You heard me. Dismissed," Niles barked, and all of them, civilians, Navy, Air Force, stiffened their spines, the words and the look he accompanied them with pushing them out, exhaling and jostling, into the hall.

# II

# THE WEAPON

# 5

Dan woke over Nevada with his head rammed against the window. Between double scotches and jet lag, he felt as if he'd left most of his neurons in the stratosphere, whirling in the slipstream of the 747. He yawned, glancing toward where Westerhouse, Burdette, and a civil servant from Contracts were sitting together. Admiral Niles was several rows forward of them, sitting alone.

The Tomahawk Program Review was a "floating" meeting that rotated among the contractors and test sites. This time, it was in San Diego, hosted by Convair. He'd worked late getting everything together for the trip, then had to rush to Dulles to make the flight.

He was still short sleep from a late date the night before. He and Mei had gone to dinner in Georgetown, then to the Folger to see *Richard III*. She said she was the daughter of an assistant economic attaché. Her parents had been called back to China, but she'd stayed to finish her degree. Back at his place, she'd let him kiss her, but that was all.

Workwise, things had picked up fast. He was now in charge of a $6 million subcontracting effort, along with his integration work.

Immediately following the meeting with Niles, he'd gone to Westerhouse's office and apologized. If he'd spoken out of line, it was because he was so new. Westerhouse had been cool — no question Dan had started off on the wrong foot — but he'd unbent enough to tell him what he had to do in order to get bidding started on the ABL.

The priorities were clear, so he'd started working that issue right away. He went to Contracts to find out how to structure a competitive request for proposal, then went to *Commerce Business Daily* and took out a quarter-page ad. He got three responses. The first was from FMC, a company that had gone from making doughnut machines to automatic guns during World War II and never looked back. The others were from companies he didn't know, Unidynamics, out of St. Louis, and Vimy Manufacturing, in Texas. He was going to meet the reps in Point Mugu and give them a look at what they were bidding on.

He got up and roved down the aisle. Westerhouse was slumped into his seat, a pillow clamped over his eyes. A sheen of perspiration gleamed in the light from the reading lamp. Dan was hesitating, wondering whether to disturb him, when Westerhouse lifted the pillow. "Dan. Clear that stuff off the seat and sit down."

"You sure? You look tired, sir. Look, again, I'm sorry about putting you on the hot spot with the admiral."

"Forget it." Westerhouse rubbed his face

with the tips of his fingers. "Water over the dam, okay? This thing's too important to let egos get in the way."

"That's a pretty . . . mature attitude, sir."

"I've been working this a long time. See down there?"

"Down where, sir?"

Westerhouse pointed out the window. "Down there. In the desert. I did the survivability testing down there, and warhead lethality. . . . Then off to the coast; we took a *Belknap*, tuned its systems to look like a Soviet. To try out different terminal maneuvers. I've only been in Crystal City since February, but I've been on this project, one way or another, for almost seven years." He closed his eyes again. "You might want to think about changing your designator. There's a pretty good promotion rate in the acquisition development community."

Dan said it was worth thinking about, and soon they had their heads together, going over what they were going to present the next day.

Outside the terminal, the evening was rich with flowers. Palm trees swayed against the lustrous blue of impending night. The very air felt lighter, sweeter, as if composed of a different gas from the heavy, wet atmosphere of Washington.

Headlights wheeled in, and Burdette, Dan, and the Contracts guy tossed their bags into

67

the trunk. Niles, silent as ever, took a seat in front.

They had reservations at a Holiday Inn in the suburbs. Vic explained, "The contractors all stay at the Hyatt. It's a cost-plus contract. They get back whatever they spend, plus ten percent profit."

Dan nodded, seeing the point. Why shave dollars when the more you spent, the more you made?

Westerhouse announced they'd meet in the lobby in half an hour and go to a Mexican place he knew. Dan let himself into his room and hung his uniform up to shake the wrinkles out. He sagged into the bed. He looked at his watch, then at the phone. He hadn't called his daughter since he got to D.C.

His ex-wife answered. She sounded sleepy, and for a moment he wondered if he'd miscalculated on the time zone. But she said no, she just had a cold.

"Sorry you're not feeling well. Has Nan got it?"

"She had this one already. She picks up everything at school."

"I can't believe she's in third grade already."

Susan's voice sharpened. "She's in *fourth* grade, Dan."

"Maybe if I got to see her once in awhile, I'd be more up-to-date."

"Don't give me that bullshit. You can come out here anytime you want. I've never made any objection to visitation."

"No, you just had to drag her off to Bumfuck, Utah."

"Archaeology jobs aren't easy to find. And I hope you don't use that kind of language to her. Where are you, anyway? This isn't a very good connection."

"I'm in San Diego."

"I thought you were stationed in Charleston."

"I was, but I got transferred to D.C."

"Then why are you in San Diego?"

"I have to go to a conference, okay? Look, is she there? I can only take so much of the sheer fun of talking to you."

"Fuck you, too, Dan. Wait."

A long pause. Then a voice said, "Dad?"

"Hi, Punkin. Are you feeling better?"

"Better?" she sounded uninterested. "Better than what?"

"Mom said you had a cold."

"Oh, that. Look, I can only talk a minute. I have to go and practice, all right?"

"Are you still in ballet?"

"I haven't been in *ballet* for years, Dad. I play tennis now."

It went downhill from there. When he finally said, "Bye, Punkin," he felt more distant from her than before the conversation. As soon as he hung up, the phone rang again. It

69

was Burdette, telling him they were waiting in the lobby.

The desk called at 0530 the next morning. Westerhouse said Admiral Niles had taken a taxi over early. The rest had a quick breakfast, then piled into the rental. Dan leaned back, watching the boulevards, the palms, the traffic go by.

The program review was at Kearney Mesa, in view of the mountains. As they waited at the gate, he saw immense white hangar structures. They signed in at the main office building, then filed into a second-floor amphitheater where a couple of dozen men and women stood drinking coffee and eating doughnuts. He got a cup of coffee and put a quarter beside the carafe.

He checked out the other players while he waited for the coffee to cool. The civilians were in engineer outfits, too-tight sport jackets and polyester slacks and ties. The women wore sensible suits with thick-looking panty hose. He caught introductions: Johns Hopkins University Applied Physics Laboratory; Vitro; Williams Research. Then the lights flickered, and everyone drifted toward seats.

A white-haired executive in gray pinstripes introduced himself as Rich Larramore, the Tomahawk program manager. "Admiral Niles, military guests, fellow engineers, ladies and gentlemen, welcome back to Convair. I'd like to start with film. Jack, roll 'em."

The first clip showed a ship's superstructure being penetrated by a missile. Sheets of torn metal cartwheeled along the deck in slow motion. Abrupt shift to a swept-wing airplane sitting on a desert field. A blur was masked for a frame or two by smoke. Tiny black objects tumbled through the air. They detonated in a rippling dance of fire, obliterating the plane.

A jumble of images cleared, showing rugged terrain whipping past the camera. Dan tensed as it wove between bare, dry hills, so close that he could make out twisted ancient pines. Sometimes the cliffs were *above* it. Then a square loomed ahead. In the last instant, it grew into a concrete blockhouse. Then the screen went suddenly white.

Larramore cleared his throat as the lights came up.

"As you know, the original task set us by the Navy was pretty daunting. Essentially, it was to design a weapon you could fire off a submerged sub off San Diego, fly cross-country so low, it had to dodge pinecones, and, on reaching Chicago, impact inside the base paths of Wrigley Field.

"Well, first we tried to put wings on a torpedo. Then we tried to extrude an MX through a twenty-inch opening. Finally, we sat down and designed the Tomahawk. We've had to go back to the computer-aided design terminals several times. But we're finally ready

71

to put something revolutionary in the field."

Things got technical fast after that. Dan made notes:

*Missile is wrapped in stainless-steel cocoon for launch. On exit, lanyard fires solid rocket booster after checking for correct attitude and velocity. Mk 106 booster: 303 lb. Arcadene 228E, develops 7,000 lbs. of thrust.*

*After launch: inlet cover jettison; wing slot/booster fairing jettison; tail control fin deployment; wing opening; booster burnout; turbofan inlet deployment; engine start and transition to cruise phase. Time-sensitive sequence of events. One glitch can wreck launch.*

*Majority of structure fabricated from cylindrical forgings. Each forging automatically machined from center out to a one-piece skin with stiffeners. Internal structure: attached by electron-beam welding.*

*Engine: 144-pound, 12-inch-diameter Williams Research F107-WR-400. Outgrowth of small engines developed for drones and James Bond-style jet belts. 600 pounds max thrust pushes 2,500-pound missile along at up to 540 mph.*

"Now I'm going to pass you off to Missile Engineering."

"Actually, Bob, you've stolen my speech. It's true, we've done some amazing things with this machine. We pump the fuel supply through the chassis of the electronics to cool them. We've used Air Force-developed high-energy fuel to get ten pounds of range out of a five-pound bag. We've designed it with modularity so we can bring new versions on-line fast. And we've already got a team at work on the 'B' model.

"Once we had the airframe and engine, we had to find a way to navigate it accurately at a low altitude. The antiship version skims the sea fifty feet up, slipping underneath the enemy's radar coverage. Near the target, an active-radar terminal guidance head boots up. Then there's the land-attack version — but that's the next brief."

The McDonnell Douglas guidance guru was one of the women wearing thick panty hose. Dan kept writing as she said, "As most of you know, the Achilles' heel of previous cruise missiles has always been straight and level flight. That made them vulnerable to antiaircraft and fighters.

"Tomahawk's smarter than that, and it's designed to take advantage of the low-altitude window Soviet air defenses leave open. The land-attack missile utilizes terrain compari-son-aided internal guidance with digital scene-matching terminal guidance. In es-sence, the missile follows a 'road map' programmed into it before launch."

She dimmed the lights. The slide showed a hilly terrain as it would be seen by the eye, then sliced into digitized squares. "As it flies, the system compares its radar returns with the terrain it expected, then computes corrections when it wanders. During the last seconds of flight, an electro-optical system called digital scene-matching area correlation takes over. It compares the expected image of the target area with the actual infrared it observes."

Dan looked around, then put his hand up. "There, in the back."

"I was wondering: We don't have any problem getting accurate terrain maps in California and Nevada, where you've been flying the tests. But what about Kamchatka, or the Kola Peninsula? Someplace where they don't like our guys coming around with surveying instruments?"

"Good question, but that's the intelligence and mapping community's ballpark. They're assembling the data you're referring to. National security assets are involved, I understand."

He nodded, understanding the shorthand for satellite reconnaissance.

She went on. "One of the continuing issue items in the minutes is the radar altimeter issue. I'm happy to say, the latest figures from the flight-test lab are —"

A heavy voice from Dan's left grunted,

"That's a vital part of the guidance."

Heads turned; a stir eddied through the room as through a school of jack at the appearance of a barracuda. "Yes, Admiral, it is."

"What's your backup for it?"

"There's no backup. It's going to work."

"Well, I have one. Litton Systems Limited, in Toronto."

"A foreign source?"

"They're letting us test in Canada. Spending money there makes sense. Just to let you know — when you read about the contract award. Are you finished?"

When she nodded, Niles clambered to his feet. He stood amid the gray-suited executives, silent and immobile as a colossus. Finally, Larramore rose, too. "Let me introduce Rear Admiral Barry "Nick" Niles, incoming director, Joint Cruise Missile Projects Office. Admiral?"

Niles didn't respond. The silence stretched out. At last, he said, "You're responsible for the airframe, and integration of the all-up round."

"Convair is, yes —"

"I mean you. *You're* responsible, Mr. Larramore."

Larramore nodded. "That's right, sir. I'm the program manager."

"Then maybe you can explain to me why your program is so screwed up."

"Excuse me?"

"Why are you so far behind schedule? Why do we have a fifty-five percent fail rate on flight tests? Why is your program so *fucked up?*"

"You're referring to the work-stoppage order."

"Yes, among other things."

"We don't have an input to that process, Admiral. Essentially, the Department of Defense is saying, we can keep working on the program but that we might not get paid for it. May I point that out? That at this point we're proceeding on good faith and our own money? We believe in this missile. All new weapons have bugs."

"Not good enough," said Niles. "I expect a few glitches early. But we're eight years into development. What I hear is, your techs are sloppy, we find rust in the actuators, cleanliness is shit, tolerances are shit, and the missiles you're sending me for test are shit." His deliberate, heavy voice bludgeoned through the air-conditioned air. "Your product is *shit,* Mr. Larramore. Explain to me why I should buy it."

Steel in his voice for the first time, Larramore said, "Admiral, maybe we'd better discuss this off-line."

"Yeah, let's take it up a level. But I want everybody here to understand this: I will not permit this program to be killed."

"We don't want that, either."

"Shut up. We're at a critical elbow in the

development process. I will not permit it to be killed due to the foot-dragging and poor workmanship of *one company.*" Larramore opened his mouth, seemed to reflect, then closed it again. "I've got authority to dual-source anything that looks chancy. That effort has begun on the ABL already. I'm putting Litton on the guidance. And as of next week, I'm putting an RFP on the street for a second airframe production line."

"Sir, the government paid for development of this missile. You have every right to buy it from whomever you want. But we designed it. We've fought through problem after problem. We have a proprietary interest —"

"Bullshit," said Niles. "You nailed it the first time: I have every right, and I'm going to exercise it. This is not Convair's missile. It's not the Navy's missile. This is *my* missile now. The minute I qualify a second source, you're going to turn over every document, every piece of engineering software, and specs on every piece of tooling. If you hold out on me, I'll cut you out of the list of competitors for every buy downstream till the end of the century."

The engineers and executives looked at the ceiling. Niles glared around once more, like Thor facing a circle of trolls, then slowly sat down, folding his beefy arms.

Niles and Larramore disappeared after the

opening meeting. The rest of the conferees broke into subgroups: missile, weapons control, launch systems. There was lots of sitting around while the engineers haggled over bit streams. Dan split his time between the launch systems group and the weapons control group. If he could get enough boxes built somehow, get them on the ship, and get the targeting and launch system debugged by next June, hell, he'd have to find someplace to sacrifice a calf.

After a cafeteria lunch, they headed over to tour the production line. It was a quarter-mile walk in the brilliant California sunshine. A fresh wind smelled of the sea, and Dan yearned for it. The open sea, free of all politicking and moneymaking. What the hell was he doing ashore, anyway?

Then he remembered. To decide what he was going to do with the rest of his life.

The hangar doors yawned, and he joined a queue for hard hats with the Convair/General Dynamics emblem.

Far above, girders webbed the underside of light-admitting panels. The distant rattle of air-driven tools merged with the whine of electric motors. He'd expected clamor, shouting, but the first thing he noticed was the quiet. He followed the group, then rejoined them as they spread themselves around something at the end of the line. He knew its dimensions by heart, yet somehow it was smaller than he'd expected.

The first assembled Tomahawk he'd ever seen was as long as a full-sized car, yet no bigger around than a woman's waist. As he trailed his fingertips over cool painted metal, over plastic inserts that faired rivets and accesses into air-cheating smoothness, a chill ran up his back.

"Beautiful," said the guidance engineer, running her hand across the outer edge of the wing, and Dan thought, It isn't just a guy thing, then. This perception of beauty in an instrument of death. He'd felt it before, admiring the raked lines of a destroyer, the half-submerged deadliness of a submarine.

For a moment, he looked back through an endless hall lined with armor and floored with bloody straw, where warriors caroused as the bard howled the paean to destruction. How many weapons — swords, spears, guns, knives, aircraft, bombs — men had made, and all but worshiped before. Now it was missiles; and someday soon, it would be lasers, burning through the atmosphere like lightning drawn with a ruler. And his weapons had made him, refashioned him from a frightened plains ape to master of the planet.

And here they stood, gathered around the newest idol to frighten the tribe in the next valley.

The cart whirred and moved past them, and another cart and another missile took its place.

★ ★ ★

He and Burdette drove Niles back to the airport after the meeting. The admiral didn't say anything, just stared out the window. Dan contemplated wiry black hair salt-and-peppered with gray. What went on in there? He didn't have a clue.

He'd had to face admirals before. But this was the first time he'd worked with one. It was true: They were different. As if those broad golden stripes lifted them to a different plane of evolution. They seemed to think in a different way, knowing instantly and intuitively what junior officers had to grope toward. Did it happen suddenly, when they were selected? Or were those the ones the board anointed, bestowing on them only the acknowledgment they were superior beings? If it was the latter, he ought to have met people like that at the lower ranks. And he hadn't. He'd known effective leaders. But none of them had been guided by some perfectly isolated and frictionless internal gyro, like the man in front of him seemed to have.

When they got to the airport, he started to help Niles with his bag. The admiral grunted something and took it away from him. He headed off without a backward glance.

"Whew," said Burdette. "Fun guy."

"Yeah, a real teddy bear," Dan said. "Well, you ready to head north?"

"Light the burners; let's launch."

80

★ ★ ★

The Pacific Coast Highway took them past rugged cliffs, dramatic views out over the gleaming sea. He wished they could stop at San Juan Capistrano. Maybe next time. . . . The ocean spread below him out to the world's edge, charged with the silver waning light like high voltage. It looked different from the Atlantic — a dark, heatless, somehow threatening hue. The hydrography was abrupt here. The bottom plunged deep just offshore. One reason, of course, why the initial tests had been flown from the Pacific. A sub could launch only a few miles offshore; then the missile could head for the deserted fastnesses of the federal reservations in Southern California and Nevada.

He asked Burdette, "Hey, you been out here before, right?"

"Sure, back when we were launching from *Guitarro*. Postshot, we're en route to Mare Island when the impulse tank in the torpedo tube blows up. Shorts out a bank of batteries, then starts a fire in the torpedo room. We were all jumping through our grommets there for a while. Anyway . . . this new engineer, he's gonna meet us at the ship, right?"

"He's supposed to've been there a couple days now. Name's Sakai. ME in electrical engineering out of Rensselaer. Dahlgren lent him to us for a year."

"Sounds good. What you want to do about

81

dinner? Want to pull off here, or wait till we get to Long Beach?"

The next morning, he stood looking up at one of the last four battleships on earth.

USS *New Jersey* lay in a dry dock huge enough to swallow a small town. Beneath its massive hull, the concrete floor was dotted with pools of water that reflected the clouds and the sky. He stared into the leveled gaze of sixteen-inch guns in slab-sided turrets. Above them poked out a bristle of five-inch dual-purpose batteries. Then bridge levels, more guns, directors, yet more levels, yet more guns, a mountain range of steel tapering into heaven. At its crest, a lacework of radars and radio antennae fretted the air, as if the ship were an enormous plant, thrusting metal as high as possible toward the sun.

He lowered his eyes again, noticing this time huge canvas screens and construction staging. Only then did his eye pick up human figures, clambering tiny as gnats about the immense fabric as compressors and paint strippers buzzed and clattered. He eased his breath out. She was from another world, another time, and encountering her here amid the hissing steam and grinding of engines was like coming suddenly upon a live tyrannosaur in its lair.

As they stepped off the steel-ringing brow, Dan looked around for the quarterdeck watch, lifting his hand to salute, then remembered she wasn't in commission yet. "There's our escort," Burdette said. "Hey! Dan, this is Perry Kyriakou, the prospective Tomahawk officer. Perry, Dan Lenson. There a guy named Sakai here?"

"Yeah, he's down tracing hydraulics. We're gonna all meet in the captain's in-port cabin. Want to come with me, I'll show you the spaces."

The passageways were hot and close and filled with noise, cables, paint chips, welding fumes, dirt, sparks, sailors, and yard workers in hard hats and coveralls. Dan asked Kyriakou how long she'd been in mothballs. "Twelve years this time," the lieutenant said. "Actually, she hasn't spent that long on active duty. They broke her out for Korea, then Vietnam. But what makes a ship old is steaming and shooting, and she's still got a lot of hours left on her." He thumped solid steel. "The only thing that was ever wrong with these, they couldn't hit a target at really long range. And that's what we're gonna add. Okay, this is gonna be the Tomahawk equipment room."

Dan looked around the gutted compartment, then took his diagrams out. He measured everything, checked everything, traced ventilation and power. Finally, the lieutenant looked at his watch. "We better get on up. I'll call the chief, see if he can find your guy Sakai."

★ ★ ★

They had half an hour with Captain Foster. The commanding officer fiddled with an unlit corncob pipe as he filled them in on the reactivation program. Then he told Dan something he hadn't realized about the Tomahawk spaces: that when Adm. Bill Halsey had commanded Third Fleet and Task Force 38 in 1944, those had been his flag spaces and his personal mess. Glancing at Sakai, Foster ruminated about how Halsey had let Jisaburo Ozawa sucker him away with a decoy force at Leyte Gulf. "My dad was on the *Samuel B. Roberts*, and he's never forgiven Halsey for leaving the San Bernardino Strait unprotected off Samar. This ship could have done what she was designed for — slugged it out with Kurita's, battle line to battle line. Four U.S. battlewagons against four Japanese. And one of those was *Yamato*. Eighteen-inch guns . . . Think about that."

But at last, Foster hoisted himself from his chair, apologizing. He had to leave, but he insisted they use his cabin for their conference. He invited them back for the commissioning ceremony.

Dan, Burdette, Sakai, Kyriakou, and the Naval Sea Systems Command representative spent the day going over the master arrangement drawings. Everything seemed okay on the command and control arrangements, but they ran into a shoal on ABL siting. Specifically, the location between the stacks, with a clear area outboard to allow for the missile-loading platforms to be set up. Sakai set the tone when, looking at the diagram, he said, "Uh, guys, this ain't gonna fly."

Dan looked at his new engineer. This was the first time he'd met him; he'd gone through résumés on the Internet and pulled him sight unseen out of the Navy weapons lab at Dahlgren with a Brickbat personnel request. Sakai looked to be about eighteen, though he was actually in his late twenties. He had long black hair and a flowing mustache, with close-set eyes behind Navy-issue birth-control frames. He had on green coveralls and brand-new half Wellingtons. He didn't want to be called by his first name, which was Yoshiyuki, and Dan was happy to go along. "What ain't, Sparky?"

"This siting plan. How hardwired is this thing?"

The NAVSEA rep said the weight and moment calculations had been done, the Surface Combatant Design Office had signed off on it, and that was that. Dan said, "Why can't we go as designed?"

"See this? Look at how close the ends of the ABLs are to the blast shields. Five buys you ten you're gonna exceed overpressure during launch."

"These clamshells are armored against fire and impact."

"Sure, but only if they're closed. I bet that's

85

how they designed it, one open to fire, all the others closed. But that's not gonna be your typical tactical employment. Let's say you're gonna do a two-ABL launch, get eight missiles in the air. That means you got the clamshells open on number one when number two fires. Not only that, you're gonna be dumping a hell of a lot of toxic exhaust right on the centerline."

"What do you suggest, Sparky?"

"Split them up. Put half between the stacks here and the rest down on the lower deck, pointed forward. The way the Soviets do it on the *Sovremennys*. Or, you don't like that, turn them end for end." He shook cigarettes out of a pack and demonstrated as the steward came out with fresh coffee.

"They fire across the ship?" Dan said doubtfully. "Left to right, right to left?"

"Sure. Why not? That way, the blast and the exhaust goes outboard instead of inboard. Your loading equipment goes in the center. Which is better, too — you get more wind and spray protection."

"You'd need two blast shields instead of one," the rep pointed out.

"But each can be lower. Who cares how much blast you dump outboard?"

"How about these Phalanxes? What's the arc of fire on them when the clamshells are open? And what are we going to do about the ship's boats?"

Dan said, "Look, we don't have all day. Will Systems Command take on the redesign? If we can come up with an improved siting plan?"

The NAVSEA rep said no, that would delay delivery.

They went around for two hours on how to resite the boxes and add additional structure to reposition the Phalanx to fire over them. Dan tried to reason with the guy, but he wouldn't even negotiate handrail locations. Finally, he pointed to the phone on the bulkhead. "Is that connected?"

"I believe so."

"I want you to do a mod to the design, grouping four launchers on the oh three level, firing over one another, and the other four aft on either side of the sixteen-inch director, facing forward and outboard forty-five degrees. Listen up now, because this is your big chance to make a speed bump out of yourself. Your boss is Admiral Obuszewski. You tell me no can do one more time, and I'm going to pick up that phone and call Admiral Niles. Niles has got Admiral Willis shitting in his in-box every day because SECNAV's shitting in his. Then Willis can call Obuszewski and we can let two three-stars do our jobs for us. Or does that sound like a bad idea?"

The rep sat mute, scowling. Finally, he muttered, "We'll redesign it." But the look he got told Dan he wasn't ever going to get anything else out of NAVSEA again.

He couldn't leave — this was essential stuff — and he realized late in the morning that they weren't going to make it to Point Mugu that day. He called over to get word to the contractors that the meeting was postponed until tomorrow. He asked the site rep to let them in to see the launcher, and help them get whatever measurements they needed.

The next morning dawned misty. Sakai put the headlights on as they headed down toward the sea. Dan asked him about what he'd been doing at Dahlgren, and he got an evasive answer, something about an electromagnetic gun. Whatever it was, he sounded anxious to get back to it. "Not that I don't want to help you guys," he said. "Just that stuff stops getting interesting for me when the theory's cold and you're just down to twisting wires together." Dan and Burdette exchanged eye rolls.

What everybody called Point Mugu was officially the Pacific Missile Test Center. It was on a peninsula fifty-some miles north of Los Angeles. Low buildings squatted between bluffs overlooking the ocean. Sakai said he knew his way around, but Dan tried to keep oriented as their security escort took them to what he called "the blockhouse." When they found it, not far from the beach, a group of men in civvies were standing near the doorway.

"Lenson, I presume? Project Office?"

"Dan Lenson. This is Sparky Sakai, Vic Burdette."

"J. J. Slater, Convair. I built this beast."

"Nice to meet you." They shook hands; Slater introduced the others, from FMC, Unidynamics, and Vimy. Dan asked if they'd gotten the bid package. "Yeah, we did. Thanks," the man from Vimy said. He looked tough, with a sun-seared Irish face.

"Sorry I got held up. You fellas had a chance to look it over?"

"There was a launch crew here drilling yesterday. We got to see some of the loading."

"That's good. I haven't. J. J., want to give me the tour?"

The prototype was about the size of a tractor-trailer container, painted haze gray. The welded seams were unground. Slater gave them a walkaround, pointing out the exterior connections and power and hydraulics requirements. "Stand clear," he yelled, then hit a button.

Bells shrilled. A rotating beacon began to flash. Two thuds echoed off the bunker.

The clamshelled upper section came up surprisingly fast. The only indication of the effort it took to lift those tons of metal was the muffled hammer of a prime mover back in the power room. A shining steel rod carried the launch tubes up with it, till they pointed at the empty sky.

Slater said, "Okay, she's open. Elevation

angle thirty-five degrees relative to the deck. You can see the canister support assembly and the fronts of the four tubes. The top two have the frangible covers in place. Those are the starred discs, look like the front of a shotgun shell. The bottom two, you can see the nose of the missile. All four have the same electrical and data connections, so you can put any variant in any tube. The heating and cooling system maintains storage temperatures from minus forty to plus one hundred and twenty degrees in direct sun. Fire and security alarms tie into existing ship systems. Any questions?"

Sakai asked, "How about pitch and roll?"

"We sized bolts and shear forces for a sixty-degree roll. I don't think you're going to get that on a battleship. Actually, I seem to recall the *Iowa* class, you roll 'em too far, the turrets drop out so you don't capsize."

Dan was thinking that one over when Slater added, "Let me say one more thing, Commander. I wanted to bid on the production units. We could kick you out a nice product. But I got overruled. The company doesn't want to commit on the time frame you're laying out. It's better just to say up front we can't do it than to look stupid later." The other reps looked at the launcher, ignoring the taunt.

"Are those actual missiles in there now?" Dan asked him.

"No, those are blind rounds — identical shape, size, weight, but no internal structure. Used them to work up the loading equipment." Slater pointed at an assemblage of metal rods and beams by the bunker. "I recommend you order your loaders from the same guys you get your boxes from. Otherwise, one company's loaders are going to be a quarter inch off, or the bolt will have different threads."

He noted that. "Okay, thanks for the show. Have you guys got any questions?"

"I do," said the FMC engineer. He had on a Bills windbreaker. "Can we streamline the design? And fix a couple things? Like these dual latching mechanisms — you get any kind of torsion, they're gonna dealign and jam. We can do better than that." He grinned at Slater.

Sakai said, "The latching mechanisms are probably mandated by the nuclear weapons security program."

"That's right," said Slater. "You want to improve the design, fine, but make sure you meet those specs. They also approved our nuclear surety link. Those you can buy from us, by the way."

A middle-aged Unidynamics guy in a sport coat asked, "Command and control?"

"It's called WCS EX mod three and that's all I know about it. Except that there's a lot of glitches in the software build. What bit stream comes through the wires, you're gonna have to ask the commander here."

Sakai said, "The back end of the launch control system processing is thirty-two signal data translators, one per tube. Each one provides discrete logic-level translation of the flight and firing data direct to the missile. Don't sweat it. All you guys need to do is put in the specified connector."

"You know, I'm starting to like you, Sparky," Dan told him. "Any other questions, fellas? . . . Yeah, you can take pictures if you want."

The Vimy engineer said, "And a bid deadline, end of the month. Gonna be late nights, next couple weeks."

"I know. We've been pulling all-nighters, too." Dan said to Slater, who was leaving, "Can we leave it open like this?"

"Sure. Just power down the console and then tell the guys in the bunker you're securing."

The Vimy engineer caught up with Dan as he was heading toward the bunker. The others were still grouped around the ABL; a strobe flashed as one leaned in under the raised clamshell, a Jonah peering down the gullet of the whale. "We're hungry for this one. Got a lot of guys down in Texas looking for this work."

"You think you can do it, get that bid in. We're definitely gonna award it, thirty-two units first buy, a lot more downstream."

"Who makes the final decision? You?"

"I don't know if I should answer that," said Dan. "So I guess I won't."

"Any way we can get an edge? Anything special we can put in there?"

"I don't think so. You've got all the same info the other guys have."

"We've done a lot of Navy work. We're pretty hungry." The man waited, then, when Dan still didn't respond, handed him a card. "Well, you think of something, call me, all right? Doesn't have to be an official communication. Just give me a call."

"Sure," said Dan. He finally got the attention of one of the enlisted men, and he yelled, "We're through. It's yours."

A few minutes later, as he was getting into the car, the card fluttered out of his pocket as he pulled out his keys. He picked it up off the floor. A newspaper clipping was stuck to the back. The headline read HOUSE DISCUSSES CUTS IN MILITARY RETIREMENT PLAN.

"The hell's that?" said Sakai, glancing at it as Dan wondered if it was what it seemed to be. Or if it was just an accident — that two unrelated things had gotten stuck together in the vendor's wallet. But it wasn't anything you could actually call an inducement. Finally, he crunched it in his fist and tossed it over his shoulder into the back of the car.

"Trash," he said. "Let's go, we got an eleven-fifteen departure."

# 6

And rapidly and smoothly as a Metro train accelerating, autumn was on them.

He hardly had time to look up from his desk as the weeks flicked by. Between trips, he was pulling fourteen-hour days, working Saturdays and often Sundays, too. He had to put two of his evening classes on hold; there just weren't enough hours. He still kept making Szerenci's, though. And there was always time for a few beers at Mr. Henry's. He even managed to convert some of the analysis he was doing into papers for class, scrubbed to remove classified information.

Now late on an October afternoon, he lifted his head and stared at the window. Then checked the wall clock and whispered, "Hell."

He got up suddenly and slid his drawer closed and locked it. He shot a glance into the corridor, then pulled his blues off and hung them. He slid his gear bag out from under the desk and pulled a set of worn gray Naval Academy sweats over his skivvies. He laced his running shoes and tried a stretch. His muscles felt like overtightened guitar strings.

"Going running?" Sakai turned his head from a Lotus display.

"I'm going stir-crazy, got to break a sweat.

You still on those slides?"

"Couple hours yet."

"Tomorrow's Saturday. I'll just come in and change here. Don't forget to lock the safe."

The engineer didn't repond. Dan tucked his ID and apartment key into the lacing of his shoe, checked his drawer again — the lock didn't always catch the first time — and left.

Outside, the sidewalks were thronged with tired-looking people heading for the Metro, for their cars, parked along the narrow streets west of Jeff Davis Highway. He did a few more stretches and twists, then punched his Casio and pushed his reluctant body into motion.

He wove between pedestrians, then broke out at a crossing light. A dark blue sky opened. Glancing at the sun, he figured he had an hour of visibility left. Enough, if he kept up a good pace.

He usually ran along the C and O Canal, a long-abandoned waterway that paralleled the Potomac. Instead of heading directly north, though, he swerved east, heading up onto the overpass to National Airport. A longer run, but it got you to a riverside path that was both more visually appealing and safer than trying to second-guess rush-hour traffic. A narrow sidewalk jammed him against the edge of the flyover. He sucked air, leaning into the climb as his shoes scuffed on grit and butts and fragments of disintegrated tires. He felt strong now. Maybe he'd try a couple of timed miles once he got warmed up.

For the first mile or so, he was always right there, but then his mind would detach from his body and the two would travel independently, the sweating, panting animal and the thing that thought a few inches above its heart. Now as his feet thudded on concrete and the hangars came into sight, tapered fuselages glittering in the rosy evening light, his mind reverted to planning conferences, due dates, milestones, reports.

The contract award on the launchers had gone through, with bonuses for early deliveries and penalties for delays. FMC came in with the high bid, with Unidynamics next and Vimy the low bidder. The board had split the buy among all three. Dan had visited each plant, making sure everyone was working to the same set of plans. FMC had a modern production line in Minnesota. Unidynamics had an older factory in St. Louis, with engineers and machinists with German names. They didn't have the latest numerically controlled equipment, but they made up for it in craftsmanship. Vimy Manufacturing had impressed him less favorably. It was a converted auto-parts factory west of Austin.

A wide curve left, and a bike path came into view. Asphalt with occasional stretches of worn grass, it followed the Memorial Parkway along the Potomac, over a bridge beneath which sailboats entered and left the marina. Sometimes he stopped there, leaning on the rail while he watched their graceful passage, listening to the fluttering luff of the sail edge as it passed a few feet below him.

Today, though, instead of slowing, he stretched out his pace. The cool air soothed his lungs, and his muscles felt loose and his head was clearer, as if the wind off the river were blowing off the work haze from a week of grinding his brain against documents and telephones and other human wills. Across that turbulent darkness, the Washington Monument pricked the sky, and beyond it the scoop of vanilla ice cream that was the Capitol.

He swung left as he reached the roundabout at the Arlington Memorial Bridge, climbing gradually into the groves and hills of the National Cemetery. Ranks of headstones came into view, then wheeled like soldiers passing in review. The trees swayed to a chilling wind, and shadows grappled on the pathways.

A distant note reached his ear. He almost kept on — no one would notice or know — then something slowed his steps. It was these silent graves. Each stone marking what had once been a living man. Each knowing fear, pain, grief . . . but still doing his duty. He knew men who slept here. High school classmates who'd died in Vietnam. Academy friends — some gone down in burning helicopters, others who'd missed the wire or tumbled into the sea on cold cat shots, one who'd been shot in the head in Panama as he waited at a stoplight.

He halted, faced the invisible bugler, and put his hand on his heart.

*Go to sleep, Go to sleep, Go to sleep now and rest in your tents. . . .*

He stood at attention, alone. Alone, yet surrounded by men who had offered themselves to death, in the belief something was worth more than their lives.

A chill searched his back. After all, it was Halloween . . . the night when spirits walked and the unexpected happened. He didn't believe in ghosts, but he still felt better when the last note trailed off.

He pushed his now-wearying legs back into motion. They went *shuush, shuush* through drifts of maple leaves. He thought, At least in their day, war could settle something, win independence or free a race or destroy fascism. A war today . . . How many nuclear weapons were targeted on him right now as he ran? Szerenci had compared the Soviet and U.S. strategic forces. The USSR had 7,000 warheads, according to CIA estimates; the United States had over 9,000, building fast toward a goal of 13,500. To make up for their lag in numbers, the Russians loaded their gigantic boosters with warheads yielding the equivalent of 20, 30, 50 million tons of TNT. The zones of destruction covered the whole District of Columbia. Even those who survived the toppling of the crystal towers would die, poisoned by fallout from deliberately dirty Soviet bombs.

His feet brushed through the dead leaves. Millions of dead leaves . . .

He picked up the pace to escape his gloomy imaginings, winding now downward past titanic warriors straining against a flagpole, past marines in dress blues folding a flag.

His mind returned to what occupied it nearly every waking moment.

The program was emerging into the public eye, and in no positive light. The *Post* had begun it with a scathing review of flight-test results. Subsequent articles, by a defense writer and aerospace analyst named Martin Tallinger, had pursued the story into the forced participation of the Air Force, allegations of payoffs, and objections from the arms-control bureaucracy. The series ran for day after day, painting Tomahawk as a financial sinkhole, a technological pipe dream, an escalatory provocation. The latest news was that the House was scheduling hearings, called by a congressman and Congressional Medal of Honor holder named Dwayne Harrow. Harrow had spent five years in captivity after his spotter plane was shot down in Vietnam. He'd escaped once and made it across the DMZ, but was recaptured by the Vietcong and returned to Hanoi, where he was tortured and beaten so severely, he'd never walked again.

And another, possibly even more dangerous opponent was stirring.

As he cut back toward the river, running along darkening paths past Roosevelt Island, he remembered the background — far back, to the early days of World War II.

When the battle line had been destroyed at Pearl Harbor, the Navy's few aircraft carriers were left to hold the line in the Pacific. They had, and as the war progressed, a growing armada built around them struck and moved and struck again till the Japanese fleet was erased and the Imperial Army lay stranded and stunned on its islands. And the future belonged to planes and those who flew them.

Ever since, these mobile concentrations of self-contained force had been the spear point of American might. Destroyers, cruisers, and frigates were their shield. The sword was the aircraft on the flattop's decks, able to strike hundreds of nautical miles, not only at enemy ships and aircraft but at land installations, airfields, communications. Wherever unrest or aggression threatened, the gray ramparts rose from the sea. And the aviators' lives were tied to them, first as fliers, then as carrier skippers, then as commanders of the great battle groups.

Those men led the Navy now, and they

were waking to a threat. You saw it not in public, but in a professional note in the Naval Institute *Proceedings*, a skeptical letter to the *Naval War College Review*. Dan had trouble at first believing he had to worry about the naval aviation lobby. Then he remembered what Munford had told him: how they'd helped kill the other cruise programs.

He pondered as he ran, till the towers of Rosslyn rose twinkling and he began the climb toward his apartment, still a couple of miles distant, but uphill all the way.

As he neared the Key Memorial Bridge, he slowed. Red lights flashed. Police cars were blocking the bridge. Instead of traffic, the entrance ramps were thronged with people.

He slowed to a jog, to a walk, and finally to a bemused halt.

Below a waning moon, a man with the head of a crow lifted a bottle to his beak. Leaves crunched beneath Godzilla's claws. A Red Death staggered. Beyond them hundreds more drifted downhill through oak leaves and wind. The murmur of a great throng surged from the far side of the river. He caught conversation as one knot drifted past. The voices were young, excited.

"Spooky."

"Dark as the inside of my asshole."

"Keep it tight," a masked headsman advised. "We close on the hour when things hidden ooze into the light. When dooms long

101

in fruition wake to life. When spirits come."

"Do spirits come?" A penguin belched and rifled his can into the underbrush.

Three weird sisters loomed from the night: witch, baseball player, infant. A vampire grinned his way alongside. "Hey, baby, need that diaper changed?"

"Piss off."

"Halloween is the time of change, the time of revelation."

She screamed as the rear of her diaper ripped free. Suddenly, they were running, the vampire's cape flapping, the headsman's heels unsteady castanets, a giggle from beneath the penguin's mask.

Dan glanced uphill, toward the promise of a shower and a drink. Then he looked toward the bridge. Over there, darkness, the bobbing glimmer of flashlights, and — were those torches?

He joined the snaking line that moved out over the black water.

The last hill dropped away from his feet. Beyond the Potomac, Georgetown was chandeliered red light. The windows of the Watergate trembled like a thousand jack-o'-lanterns. He whiffed marijuana and perfume, rum and the dank miasma of river. The penguin grabbed at the count's cloak, rolling in a drunken shamble. Showgirls, Zorros, pickles, magicians' assistants pushed along in jerky peristalsis. Toward the city glitter, they pilgrimed together above chthonian chaos. A proffered fifth of Seagram's; he hesitated, then shook his head. A barge burned red and green below. Bottles snapped out from the crowd, bubbles of glass spinning down into darkness, each querying the night, *Who — who — who*, till they burst on sudden steel.

On M Street, smoking fusees smeared scarlet light over the face of a bleeding Jesus who walked with the back of his hand on his hip. Dan pushed past Santa Claus, androids, whores, zombies, generals with three-foot penises. At the corner of Bank Alley, a party of impassive Chinese in blue Mao suits stood watching giant rats, clams, androgynes dance and gyrate past.

At Thirty-third, the crowd jelled solid into six lanes of partying flesh. Beneath the clock on the Riggs Bank, a woman's immense rubber breasts proclaimed her a Mutant for Nuclear Power. Undertakers, punkers, Arabs in Saran Wrap rocked and tottered under sodium fluorescence. A black woman in jodhpurs led a blond savage on a chain. Three Girl Scouts with Reagan masks staring from crotchless panty hose offered him a liter of Popov's. Hands and paws clawed at it, but he lifted it from their reach. Abandoning at last all thought of going home, he sucked clear fire till his lungs ached for air.

The night was advanced when he found a

103

clear space again. He was leaning against a tree, watching a train of elephants sway past by firelight. The stars swayed crazily above drunken pullulation. Women swayed by, stripped to the waists. The freezing air packed his nose with burning garbage, beer, grass, and greasepaint, the commingled smells of a balls-to-the-wall riot of four thousand in one square mile, commingled din of forty rock bands in a street ten blocks long.

"You dropped your hat."

She was nearly as tall as he was, and her voice was cool as autumn through the mask. "Thanks," he said, taking the watch cap. "Uh, nice costume. A witch?"

"Close enough. What are you — a thug?"

"No. Actually, it's not a costume. I was just out running and saw everything going on."

"Sometimes you need to become somebody else."

"True. True." He was musing on her black domino when a crash came from the next street, the shatter of glass and hammer of metal. He remembered an unwisely parked Jag. "It's getting rough."

"Last year, they burned two squad cars. The cops pulled out at eleven." She laughed, half-innocent, half-cynical. "This your first Halloween in Georgetown?"

"That's right. Where are you from?"

"Northeast. Out by Catholic U."

"You go there? Catholic U?"

She shook her head no. The black mask gleamed under the streetlight. He sensed the warmth of her body through a foot of cold air.

"Go for a walk?"

"Maybe."

They crossed a footbridge over the abandoned canal. Yelling and screaming fell away behind them. The moon glimmered dim on waterlogged leaves, quivered on stagnant water. They stepped over drunken men, asleep on cobblestones in October. The light waned as the moon slipped on a mask of cloud. "Where are you going?" she murmured.

"Nowhere."

"It's too dark here. I'm going back."

He stopped. The corner of an old building cut off the sky. She hesitated, then leaned against the rough stone wall.

"So, what's your name?"

"Do we need names?"

He reached out to hold her. Her hair was a black wave against stone, her perfume a black flower against the smell of piss in corners.

"You feel so good," he whispered.

"Are you drunk?"

"Yeah." He x-rayed her mask. "Why don't you take that off?"

She was shuddering in the cold. Sirens ripped by on the parkway. The stars shivered.

He muttered again, "Let me see you."

As she lifted her hands to the mask, the moon came out from its shadow. Her lips appeared first, full, glistening. Then the lunar light silhouetted an almost-masculine chin, high cheekbones, a heavy dark curve of eyebrow. Her eyes waited, wide and dark as silent water.

"What's your name?"

"Why?"

"I want to see you again."

"Are you serious? What's yours?"

"Dan. Dan Lenson. I live in Arlington. I'm divorced, in the Navy, one child —"

"My, you *are* serious. Well, I'm Kerry Donavan. Kerry, with a *K*."

"Hi, Kerry. Funny way to meet, huh? Tell me about yourself."

"You might not like what you hear." Her mouth was too wide and her chin too broad for her face to be beautiful. But it was striking, a face that would make men look at her and then, most of them, look away. Her body was strong, too, under the cloak, solidity and purpose in her shoulders and arms. "Anyway, I have to go home."

"What, now? Can't we go someplace?"

"Not tonight."

"Well, look, can I get your number? Can I call you?"

She gave him a string of digits. He didn't have a pen, so he tried to memorize them.

"I've got to go," she said again. "Walk me back to the light."

"How are you getting home?"

"Just get me back to M, all right?"

She turned to look back, heading away up Wisconsin, and he waved. Then she was gone. He rubbed his face, suddenly depressed, less at her departure than at his own solitude and desperation. Grasping at anyone who might fill that emptiness . . . He should be home, getting some sleep, not drinking so much. . . . He spat angrily, then stumbled into an uncertain run.

# 7

The word telegraphed through the building. Niles was going after the Air Force. Two light colonels and a female master sergeant were cleaning out their desks. Dan didn't understand what the director was doing, but he had to admire his tactics. He'd slashed and burned through his own service first, then gone after the contractors. Now it was the turn of the boys in sky blue, they couldn't say they were being discriminated against.

"Okay, you're on-line," Sakai said, sliding back from the new personal computer on Dan's desktop. There were rumors of new carpeting, too.

He worked till 9:00 A.M., broke for a meeting on supportability, then talked on the phone with a systems analyst from Johns Hopkins about the weapons control system software.

He looked at his "things to do" list and remembered he hadn't called the woman he'd met in Georgetown. Kerry. If that was really her name. He took the elevator down to use the pay phone in the lobby. It rang and rang. He was about to hang up when a man's voice said, "Day House, hello?"

"Sorry, wrong number."

"Colonel Evans wants to see you," Burdette

said when he got back to the office.

He wondered what the deputy director wanted. He checked his ribbons and tie, made sure he had his wheelbook and a pen, and headed down the hall.

The deputy's office looked the same as it had the day he reported in: the pipe haze in the air, the aircraft photos on the walls. He knew more about the trim, fair-haired colonel now. Knew, for example, that Scott Evans had shot down three MiGs in Vietnam; had been an aide to the Secretary of the Air Force; had had highly successful command tours at the squadron and wing levels; and had just been selected for promotion to general, though he wouldn't actually pin his stars on till next year. The Air Force ran things casually compared with the Navy, so instead of sounding off, he just said, "You wanted to see me, sir?"

Evans turned from the window. "Dan. How are you doing with us? Getting along okay with Dale and Vic?"

"Yes, sir."

"That's great." Evans eased down behind his desk and leaned back, hands behind his head. He didn't look as if he was worried about getting fired, and for a moment Dan wondered why; everybody else was running scared. "Have a seat, okay? Look, I wanted to talk to you about doing something for Test and Evaluation. I'd go through your boss, but

109

he's been out of pocket for a few days."

"Yessir, haven't seen him all week."

"Well, this is a G/R issue anyway."

"G/R" meant common both to the Navy missile and the GLCM, the Air Force-owned nuclear Tomahawk slated for deployment to Europe.

Evans started with a recap. Most of the developmental glitches had been worked through, but there was still an occasional failure to transition from launch to flight — the same problem the sea-based Tomahawks were experiencing.

"How close are they to a final design, sir?"

"I'm crossing my fingers this is it, the bird we're gonna fly next month. The Brits are set for a deployment at Greenham Common next December."

"What do you need me to do, sir?"

"The admiral wants somebody from this office to observe the tests at Cold Lake. Can you help us out? The T and E side will take care of your travel arrangements."

"Well, I guess so, sir. If Admiral Niles wants me to. Any specific direction, other than observe?"

"The prime contractor's actually going to run the launch, under direction of the operational test and evaluation community. We just want to keep the system honest, make sure that if there's some little problem, the OSD guys don't give them an *F* when they actually ought to be getting a *B*. Like what just happened to that Army air defense gun, and they canceled the whole project."

"I thought the test people were supposed to be independent. Give DOD an objective look at whether or not the system works."

"Sure, we're not going to drive that. If the transporter gets a flat tire, it gets a flat tire. But is that a mission limiter? That's the kind of question you can help them out on." Evans got up and took a turn around the room. "Leave room in your luggage to carry classified material back, data tapes. Hot tip: Cold Lake is gonna be about eight feet deep in snow."

"I hope you're kidding, sir."

"Not by much. Oh, and not everybody up there's happy about us flying these things over their country. Just to give you a heads-up. Anyway, let me go back to this flight transition problem. Some suspect the booster, but —" The colonel shoved papers and reports aside on an adjacent table and came up with a transparency. The title read "Booster separation redesign 10-D." Evans said, "I don't have the most recent one. I think they're up to twelve or thirteen by now."

"So you want me to watch the tests, and be alert for any glitches —"

"And if they occur, get us some idea why."

Dan thought that was actually the contractor's problem, but the message he was getting was that somebody didn't trust somebody else. So Niles was asking him to be his eyes on the scene. "All right, sir, I'll give her a try."

Evans knocked his pipe out into the ashtray, keeping the burnt tobacco carefully distant from his spotlessly crisp Class A's. "Thanks, Dan. That's all, I guess."

He only remembered when he was locking his desk that he had to give a presentation that night. "Shit," he muttered. He riffled through his file drawer, pulled out three folders and stuffed them into his briefcase.

The class had shrunk from twenty to nine. Sliding into his chair, closing his eyes in exhaustion, Dan understood. Szerenci assigned work ruthlessly. Each project entailed first study, then creative thought, then endless calculation. They'd written computer programs that reproduced the entire armored battle in central Europe. The finished paper was two pages long, but it had taken him eight nights.

Szerenci looked tired, too, as he threw his coat, damp from a slow, cold rain, onto his desk. This time, Sandy Cottrell didn't go up to greet him. She didn't even look at him, just sat with her legs crossed and her eyes on her notes.

"Okay, tonight we've got a treat — a presentation by Mr. Lenson on Navy weapons development. Dan?"

He started from memory, with a description of the missile. Nothing classified, but you'd have to dig around to put the figures together. He outlined range, speed, accuracy. He explained the different versions and how each would fit into Navy and Air Force inventories.

Szerenci asked, "Let's hear more about the TLAM-N. What does it do for our nuclear strategy?"

Dan reoriented. "Uh, that carries a two-hundred-kiloton W-eighty warhead. It was part of President Carter's program to upgrade the B-fifty-two."

"Right, but what exactly does it *do?* What does its addition to the strategic arsenal buy for us?"

Szerenci went to the board. In five minutes, he had outlined the Soviet air defense system, reduced it to a mathematical equation, and shown how a cruise missile could triple the number of U.S. warheads arriving on target. Dan was awed; in all the time he'd spent at JCM, he'd never heard a concrete justification for the nuclear Tomahawk. Now it lay on the board, spare and unequivocal as $E=MC^2$. Szerenci raised an eyebrow. "You look like this is new to you."

"It is."

"But obviously somebody did this work at some point. Right? You could burrow back and find the roots of this at Program Analysis and Evaluation, a Secretary of Defense named

Mel Laird, a study for Harold Brown. And the internal politics are fascinating. You've got SecDef and Congress fighting the Chiefs to get a weapon the services don't want. You've got an Air Force program assigned to Navy sponsorship so the Air Force can't torpedo it, and elements in the Navy using the Air Force as cover to get a weapon for the surface fleet without their own aviators shooting it down.

"But this isn't a course in political maneuvering. Sorry, I'm interrupting your presentation; please go on."

"That's all I had on the weapon. Let's talk about the developmental process next."

He flipped slides, going through interorganizational relationships, then the budgeting process. Heads bent over notebooks. He caught a smile from Mei. Maybe he should try again with her. But did he really want to get involved with somebody who'd already told him she was going back to China? What was he trying to do, replicate his failed marriage?

He jerked his mind back like a disobedient dog, described the *New Jersey* installation, then closed and asked for questions. He took his seat with relief as the prof began his lecture.

"Calculating the possibility of a disarming first strike. Is it theoretically feasible, or not?" Szerenci asked.

They straggled toward Mr. Henry's in a misty rain. Szerenci took one schnapps and pushed the other across the table. "Nice presentation."

"Thanks." Dan tossed the fiery sweet liquid back as Szerenci signaled the waiter for more. Cottrell looked away from them. They were all at the same table, but she seemed distant. Hectic spots flamed in her cheeks as she hand-rolled another cigarette. Not for the first time, he wondered if she was in the best of health.

"Mei, are we talking too fast? Are you keeping up with all this jargon?"

Mei fingered her wineglass. "I understand what you are saying."

"We'll be getting into the Chinese strategic position in a couple of weeks. Maybe you can talk about how your forces are set up."

"I will try. Perhaps my uncle can help me."

Dan finished the second schnapps, feeling the glow. Two lit the fire. Should he go for another? Why not, he thought.

"You career Navy, Dan?" the prof asked.

He glanced at his Academy ring, glowing golden in the bar light. "Trying to make a decision on that."

"Thinking about the executive side? Consulting? Academia? A law degree can buy you time. And it'll come in handy, whatever you do."

The idea of law horrified him. Being locked

in an office with stacks of dusty books, helping whoever paid you to rip people off. . . . Szerenci flipped a card onto the table. "Or, I know some folks who are setting up a new research institute. Going to take on RAND and Brookings and CNA. . . . You decide. If I can help, come and see me."

Dan caught Cottrell's eye, and was startled to see hatred plain in it. She said casually, "I'll have to get him over to my side of town, too. Show him what goes on up on the Hill. Would you like that, Dan?"

"Uh, I guess."

"Good. I'll call you. Sometime soon."

He looked after them as she and Mei headed for the ladies' room. Something going on there, but he wasn't sure what. He slipped Szerenci's card into his wallet, said thanks again, and got up.

Outside in the rain, he looked up at the buildings around him, envisioning how a fifty-megaton warhead would turn them instantly into incandescent gas. Then he headed for the subway, feeling secure only when he was shielded by a hundred feet of solid rock.

# 8

A couple of days later, Dan found Westerhouse sitting at his desk when he let himself
in. The captain rose when he came in, clearing
his throat in a way that might have been self-
conscious. Dan saw he'd lost weight; the tab
of his uniform belt came a couple of inches
out of the buckle.

"Hi, sir. You back?"

"Oh, hi. I wonder if we could get together
later in the day, go over what you've got on
your plate."

"Will do, sir. How about if I stop by around
eleven?"

They agreed on that and Westerhouse left.
Dan sat, and there was a couple of seconds'
worth of silence. Then Sakai said, "Hey, you
see Peter Jennings last night?"

"Uh, no. What'd I miss?"

"Hour-long special on Libya. Khaddafi's
building a nuclear weapon."

"Jesus Christ. That's all we need."

Burdette leaned back from his cubicle.
"Dan."

"Sorry. Forgot I was being monitored by
the Moral Majority." He looked at his list
of things to do and remembered the Halloween girl again. She'd probably given him
a string of random numbers just to get rid

of him. One last try.

This time, to his surprise, she answered. "Hello."

"Is this Kerry? Kerry Donavan?"

"Yes?"

He could tell she had no idea who he was. "We met the other night, in Georgetown? The guy in the sweats. We went down to the canal together."

"Oh. Oh, yes. I remember now."

"I called before, but a guy answered."

"You must have talked to Carl."

He wondered who Carl was, and why they lived in the same house. "Look, I thought maybe we could get together, for a drink or something."

"Are you serious?"

"Sure, why not?"

"I told you — you might be surprised by what you find."

"Sometimes surprises are fun. If it doesn't work out, it doesn't work out."

"I guess that's a reasonable attitude. This afternoon?"

"*This* afternoon? I'm at work."

"You work downtown, right? I have to be there a little after three. Can you meet me at three?"

He thought fast. "Maybe. Maybe I can."

"All right, meet me at Federal Triangle. The subway exit. You can go with us. Then after, we'll see, maybe come to dinner."

Someone called. A man's voice? "Gotta go. See you."

She hung up. After a second, so did he, thinking, That was strange. Where were they going? Who was "us"? He faced his desk again, picked up a piece of paper, then put it down. He looked at his watch, then at the stack of reports and messages.

He cleared everything else out of his mind and went to work.

At ten to eleven, he turned his classified material facedown on his desk, locked his file drawer, and told Vic he was going to the program manager's office.

Westerhouse was sitting with his head propped on his arm. He pointed silently to the seat opposite. Dan sat and waited. Finally, he cleared his throat. "Sir, you got my note about my going to Canada, didn't you?"

"Yeah, I did. Sorry, I had to be out. How are we looking on the schedule?"

"It's actually looking up, sir."

Westerhouse examined him. "An optimist?"

"No, sir. It'll be close, but we just might do it."

"Are we going to get the ABLs in time for *New Jersey*?"

He outlined the status, the split buy among the three contractors. "I'm riding herd on them. They'll deliver the first unit in March."

"Maybe. My experience has been that when

you're working from redlines, there's always some woodchuck that pops out and stops the show. How about the other hardware?"

He described the status of the operator interface display terminals, and the rest of the gear set being built for *New Jersey* — five separate pieces of electronics for the equipment room, four more racks for the control room. Westerhouse said, "Are you telling me they'll be ready on time?"

He bit the bullet. "Barring any unforeseen problems, they look on track, sir."

"Okay, the software?"

"That's the long pole in the tent. It's written in assembly language and it's a disaster. I've got Sakai on it about eighty percent of his time. Got an assist visit scheduled next week. Sparky and I'll try to find the bottleneck and ream it out."

"We've got to get it on the rails. You work it at the technical level. I'll set up a CEO-level meeting."

"Okay, sir. How's the missile doing? How's Convair reacting to Admiral Niles's cattle prod?"

"Larramore's got a gold team taking apart their quality problem. About all we can do now is wait for them to get their ducks in ranks. Other hard spots . . . well, we've got the transition-to-flight problem." Westerhouse said the Canadian tests should show whether the booster changes worked or if they had to go at it from another angle.

His boss turned over a message blank and sighed. "Okay, new subject. These congressional hearings. The public relations types prepare the testimony, but they're gonna need technical help. Can you take that on?"

"I've never done anything like that, but I'll try."

"Go on up and see Carol, get a window set up."

"Aye aye, sir."

Westerhouse turned over another page. "You're going to Cold Lake?"

Didn't we cover that? he thought, but he just said, "Yes, sir. Colonel Evans asked me to go up there and keep everybody honest."

His boss tapped a pencil. "Is there anything else that if you got it, it could speed things up, make your job easier?"

"Just about six extra months, sir."

Westerhouse crinkled his eyes but didn't smile. He got up, said thanks. Dan said, "Oh, if it's all right, I've been working Saturdays, and Sundays, too, sometimes. Can I get off a little early this afternoon? Personal stuff."

"I don't see any problem with that. As long as you're caught up on the preps for your trip."

As the sky grew from a shining blue egg far above him, he wondered why his heart was speeding up, why his fingers were digging into the handrail of the escalator. . . . He pulled his mind away and watched the walls slide by. At intervals, subterranean leakage stained the new white concrete. Past him as he rose streamed hundreds of federal bureaucrats, the vomitus of the government buildings concentrated here in the center of the District. Glances snagged on his uniform, then returned to weary blankness. He fingered his cap.

He'd mulled over wearing his blues to meet Miss Mystery. Nobody who'd worn a uniform in the seventies was ever quite comfortable wearing one in public. But the only alternative he had at his office was running gear, and he didn't think sweats would look too great at what might turn into a dinner date. So finally he'd just pulled his bridge coat on against the chill.

The blue oval grew larger, and he caught a glimpse of a dome, a statue shining in the sun.

The escalator bowed like a diving porpoise and deposited him on the shining metal landing. He stepped aside, out of the hurrying District stream: men and women with newspapers and briefcases, shoppers carrying department store bags, tourists, students.

She stood by a line of newspaper-vending machines, looking out over the crowd. He threaded his way through to her and saluted. "Hi."

"Hi. . . . I didn't realize you were in the military."

"I told you I was in the Navy."

"Did you? I guess I forgot." She was wearing a dark skirt, an overcoat, and flats and her hair was up. Her face was paler than he recalled it, tilted back for a kiss beneath the Halloween moon. But he was relieved. She was attractive — he hadn't been *that* drunk.

"Where exactly are we going?" he asked her.

She pointed across Pennsylvania, and he raised his eyes to a square sandstone pile as they stepped off the curb. "A courthouse? Is that what this is?"

"Look, this might be embarrassing for you. I didn't mean to play a trick, but you called, and . . . it's a court appearance. It shouldn't take long. But if you want to back out —"

"No, that's okay, I'll just tag along and keep you company." He still didn't know what was going on. Was she on jury duty? A lawyer?

The sign changed from WALK to DON'T WALK. She ran the last few feet to join a group by the west entrance. She turned from greeting them. "These are my friends — Phil, Max, Deborah, Ken."

He nodded and shook hands, puzzled. They looked doubtful, too; the woman hesitated before shaking his hand.

"It's almost time. Come on."

He jerked his gaze away from a poster one of them was carrying and followed them up the steps.

"Hands up, Admiral," said a black guard

with a .38 on his hip. Dan lifted them as the others threw backpacks and cases on the conveyor belt.

When the search was over, they trooped through a gray marble corridor to a bank of elevators. On the sixth floor, they went through a second security check, then filed in one by one.

The courtroom smelled of frightened, unwashed people. It had a water-spotted acoustic ceiling and red polyester carpet. He took a seat with Kerry's friends in a middle row, tucking his combination cap under the bench. Up front, a cop and his lawyer were discussing something with the judge, a florid white man with a heavy, unsympathetic face.

He leaned over to Deborah, the woman who'd hesitated before taking his hand. She stared back through glasses thick as portholes. He whispered, "Hey, what's going on?"

"You don't know? It's their arraignment."

He wasn't entirely sure what an arraignment was, but Deborah's lips were compressed; she didn't seem eager to talk. He sat back, figuring the situation would clarify itself.

Finally, the cop's business was done; he and his group left. A stir at the front, the pop of briefcase catches. The judge glanced toward where, Dan saw with a shock, Kerry sat with three men and another woman. Someone he couldn't see intoned, *United States v. Beliejvak. United States v. Diehl. United States v.*

*Donavan. United States v. Haneghan. United States v. Ostlander.* The defendants will please rise."

She stood with the rest and faced the bench. The judge asked them, "Do you have counsel?"

A bearded man in a scruffy-looking three-piece suit said, "Your Honor, I represent the defendants."

The judge raised his voice. "You are charged with an indictment charging you with criminal trespass, destruction of government property, conspiracy, and destruction of national security materials. Do you understand the offenses with which you are charged?"

"No, sir, we don't." Dan focused on the man who stood beside Kerry. He was older than she, spare, erect, with a high forehead and a narrow, bony face straight from a Dürer engraving. His brown hair was prison-short. He wore a blue chambray shirt with the collar buttoned and black trousers.

"You should. Have all of you seen and reviewed the indictment with your attorney? . . . Then I'll take it that you understand the offenses with which you are charged. Do you have any other questions?"

The man in the chambray shirt lifted his hand. "Your Honor, is that considered a count of sabotage? The 'destruction of national security materials'?"

125

"I believe it is. Is that the government's understanding?"

A gray suit rose on the judge's right. "That is our understanding."

"Is it, then, the charge that, by disarming the bomber, we have disarmed the United States and put the people of the United States at risk of attack?"

The prosecutor, dryly, "That is the essence of a charge of sabotage."

"Deborah," Dan whispered. "*What* is going on?"

She whispered back fiercely, "What are you doing here, anyway? Who are you?"

"Kerry invited me."

"Well, be quiet, or they'll throw us all out. They're being arraigned."

"I can see that, but what for?"

"They carried out an action in New York State last winter. Kerry and Carl went through the fence. Tammy and Clinton drove the station wagon, so they're accessories. Erica helped, but she didn't go along. The state charged them with felony trespass. They went through the whole grand jury thing in New York. But in September, the feds decided to press charges and change venue. So the whole process starts again, only this time in a federal court."

"Why did they — what's an 'action,' and —" He stopped as she gave him a look so poisonous, he would not have been surprised to find his buttons tarnished. He rubbed his mouth and sat back.

The judge was saying in a tired voice, "How do you anticipate your clients will plead?"

The bearded attorney: "Not guilty."

"Do they desire trial by jury?"

"Yes, Your Honor, they do."

"May I make a statement relevant to my plea?" Kerry said. It was the first time she'd spoken.

"What is it?"

"I want to plead on behalf of the children of the future. That they may live in peace, not under nuclear terror —"

"I don't want to hear it. Guilty or not guilty — that is all I want to hear at this arraignment."

"I want to plead for the right to —"

"I will assign you a plea of not guilty."

"Deborah," he whispered again.

*"What?"*

"You said they carried out 'an action.' What exactly did they do?"

"They hammered on a bomber. They poured blood on it. They're facing six to eight years." She rooted impatiently through her purse, then held out a flyer.

THE STATEMENT OF THE COLUMBIA
PLOWSHARES ACTIVISTS

On February 7, enacting the Isaiah vi-

127

sion of "beating swords into plowshares," five peace activists calling themselves the Columbia Plowshares of Washington, D.C., carried out acts of nonviolent disarmament on U.S. first-strike nuclear weaponry. Penetrating the boundary wire at Griffiss Air Force Base in Rome, New York, we exposed the genocidal nature of the cruise missile prototypes being flight-tested from the air force base.

We also carried with us an indictment against the U.S. government for crimes against God, humanity, and international law. Since August 1945, the entire world has been held hostage by nuclearism and the exponential rise in military violence. With blind insanity, we have accumulated enough weaponry to eliminate all life on the planet many times over. In the past fifty years, over $13 trillion have been spent on weapons research, development, and deployment.

Disarmament is the first step toward Christ's Kingdom. We refuse to see violence as inevitable, injustice as the order of the day, and death-dealing as the only way of life. Join us in our declaration to announce the jubilee for the poor, relief for the children, and peace for all.

"Thanks," he muttered, sliding down into his seat. Now he understood the looks his uniform was drawing. A boyish-looking fellow in a loud bow tie kept glancing his way as he scribbled on a pad. He debated leaving, but he didn't want to draw even more attention. Instead, he listened to the judge assigning trial dates, then to a long objection by the government, apparently an attempt to get the defense lawyer off the case. The judge set a motion cutoff date. Then he said, "The parties are entitled to bond as originally set. It is the intention of the court that you be subject to pretrial supervision, and a limitation on travel subject to the approval of the pretrial office." Kerry started to say something, but he cut her off with "Dismissed. Next case."

Deborah and Ken and the others got up. He retrieved his coat and cap and shuffled out with them.

Kerry and the other defendants joined them in the corridor. Her face was even whiter than it had been outside. "Well, that's over."

"You didn't tell me you were the one making the court appearance."

"I know. Still want to have supper with us?"

He actually didn't, but he was ashamed to admit it. "Sure. Oh — is that the guy I talked to on the phone?"

"Carl, this is Dan. Dan, Carl Haneghen." They regarded each other; then Haneghen said, "Thanks for coming in uniform. A gesture of support?"

"Not exactly."

"Are you a friend of the defendants?"

Dan looked around, and there he was, the young fellow who'd been taking notes in the courtroom. Bright red-orange suspenders showing under a rumpled tweed jacket, bow tie, large red plastic-framed glasses on a boyish-looking face. Tousled reddish blond hair over his ears, and sun-crinkled green eyes. "Martin Tallinger," he said, shaking Dan's hand before he realized it. "I write on defense policy, military issues for various publications. I couldn't help noticing you in there. Are you a friend of the defendants?"

"I know Miss Donavan." Simultaneously, Dan recognized the name. Tallinger was the writer-analyst who'd done the hatchet job on the Tomahawk program.

"Are you a Plowshares member, Commander Lenson? That's the proper rank, right?"

Dan's hand came up to his uniform blouse. Damn it, he'd left his name tag on. "No. I'm not a member, and I'd rather not be mentioned in print, if you don't mind." Looking past Tallinger, he caught Deborah's sneer.

"You don't want your name to be used?"

"I'd appreciate it. Very much."

"So your interest is — what? Personal? Professional curiosity?"

He didn't answer. Haneghen said, "Martin, if you have any questions about our witnessing, maybe I can help you." Tallinger nodded, but his eyes followed Dan as they headed for the exit.

Donavan took his arm. "Last chance to back out. I know this isn't what you expected. But it's who I am."

"It was kind of a shock."

"Well, now you know. Deborah? Ken? You coming?"

No one in the group seemed to have a car. They waited till Haneghen came out, then trooped back to the subway. They got off at the Catholic U stop, then stood in line for a bus. When they boarded, they were the only whites on it. A leathery-voiced woman directly behind Dan declaimed for the entire trip in a loud voice, telling everyone about her abusive husbands and her rape by her oldest son. Occasionally, she reached over the seat to stroke his shoulderboards. The other passengers looked straight ahead or out the windows, or read papers or romance novels. The bus bumped and grunted over cracked, potholed streets. He considered getting off, taking a taxi back downtown, but the uneven sidewalks were deserted as evening came. The few cars were junk heaps or stripped tireless wrecks. It didn't look like many taxis would be cruising here.

They rode for almost an hour. Finally, the doors hissed open on a street lined with dilapidated houses. There were no yards, no lawns, no trees, just cracked asphalt and wrecked cars. But the others didn't seem to mind. They strolled down the street, talking about the court appearance, someone's sick child, a vigil for somebody who was being executed.

He walked silently with them, watching as their breath turned white and rose slowly under the occasional intact streetlight. What the hell had he gotten himself into? Then he ordered himself to lighten up. Except for Deborah, they didn't act unwelcoming. And he didn't think anyone from Joint Cruise Missiles would be watching from these peeling swaybacked porches and stoops.

They emerged onto the border of an open field, startling in the center of such a densely populated area. Beyond it rose the spires of a church or basilica.

"Here we are." Kerry looked over her shoulder as they opened a chain-link gate and went up a short walk. He lingered, looking up at a rather shabby old three-story house squatting in a tiny fenced-in yard, then followed them in.

Ken, who wore jeans and had a limp, showed him around before supper. The basement held a donated gas furnace, storage areas, and a chapel. The big old-fashioned kitchen smelled of soup and of the corn tortillas a stout woman was hammering out on a table. All six blackened burners were roaring on a commercial gas stove. The first floor held dining room and living room but was also a playground for a carpetful of small children. Upstairs was a warren of smaller spaces, some of the doors hand-lettered with the names of the occupants. More children peeped out at him as he went by. Twenty-five people lived in the Dorothy Day House, Ken said, most of them homeless who for one reason or another the city authorities couldn't help.

Now he sat with them at the big dining table, mostly black or Latin women and small children, though there was one old man with long white hair and eyes locked on some other planet than this.

He felt confused. Ken, whose last name was Zinkowski, had told him the house belonged not to Plowshares but to an organization called the Catholic Workers. He'd asked Ken, "But who are the staff?"

Zinkowski had smiled. "Staff?"

"The people who aren't homeless — like you — are they religious? Is this some sort of monastery?"

"We have friends in the religious community. Carl's a priest. And most of us are spiritually inclined. But, no, we're just whoever feels called. People come to try it out and look and experiment. Some leave after awhile. One of our guests asked once who someone was. 'She's visiting,' I said. 'Isn't everybody in this house?' Carl said." Ken had smiled. "And we're glad you can join us for supper. Come back whenever you like."

Now he raised his eyes to the posters and artwork on the walls. FIN EL BLOQUERO DE CUBA. Wood-block prints of Jesus in a bread-line, St. Joseph at work. Pictures of Martin Luther King, Jr., Gandhi, Mother Teresa, Albert Schweitzer. IT'S A SIN TO BUILD A NU-CLEAR WEAPON. NO SPANKING ZONE. Sign-up sheets for laundry time and cooking duty.

"Enjoying yourself?" She leaned down, flushed, hand on his shoulder. "Look, I'm glad you came. We'll have time to talk later. Okay?"

He nodded and she vanished again. A small boy examined his uniform, then reached up to touch his ribbons. He remembered when Nan was this age, and he smiled at the boy.

"Are you a policeman?" the boy said, wide-eyed.

"No. No, I'm just a friend of Kerry's."

"She knocked wi' a hammer on the bomber plane. To stop them making bad things for war."

"Yeah. So she did. How about you? I don't guess you're going to be first in line to join the Green Berets, are you?" The boy stared, then burst into laughter.

A clatter of platters announced the meal. Black beans and rice, guacamole, a spicy sauce, hot tortillas. Kerry stood back, wiping her hands on a worn towel, then reaching out to stroke a child's close-cropped head. "Getting acquainted? Okay, I guess everything is under control for a few minutes. . . . Let's eat." She sat down next to him. She'd changed out of the suit and skirt into jeans and a crewneck sweatshirt. She smelled of soap and baking. Her black hair was twisted back over her shoulder.

"Pass the rice, please. You were probably figuring a different kind of date."

"Well, you're right." He reached for another tortilla. "Your buddy Deborah doesn't like uniforms."

"She's been known to take things personally. But I figure we should be trying to reach the people in uniforms. After the guards arrested us at Griffiss, we had a very nice talk with them, Carl and I, while we were waiting for the police. For the most part, no one has ever talked to military people seriously about what they're participating in."

"Well, I don't believe in what you're selling."

He expected an argument, but she shrugged. "As long as you're satisfied you're right."

"Carl — that's Haneghen, right?"

"Yes. He was my partner for the Rome action. Have you gotten to talk to him?"

He looked across the table at the man in the chambray shirt. Flanked by kids, he looked happy. Not like someone facing six to eight years. "Not really."

"Relax. Look, don't let Deborah get to you. Okay?"

"All right," he said.

Later, after she went back to the kitchen, Haneghen took the chair next to him. He had on heavy steel-toed boots, the kind shipyard workers wore. Close up, his close-cropped scalp, light blue eyes, and long, narrow head came across as either pedagogical or penal, but he extended his hand with a gentle expression. "Carl Haneghan. We met at the arraignment, right? Thanks for coming. We don't see a lot of military people on our side."

"I'm not on your side."

"Sorry, I made an assumption I had no right to make. Do I understand you to be visiting Kerry?"

"That's right."

"What do you do, Dan?"

"Whatever they tell me to, Carl. How about you?"

Haneghan didn't seem to resent his answer, and Dan felt ashamed. He was getting defensive, and so far, the guy hadn't done or said anything to deserve it.

"What do I do? Mainly, work with people who need me. Occasionally, I paint."

"Oh, an artist?"

"No. Houses, during the summer."

"Somebody said you were a priest."

"There's truth to that rumor. But I seem to be effectively excommunicated at the moment."

"The church didn't like your 'actions'?"

"I look on civil disobedience as sacramental. The same as celebrating Mass, in a way. But you're right. Our movement is not exactly at one with the Vatican. Did you enjoy dinner? If you want to take your coat off, you can hang it over there. I don't think the kids will bother it."

"Maybe I'll do that. Dinner was good, thanks. Any chance of a cup of coffee?"

"We don't use much coffee here. Or sugar. There are those who think it's acquiescing in an oppressive peasant economy. I could probably find you some tea."

Dan told him no, that he was fine. He wanted to ask what these oppressed peasants were going to do for money if Americans didn't buy their coffee and sugar, but he figured they had an answer for that, too. Okay, pleasant conversation. "Uh, is this your first arraignment?"

"Oh, no. More like the eighth or ninth. And we have another trial coming up for a Pentagon action. Another fella from Jonah House and I, we poured blood on the River Entrance on the Feast of the Holy Innocents. The prosecutor wanted me held without bond. But O'Malley — he was the judge today, the one with the mustache — he's actually not as rough on us as he could be."

"Have you done time?"

"Oh yeah. Two years at Allenwood, making furniture for Ed Meese's office. I wrote 'Fuck you, Ed' in the varnish, where you pull the drawer out. Hope he got my message."

"Good for you," Dan said. He looked around. "Say, can I help clean up? Is that okay with everybody?"

Haneghen said that would be welcome, and Dan got up and went back into the kitchen. He offered to scrub the pans, and Kerry handed him the brush with a sigh of relief.

The kids disappeared after dinner, protesting that they weren't sleepy. There wasn't any television in evidence. When all the pots and dishes were done and stacked, Kerry suggested they go for a walk. "A walk?" he said. "Outside? Is it safe?"

"I try not to let fear rule my life," she said quietly. "We won't stay out long."

They strolled along the steel fence that barred access to the grassy plain. She told him the building at the top of the hill was a Reconstruction-era home for veterans. "They come out in the summer and garden, the old soldiers, and we talk," she said. Their breaths puffed out, drifting through the chain link as if it wasn't there. A silence, then she added, "So, I guess this wasn't what you expected."

"You keep saying that. How did you get

involved with this — with the group?"

"With Catholic Action, or with Plow-shares?"

"I guess I'm still confused as to who is what."

"Well, it's not that hard, just that the memberships overlap. I guess originally I was attracted to the lifestyle, the idea of helping people. Then I met Carl, and going to the action with him seemed like the right thing to do.

"See, I didn't plan to go in, not originally. Erica was supposed to be his partner, going through the wire. But at the last minute, she couldn't face the possibility of leaving her kids for so long — she's got two girls, eight and eleven — and going to prison for years. . . . None of us can say a word against her decision. The federal authorities are getting serious. The state courts will charge you with trespass and maybe property destruction, but the feds are hitting us with sabotage charges. A couple on the West Coast, they were tried four times. Two hung juries, a mistrial, and a conviction. They appealed from prison and their conviction was overturned, but now they're going back to court on a reduced charge. So that actually makes five."

Dan's ear turned to the distant *pop-pop-pop* of gunfire, but she didn't remark on it, so he didn't, either. He turned his head slowly, checking out the shadowed housefronts. "Is

139

that legal? I thought you couldn't be tried more than once."

"I thought so, too, but they do it. Anyway, Carl was ready to go alone. But it's better to have more than one person, in case anything happens, and it's better to have both sexes. So I went with him. Usually, there's a long process to prepare yourself — prayer and so forth. But I felt I was ready."

"And now you're looking at prison time, too."

"That's right." She looked across the dark lawn. "And do you know . . . This is something I'm not sure I could say to them . . . but I'm not sure it's worth it. It felt great when I did it. I was scared, but once I was through that first fence, it was a total feeling of commitment and justice. I'm not *sorry*. I did it freely, to bear witness. But face-to-face with the cost, I don't want to pay it. Maybe I don't have the kind of commitment the others do — that Carl has, for example."

Dan started to understand something he hadn't gotten there in the house. Why she'd wanted to be someone else on Halloween. The mask, the tights . . . maybe even her reaching out to him. "Ken was telling me how everyone at the house is a visitor. Only some visits last longer than others."

"I guess so."

"How long have you been there?"

"Two years now."

"Where are you from?"

"Massachusetts. West of Boston."

"What do you do? Other than pour blood on airplanes?"

"Actually, that takes up very little of our time. Our vision at the house is two eyes and one face — resistance and hospitality. We only spend about two percent of our time doing antiwar work. I help out at a shelter and soup kitchen we run downtown." She glanced at his ribbons. "And what do you do, in the Navy?"

"I'm a ship driver." He gave it a beat, then added, "We call it surface line. I've spent most of my time in destroyers and frigates. One tour on a staff, in amphibious ships."

"Ships that . . . crawl out of the water onto land?"

"You'd think so from the name, but actually they carry marines."

"To intervene in other countries?"

"To preserve peace."

"How do you preserve peace with a gun?"

"Ask any cop." He was getting a little sick of the sanctimonious atmosphere. "Look, your friends and I don't seem to have much in common. I don't think a lot of the stuff they're spouting is very realistic. Or even true."

"Your face made that plain. When you were talking to Ken, and Carl."

"And Josh."

"Josh?"

"The kid. He already thinks anybody in uniform's a trained killer."

"Oh, you mean Joaquin. Well, aren't you?"

"Sure. But I only spend about two percent of my time actually sticking bayonets into babies."

"I see. What ship are you driving now?"

"What?"

"You said you were a ship driver. What ship are you driving now?"

He'd hoped she wouldn't ask that, but here was the hardball, right in his face. He thought of just saying he worked in an office, but decided to save them both time. "I'm not assigned to a ship right now. I work in weapons development. I'm in charge of putting Tomahawk missiles aboard the battleships."

She was silent for a few paces. He heard sirens now, far off, but getting closer. "Shall we head back?"

Without speaking, she wheeled and they retraced their steps. He kept watching the shadows, the empty pavement, the glitter of broken glass, the piles of uncollected trash. "What's the idea locating here? Right in the middle of the crime wave?"

"It's close to the poor."

"It's that all right."

"And we're poor, too. Carl can't hold a job."

"Why not? He looks healthy."

"He doesn't want to get into the tax trap.

142

What's the good of opposing violence if you help pay for it?"

"Oh. Right." He looked away, recognizing the inevitable. He wasn't going to get anywhere with this woman. He shouldn't *want* to get anywhere with her. But something about the curve of her mouth, the sad expression of her shadowed eyes . . .

They climbed the porch steps. "Well," he said. "Look, thanks, for dinner and all. But it's getting late. How do I get to Arlington from here? Can I call a cab?"

"They won't come here at night. There's a bus stop two blocks that way. Take the Number Two H bus back to the subway." She didn't look at him, but added, "Before you go, let's sit on the swing."

The old wooden glider creaked under their weight. He leaned back, warm in his bridge coat.

"How do you feel about this?" she murmured.

"About what?"

"Seeing me here. Where I live."

"How do I feel? Well, I think you're a good person. Probably better than I am. I think we're different."

"Maybe not as much as you think."

"Oh?"

"Not everybody can live up to their ideals."

"You seem to be trying."

"Maybe it looks that way," she said, and

put out a boot and pushed the swing into motion. "I guess I shouldn't like you."

"I shouldn't like you, either." He didn't say it, but he thought, But maybe I could. He looked sideways at plaintive eyes under heavy dark eyebrows. He was remembering the softness of her lips beneath his, the glitter of the moon on black water.

"But maybe you could?"

"Yow."

" 'Yow'?"

"That's exactly what I was thinking. Same words even."

She turned toward him and he was breathing her breath again. Then they were kissing. His cap fell off and rolled away into the shadows.

His mouth against her ear, feeling her warmth in the immense cold of the night, he whispered, "What about Carl?"

"What about him?"

"Were you lovers?"

"He's a priest."

"Were you lovers?"

She answered by not answering. Finally, she cleared her throat. "It didn't work out. Now we're just friends."

He caught voices through the door, and the porch light flashed on. He bent for his cap. She flipped her collar up, looking away as he stood. "Well, anyway, good night."

"Good night," she said. He went down the

walk. He looked back at her from the gate. "Two blocks," she said, and pointed. He lifted his hand and then walked away.

# 9

Through the director's corner windows, the first snowfall of the winter made Crystal City glisten below a steely sky. Dan noted those present: Colonel Evans, the colonels and captains who headed the program offices, the public affairs staff, the civilian Ph.D adviser, the GS-14 who handled the financials. Finally, the deputy glanced at his watch. "Find yourselves seats, please. The admiral's on his way up."

It was the initial meeting to prepare for the House appearance. The senior people settled around a table set with lined tablets and sharpened pencils. He was heading for a chair by the wall when Evans said, "Dan, could you take the minutes, please?"

"Yes, sir." He got one of the spare pads and made sure he had a backup pen.

"Attention on deck." Everyone rose as Niles, looking like a blue-and-gold iceberg, hung his cap on the stand and took his seat at the head of the table.

He outlined what he wanted. A ten-minute opening statement. A three-minute video using the Tonopah footage. Separate addenda for classified material and financials. Prepared responses addressing test results, progress of second-sourcing, and cost overruns. Finally, he grunted, "Okay, that's enough to get you started," then picked up his cover and left.

They stood for a moment after the door closed. Then Evans moved over, took Niles's place, and said, "All right, let's continue. What else can they ask us?"

One by one, they dredged up the sore points: the transition problem, the nuclear safety certification, a lawsuit from a farmer in California whose fruit trees had been destroyed by a crash — every crack and niche a hostile interrogator might get his fingernails into. When they tapered off, Evans said, "Anything else? Yes — Dan?"

"I don't know if they'll ask anything like this, but why are we even putting nuclear warheads on cruisers? If we're saying they're so accurate that we can put them through somebody's window, why not go to all-conventional?"

Several officers lifted their heads to examine him. "That's a programmatic question; I don't think they'll be asking that," the deputy said curtly. "Anything else? Okay, we'll put together a draft statement and reassemble Monday to murder-board it. Thank you, ladies and gentlemen. . . . Lenson, I'll need those notes as soon as you get them typed up."

Dan stood in the hallway, angry at Evans's dismissive response. He looked at his watch. A whole morning shot. By the time he got these typed, it would be time for lunch with Sandy Cottrell.

The white-pillared dome of the Capitol rose serenely above spidery bare oaks across the street from the Longworth Building. He asked a security guard for the Ways and Means Committee hearing room.

Sandy was already holding a drink, and it didn't look like her first. A cigarette burned between short lacquered nails. Her cheeks were flushed and a low-cut blouse showed most of her chest. He inhaled perfume and smoke as they shook hands. "So you found us."

"Yeah, thanks for the invite. This is where you work?" He looked around, feeling intimidated, still getting used to being on the Hill.

"In Rog Zoelcke's office, upstairs. If you've got to have lunch, this is about as convenient as you can get. And the Restaurant Federation puts on this great winter shindig."

"Why did we have to have lunch?"

"We had to sometime. Couldn't you feel it? What are you drinking? Let's go on in, there're bar tables inside."

He felt even more out of place as they passed through a receiving line. Cottrell got hugs and cheek kisses. He got fast handshakes and eyes that darted past him to the next person in line.

The ceiling of the immense room was domi-

148

nated by huge gold relief images of eagles with spread wings. At the far end, a curtain hung behind a raised dais. The leather chairs were empty. The floor was carpeted in dark blue, with a gold eagle motif. Across it, rows of linen-covered tables were stacked with food. Chefs and carvers stood slicing and serving. A huge center table held a flower arrangement nine feet high. There had to be five hundred people talking and eating and circulating beneath the gaze of the eagles.

"What were you saying?"

"Oh, that I can't drink during duty hours. Plus, I've got a pretest meeting this afternoon, testimony to prepare —"

"House? Senate? What committee?"

"House Armed Services."

"Which subcommittee?"

"Uh, I think it's the full committee. On procurement."

"The full committee, no. It's probably the Procurement and Military Nuclear Systems Subcommittee. Mel Osborn's the chairman, right?" Dan had to shrug. "You don't know who the chair is? Then how do you know how to pitch your testimony?"

"I don't. I'm just helping Admiral Niles get ready."

A sound system harrumphed, and the assembly quieted as a jolly man made remarks. Dan was more interested in Cottrell's shining aureole of golden hair, her damp-looking

149

neck. The blouse was *low*. If he leaned over . . . Yep, there they were. "Thanks for coming to our annual winter reception. . . . Sample our finest offerings. . . . Touch base with our friends on Capitol Hill. . . . State chapter people scattered around the room. . . . Chance to discuss issues that concern us. . . . Pleased to have you here, and thanks for coming."

Cottrell asked him, "And this Niles, he's who?"

Dan pulled his eyes off her tits and outlined his chain of command. She coughed and lit another cigarette. "Sounds like you're low man on the food chain."

"I'm only a lieutenant commander, Sandy. That's heavy aboard ship, senior department head or exec, but I'm beginning to realize that just about qualifies me to take notes and run the overhead projector in this town. What are you doing these days?"

"Same thing as before. Junior staff for a junior member. But Eddie's getting me an interview with a hot new Beltway lobby and consulting shop. That'd be a big step up in salary."

"That's good. And who are all these people?" He stared around at the sea of suits and dresses, the reefs of tables, the flotsam of food.

"This is a trade association reception. Meet and greet, grip and grin. This and the Society of American Florists' reception are always packed. Oh, let's go over there — that looks so good."

He got a dish and stood with her at the corner of the dais as she nibbled. Halfway though salmon with macadamia nuts, she said, "Wait here, okay? I have to talk to those people." And she vanished.

He stood alone, eating and people-watching. A haze of smoke and steam hovered from the chafing dishes. When she didn't come back for a while, he went to the bar tables. He resisted temptation and settled for a ginger ale. He fished the cherries out and was looking for a place to ditch them when Cottrell said brightly behind him, "Here you are. Look who I found! Andy, this is Commander Dan Lenson."

A chubby man in a blue suit and mulberry tie was carrying a plate of sliced ham and small orange biscuits and various pâtés and cheeses on crackers. He offered his elbow. "Hi, Dan. I'm Andy DeSilva, work for Jack Mulholland. Office down the hall from Sandy's."

"Nice to meet you, sir."

"Do you recognize the name Mulholland?" Cottrell asked him.

"Seen it in the papers. A representative?"

"That's right. One of the guys your boss'll be getting grilled by pretty soon." She looked toward the tables. "I think I've earned dessert today."

"Try the raspberry cheesecake. Incredible."

When she was gone, DeSilva said rapidly,

151

in an offhand tone, "Sandy said you were involved with Navy missiles. Where exactly?"

"I'm with the Joint Cruise Missile Project."

"Quick question. Something Jack asked me to look into, and Sandy happened to mention she knew somebody on the operator level."

He was instantly on his guard. Everything he'd heard around Crystal City had cast congressional staffers as the military's number-one enemy. "I can't tell you much."

"I'm not interested in anything technical. My question is more directed to funding."

"You want to ask somebody who —"

"Dan, this is not official testimony. This is called 'background.' Sandy, reassure him."

She said around cheesecake, "Andy's right — this is off the record."

DeSilva said between crackers, "One of the subcommittee staffers told me they're thinking about a supplemental bill. What I need to ascertain is the linkage between changes in funding and the missile buy itself. Kind of to see into the admiral's head. What if he got, say, twice as many procurement dollars as he's requesting at the hearing? Would he then be prepared to buy double the number of missiles you are talking about in the total procurement?"

"Well, I don't know why not. But actually, we're still in the testing phase. So maybe it would be better to hold off on a big buy."

"In my experience, the best time to spend

money is when you're offered it."

"True, but if a design's not finalized —"

"What's the IO?"

The IO was the inventory objective. Just hearing the acronym outside the office was startling. "I don't believe I'm supposed to reveal that."

"Oh, you're not? Funny, I read it in a DOD press release. Okay, I'll tell you: the Navy's Tomahawk IO for the current fiscal year is forty-eight. That's not counting the maintenance pipeline, or training, or any war reserve requirement. But not only do you not have that number; you're not even requesting that many in *next* fiscal year's buy."

"You're talking way beyond my pay grade. Something like that, you'd have to approach Admiral Niles. Or maybe even his boss, Vice Admiral Willis."

"The question isn't whom to approach, it's whether you can find a use for the funds if you get them. And what that use is going to be — whether it's to acquire additional missiles or something else — I don't know. What would you say it would be?"

"Mr. DeSilva —"

"He wonders why you're asking him this," Cottrell said half-smiling, eyes narrowed.

"I have no problem telling him. Dan, there are certain parts in the engine that are fabricated from a high-density ceramic only a few companies in the country can work with. The company that supplies those blades is at capacity right now. If we can get procurement up, they'll have to look for another source. The best candidate's in Jack Mulholland's district. They also make turbine blades for the new Army helicopter engine."

"Okay," Dan said. "But we aren't in full-scale procurement yet. We're still working on the booster and the weapons control system software, and —" He stopped, realizing he'd just outlined the program's major problems. "I'm not discussing this any further."

"Well, you've told me what I needed to know. I'm a little confused, though. All through the Carter years, you people were screaming how the forces were being gutted. If I were you, I'd take as much as I could get. Or would you rather the Army got it?"

Dan started to respond that the Army didn't deploy 365 days a year, but he realized DeSilva was punching his organizational loyalty button. He said again, "I don't feel comfortable discussing it."

"Hopeless," said Cottrell. She raised her glass to a passing waiter, who handed her another and took the empty away.

"Where's all this money coming from? I thought Reagan just cut taxes."

"He did. The economy will grow, and receipts will rise, and that's how the deficit will get paid back."

"So we're just borrowing it?"

"What do you care?" DeSilva tossed his plate onto the dais and kissed Cottrell on the cheek. "Got to get over to Energy and Commerce. Thanks, beautiful."

"Wait a minute, Mr. DeSilva —"

Dan looked down the assistant's chubby upraised finger.

"Commander, I don't think you realize how many heavy hitters are gunning for your little buzz bomb. The whole issue of the General Dynamics-Navy relationship, the Electric Boat settlement and the Trident work, there's even F-sixteens and tanks in the pot. Are you aware that if that blows up, you're toast? I'm just trying to help. Tell your admiral that if he ever wants to go to production, he'd better do it now." He gave Dan a possibly friendly but also possibly mocking salute and left.

Dan said angrily to Cottrell, "So this was all business?"

"It's *all* business, Dan. Don't tell me you haven't realized that yet." She looked around, then up at the big leather chairs. "Those look comfortable. Come on."

He eased himself down into one. The leather was soft. He looked out over the thronged floor, imagining himself as a powerful committee head. Cottrell said, "Let me tell you a little story about Roger Zoelcke."

"The guy whose staff you're on?"

"Right, right. Well, he tried to run a clean

155

shop when he first came in. He got put on the transportation subcommittee. Not sexy, but important stuff, roads and bridges. Then one day, Transportation comes in with this proposal. They did some experiments, and they proposed that the federal government, on the interstate highway system, require that the contractors have to add old chopped-up tires to the concrete or whatever they used for paving, as a filler."

"Sounds like a good idea."

"It *was* a good idea. Not only does it give you someplace to put all the fucking tires but it makes the road more flexible or something too; it actually lasts twice as long. But the contractors had a problem with that. They don't *want* it to last twice as long. So their association had a talk with him. And good old Rog, he told them no, they'd just have to get with the program and start putting rubber in their cement.

"Instead, they raised a quarter of a million bucks and gave it to a banker in his district and he lost his seat.

"He came back two years later, but it was like he'd had a brain transplant. Now the asphalt association guys come around before every election, have their little fund-raisers, five hundred a plate. And there's no rubber in the roads anymore."

"What's the message?"

"The message is that the government

doesn't buy things because anybody needs them, Dan. They get bought because the ship-builders and the guys who build tanks have a drink together. They cut checks for Representatives X and Y. Then Y says to X, 'You help me get these cruisers built in my state, I'll help you out with the tanks they build in yours.' Then some summer intern writes it into the budget."

"Some of them must have the interests of the country at heart."

"I love it. Childlike faith. Sooner or later, you learn people around here have only one goal: to stay in office. Now, you were looking for a job, weren't you? When you get out?"

"I was thinking about it."

"Eddie found something for you."

Dan drew a diagram on the arm of the chair with his finger. He said, "What?"

"It's called the Senior Executive Service. You rotate every five years, but you stay inside the Beltway."

"And he and your other friends can help me get in?"

"Oh, it's mainly Eddie. He can get you in at the Office of the Secretary of Defense, or Program Analysis and Evaluation. You might be better at PA and E, actually."

"What do I have to do?"

"I told you before — he just wants to help his students. He has a lot of respect for you.

Do you want me to tell him you're considering it?"

"Let me think about it. I've still got some time before I have to make a decision."

She leaned back in her chair. Then he felt her shoeless nyloned foot slide up his leg. "That isn't the only reason I invited you here."

"To introduce me to Andy?"

"And to talk about our careers. No." Her foot moved up his thigh, onto his lap. He leaned back too and wiped his hair back, glancing around. No one was looking at them. The long table shielded them both from the chest down.

"Here's a member of the standing committee," she murmured. The colored spots flamed in her cheeks.

"I thought you were dating Eddie . . . Dr. Szerenci."

"I don't need help keeping track of my relationships. Let's go up to Ron's office and do it on his desk."

"Jesus, Sandy."

The toes stopped. "Wait a minute. You've been coming on to me at Henry's, and that's okay, but when I come on to you, it's 'Jesus'? Tell me you haven't been brain-fucking me since the first night of class."

"I'd better get back to work." He pushed her foot off his crotch and got up, knocking over his ginger ale. "Shit. . . . Look, I'll think about the SES thing, all right?"

"Coward," she said, but she didn't look displeased as he stumbled away, mopping at his pants with a napkin. She looked off over the hall and coughed, then leaned back and lit another cigarette.

Sitting in the Metro on the way back to Crystal City, watching the lights flash past in the subterranean darkness, he couldn't say why he'd reacted the way he had with Cottrell. She was good-looking and smart and, yeah, he *had* fantasized about her. But face-to-face with an invitation, he'd wilted. No, that wasn't exactly it. Pondering it, he realized that some wary and self-preserving instinct had warned him to steer clear of her. He smiled sardonically at his reflection in the window as around him other passengers gathered papers and briefcases, preparing to depart. And for once, goddamn it, he'd listened! Was he getting smart at last?

The afternoon pretest meeting for Primal Thunder was at a conference room in the Crystal City Marriott. When he slid his hat into the rack, it was the only Navy cover there. A line of Air Force officers and Canadians in their dark green single-service uniforms stood in line at a folding table. Behind them, noncoms were checking IDs against a list. They found his name on it, but there didn't seem to be a briefing package for him. He protested and they found a spare. He got a seat and flipped through it — schedules, a welcome-aboard package, maps, an operation plan.

He closed it as a Canadian colonel took the podium. The colonel made a short statement in French, then switched to English, as if having made his point. "In cooperation with our NATO allies, and in pursuance of a bi-lateral agreement signed in Ottawa last year, my government and armed service are com-pleting preparations for tests of the U.S. Air Force AGM-eighty-six air-launched cruise missile over the territory of Canada.

"First a brief overview of what we are calling Project Primal Thunder.

"Starting on January fifteenth, a test series of eight missiles will be launched from B-fifty-two Gs in the Beaufort Sea, fly a fifteen-hundred-mile corridor through the Northwest Territories and British Columbia, and be parachute-recovered at the Primrose Test Range, Cold Lake, Alberta. The decision to test the cruise in Canada will take them over terrain and through air masses and weather conditions similar to those a missile would encounter launching over the Barents, Kara, or Laptev seas on penetrations of northern Russia to Soviet Siberia.

"Two other programs will be carried out simultaneously with the ALCM tests. The first is to permit the Canadian armed services to evaluate the ability of the DEW line and the Pinetree line to detect launch aircraft and the missiles themselves, and the ability of the Canadian Region of NORAD to detect, track, and destroy. The second is to test the ground-launched U.S. Air Force BGM-one oh nine G, with this missile flying along the same route but in the opposite direction: launching at Primrose, then impacting on-ice targets just north of the Yukon coast."

He turned the meeting over to a USAF general, and Dan leaned forward, squinting as the graphic went up.

The corridor was shaped like a hockey stick, with the bottom of the L facing east. A hundred nautical miles wide, it began north of the Canadian coast, three hundred miles north of the Arctic Circle, in the ice-locked emptiness of the Beaufort Sea. Section A extended from the air-launch point to just within the coast. B and C curved southeast, west of Great Bear Lake. D and E turned south, section E crossing the border into British Columbia between 121 and 124 degrees west. F was a snaky bend east again, leaving the flat frozen tundra to thread the passes of the Rocky Mountains. G and H passed north of Great Slave Lake and Edmonton, centered on 56 degrees north. The end of segment H, the tip of the hockey stick, poked out into Saskatchewan north of Saskatoon. Looking at it, Dan had to admit that whichever way you flew it, it would be a good workout for a low-altitude missile.

At the very end of the brief, the general mentioned GLCMs again, very briefly. Then he turned the floor over to a youthful-looking Air Force major.

People began getting up even as he put his first slide on the screen. Dan craned past bodies to see it. The field tests would be carried out with launchers and battery personnel from Dugway Proving Ground, where earlier tests had been conducted. The transporter-erector-launchers, which were mounted on truck-towed trailers, would convoy from Dugway to Cold Lake in an epic cross-country journey that would double as a road test. By now most of the audience had either left the room or were standing in the back, discussing the ALCM in loud voices. The major seemed to note this. He paused, looking down, then said, simply, "That concludes my brief."

He turned the mike off and came down from the platform. Dan got up as the major passed him, and said, "Hey. Hey! I'm the Navy guy who's going along with you."

"Oh yeah? Steve Manhurin. Major, USAF." They shook hands. "You coming on the cross-country thing?"

"I don't think so. I'll be flying up, meet you in Cold Lake. How do you feel about your boosters?"

"I wish I felt better," said Manhurin. "The

results we got at Dugway weren't conclusive. I'm not exactly an expert, but seems like it's worse when the missile gets cold-soaked. Maybe we can get a handle on exactly what's wrong this time."

"Uh, do I get the feeling you're playing second fiddle to the AGM-eighty-six?"

"I get that feeling too. But I think we basically have a good missile. I'll go to Europe with it."

Dan hung around awhile, talked to a couple of the Canadians and exchanged cards. Finally, he got his hat and headed back through the Crystal Underground, thinking about what he'd just seen.

# 10

"Finished with that, sir?"

Dan flinched back from sleep. His mouth tasted foul. He slugged down the last half an inch of warm scotch and handed the cup to the flight attendant. Beside him, Sakai made choking noises. The plastic sound channels of his headphones were twisted around his neck. Dan nudged him. "Sparky. We're on final. Better wake up before you hang yourself."

As the engineer writhed into wakefulness, Dan looked down again at his notes from the latest West Coast trip. *New Jersey* was out of dry dock and moored at Long Beach, preparing for sea trials and commissioning. Rip-out and rebuild of belowdecks spaces had been completed, and Raytheon was shipping the consoles and racks later this month.

The software, though, was now nearly a year behind schedule. The *Merrill* software build was supposed to be the basis for the battleship programming, but it wouldn't be ready for commissioning and might not be for the shakedown cruise, either. Dan was recommending that the integration contractor start a parallel software development effort.

He passed it to Sakai. "Press your eyeballs to that."

While the engineer read, Dan went through

his wheelbook, making sure he'd done as much as he could. Tomorrow was the party; he had to slip over to the Exchange and stock up. Next week he'd be leaving for Canada, with the congressional appearance after that, then Canada again. Lots going on. . . . The big news this week had been Bill Perry's decision to put the Boeing ALCM into full production. Dan wondered if they'd even have a Tomahawk program left after the hearings.

"Attention, please. We are beginning our approach to Dulles Airport, Washington, D.C. Please return your seats and tray tables to their full upright position."

He'd called Kerry from California, and waited eagerly to hear her voice. But when she came on, it had been casual enough. Just "Hi, how are you? I'm coming back Saturday. Want to get together?" They'd agreed on a run and bike ride along the C and O Canal, then dinner in Georgetown.

As the landing gear screeched and the cabin shuddered, Sakai handed the memo back. "How's it look?" Dan asked him.

"I made a couple marks on it."

"It's what you said we ought to be doing. I'd like you to oversee that parallel development team. Make sure everything interfaces."

"You know better than to listen to me," Sakai grumbled. He looked red-eyed, worn out.

Dan said, "so long" and reminded him

165

about the party Sunday. He caught the courtesy bus out to the satellite lot and headed for home.

He didn't see Haneghen when he stopped at the Dorothy Day House. In fact, he didn't see anyone other than Kerry, who was sitting on the swing. When he pulled the Volvo in, she came down the steps. She wore black ski pants, a maroon parka, and a stocking cap. The parka was faded and had a sewed seam across the front, as if someone had hacked at it with a knife. "Hi," she said.

"Hi. You're looking good." He debated kissing her, but the moment passed. Instead, he cleared his throat and said, "I brought the bike."

"Where is it?"

"In the trunk. The front wheel comes off." He popped it open to show her. "I got it in France. Kept it in the fan room, aboard ship, to ride on port visits."

They got under way. A few minutes went by in silence as she looked out at the passing houses. Then she said, "Thanks for calling. I needed to get out of there for a while."

He glanced at her. "Trouble?"

"No, but little things take on an emotional charge when you see somebody every day. How was California?"

He wondered if "somebody" was Haneghen, but he didn't ask. "Warm. It's like

166

climate shock when you come back and it's winter here."

"Where are you going next?"

"Canada. Way up north."

"Is that when you test your new missile?"

"Uh-huh." He felt guilty discussing his work. Their lives, their convictions were so different. . . . But he had to admit that of all the women he'd met since he came to D.C., she was the only one he could see taking seriously. The more time he spent with her, the more he liked her.

But was that a good thing?

He parked the car on M Street and carried the bike down to the path. He couldn't help saying, "Remember when we kissed, over there?"

"You must be thinking of somebody else."

"Somebody in black net stockings?"

"Somebody who only comes out once a year."

"Does that mean I don't get another hug till next Halloween?"

She raised her eyebrows, then bent to pick a pebble from the front tire.

He started his warm-up exercises as she pedaled down the towpath, then came back. She looked good in stretch pants. She had a green scarf wrapped over the lower part of her face. "Are you warm enough?" he asked her.

Her voice came out muffled. "You mean the scarf? I get coughing fits in the cold. It's better if I can heat the air up before I breathe it."

"We don't have to go far. Four or five miles —"

"Go as far as you want. Seems like I haven't been outside in weeks. I should probably get more exercise."

"Okay, ready? Watch out for those icy patches."

She said all right, and he started out slowly — didn't want to tear anything. A mile to warm up; then he could do another for time.

The path wound back and forth, following the snow-dusted surface of the frozen canal. Once mules had towed boats and barges along it, carrying freight and passengers past the Potomac rapids into the newly opening hinterlands. Now it was a bike path, a walking path. In the summer, it was filled with strollers, though it emptied fast near dark. Today they passed only an occasional walker, heavily dressed and booted, and once in a long while another biker, bent low against a chill wind. Crushed shell and gravel crunched under his Nikes. The milepost, ahead. . . . Here it came . . . 6:40. He always ran better in the cold. Heat engines were more efficient when there was a thermal differential. What were human beings, anyway? Heat engines, economic units, individual expressions of the collective unconscious? So many ways you could see the world. Her tires crackled behind him.

"You said you were married before?"

"Uh-huh." He cut his pace back till she was beside him.

"What happened?"

"Oh, it didn't work out. We got married out of school; we were separated a lot."

"Any kids?"

"A daughter. Lives in Utah now, with my ex."

"Do you call? Are you involved in her life?"

"In Nan's? Not as much as I'd like to be. But, I guess, as much as I can be this far away." He gave his breathing a few strides to catch up, then said, "How about you?"

"I was married, too. I had a son."

"Your ex get custody?"

"No. He died, when he was eleven months. Choking on a toy."

He slowed to a jog. "God. I'm sorry."

She was looking into the trees. "That's pretty much what broke us up. I blamed him. He got him the rabbit. Its head came off. And I blamed myself, too, for not looking into the crib often enough. . . . You know what I'm trying to say."

"Uh-huh."

"Then I met Carl. And I thought if I could help save other kids, maybe it would make up for it. Looking back, it doesn't make much sense —"

He said, "It makes sense. Sense of the heart." And then he thought, surprised, Did I say that?

169

"You think so? Anyway, that's how I got into activism."

He figured this was a good place to bring up something he'd meant to ask. "I wondered about that. And about how it made you feel about what I do."

She didn't answer right away. He slowed, coming to a section of path where it looked like road graders had been at work. The puddled water had frozen in the ruts, and he picked his way across. Her bike rattled across ridges of frozen mud.

"About you being in the navy?"

"I guess so. Yeah. That's the message I get around the House."

"I never said we don't need a navy. Somebody's got to rescue people when their ships sink, I suppose."

"That's actually more the Coast Guard's job, Kerry. We're more focused on fighting."

"Well, maybe then we *don't* need one. Dan, I may not like what you do for a living, but that doesn't mean I think it's all your fault."

"Okay."

"And don't be afraid of me. All right?"

He didn't answer that. Instead, he said, "How are your lungs doing?"

"Don't worry about them. Look, you're always worrying. Why? What are you afraid of?"

He could tell she was smiling by her eyes,

even though her mouth was masked by the scarf. He muttered between breaths, "I'm not afraid."

"Then why aren't you happy? Don't you think God's got everything under control?"

"He's not doing such a great job of it."

"Or maybe She knows more than we do? Don't you think that's a possibility?"

He was thinking this was strange, talking about God while you were running, and then he thought, Why not? And suddenly he felt he was where he was supposed to be, out in the icy wind on this bright, cold day, with her wheeling along beside him, talking about children and death and fate. A bright, slow joy like the reflection of the sky on the ice stole over him. Maybe it was a runner's high, or maybe that she thought these things were important and he did, too, but you couldn't talk about them with just anyone. She seemed to have a peace he didn't, or that he'd only glimpsed from afar.

But at the same time, he was afraid. If you loved someone, she could hurt you. The way Susan had hurt him, cheated on him, left and taken Nan with her —

"You're worrying again."

"Sorry. Hard habit to break."

"Let's try an experiment, okay?"

"What kind of experiment?"

"For the next fifteen minutes, or, say, till the end of this run, just accept that everything is the way it's supposed to be and that you don't have to fix it or do anything except be here. All right?"

It didn't sound like the kind of philosophy he wanted to live his life by, but he said, "Okay. Till the end of the run."

"Good."

"You warmed up? Ready to pick up the pace again?"

"Why don't you try to catch me," she said, and he heard the accelerating click and hiss of pedals and gears, the high-pitched crackle of gravel under her tires. A moment later, she swept past, legs thrusting like pistons, and he went to a sprint. Up on his toes now, sucking air that turned to ice as it hit his throat. Closing, feeling the sting of rock bits whirring off her rear wheel. A swerve, and they were level, but this was as fast as he went.

He ran even with her front tire for ten seconds, fifteen, before he hit the wall and had to drop back, sucking air as she sped away down the path, growing smaller and smaller, until she went around a curve and the path was empty under the nodding snow-laden elms. Then as he jogged on, a maroon speck reappeared in the distance. It grew larger and larger, until she skidded to a stop in front of him, her eyes crinkled. He jogged up to her and put out his arms, meeting her cool lips under the pulled-away muffler and her hot breath under the chill gray sky with an utter inevitability, to which he finally let himself surrender.

The next morning, they stayed in bed late, looking out his apartment window at the cloudy winter sky. But even when they weren't talking, just lying side by side drinking coffee and reading the funnies, he felt happy.

They walked to a deli for brunch. Then, when they got back, started getting ready for the party.

He'd planned it for weeks, to celebrate the end of finals, and the holidays. He'd invited his classmates from Szerenci's course, neighbors from the other apartments, and the guys from the office; he'd put a notice on the board inviting one and all. Kerry had made a couple of calls when he asked her to invite her friends, too.

Now, waiting for the first guests to arrive, he looked around the apartment. It was cleaned and vacuumed, but his furniture looked tacky — cheap, battered, the kind of chairs and end tables divorced officers hauled from apartment to apartment. The couch still had the shipping sticker on it. Too late to do anything about that. . . . The main attraction for the guys would be the four cases of brew in the tub, with forty pounds of ice from the 7-Eleven. He wanted a beer now, but he reminded himself to watch his consumption.

He'd noticed a tendency to let it get away from him.

Kerry came out of the bathroom, brushing her hair. He recalled it falling across his chest in the night. Looking at her now, tall and stately, he wanted her again. But when he put his arms around her, she fended him off. "What kind of food did you get?"

"Party stuff. Chips and pretzels and dip —"

"If they're coming at six, they'll expect something more substantial than that."

"You think so? Most of the parties I go to, that's all they have."

"An evening party, yes. You're giving a dinnertime one." She went into the kitchen. He heard the fridge door opening, closing, then a rattle and slam of cupboard doors. "There's not much in there," he called.

"The understatement of the century. Unless you're talking about booze."

"I can order pizza, if you think they're going to want dinner."

"It's not great, but let's at least get frozen ones, and some fresh cheese and vegetables. Give me your keys. I'll go to the store while you finish cleaning up."

The Navy guys were the first to arrive. Vic arrived with his wife, Lucinda, a hefty, attractive woman who wore lots of silver. Sparky brought a girl he introduced as Honey. A couple of lieutenants and lieutenant commanders showed up from the sub-launched side. To his surprise, Carol came, Niles's secretary. She said she'd seen his invitation on the board and lived just three blocks away. He ushered them in and started organizing drinks.

While he was slicing the cheese, a glass of rosé on the countertop, Cottrell arrived. "Who's the nonblonde?" she hissed, cornering him against the sink.

"That's Kerry Donavan."

"Who brought her?"

"Me."

"Not bad — if she lost twenty pounds."

"Did you bring the music, Sandy?"

"Uh-huh. Kiss, Garth Brooks, and Metallica. That my wine?"

"No, but there's the bottle, and the glasses. Plug that in by the sliding doors, all right?"

More students arrived, then the neighbors from the building. The rooms filled with people and cigarette smoke. Despite the cold, some went out on the balcony. He kept bringing things out, wine and cheese and crackers and nuts.

A tap at the door. "Can somebody get that?" he called.

It was Ken, from the Day House, in the same frayed blue jeans and fatigue jacket with the peace symbol on the back that he'd worn in court. For the first time, Dan wondered if inviting everyone at once had been a smart idea. Too late now. . . . "Come on in," he said. "Ken, this is Vic Burdette, works with me. Ken, he . . . uh . . . he's active in social causes. Vic, show him where the beer is, okay?"

"It's not Coors, is it?" Ken said. "I don't drink Coors because . . ." The rest was lost in a rising buzz of conversation.

Another rap at the door. This time it was Colonel Evans, in a sport jacket and turtleneck, with a dignified-looking wife, taller than he was. Mei Zhou smiled shyly behind them. She was in a black dress. Grinning, Evans said, "We found her down in the lobby. Is she yours?"

"Hi, sir, come on in. Yessir, she's a classmate from GW."

The Air Force officer introduced his wife, Jeannette, then presented a bottle. "Brought you this."

"Thanks, sir, we're short on vodka. Go on in. You can put your coats in the bedroom."

He felt awkward returning Mei's kiss. He hoped she and Kerry wouldn't start trading Dan Lenson stories. Or worse yet, Cottrell. Then he ducked back into the kitchen. He finished his wine and poured another, then checked the pizza.

"Help you cut that?"

"Thanks, Sparky. Watch out, it's — Shit! Ow, God, that's hot."

The party started to roll. Running back and

forth to get the goodies out on deck, he could have told the players apart just from what they wore and how they stood. The Navy guys were in slacks and dress shirts, and they stood alertly against the walls, as if on watch. A couple were even wearing shiny black Corfams. The students were in suit jackets or dresses, and they talked about Abscam or the Sandinista government. The Catholic Worker people looked smaller by contrast, more careworn, and they had terrible posture. They were mostly beer drinkers. Dan saw Haneghen on the balcony with Burdette. That would be an interesting theological discussion.
. . . Westerhouse was saying to Deborah, "Yeah, but isn't it rewarding failure, to keep subsidizing that kind of behavior? What happens when their kids have kids?" Dan hurried past before the return salvo was in the air. He finished the second glass of rosé and decided he really wanted a shot of Cutty on ice. He looked into the bedroom. Three of the Navy wives were sitting there comparing private schools with public ones. Thank God he'd changed the sheets.

But everything was perking; the nuts and chip levels were dropping. He checked the bathtub and submerged another case under ice slush. Then he circulated, beaming benevolently as fragments of conversation hurtled past.

"The last episode of *M*A*S*H* . . ."

"The emergency jobs bill . . ."

"But the assembled U.S. bishops have denounced their deployment, testing, and manufacture. If you call yourself a practicing Catholic . . ."

"Did you read the analysis? The way I read it, there's no survivable basing mode short of putting it to sea for forty billion dollars."

"I knew Rita Lavelle. My brother worked for her, and he said there was no way she couldn't have known."

"We're providing them with the latest technology. LM-twenty-five hundred gas turbines, Mark forty-six torpedoes, new sonars. They'll be a counterweight to the Russians."

"She and two other nuns stayed with us at the house last summer. We'll be going to El Salvador to help with the clinic."

"Only a matter of time before something happens in Beirut."

"The way around that is, you go the frozen-embryo route, select the best, and pay them to . . ."

"Put in for the midlevel Naval War College course."

Colonel and Mrs. Evans loomed up, Jeannette smiling like Edwina Mountbatten among the untouchables. Evans beckoned to him and he bent. "This Haneghen . . . where'd you meet these people?" the deputy murmured. "They're dangerous."

"I don't think they're *dangerous*, sir. They're

just friends of friends."

"We're often judged by our friends, Dan."

"Yes, sir. . . . Can I get you another glass of wine, Mrs. Evans?"

Damn, he thought. He refreshed his scotch and carried the glasses back into the living room. Every chair was occupied and now it was getting hard to slide among talking people. . . . Where had he left his drink? He got another.

He was washing down some chips with another scotch when the roar took a dip in volume. He turned.

Edward Szerenci was taking off his coat. His teeth flashed as his students converged, calling out, bringing drinks or food. He accepted a Heineken and a slice.

"Hey! Dan!" He whipped his head around at a familiar voice. Then he and Larry Prince were pounding each other's backs.

Larry was an Academy classmate. They'd run into each other again in the scratch battle group that had faced down *Kirov* and her escorts in the Gulf of Mexico. Prince had been carried as missing, presumed dead, when his ship had taken a missile in her bridge. Actually, he'd been blown overboard and had drifted for twelve hours before being picked up by Vietnamese shrimpers and taken into Pascagoula. He'd written an article about it for *Shipmate*. They caught up on their classmates, who was where. Prince told him he'd run into Ritter Mingo, who was making a name for himself running anti-Nicaraguan operations out of the White House staff.

One of Dan's neighbors in the building came up after awhile, cutting her eyes at Prince, and Dan caught the message and introduced them. Then he excused himself, thinking she wouldn't make much headway with Larry, but she was welcome to try.

Sometime later, he straightened from his slump against the wall, almost spilling his drink.

Apparently, Szerenci had been talking about nuclear strategy with one of his students. Donavan must have overheard them. Now she stood at the heart of Szerenci's coterie, face-to-face with him, and Dan saw her head lift and her cheeks go that familiar shade of white. His heart sank as he heard her say, "A hundred megadeaths. Does that mean what I think it does?"

"A hundred million deaths. Those are the numbers for a major countervalue strike."

With deceptive softness, Donavan asked, "Of those megadeaths, how many are under four years old?"

"How many?"

"That's right. How many of these enemies of yours are little children?"

Szerenci said dryly, "From age zero to four would be around six to eight percent, if we

180

assume a standard population model."

"And planning their deaths is what you call 'defense.'"

"No, that's what we call 'deterrence.'" Szerenci glanced around the room; for a moment, Dan thought he was looking for chalk. "If it's not too horrible to contemplate, then it's not a credible deterrent, is it?"

"So it's more like a threat than a working weapon?"

"The weapons have to work. Or it isn't a threat."

"Uh, has everybody gotten pizza?" Dan said. He said to Kerry in an undertone, "Look, not now, it's a party."

"That's all right, Dan," said Szerenci. "She may be savable. So, Kelly —"

"Kerry."

"Kerry, you don't like the idea of nuclear deterrence. What do *you* think we do faced with a hundred-and-twenty division-equivalent Warsaw Pact threat on a six-front attack?"

"Jesus said, 'Love your enemies, do good to those that hate you, pray for those who calumniate you, so that you may be Children of God.' I believe in those methods, in Paul and Gandhi and Christ, not your analysis."

"You don't seem to understand what analysts do. We don't determine policy. We try to make policy choices subject to rational analysis."

"What if the policy itself is irrational?"

Szerenci smiled. "I suppose, then, we try to make it more efficiently irrational. But I don't think it's an irrational policy."

"Can anyone win a nuclear war?"

"Under certain circumstances, we can envision a counterforce strategy that would lead to war termination on favorable terms."

"With how many dead?"

Szerenci shrugged. "Is it a decapitation scenario? Counterforce? Countervalue? RAND or SAI models?"

"Are you saying you don't know?"

"I'm saying the models are squishy and our numerical values are shaky. After all, we have only two pieces of hard data on the graph — Hiroshima and Nagasaki."

"Give me a rough guess. Ten million?"

"Prompt effects, not counting fallout, disease, and famine? Sure."

"A hundred million?"

"Conceivable."

"A billion?"

Szerenci said, "There's been some work on nuclear winter that suggests it might be everyone on earth."

Nobody said anything. Then Kerry said softly, "And you say this is rational?"

Szerenci swirled his glass. "But let me add one thing. When we play these scenarios, the heuristics are interesting. It's very difficult to get the teams to initiate a nuclear conflict.

The control team practically has to push the button for them. Not only does deterrence work in reality; it works even in the game room."

"So we keep building weapons, and impoverishing ourselves. And not only that; we realize it's futile."

"It's not futile. It preserves the status quo."

"Which stinks. Instead of walling off our 'enemies' with arms, what if we used those billions of dollars to give everyone a job and a home?"

"Are you really willing to gamble our survival on the benevolence of our opponents?"

"You're reasoning backward. Our weapons make our enemies."

"You should read Lenin," said Sandy. Her cheeks were flushed, and she sipped wine, casting a flat glance at Dan. He could read it: You prefer *this* fruitcake to me?

"And Hitler," said Szerenci. "Of course, according to you, the Allies should simply have submitted to him. The Israelis have learned their lesson — about trusting in nonviolence."

"Do you think we defeated Hitler? We *became* Hitler. We fund wars around the world. We're the world's biggest weapons supplier, and out of the top fifteen countries we sell to, twelve of them are dictatorships."

"It's better to fight a war on someone else's territory."

"You can't isolate war and hatred and ship it somewhere else. Go to the ghetto at night. When you put your faith in violence, violence becomes your faith. Martin Luther King, Jr., said, 'The United States is the greatest purveyor of violence in the world today.' "

"You don't ensure national security with mottoes and pious quotations, Miss Donavan. So far, that's been the level of your reasoning," said Szerenci. "We're facing an ideology that states plainly its ultimate goal is our destruction."

"If we devoted those resources to the poor, communism would stop being a threat. No one would be attracted to it."

"There was poverty long before the Cold War."

"And there will always be, no matter how much 'progress' we make, because the progress is not in God's direction. Whoever has two shirts has to give one to someone without clothing. That's the only 'strategy' that will actually give us peace."

Dan looked around quickly. Everyone was staring, mute, glasses and plates balanced on knees or held suspended. As his eyes followed theirs back to her, he saw her cheeks were flushed now; a strand of dark hair fell across her forehead. She held herself erect, intent on battle, nostrils flared as she caught her breath. To him, in that moment, she had never looked more beautiful.

184

She said, "You, Professor, are part of the machine. These students respect you. Your bosses do, too. What if you told them what we needed was not more arms, but more love?"

"They'd get another analyst."

"And if all the analysts told them that?"

"Then they'd do without us, because we'd be wrong."

"But it wouldn't be as efficient, would it?"

"And we might lose," said Szerenci, and for the first time, anger darkened his face. "I grew up in a country that lost a war. There's nothing worse."

"How about losing your soul?"

He stood in the kitchen alcove, wanting to step in but knowing he couldn't. It was a duel, a *mano a mano*. Listening to them parry and thrust, he thought, Is it possible — can both of two diametrically opposed viewpoints be true? Because when Szerenci spoke, rationally, with a sardonic disdain, he recognized truth. And when Kerry answered, passionately, with the spirit of love, he knew that was the truth, too. A deeper one, one he'd suspected all his life. But he'd always looked away. Because to follow it meant throwing away everything he'd worked so hard for: his commission, his profession, his career.

Evans was right. These people *were* dangerous. Because he was starting to wonder if they were right. And he realized something else, looking across the smoky room as Szerenci turned away and Kerry met one by one the skeptical objections of his students.

He realized he was in love.

# III

# HAMMERS AND BLOOD

# 11

The snow whirled down, heavy, devoid of light, cutting them off from the world as they stood together on a back street west of Howard University. As she studied the newspaper, Dan watched snowflakes landing on her hair, on the tatty knitted beret she'd found at a yard sale for a quarter. One fell on her eyelash and clung, till she raised a glove and brushed it off.

Early January, and she was looking for a room. Things were getting too heavy at the house. Too many people, squirrels in the attic, noise at all hours. She didn't say so, but he figured it was Haneghen, too.

Late one night, she'd told him the whole story of her involvement with the priest. She'd only gradually realized his vision excluded a lover, a family. "He was committed to the Church. Now he's committed to nonviolence, and everything it means. There just isn't room in his life for anything else."

Dan had said, "Have you talked to him about it? About us?"

And she'd whispered, lying in his arms, "Yes. He understands."

"Thanks for helping me look," she said later as they inched through uncleared snow toward a Quaker-sponsored rooming house that might or might not have a room available later that week. "I don't know how I could do this without you. But you just can't do much on what I make baby-sitting."

He glanced at her profile and took a fresh grip on the wheel.

He was thinking of asking her if she wanted to stay with him. But once the words were said, it wouldn't be easy to unsay them. A movie, dinner, sleeping over was one thing. Having her move in — that was a new ball game.

But he wasn't seeing anybody else now. He'd even stopped reading the personals.

"Would you mind if I asked you to go back to the first place we saw? The one out by the Medical Center?"

"That was a dump, Kerry. You aren't seriously thinking of living there, are you?"

"Well . . . I thought so, too. Okay, we'll keep looking."

He cleared his throat. Staring through the windshield, he murmured, "Or you could move in with me."

She didn't answer. He was about to repeat himself when she said, "I heard you."

"It was just a thought."

"It doesn't sound like it's exactly what you want most."

"Sorry. But it might be fun. At least till you found a place you like."

It floated there while he concentrated on

not skidding into the truck in front of them. Finally, she said, "I seem to be spending my weekends with you anyway."

"I didn't mean to sound unenthusiastic. If you want to come, I'd like to have you. And it's close to the subway."

"You don't have to give me a sales pitch."

"Sorry."

"If I did, I'd pay what I'd pay for a room. A hundred a month."

"If you want to."

"And you'd take it."

"All right. I'll take it."

"Maybe we could try. . . . Are you getting hungry?"

"There's an Indian place," he said. "Help me look for a parking space."

That was how it went, as if neither of them wanted to make it too dramatic. That evening he went by the house and helped carry her things down. There wasn't much. Two armfuls of clothes. Three pairs of shoes. She left the mattress and linens and towels for the next guest. "You move light," he told her on the narrow, worn stairs. Somewhere a child was crying, a mother crooning in Spanish. The murmur of talk came from downstairs, around the big table.

"I try to live light. Whatever you have beyond what you need, that's something less for someone else."

He pondered that sobering thought on the

191

way downstairs. In the military, success was measured in other terms than money — rank, command, awards. And compared with how he'd grown up, an officer's pay seemed generous. Now he was paying child support, there weren't many luxuries. But he'd never thought of making more than you needed for used clothes and a bare room as an actual evil.

If he left the service, he wouldn't have that paycheck every month. He wouldn't have that guaranteed retirement.

After he locked the trunk, he went back in, to find her in the kitchen, having tea with Haneghen. Carl glanced up as Dan came in. Was that anger in those light eyes? "Dan. Understand Kerry's going to stay with you?"

"Hi. Yeah, till she finds a place she likes."

"That'll free you up a room," she said, looking into the tea mug, and not at either of them. "How about that veteran who wanted out of the city shelter? You said he knew something about plumbing."

Haneghen reached out across the table. "Take good care of her," he said. Kerry took his hand. His knuckles whitened for a moment. Then he let go and sat back. "Will we still see you down at the kitchen?"

"Every morning."

"Okay, then. Yeah, I'll call the shelter, tell them to send the sarge over. Dan, you free Tuesday night? We need to beg a ride."

"Tuesday? Oh, sure." He felt expansive; it felt like victory; as if he'd won Kerry from him. "No problem."

That night, he carried her things up in the elevator and gave her a key. They heated up potpies for dinner. But then she made up a bed on the couch, in the front room. He thought she was going to sleep there, but he woke later and found her next to him. He didn't move or say anything, just lay there pretending he was asleep until her breathing slowed, too, and a faint snore came from next to him. Then he turned over, carefully, cautiously, and looked for a long time at her face, at her closed eyes, by the blood-colored radiance that came through the window. The light of the city, reflected from the clouds.

At NC-1, he worked nights revising budget estimates. He flew to St. Louis for Unidynamics' demonstration of their first complete ABL, and to Titusville to check on McDonnell Douglas's progress on the airframe second-source. He put in more hours polishing Niles's statement and role-playing the upcoming hearings.

Usually, he didn't think much about what he was doing. But once in awhile, deep in analysis of allocation strategies of runway-kill munitions, he saw himself suddenly as a gear in a machine whose end product was death. To be able to put explosive anywhere on earth, with a little cartographic work and the press of a button — at first it had sounded exciting.

He went downtown with Kerry and stood in line serving out potatoes and bread and a savory bean soup. The storefront smelled like cabbage and sour milk, but it was warm, and when the doors opened, the people thronged in, pushing and elbowing. A lot of the "clients" acted drunk, drugged, or deranged. Loud women in tight clothes dragged expressionless children, threatening and slapping them. They didn't look at or talk to the people who stood in line to serve them. They just grabbed their food and headed for the eating area, and when they left, paper plates and spilled chow littered the tables and the floor.

"They don't seem very grateful," he said to Haneghen in the back room.

"Why should they?"

"Why should . . . Because they're getting free food?"

"Which is the least of what they need. They despise one another, just as they're despised. Why should we expect the poor to act any different from anyone else? Ken was attacked last year, on the line. You know his injured leg? He was talking to a man about pacifism. The man attacked him with a knife."

"Why? Because he wouldn't fight him?"

"I guess to see if he was serious."

"I can't buy it, either," Dan told him. "Not

194

total nonviolence. I mean, how about when somebody's killing innocent people? Like what's happening now in Cambodia, Pol Pot's killing everybody who can read. What do we do, just stand back and let it happen?"

"How will killing more help?"

"Well, how about the Nixon doctrine? Can't we arm them, so they can defend themselves?"

"So twice as many will die, you mean?"

"What if somebody's about to kill you, or your family?"

"You reason with them. You don't meet force with force. Can you take the other end of this?"

He helped carry the tureen out, then went back to replenish the bread stack. When he came out, the ex-priest was stacking cans of infant formula in a shopping bag. Dan asked him, "No matter what, you turn the other cheek, huh?"

"Ask yourself this. If you can persuade, by your example, one or two people to act with love, and they each convince others to do so, then how soon will it be before the whole earth is free of war and violence?" The woman waiting for the Enfamil blinked slowly, as if they were speaking a foreign language.

"That depends on what's called the 'doubling time.' Like a nuclear chain reaction." He looked back at the line. "But it doesn't look like you're making much progress here."

Haneghen handed over the sack, and the woman left. "I don't judge them. We're sowing seeds of love, and the harvest isn't going to come in for a long time. I have to remember what St. Vincent de Paul said: 'It is only by feeling your love that the poor will forgive you your gifts of bread.' "

"What's that supposed to mean?"

Haneghen just shrugged and smiled. "Let's get the rest of the juice up front. Bring that drum of peanut butter, too."

Tuesday night, he had the Volvo at the house at six. The members came down the steps carrying sticks with rolled-up cloth. They stacked them in the trunk. Kerry got in the passenger seat. Deborah, Carl, and Ken squeezed into the back. Dan started up. "Where to?"

"Sheraton."

"What's going down?"

Haneghen said, "It's better if you don't know. Then you're not an accessory."

He shut up and concentrated on driving.

When they got there, Kerry stuffed a banner under her sweater. The others looked grim, like troops before an assault. "You don't have to come in," she told him.

"I can watch, can't I?"

"I don't want you to do anything you don't want to do."

He didn't feel great about this, but he'd

volunteered his ass already. It was a matter of following through. He locked up and followed them into the hotel. At least he was in mufti this time: jeans, flannel shirt, a civilian-style parka.

Signs in the lobby said the MilTech International Show was in the main display area. Letting them go on ahead, he followed a trickle of attendees down to a display floor. A hum and rustle echoed beneath the vaulted ceiling.

This was the American section. Over the booths hung logos for Northrop, General Motors, EG&G, Kaman, Singer, Rockwell, Bendix, Texas Instruments. He passed Arabs, Chinese, Latin Americans, and Africans examining displays, reading brochures, quizzing the salespeople, who stood beside mock-ups of grenade launcher/turret combinations, dynamic armor, electromagnetic pulse-resistant cabling, tactical missile targeting systems.

Past that was the international aisle. Blond Norse maidens beamed smiles for Mauser and Rheinmetall and Nobel and Oerlikon. There were booths for Aerospatiale and Saab, Philips, and British Aerospace. A Kärcher mobile kitchen was serving hot finger food. He lingered in front of a South African display marketing advanced restraint systems, electronic shock wands, the latest "crowd control technology." Italian antipersonnel mines promised "area denial through psychological

197

shock." There were no photos of burns, wounds, or bloody bodies. He felt more comfortable in front of the naval displays. No matter what, he still couldn't believe being able to take out a Soviet sub that was trying to sink you was anything to be ashamed of.

He was at the Unidynamics booth, examining a model of the ABL and talking with one of the engineers, when he heard shouting. Security guards trotted past. Walkie-talkies crackled.

They'd found an open mike, set up for welcoming remarks. Haneghen's voice echoed under the vaulted roof. Behind him, Deborah and Kerry held the two ends of a blue banner. It was lettered in a hand-scissored alphabet of yellow felt, crude, as if cut out by children. Then he remembered seeing the kids at work, at the house; they *had* been made by children.

BUT I SAY TO YOU
* LOVE YOUR ENEMIES *
BLESS THOSE WHO PERSECUTE YOU

"What the hell?" said the engineer, coming out to stand beside Dan. "Where did those nuts come from?"

Haneghen didn't speak for more than a few seconds, though, before the mike went dead. Then the guards reached them, unsheathing billy clubs. The protestors lifted their arms, locking their fists behind their heads, as if they'd done it many times before.

The security force came down Dan's aisle, leading them out. Their captives were spattered with blood, and he tensed before getting the picture; they must have thrown it on one of the displays and gotten the back spatter on their clothing. Haneghen was in cuffs, but he looked relaxed, joking with an extremely fat guard. Kerry caught Dan's eye. He waved at her.

The engineer looked at him strangely. "You know those assholes?"

He started to say no, then caught himself. "Sort of. I mean, some of them."

"You better get your head straight, buddy." He gave him a quizzical, hostile look. Dan wheeled and jogged off after the disappearing backs.

The trouble was, he wasn't sure what he was feeling.

As he spent more time around them, he discovered they were neither saints nor nutcases. Deborah had a bad temper. Haneghen was single-minded to the point of fanaticism; he didn't seem to understand not everyone could be dedicated twenty-four hours a day. Sometimes they were intolerant. Occasionally, their attitudes of moral superiority got irritating. But when it came down to what they valued, they were ready to sacrifice for what they believed in.

In other words, they weren't all that different from professional military people.

He had more trouble accepting what they called "personalism" — the idea that to do any good, charity had to be extended in the form of one hand to another, not through bureaucracies and government checks. He liked their politics even less. It seemed whenever force was used by the United States, or anyone supported by America, it was wrong. But when leftists or revolutionaries were doing the killing, it was justified outrage, and we were even more to blame. He had arguments with Ken about that.

What he couldn't argue with was their idea of voluntary poverty: that keeping for themselves anything in excess of their immediate needs — a spare pair of shoes, a second coat, a spare room — was a kind of sin, and that their first priority was helping those in need. It sounded crazy, but watching them do it, not talk about it or listen to sermons about it but just *do* it, had more impact than anything they said. The house was a noisy, messy, happy place. At night, others came by, Quakers, Unitarians, and they shared. One old fellow had spent World War II in a mental hospital for being a conscientious objector. A couple from California told chilling stories about their work in Central America. Not many held what the IRS would consider a job, though they all worked, most at shelters or with the retarded or at hospices, and most had some manual skill: carpentry, bricklaying, sheet-metal repair.

Sometimes they seemed naïve. They didn't seem to believe there were people out there who weren't as well disposed toward their fellow man as they were. Sometimes they amused him; sometimes they irritated him; sometimes they appalled him with tales of injustice, oppression, things he hadn't realized were going on.

He slowly understood that this wasn't just a handful of people. It was a movement, diverse but loosely linked, and what they actually had in mind was not just to save people here and there. It was to change everything.

Meanwhile, he was with Kerry every day. They didn't spend all their time at the soup kitchen or at the house. When she wasn't meeting with lawyers to prepare for the trial, she cycled beside him when he went running. They went to foreign films with subtitles that made them laugh. She woke cranky, and he learned not to take anything personally till after she had coffee. He remembered how angry Susan had gotten with him for not helping out, and he resolved this time would be different. He did the laundry, made dinner twice a week, shopped on his way home from Crystal City.

It was the first time he'd lived with a woman since Susan left. Sometimes it was scary. And sometimes, just sitting together at the café table they'd bought secondhand in Alexandria, it was nice.

Sometimes it was really nice.

"This is Maryland Avenue," he said, peering ahead as the Volvo shuddered over cobblestones. "This'll take us right in to the Academy."

He'd been surprised to find she'd never been to Annapolis, and had suggested a weekend trip. Now he drove past the governor's mansion and the State House, into the Yard. The jimmylegs waved them through, glancing at the base pass on his fender. He parked by Mahan Hall, and she took his arm as they started down Stribling Walk. He started to detach it — public display of affection, fifteen demerits — then let it stay.

"This is it. Those guns were captured from the British in the War of 1812."

"The grounds are pretty."

"You should see it in the spring; these snowy patches are all flowers then."

They walked against a bitter wind. A few mids were out in reefers, chin straps down. They glanced at him incuriously. He knew that as soon as they saw he was in civvies, and they didn't need to salute, he vanished from their perceptual universe. Not long ago, he'd been one of them, toting his books off to class: leadership, statics and dynamics, calculus. . . .

Kerry said, "I didn't know there were women."

"Since 1976. One's Brigade Commander this year."

"How did you end up here?"

"They have exams for admission. I got lucky."

"Is this where you wanted to go?"

"I didn't have a lot of choices. But yeah, I wanted to come here."

"It's cheap?"

"Actually, they pay you. Course, you have to commit for five years after you graduate."

"So it's a trap. In a way."

"Oh, they explain it up front. You know what you're getting into."

She said, "That's the dorm?"

He raised his eyes to the French Renaissance frontage of Bancroft Hall. Snow-devils scoured the brick expanse of Tecumseh Court. The windows looked blank and dark. He pointed out his Plebe Summer room, then, seeing her shivering, went on up the steps into the echoing solemnity of Memorial Hall.

They looked up at the murals of sailing-ship battles, at the flag Perry had flown at Lake Erie. In the hush, he recalled the awe he'd felt as a plebe, contemplating the roster of fallen heroes shrined under glass.

"You believe in this," she murmured. "I can see it in your face."

"Yeah, I do."

"But you're not as sure as you were once. And you're trying to work it out in your mind. Is that right?"

"I guess so. Yeah." He took a breath and paced the creaking parquet where he'd learned to dance. In a side alcove, a mid was playing the piano, and the slow notes echoed like time itself beneath the crystal chandeliers. "See, I knew some of the guys on that list. They didn't fight for the reasons your friends think they did — for money, or some kind of blood lust. They did it for their country, because they thought it stood for justice and freedom. And that means for the right of people like Haneghen to say what he thinks. America's not perfect, but at least we're trying. The things they teach you here — they *feel* right. Duty. Honor. Responsibility. They're hard to live up to. But that doesn't mean we can't try."

"Have you ever wondered why they're so hard to live up to?" she asked him.

"Sure. Because we're human."

"Right. But also because, maybe, those noble ideals — are they dedicated to the right end? Nobody can argue with doing your duty and so forth. But when the goal of all that is doing violence, to serve a state based on injustice and evil —"

"That's not the *goal;* the goal is to avoid war by being ready for it. And if the state's based on injustice, we can change it. You

204

make it sound like we're Nazis. If we were, Mr. Haneghen wouldn't be running around loose, that's for sure."

"He may not be 'running around' much longer. Don't forget, we're going to trial next month."

"Shit. I forgot."

"I might go to prison. Depending on whether that sabotage charge sticks. The prosecutor's filed a motion that he doesn't have to prove motive, only intent."

"What's the difference? Isn't motive the same as intent?"

"Not according to him. It's called an *in limine* motion. If the judge grants it, we won't be allowed to present any evidence based on political or religious beliefs." She shrugged. "Then it'll be open-and-shut. We can try to testify, but they can gag us."

"I can't believe they'd do that."

She looked up at him then, and he saw doubt — and was it fear? — in her eyes. "Oh, it's been done before. They're portraying us as terrorists. And . . . I thought I was ready. But you're not the only one around here who's not sure what they're doing is right. And you're not the only one who has a decision to make."

"What do you mean?"

"The prosecutor's offered me a deal."

"What kind of deal? Like a plea bargain?"

"No. He's offering me immunity."

"What do you have to do?"

"Plead guilty to a charge of property destruction. He promised I'd get off with community service. Something new, huh?" She laughed, but it didn't sound amused.

"That doesn't sound too bad."

"And testify against the others."

While he thought about that, she went to the French doors.

A bust studied them from a niche as they leaned on a granite bulwark. Snow whipped their faces. "That's the Bay," he said, studying whitecapped gray beyond playing fields. "The Severn's to the left. Those antennas on Greenbury Point are for communication with submerged submarines."

"Nuclear submarines?"

"Uh-huh."

"Well, that's one difference. When those heroes of yours were sailing their ships, war didn't mean everyone on earth could die." She rubbed her cheeks, and he leaned behind her and put his gloves over her face. She said, muffled, "And you know, someday it's going to end."

"What, war? It's a nice thought."

"It's going to happen. I'm not saying your friends were evil. It's just that, sooner or later, we're going to outgrow it."

"Someday the sharks out there are going to stop eating fish, too."

"People aren't sharks."

"I think we are. We've got an aggressive instinct that just won't stop. Unless they come up with some kind of medication or something. And make everybody on earth take it."

"Or unless we change our hearts."

He didn't think it was going to happen soon, but he saw her point, too: that it had to come one person at a time, and that all you were responsible for was your own actions. And he couldn't disagree with that.

"What do you think I ought to do? About the deal?"

"I've been thinking about it. I can't tell you what to do."

"I know. I just wanted to know what you thought."

"I'd like to have you with me. But . . . you really think that's what they have in mind? Prison?"

"Absolutely. Conspiracy, and destruction of national security materials? Actually when you put it together, it could be up to forty-five years. But six to seven is more likely, our lawyer thinks. That's the sentencing minimum on the sabotage charge."

Dan looked out over the Bay. He said slowly, "I don't think you should bilge your friends."

"Bilge?"

"I don't think you should testify against them. I want you with me, but I don't want you at the price of your convictions."

"I'm coming to that conclusion, too," she said. "But I'm afraid. I don't want to go to prison, especially now."

He said quietly, "If you do, I'll be there when you come out."

She blinked into the icy wind. "Thanks, but I'm not going to hold you to that. I'll be a different person then. You'll be different, too. Let's not make any promises we can't keep."

When she began to shiver again, he kissed her hair. "We'd better go in. You need something warmer to wear — a sweater or something."

"Did you say you wanted to see somebody?"

"Yeah, let's see if Charlie's in. Then we'll go out in town for lunch."

The second batt officer was a classmate. He and Dan caught up, sitting in his office. Then he said, "You up for noon meal in the mess hall?"

"We were thinking about Middleton's, but —"

"Whatever," she said, in response to his look.

So they ate with the Brigade. King Hall looked smaller now, the arched overhead dingy. The mids at their table looked young. Even the first class looked like kids. Could this really have been his world, not that many years ago? But even as he asked it, he knew it had; that he'd always measure himself and those around him against the calibrations the Academy had etched into his heart. Maybe he and they would always come up short. But without the ideal, the example, the benchmark to measure their lives against, they would all be well and truly lost.

After lunch, he took her to an Irish shop in Crabtown and insisted she pick out a sweater. She chose the plainest, cheapest they had, but it was thick and warm. "And don't give it away," he told her. She smiled, sort of admitting he was right. They walked all over town in the cold and saw everything, and he told himself, holding her hand, swinging it like kids, This is what it feels like to be happy.

But that night in McGarvey's, he got to drinking hot rums, one after the other. She watched him, the beer in front of her untouched. And later — how long, he couldn't tell — he found himself lying helpless on the bed while she cleaned his face. He rolled his head away, and after that, everything was black.

At breakfast, she said, "You drank a lot last night."

"Yeah. Too much."

"So much, you passed out. Do we have a problem with that? With drinking too much?"

He pondered it. He felt weak and sick and guilty. He couldn't understand why he'd done it. He hadn't meant to.

"I guess we do. Have a problem, I mean."

"Then what are we going to do about it?"

"I need to cut down."

"Do you think you can?"

"I'll try. I'll promise you one thing — you're not going to see a repeat of last night."

She nodded, then changed the subject. He felt relieved and grateful. No more, he thought. Cut out the hard stuff. Just wine from now on.

He drove her back to Main Street and parked. "I thought we were heading back to Arlington," she said.

"Will you be okay in the car for a minute?"

"I guess so. Why?"

"I have some business."

She got the message that he didn't want to tell her, and said she'd wait. He went around the corner, into Bailey, Banks and Biddle's. The clerk looked up expectantly.

He said, "I'd like to look at engagement rings, please."

# 12

Monday morning, and another Primal Thunder pretest meeting. This one was internal to the project office, but most of the attendees were Air Force, including Manhurin, the major he'd met before. Another, thicker package was handed out this time. This time, one had his name on it. Colonel Evans ran the meeting, and he spent most of it reviewing the time line and status of the AGM-86.

Dan started out not listening very closely, but he tuned in as he realized the Boeing missile had problems, too, including the engine, low-altitude maneuverability, and the navigational system.

Evans briefed without notes, smooth and professional. Dan thought he looked like a general already, calm and compact and very, very competent. "To date, terrain comparison navigation works best where it can establish uniqueness. Against the USSR, though, our flight path lies over the relatively flat northern steppes. So we'll concentrate on calibrating for flights over flat snow and ice-covered terrain, adjusting for the Coriolis effect, and testing the B-fifty-two/missile interface."

At the end, almost as an afterthought, he took a few minutes to discuss the GLCM tests.

As the meeting broke, Dan caught up with Manhurin. The major said that despite breakdowns on the road, the convoy would be mushing into Cold Lake in time for the tests. Dan brought up a couple of his concerns, such as how applicable test data from the Air Force weapons control system was to Navy software. Manhurin said it had been developed from the Navy product, so results should be pretty much applicable to either one.

"I'll be there," Dan told him.

"Actually, we don't need to cook a missile for most of what we'll be doing. The extreme cold weather ops, dispersal and security and so forth. So if you wanted, you could hang here, only come up for the actual shoot."

"Maybe. Or maybe I'll go up early, get familiarized with your system."

He got back to his cubicle midmorning and settled in. Lucille had left a stack of mail on his chair. Vendor brochures, *Naval Engineers Journal*, conference flyers, an envelope with a handwritten address, Arlington postmark.

It was a card from Kerry. When you opened it, there was Pepe Lepew kissing a female skunk on the plaza of a Parisian café. The caption read "Love. . . . she is blind, no?"

Dear Dan,

There was no card with exactly the right words to tell you how much I enjoy being with you every day. Perhaps when we've had more time together, I can explain myself better. But for now, thanks just for loving me, just as I am.

And if you're confused sometimes, you're not the only one.

But I want you to know that whatever problems you have, you don't have to work through them alone anymore.

Love, Kerry.

He read it through again, then propped it on his desk by the Pentagon phone book and the *Government Printing Office Style Manual* and his purple-jacketed *Joint Staff Officers' Guide.*

Burdette leaned from his cubicle, wanting to know if Dan had seen a message about pin corrosion from *Merrill.* He snapped back long enough to find it in his incoming, then reverted to daydream mode.

She'd said it first — the *l* word. He was going to hold off till he got the ring, back it up with something concrete. But she'd beaten him to it. He leaned back, letting it warm him.

Then he winced, remembering his shoddy performance in Annapolis. But since then, he'd kept away from anything stronger than wine, and counted each glass of that. She hadn't said anything else about it, till now —

that oblique reference at the end of the note. She was too good to lose. She cared about people in a way he didn't but wished he did. He had a nurturing side, but up to now, he hadn't been operating in an environment that exactly encouraged it.

His phone rang and he grabbed it automatically. "JCM, Lieutenant Commander Lenson."

"Commander Lenson. Don't know if you remember me. Martin Tallinger here."

He leaned forward, instinctively turning away from the others in the space. Remembering the dingy courtroom, a bright-haired young man in a bow tie boring in as he'd stood there, angry and embarrassed amid people he'd thought then he had nothing in common with. "Yeah. I remember you. How did you get my number?"

"It wasn't that hard, you're in the DOD directory. I was going to call JCM anyway, and when I saw your name, I thought, I know *him*. . . . Look, I'm trying to pull together an article about what the budget's going to look like next year. Specifically, missile programs. Maybe something about how the new director — Nick Niles, right? — how he's doing on fixing what sounds like very serious problems over there."

"I'd better not discuss that. Most of what I know's too technical for —"

"I won't quote you. The last time we met,

you asked me not to print your name. And I didn't, did I?"

He got the message. Tallinger was saying Dan owed him. He said unwillingly, "No."

"So you know I protect my sources. Look, I'm going to publish anyway, so if you want the program's side of the story in print, you might want to talk with me. Let's get together after work. The Tune Inn, at six? They do a great burger. Meet you under the deer's butt —"

"Sorry, I can't make it. I've got a test series to get ready for. I'll be working late. Got to go." Tallinger said something he didn't catch, sounding disappointed, as he hung up.

After thinking that exchange over for a few seconds, he dialed the program's Public Affairs office. The PA type who answered said sure, he knew who Martin Tallinger was. He had one of his books there in the office.

"He just called me. What's the deal? Who's this dude work for?"

"Hold on a second. Let me pull this thing down, see what it says on the back flap. . . . Hotchkiss. Yale. Rhodes scholar. Served in the Office of the Secretary of Defense. 'Writes regularly on defense policy and aerospace issues.' Won something called the Edward Weintal Award. Fellow at the Johns Hopkins School on International Studies. Says he lives here in Washington. Picture of a kind of weenie-looking guy with glasses."

"That's him. Uh, what's the book about?"

"Title is *Aerospace Readiness and Coalition Defense*. Brookings Institution put it out, if that's any help."

"Uh-huh. Well, look, I basically stonewalled him. What should I have done?"

"Well, you got to deal with the press. He calls again, refer him down here. He wants an interview or something, we'll set it up officially and I'll sit in. Okay?"

He said thanks and hung up. Leaning back, he thought about it for a couple of minutes more.

Burdette came back in and gave him back the original of the pin corrosion message. "Did you make a copy?" Dan asked him.

"Got it right here. And one for Sparky."

"Uh-huh. Where *is* Sparky?"

"Over in the head shed. Captain W. wanted to see him."

He contemplated Kerry's card again, his brain transitioning back from the interruptions to wonder again what he was going to do. Burdette's chair creaked. He stared at the black officer's back. Then cleared his throat. "Uh, Vic?"

"What?"

"You read that Bible on your desk?"

Burdette turned a wary look toward him. "Every day. Why?"

"I could use some moral direction, that's why. You're a Christian, right? You're in the military, too. How do those two go together?"

Burdette put the message down. He looked at it, then at Dan. "You serious?"

"Just curious. I just wondered what it says about the kind of stuff we do around here."

The engineer laced his fingers over his stomach. "How long have I got?"

"Till lunchtime. Hit me."

"Well, there's — give me a second, let me get my head out of this other stuff. Okay.

"There's an awful lot in the Book about the morality of force. The Old Testament is a history of God's people in conflict. And at times, yeah, He sent them to war."

"In spite of 'thou shalt not kill.' "

"Exodus, Chapter twenty, verse thirteen. But 'murder' is a better translation of the Hebrew. Don't get confused between murder and killing. Sometimes God directs us to kill. 'Whoever sheds the blood of a human, by a human shall that person's blood be shed; for in his own image God made humankind.' "

"What about 'They shall beat their swords into plowshares, and they shall not study war anymore'?"

"Uh-huh. Isaiah, chapter two, verse four, which is backed up by Micah, chapter four, verse three. But then you got Joel, who says, 'Beat your plowshares into swords.' You could preach on both. But that's all Old Testament. Let's go to what Jesus said."

"Okay."

"The passage you hear most often is Matthew, chapter five, verses thirty-eight to forty-two." Burdette pulled the Bible down, thumbed through it, then read, " 'You have heard that it was said, "An eye for an eye, and a tooth for a tooth." But I say to you, Do not resist an evildoer. But if anyone strikes you on the right cheek, turn the other also; and if anyone wants to sue you and take your coat, give your cloak as well; and if anyone forces you to go one mile, go also the second mile. Give to everyone who begs from you, and do not refuse anyone who wants to borrow from you.' Jesus is replacing the old law with the dispensation of grace."

"I've heard that quoted to justify pacifism."

"That's not how the Book works. You got to consider God's plan and Jesus' mission."

"Okay. And what's that?" He hadn't meant to get into a theological discussion, but obviously Burdette had given the subject thought. He decided to squeeze and see what came out.

"Well, let's start with what you asked me, the morality of self-defense. First off, loving your enemy doesn't necessarily mean giving him what he wants. How else is he going to learn violence don't pay, and that he has to reform his will? When a cop pulls some drunk off the road, it's for his own good, as well as others."

"But Jesus made Peter put away his sword.

He went to his death instead. That passage you quoted from Matthew — it specifically says, 'Do not resist an evildoer.' "

"Does it?" Burdette read the passage again. "Actually, none of these examples are direct threats to anybody's life. To hit somebody on the 'right cheek' — if the guy who's hitting you is right-handed, like most people, the only way he can hit you on the right cheek is with the back of his hand, right? That was a formal insult in Jesus' day. He's not saying, 'Let someone kill you'; he's saying, 'Don't retaliate for petty injuries.' He's not saying, 'Submit to being enslaved'; he's saying, 'Go two miles instead of one.'

"Second, this passage is addressed to the person who's getting insulted. It doesn't say that if a child is being murdered before your eyes, hey, not your problem! Does it?"

Dan said, "No, but —"

"Especially if you're executing governmental authority. Romans, Chapter thirteen: 'The powers that be are ordained of God.' Next, the military. Jesus was up front with people who were on the wrong path. He confronted the Pharisees. He warned the priests not to profane the Temple. But he never told the centurion to stop being a centurion. In Luke, John the Baptist tells the soldiers, 'Rob no one by violence or false accusations, and be content with your pay.' It doesn't say not to be a soldier; it says to be a *good* soldier."

Burdette moved a couple of papers around, glanced at one, tossed it into his out-box. "The question isn't whether force is right or wrong in itself. It's like everything else in God's world: We can use it for good or evil. It's a question of authority. The biblical principles of authority — and you want it before lunch? Well, start with the idea of the covenant. The deal God makes with his people.

"Because God is the creator, any authority one man has over another has to come from Him. We have three human-to-human covenants: the marriage covenant, the civil covenant, and the church covenant.

"The civil covenant's the one that says the king or the government has authority and the people submit, as long as the government acts in accordance with the laws of God. Our government was founded on a scriptural basis. Now, it's departing from that — tolerating abortion, homosexuals, promoting sexuality and secular humanism. If we don't turn back, authority will be taken from it. But so far, it has the civil authority."

"Okay, what about nuclear weapons?"

"God used them."

Dan said, "What?"

"On Sodom and Gomorrah. Those were God's nuclear weapons. . . . Look, the Bible says the government has the authority to defend us. The other side has nukes. End of argument, far as I'm concerned."

"And you think this is what Jesus would have said?"

Burdette sighed. "Dan, we don't live in the millennium yet. We live in the 'between times.' The Devil's at work all around us. I'm going to fight him at Armageddon. The way I read this Book" — he put it gently back on the shelf — "I'm convinced what I do here is totally and completely in accordance with the teachings of Jesus and the will of God."

Dan was going to ask for clarification — there still seemed to be a gap there somewhere, either in Burdette's reasoning or his own — when Sakai came in and went silently to his cubicle. "What'd the captain need?" Dan asked him.

"Huh? Oh, nothing. He wants to see you next."

"Who, me? Now?"

Sparky nodded, and Burdette said, "Well, Commander, we'll talk about it some more later, okay? And maybe I can share with you the good news, about Jesus Christ's atoning death on the cross."

The first hint he had something was wrong was the woman standing outside Westerhouse's closed door. She was stocky, unsmiling, in a gray suit jacket and plaid skirt. She had a visitor tag but no escort in sight. He was about to ask her who she was when the door opened and one of the submariners came out. He looked stunned. She caught the door and held it for Dan. He looked through and saw a large black hand resting on the table.

"Lieutenant Commander Lenson, sir."

Westerhouse said, "Sit down, Dan."

Admiral Niles didn't say anything. So Dan looked at the others, trying to figure out what was going on. Westerhouse, looking as tired and hollow-cheeked as he did these days. Mrs. Toya, Security. And two civvy guys in suits and ties.

The door closed softly behind him. Then he heard it lock.

Westerhouse said, "Dan, this gentleman on my right is Special Agent Sheck Attucks, from the Federal Bureau of Investigation. The one on my left is Special Agent Patrick Bepko, from the Naval Investigative Service. They inform me we have a leak from inside this program. We wondered if it might be you."

He just stared. Finally, he said. "No, sir, it's not me."

"Captain, if I may —"

Westerhouse fell silent. The older civilian, Attucks, said, "Mr. Lenson, I work in the counterintelligence arena, out of the Washington field office. This is not an interrogation. Consider it a friendly warning. It has come to our attention that on at least a couple of occasions, information has been passed by someone within this program to an outside

222

intelligence service."

"Jesus," said Dan. He didn't like the way they were all looking at him. Even Niles, now. "Uh . . . who to? I mean, what kind of data? Who's it going to? How did you find out?"

"I can't be more specific. We're simply passing the tip on to the NIS. So, Pat, he's yours." Attucks sat back, but Dan saw the point: Start with the FBI and you got someone's attention. It worked. He sat up, wiping his suddenly moist palms on his trousers.

Bepko said, "Agent Attucks can't disclose how this leak was detected. That would compromise an intelligence source. The data wasn't classified. You might think, Then what's the problem? What concerns us is that where a pipeline for open information is established, classified usually follows."

Silence. Finally, Dan cleared his throat. "I'll be happy to cooperate, if you'll tell me what you need."

Attucks leaned in. "Answers to a couple of questions. First, are you sharing or supplying information to any outside activity or organization? Anyone who doesn't have a clearance and a need to know?"

"No." But the instant the denial left his mouth, he remembered.

"Something come to mind?" Bepko said softly.

"His name was Andy DeSilva. I met him

at a reception. He's a staffer for a guy named Holland, or — Mulholland, that was the name. A congressman. DeSilva was asking about Tomahawk. He wanted to know if we got a supplemental, whether that money would go into procurement. There's a factory in his district that makes parts for the engine."

A hand, immobile till now, stirred. "I could have benefited by knowing that. Did you think of reporting that congressional contact?"

"No, sir, Admiral. I'm sorry. It was all so casual. It was at a party —"

"A lot of very uncasual things happen at Washington parties," said Attucks. "What did you tell this Mr. DeSilva?"

"Nothing . . . except that I inadvertently mentioned two soft areas in the program. The booster and the WCS software."

Nobody spoke; at last, the agent shook his head almost imperceptibly. Bepko switched his attention back to Dan. "Thanks for that, but search your memory, Commander, for any other indications you might have of activity or conversations you might have had in the last six months that could have resulted in communicating information about the program. Especially with anyone possibly hostile to the United States or the military services of the United States."

He sat silent. That last part of the question made him think of the Plowshares people. But he couldn't recall telling Haneghen or Ken or

Deborah or even Kerry much about the program. He'd always been on his guard around them. Should he mention them anyway? It seemed so unlikely, and it would reflect so badly on him, that he decided not to, subject to further thought at least. "I can't think of any."

"What about your associates? Have you noticed any unusual or suspicious behavior? Such as making excess copies, bringing a camera to work, checking out references for use at home, excessive overtime, curiosity about other people's work, evidence of heavy drinking, drug use, homosexuality, sudden affluence?"

He searched his memory. Sakai was an unconventional guy, but Dan didn't think he'd be passing information. Burdette, not unless he was a hell of an actor. Lucille? Westerhouse himself, sitting across from him? Finally, he said, "I'm not coming up with anything."

"Okay, what do we do about this?" Niles grunted.

Toya flipped open a notepad. "Well, Admiral, the commander was the last prospect. As to what we do — we've got to heighten our security consciousness. I'll want all hands made available for training on how to recognize and deal with approaches from intelligence adversaries. I also recommend tighter physical security precautions. Step up pass checks. Implement two-man control on all secret and above. Increase compartmentaliza-tion."

Dan thought, Great, just what we need. The program was on the knife edge, and now they were going to get pulled off on briefings and training, have to get special clearances before they saw one another's paper. He said, "That'll slow things up."

Westerhouse: "We'll just have to work longer to make up for it."

Niles nodded ponderously, and Dan knew it was no use arguing. Bepko said, "Thanks for coming in, Mr. Lenson. This may strike you as odd, that we call people in, rather than trying to catch them in the act. The reason is that we'd rather stop this leak before essential information escapes than try to close the barn door afterward. We're devoting resources. We'll find the leaker eventually. It would be better for whoever was concerned if we got that information voluntarily."

As Dan got up, Bepko added, "Before you go, let me give you a number."

Dan took out his wheelbook. He clicked his Skilcraft and waited.

"Here it is: four three three-nine one nine one. If you remember anything — or notice anything — or want to tell us anything — you can either contact Mrs. Toya here or call that number." He held Dan's eyes. "That's the espionage hot line. What comes in on it is confidential."

He stopped halfway back to his office, standing in the corridor, staring at a paper clip someone had dropped on the carpet.

Could it happen? Was it possible someone he worked with was passing stuff to an enemy?

He remembered a rangy, salty chief warrant in faded khakis. A man you'd have thought would be the last to sell out his shipmates. Remembered an airless day, the stern shuddering as *Barrett* drove at flank speed away from the coast of Cuba.

Yeah, it could happen.

Face sober, he went on down the passageway.

# 13

A few days later, he looked down on plain and muskeg, the flattest, whitest landscape he'd ever seen. The C-130, a direct flight out of Andrews for Primal Thunder personnel, had overflown several winter storms along the way. It was a long flight, and standing in the narrow urinal he'd wondered what they'd do if they went down. Like that South American soccer team that had crashed in the Andes. Who would eat whom? Would they go by rank? Size? Age? Or service?

But eventually, the pilot came on the intercom. He told them they were approaching Canadian Forces Base Cold Lake, courtesy of the 130th Airlift Wing, Air National Guard, out of Yeager, West-by-God Virginia, and to fasten their belts, please. Dan twisted around to stare down as the transport banked. A frozen-over river snaked in tight loops. Then came runways in an L pattern, hangars with snow-covered roofs. Beyond the hangars and repair shops sprawled barrack blocks and tank farms and the familiar grid of military housing. It was all covered with snow, hard-looking and somehow whiter than white under the overcast.

Then the earth rose up to seize them again, snow-scoured concrete grooved with transverse lines, as if it had been poured in long slabs, and beneath him the wheels squealed and the engines went into reverse.

The moment he stepped outside, he couldn't breathe. Even in the lee of the terminal, the air was a searing, throat-numbing fluid. He coughed, then clamped a glove over his mouth. Snow whipped off the road into his face.

Base Accommodations had him in a double with a major he didn't know. He threw his gear on the bed, then leafed through a booklet titled *BFC Cold Lake Information Générale*. The place wasn't quite as isolated as he'd thought. There were towns, Grand Centre three klicks east, and Cold Lake to the north, on the lakeshore. The pictures of people sunning themselves on the beach made him shiver. He pulled out his shipboard steel-toes and melton reefer and gloves, then hung the rest of his uniforms and went looking for dinner.

At the Officers Mess, he joined a table of Air Force and Canadian Forces uniforms. They were talking about the possibility the weather might delay the testing. "Not here, but down south," one of the U.S. guys said. "The Buff's flying out of Arkansas — no problem there — but the support and chase guys are out of Tinker. They don't get off, we can't have a launch."

"Hell, that's exactly when we *want* to launch," said a light colonel wearing Strategic Air Command insignia. "This is what we'll have to fly in against the Bear."

"Where are you guys dropping your birds?" Dan asked them, wondering how they were going to avoid fouling one another, with two different series of tests going on.

The SAC guy examined him. "Navy?"

"Here for the GLCM test."

"Oh. Anyway . . . there's a big range north of the airfield. Four thousand square miles. Your impact point's out on the west edge."

He spotted Manhurin, then carried his coffee over. "Hey. Steve. Mind if I join you?"

"Hey, Dan. This is K. T. Thompson, our Canadian liaison; Eugene Decker, my security force commander; Doug Geddes, the missile combat crew commander who'll be firing first. Guys, this is Dan Lenson, runs the Tomahawk shop up in D.C."

"What you doing up here, uh, Commander?"

He told them. "Since we have so much commonalty, my CO thought we should have an observer here. Plus, I can learn to talk joint Tomahawk. How'd your road march go?"

"Reasonably okay. The turbine generator got knocked off-line a couple times. That tractor'll pull eighty thousand pounds at fifty-five miles an hour, but you hit a pothole cross-country, you'd kill everybody. . . . Gene, you about done? Anybody want to go out to Five Hangar with me, catch a beer? I got a jeep. We're gonna go change first."

"Sure," he said. "Count me in."

They were slowing for the car ahead, stopped at the gate, when he saw the shadows in the blowing snow. "Oh, what now," said Decker. "Not these idiots again."

Dan squinted out into the sourceless light. Past the gate was open field and then woods, winter-stripped alders and poplars standing gray and dead-looking in the snow. Four figures stood ahead of them on the road. They held close-gripped placards and what looked like a badminton net, though it was flapping so hard in the wind, he couldn't identify it precisely. He caught placard text as one turned from the car ahead: THANKS CANADA FOR MAKING WAR INEVITABLE.

"Holy shit, these assholes still here? It's gotta be thirty below."

"Run over 'em, they're stupid enough to stand in front of a car."

Dan looked out at four very cold-looking people in heavy coats and boots. At the woods' edge, an orange mountain tent vibrated in the wind. White smoke whipped off the tailpipe of an idling truck with RCMP insignia. He leaned forward. "Hey, pull over. Get me one of those."

Decker, who was driving, started to say

231

something, then cranked down the window. A cold-reddened face appeared. It spoke four or five words, but they were blown away by the wind. A mitten pushed the flyer through. Decker passed it back, holding it by the corner, as if it was dirty.

The cover showed a crane piling more rockets and bombs onto an impossible stack of armaments. Dan saw that the peace movement had mastered bulletized presentations.

• The Cruise missile is the latest thing in nuclear weapons. It's compact, accurate, sneaky, and deadly. Thanks to Canada, it makes nuclear war more possible — even probable.

• The Cruise missile is small enough to fit in your garage. Yet it is deadly enough to kill fifteen times as many people as the atomic bomb dropped on Hiroshima, Japan.

• The Cruise missile is designed for sneak attacks. It flies so low, it is undetectable by radar. It is meant for attack and not defense

**Millions die though no shot is fired.** Spending on arms diverts money and resources away from relieving disease and starvation. Global military expenditures exceed $600 billion annually. Just two weeks' worth of that spending (about $23 billion) could provide food, fresh water, housing, health care, and education to the neediest of the human family.

**People can't win in an arms race.** The arms race fuels inflation and unemployment. This results in cuts to social service programs as money is diverted to feed arms production. We are all asked to "tighten our belts" while arms spending goes unchecked.

**It will be a great day when our schools get all the money they need and the air force has to hold a bake sale to buy a bomber.** What is more, a million dollars spent in almost any other sector of the economy creates more jobs than a million dollars spent in the military sector. The arms race does nothing but encourage the expansion of militarism and antihuman technology.

Be heard! Be a peacemaker!

"What's that?" said Manhurin.

"Peace flyer."

"What are you reading it for?"

"They looked cold," Dan said. "The sooner they give 'em all out, the sooner they can go warm up."

"Why don't they get another hobby?" said

one of the others. Dan looked for a moment longer at the flyer, at the damp, cold, soggy paper, then folded it and put it away.

"Five Hangar" turned out to be a bar called Shank's, at the Grand Centre Hotel. It looked like a set from *Gunsmoke*. The oak walls were covered with crests and plaques. Wooden beams braced the darkness overhead. At the far end, a big TV was on. Players glided about, muffled and padded, in a sport midway between ballet and brutality: the Edmonton Oilers versus Detroit. The Air Force officers ordered beer and Canadian Pride. Dan started to order whiskey, then remembered and asked for a LaBatt's instead.

"Not so bad. Just like home."

"At least it isn't Wednesday. I hate that karaoke shit."

"Hey, Dan, ever heard drunk-on-their-ass Canadians doing karaoke? How about it, K.T., want to give us a sample?"

"You fellows will have to provide the entertainment yourself."

Dan watched the game for a while, then looked around the bar. There were two groups. First, young guys with crew cuts who were wearing combat boots and short jackets and had big watches. Fighter pilots, he guessed, though they might be ground crew. Second, older men in rough boots, plaid shirts, Imperial ball caps, and heavy belts with fancy-worked knife sheaths. The two contingents avoided each other, oil and water.

"Speaking of snow, we're going to have to get you cold-weather gear," Thompson told Dan. "What you're wearing's not gonna cut it. We're gonna be deep in the field tomorrow."

Decker said, "I'll take care of that for him, K.T. Have you got long underwear, or do we need to scramble some of that, too?"

"I could use a spare pair. How're we getting there?"

"Base Flight's got an Iroquois laid on for zero-eight-thirty. Sounds late, but it's gonna be right at dawn. We're only getting about seven hours of daylight."

Dan asked Manhurin what he'd done before GLCM. The major said he'd been a missileer since he graduated from Auburn.

"You guys are divided into pilots and missilemen."

"Uh-huh, but everybody plays second fiddle to the pilots. Anyway, I went to undergraduate missile training at Vandenberg. Was a crew dog at Grand Forks, the Four hundred forty-sixth Strategic Missile Squadron of Three hundred twenty-first Strategic Missile Wing. Minuteman II."

"What's Minuteman duty like?"

"You stand duty down in the center, where you have like — you've seen it in the movies — the two-man launch procedure. 'Three,

235

two, one . . . mark. . . . I have a tile; release.'
Right now, I'm attached to HQ, Tactical Air
Command, as GLCM program manager. As
well as commanding Flight One of the Eight
hundred sixty-eighth Tactical Missile Training Squadron. Sixteen nukes, sixty-nine people, twenty-three vehicles."

"That's what you're calling a 'flight.'"

"Right, we're modeled on the Army
Pershing battery. Two launch control centers,
four transporter-erector-launchers with four
all-up rounds each."

Dan said, "I got the impression from that
SAC guy at dinner —"

"What SAC guy?"

"Some light colonel. Anyway, I got the impression they barely knew you were here."

Manhurin said, "Well, it's a flyboy-missileer
kind of thing. Like in Grand Forks — there're
even two bars, but you'll never see a fly guy
in one or a missileer in the other." He swigged
his whiskey and inspected the glass. "Should
I have another? Probably not."

"That sounds like the black shoe-brown
shoe squabbles we have in the Navy."

"Yeah, but you guys have had a lot longer
to grow apart. Sometimes I think they just
should have given all the missiles to the Army.
Or do like what the Russians did, set up a
separate branch of the armed forces. Call it
Space Command, like in Heinlein."

Dan almost agreed, then remembered all

the missiles aboard the subs. He got up and went in search of the head.

When he got back, they were discussing the Strategic Defense Initiative. Pop-ups and X-ray lasers and kinetic kills. Till Decker said, "Uh-oh. Here they come."

He looked up, to see another handbill, this time being held out by a hefty blonde in a figured Indian sweater. "We got one at the gate," Decker said. Dan tracked her on and off as she worked her way around the room, getting rebuffed or ignored. One of the pilots caressed her ass; she pushed his hand away. They laughed as she left.

"Excuse me a minute," said Dan. He got up and went after her.

They sat apart from the rest, parkas hanging off the backs of their chairs, steam rising from mugs. Two guys, three gals. One was so bone-cold, she was shuddering even in the hot air of the bar.

"Hey. You the folks from the gate?"

"That's right. Just came in for the night."

"I've got some friends in Plowshares in D.C. Where you folks from?"

A young guy with a mustache said, "Oh, here and there. Mainly from Canada, but we've got some imports. Even a fella from Britain, from Greenham Common. Sit down, have a LaBatt's."

"Thanks, I can only stay a minute." He pulled over an empty chair as they introduced themselves, setting it on the far side so Man-hurin and the others couldn't see him. The young guy was Holden Murdoch, the coordinator. The woman in the sweater was from British Columbia, a member of Peace Caravan. Another man was a Minnesota native, born in St. Paul, but had put in four years in the Canadian armed forces. Catherine was from Halifax. Nancy was from right here in Grand Centre.

Murdoch was saying, "We call it the Cold Lake Peace Camp. It's small, but it'll grow. We've got a house downtown we stay in when we're not actually taking our turn on vigil. Cramped, but warm. We've got a store-front on Main Street, too. You might have seen it."

"Not yet. How long are you planning on staying?"

"As long as they keep testing, we'll keep protesting."

"You really think you can stop the flights?"

"We've got to try. Actually, when they were going to fly it in Utah, so many people showed up, they moved the site up here."

"I thought it was because the terrain was better."

"No, it was the protests. So it's not impossible. We've just got to get people to say enough's enough." Murdoch flicked the stack of flyers. "We're going to saturate the place with these. We've done press releases. And we started fasting. We'll each do a week, have a rotating thing. We're going to do a rally. People from the Lakeland area, Alberta, Saskatchewan. Soon as the weather lets up, we're planning a three-hundred-kilometer walk from Cold Lake to Edmonton. We've got fifteen groups signed up for that."

Nancy said, "We'd be glad to have you, if you wanted to come."

"I won't be here then. And I wouldn't march with you if I was." He hesitated. "I'm actually here with the military side."

They looked doubtful. Jeanne said, "And you said you had friends in Plowshares?"

"Uh-huh. Carl Haneghen, Kerry Donavan —"

"I know Kerry," said Jeanne. "She was on the Griffiss action. They're facing federal charges, aren't they?"

"That's right. I'm surprised you know them."

"Word gets around," Murdoch said. "Look, even if you don't want to be part of the vigil, you could pass out leaflets, inside the base. Or just put a stack in the chapel, or the cafeteria, anywhere people could pick them up."

"I don't think so. I'm not really on your side."

"Are you in favor of nuclear war?"

"No."

"Then we're on the same side."

"I don't think it's that simple."

"Oh, you can't get much simpler than non-violence and cooperation," said Murdoch. He gave Dan a smile. "Now, depending on weapons to give you peace — *that's* complicated."

Jeanne, the one in the sweater, said, "You're obviously doubtful. You know Carl and Kerry. What are you doing on the other side of that fence?"

"My job."

"Developing the weapons that will kill millions?"

"The weapons that will keep the peace."

"Even you can hear how absurd that is," Murdoch told him. "That's why you came over to talk to us. Your heart's gradually leaving the side of war and coming over to the side of peace. Someday you're going to have to decide. Why not now, when you can make a difference?"

"I don't think so," he told them again.

"Well, as long as you're here, let me ask you something. About blockading the gates."

"I wouldn't try that. They'll probably just arrest you."

"I already talked to the base administration officer. They'll arrest us all right. But if that's what it takes to get heard . . . Anyway, my question — when should we do it? We're reading in the papers they're going to start the tests soon."

"I don't know," said Dan. "I mean, I know the tests are starting, but I don't know when

240

the best time would be to schedule your . . . action." He thumbed through his wallet, saw a twenty, and passed it to Jeanne as he got up. "To help out. Anyway — maybe I'll see you again at the gate. Good luck on your vigil, and on your march."

He was standing outside with the others, waiting for Geddes to bring the Jeep around, when Decker put his arm around his shoulder and walked him a couple steps away. "What?" Dan said.

"I saw you talking to them. The peaceniks."

"Oh. I just had a friend I thought they might know."

"Hey, I plan to forget it. Although if I'd seen you grab a bunch of leaflets, maybe plan to distribute them on base —"

"I didn't take any leaflets."

"I said no problem, okay? I just want you to know these creeps aren't what they tell you they are. We have some interesting intel on them."

"Intel? What kind of intel?"

"All the anticruise groups are funded from the East Bloc. There're trained agitators at Greenham Common."

"One of these guys is from Greenham Common."

"Is that right? Interesting. Another thing: This 'peaceful protest' stuff is bullshit. The Germans found weapons when they raided

241

the 'peace camps.' I expect an attempt to disrupt the tests here."

"Wait a minute. Are you trying to tell me these people are Communist-funded? That's why they're standing around out there freezing their asses off, putting up with pilots groping them? I don't know if I can buy that, uh, Gene."

"Not all of them. But there are those with other motives there, too. Just to help you decide which side you're on."

Dan glanced at him. Had he heard that last part of the conversation with Murdoch? The security officer didn't give him any indication, just slapped him hard on the back as the Jeep drove up. "Remember, base flight out in the morning. Be at the hangar, zero-eight hundred."

# 14

They were airborne at the first suspicion of dawn, despite a threatening overcast. The Huey lofted them out over hills and lakes and rivers, miles of frozen marsh, then more lakes and more forest. They floated and vibrated at three thousand feet as light came to a bleached-out world. In the latter part of the flight, Dan made out targets below them as they windmilled onward, make-believe aircraft and pillboxes. But nothing moved, not even a deer. Isolated by the roar of turbines, buckled so tightly that he could barely shift his weight, he thought of what Murdoch had said last night in the bar. And suddenly, it seemed as if the desolation below was a warning, a foreshadowing of the future men were bending all their inventiveness and skill toward.

A world at peace at last, because every living thing was dead.

They pitched down and dropped, descending to five hundred, four hundred, three hundred feet. He saw what it must look like to the missile, hurtling between hills, pulling g's as they banked, the forest speed-blurring below. Then the chopper slowed and drifted gentle as a falling marshmallow toward a tracery of wheel ruts. Not till then did he realize that what his eye had taken for irregular protrusions of forest and snow were actually vehicles concealed beneath camouflage nets.

The skids thumped down in a rolling cloud of blowing snow. Grabbing his bag, he ran after the others toward a dimly seen pair of Hummers. Got there, damn near frozen, to be handed clothing and boots. He pulled them on in the close quarters of the vehicle: woodland cammies, parka, brown leather gloves with wool inserts, green mukluks — canvas rubber-soled boots with heavy felt inserts. He rolled his steel-toes inside his reefer and thrust them into his bag.

Not long after, he followed Manhurin up steel steps into a camouflaged van. Stamping snow off his boots, he looked around the interior of the Launch Control Center.

It was long, narrow, and walled with equipment, eight by twenty at a guess, with a huge chair at each end, mounted on rails. Dark blue indoor/outdoor carpet, stained and mushy underfoot. Behind him, the flight commander said, "Doug, this is your universe. Why don't you tour him."

"Right." Geddes took him down the aisle. "Let's start this end. Beyond this wall is the generator. These chairs are from C-one forty-ones. You get a four-point harness so you can ride out the blast from an SS-eighteen. Air conditioning. Chemical-bacteriological-radiological filters. Emergency lighting. Everything's shock-mounted." As he pointed to the racks and consoles, Dan noticed he was wearing a sidearm. "Recognize any of this?"

"Oh yeah." He was looking at the same equipment he'd been sweating over to get installed in *New Jersey*.

"We only had four billion to build this system, so we stole shit from everywhere. Those clocks up there are from Poseidon submarines. The sat comm's Army." Manhurin leaned to a display. The same orange-on-black touch screens, Dan noted, that the Navy used. "Pull up the system status. There we go. . . . We're going to drill this afternoon, then get a launch window and fire our first test round sometime after nightfall."

"How's your experience with maintainability? We've had some problems."

Geddes said they had bit losses on the fiber-optic cable; comm outages, especially on uncovered HF; and the electronic surge assemblies on the VHF tended to trip and blow up, which cut the comms between the flight commander and the security force. But the system worked reasonably well, considering it had been thrown together from off-the-shelf components from different source activities. "Let's just say I've seen a lot worse. Like Titan, all bolts and tubes and hypergolics."

"How about the DTDs?" The data transfer devices were the way the land-attack mission data got from the planning activity to the firing unit.

As if it helped him talk to have the equipment actually in his hand, Geddes reached down to slide it out of the RASS. The data transfer device was a rectangular box the size of a small suitcase, with a gray metal baseplate at the bottom. The sides and top were smoky plastic, through which Dan could see the platters.

"Only hitch is, we get head lockups occasionally. Your screen freezes; then you look in and the platters aren't spinning. I think it's the vibration does it."

"How do you unlock it?"

Geddes glanced at Manhurin, who grinned, and the crew commander said, "Well, this isn't in the manual, okay? But it locked up back at Dugway, and we were taking it out to work on it, and one of my guys happened to drop it. So then we said, 'hey, let's put it back in and see if it spins now.' And it did. So when it locks up, we take it out and knock it against the rack. Usually, that frees it up."

When he'd seen enough of the LCC, Decker took him across a field, following what he said was a fiber-optic cable under the snow, to one of the transporter-erector-launchers. Beneath the tented camouflage, it was reminiscent of the armored box launcher, but mounted on a trailer, with a big German-made tractor up front. From there, the security officer took him past the support vehicles, the vehicle park, the fuel farm, the cluster of twenty-man tents where the guys lived in the field. Then he led him out into the winter woods, tramping slowly through crisp, squeaking snow. His breath crackled as the moisture in it froze.

"Halt. Password?"

Four ghosts rose from the ground. White oversuits, M16s, grenade launchers. Behind them, the preying-mantis crouch of a machine gun. Decker gave the password, then explained their perimeter deployment, the ground radars, how they sited the vehicles and TELs. "In Europe, we're going to have to strike a balance between the ground threat and the air threat. If there're terrorists or Spetsnaz, we bring the perimeter in close. If things really go to shit, we fall back and go to close-in defense.

"Right now, we're set up for an attempt to infiltrate. Remember what I told you last night? About those Peace Posse types you were sippin' tea with?"

"That they were Commies. I still don't buy it."

"Buy it or not, they're going to try to disrupt these tests. We have firm statements of intent. Idea is to pressure the Canadians to call them off. The Liberals have already passed an anticruise resolution. So they could actually poke a pretty big stick in our wheels. . . .

Anything you feel like telling me?"

"No."

"Want to play intruder tonight? We'll give you a night scope, see if you can penetrate our position."

"Maybe some other time."

When they got back, it was lunchtime. MREs — meals, ready to eat — and hot coffee. He talked to the techs and took notes, tips he could forward to *Merrill* and the battleships.

Finally, he went back to the tents and found his bunk. It felt strange to be staring up at green canvas, to hear the wind rattling the fabric, the hiss of a Coleman heater, instead of the steady hum and whir of a ship.

When he woke, it was dark. He checked his watch, afraid for a moment he'd missed everything, but the time reassured him. He pulled parka, boots, and gloves on again and left the tent.

The overcast sealed off the stars, and he crunched across the snow in darkness so complete, he had a moment of disorientation. He walked with his hands out, so he didn't run into any trees. Then he felt something yielding. He ducked under the camo netting and went up the steps into the van.

The red lights filled the interior with blood and shadows. Geddes and his second in command were strapped in. Manhurin wasn't around; he was probably in the flight commander's vehicle, overseeing things. Dan found a folding chair, set it up in front of the launch console, and settled in to watch.

It was like the Navy launch control group, except that there weren't as many display terminals. One flat panel displayed different screens of data: weapons system status, mission status, missile status, calibration status. As the crew commander flicked through them, Dan leaned back, random screens of thought sequencing through his mind. Wondering if what Decker had told him about the protesters could be true. If it was, did it mean the same was true of Haneghen? Of Deborah and Ken, and the others whose motives seemed so pure and transparent?

Or was it just a smear? Defining the others as evil, and thus of necessity directed by what the leader of all just crusaders had called "the Evil Empire"?

Was he being enlightened? Or contaminated?

He sat musing as numbers flickered on a heatless screen.

"We're gonna take it from the start, just like a combat launch," Geddes told him. "Here's the scenario. We dispersed a couple of days ago, been waiting for the word. And here it comes." The Teletype began to clatter. Dan was taken aback; he'd expected something more high-tech, but the sergeant came over with a regular old high-freq message.

"Gimme the procedure book. . . . Okay, that breaks: Execute missile C-three on mission one thirteen. Your launch window is zero-two-ten-Zulu to zero-two-thirty-Zulu." He glanced at the clock. "Pull out the authenticators. Here come the numbers."

Plastic popped. "It's a match," his second said from the far end of the trailer.

The deputy crew commander got busy on the radio, letting everyone know launch was imminent. "Double-check, make sure nobody's hanging around the TEL," he added. Dan had an unpleasant vision of some unwary cook being blown into the trees.

"The security cops'll clear out the path downrange on the fly-out vector," Geddes told him. "Likewise around the back-blast area. That booster burns through the end of the canister, it sends a lot of shrapnel flying around. Okay, let's power up this sucker."

There were seven steps to the alignment. Meanwhile, Geddes was downloading the mission into the missile's guidance set. "Erecting the TEL."

He read off the elevation, and stopped it at forty-five degrees.

"That's higher than our box elevates," Dan said.

"We got to shoot over trees and hills. Okay, come on. . . . There it is. Alignment complete.

Green missile on C-three."

Geddes reported mission download. His assistant took his hands off the console, held them up like a chef contemplating a casserole ready for the oven. "That was expeditious. Seventeen minutes till window opens. Keep me honest on this, Dan."

At 0208 military time, they started reading off the final checklist. One man set the touch screen and the other confirmed it before going on to the next step.

"Confirm mission load. Push mission IDT TEA. Confirm mission number against initiating message."

"Confirm, one thirteen in the missile, one thirteen on the message."

"Confirm within launch window."

"Check, check, check."

He'd expected something dramatic at the moment of putting a nuclear-capable missile into the air. But all that actually happened was that Geddes said casually, "Everything look good to you? Did Gene report back range clear? Prepare to launch. Three, two, one, press." He laid his thumb firmly on the screen. At the far end of the van, his assistant did the same.

A sudden roar made the equipment judder in its racks. Dan flinched. Through it, he dimly heard Decker yell, "Missile away."

He unlocked the door and swung himself under the camo net. The roar was already dwindling, but it was still so loud, he clapped his hands over his ears. He swept his gaze around above the trees as an acrid, powder-smoky cloud swept over him. Then saw it, a flickering, swiftly rising white-orange meteor that winked out even as he glimpsed it, absorbed by the overcast night.

Yet still he stared upward, shielding his eyes. And for a suspended few seconds, it was as if, even though he couldn't see it, he was still riding with it, a ghost in the machine.

*As the missile emerges from the canister, four tailfins pop out. But still the climbing rocket is steered, not by fins, but by thrust vector tabs that aim the flame of the booster exhaust like a yards-long torch.*

*At thirty seconds of violent acceleration, two or three nautical miles downrange, transitioning from pitch-up into level flight, the guidance set approaches a crucial decision. Both airspeed and attitude are critical for engine start. With only forty-two square inches of intake feeding an engine the size of a pony keg, the missile has to have an exact vector and velocity of airflow down the airframe.*

*There will only be one chance to start the engine.*

*At 475 nautical miles an hour, the guidance set decides it is within the envelope. The missile jerks as explosives fling the booster free.*

*An instant later, the air scoop blows down into its flight position. Stubby, sharp wings snap out like switchblades. Another signal triggers the starter cartridge.*

*Alone in the darkness, the missile rocks at the threshold of flight, half rocket, half aircraft. Now it must fly, or surrender to the reign of gravity; arch ballistically downward, returning to the earth's embrace.*

*A roar, a whine, a trail of black smoke. The missile drops its tail, quests with its nose. Radar beams finger the darkness, tracing hill and valley with invisible cat whiskers. Within its computers, patterns flash.*

*Its long flight has begun.*

The van door opened behind him, spilling red light. Figures looked skyward, as if they could tell something about the missile, already miles away.

"Looked like a good launch," Dan said to the shadow he thought was Decker.

"Yeah, looked sweet. But a couple times we've had good launches, and then the thing goes bonkers."

"Bonkers?" He'd read the summary stats on the Air Force shots, but he hadn't seen anything detailed.

"Sometimes you get a pitch-over, it flies for a while, then sort of falls out of the sky. It'll hit level-out and something happens. T-one ninety-six did that. Total wreck, the chute didn't deploy and it went into a canyon."

Geddes joined them. "She's on her way," he whispered. "Fly, baby, fly."

They stood around watching the sky till it got too cold to endure, then dispersed. Dan trudged over to the telemetry van with Manhurin, but the men within motioned them angrily out. So they went back to the mess tent. After a thawing-out period, they ate more MREs off their laps, sitting on the bunks. Somebody went around bumming the miniature Tabasco bottles from the condiment packs. Then they just sat waiting.

It came in three hours later. Short and simple, relayed from the impact point via the AWACS aircraft that had tracked the missile through the whole 2,200-kilometer flight.

GLCM C3 FLYING MISSION 113 TRACKED VISUALLY BY CF-18 THROUGH FINAL LEG. PASSED OVER AIM POINT TOKTOYAKTUK PENINSULA. RECOVERED BY PARACHUTE.

"There it is," said Manhurin, getting up. "Good work, everybody. Especially the maintenance guys."

Dan joined them in smiles and handshakes. After all this work, to actually see the thing fly, to know it could do the job! But almost instantly, from what felt like another half of his brain, a darker thought quenched his elation. Was this really something to celebrate?

He went to bed and stared for a long time at the canvas, stretched close and taut and dark above his face like an already-fitted shroud.

# 15

A bang, the scream of landing-gear tires, and he returned to earth again, not as disoriented and sleepless as usual. Maybe he was getting used to this. Or maybe it was that he'd stuck to orange juice on the flight. He got his briefcase out of the overhead compartment, checked the lock — he was carrying the preliminary results from the first series, double-sealed in taped envelopes — and carried it out, past the gate, and into the terminal.

Friday morning, and through the huge viewing window was the Potomac, and beyond it the gleaming dome where Monday the hearings would begin. One thing after another. But at least he'd have the weekend off, with Kerry.

Then he saw her, waiting at the end of the corridor. A moment later, his arms and his heart were full. "Gosh, this is a surprise. You didn't have to come and meet me."

"No big deal. I told them at the kitchen you were coming in, and Deborah said she'd cover on the sandwich line."

"Amazing. *Deborah* said that? Hey, and look at this. You're wearing the sweater."

"Do you have to go right in?"

"Shoot — yeah, I better. I have to turn this stuff in, can't take it home. And I got to check my box, my messages. . . . We could have a bagel or something before we go over, though."

They sat together, watching the airport crowd stream by like schools of anxious heavily burdened fish. The snow had melted and the grass outside was a lifeless brown, the sky gray, the windows dirty. Still he felt happy sitting across from her, looking at her in her worn old coat and her yard-sale tam and the new sweater.

"How was your visit to Utah? It was Utah, right? How long did you get to spend there?"

"Just a one-day stopover. Flew in, slept on the couch in the rec room, flew out the next morning. It was kind of . . . strange."

"How's your daughter?"

"Oh, Nan's doing great. Smart as hell. Pretty as hell. She's into tennis, and doing real well at it, plays way above her age level."

"And your ex-wife?"

"She's still my ex-wife. She's doing archaeology full-time now. She's seeing a doctor. I mean, living with him. A dermatologist. That's whose house I was at. He's got this big place out in the desert, Mexican tile floors, pool, all that shit."

"Jealous?"

He shifted on the wire chair. "Not exactly. But not comfortable, either. It's easier not to think about it at all. So mostly, I don't."

She studied her muffin. "Do you still love her?"

He pondered it. "I used to think I always would. Like that once you love somebody, it never goes away. You know? But after years and years . . . I love Nan. Sometimes I can't stand not seeing her. But I wouldn't take Susan back. I don't think she was very good for me, or that we were particularly great together. I don't mean she's not a good mother or anything like that. Just that she was more — oh, forget it, I'm not going to get into comparisons. But I think you and I can be friends, not just lovers."

"But you also keep saying we're different," she pointed out.

He took her hand instead of answering right away. Rubbed a red patch on the back of it. "You burned yourself."

"That's an old stove, the things that hold the pots — the burners — they're cracked off."

"Maybe I can take a look at it. Yeah, we're different, but does that mean we can't be happy? There are Republicans and Democrats who get along. People from different religions. We can disagree about other things and still love each other." He kissed the burned spot. "Actually, I don't know how much longer I'm going to be in. Like I told you, I'm thinking about putting in my letter, end of this tour."

"Because of me?"

"Not totally, but you're an input. More cream cheese?"

"No thanks. Oh, a friend of yours called. May?"

"Mei's in Dr. Szerenci's class. You talked to her at the party. The Chinese girl?"

"I remember her now. Well, she invited us to dinner tonight. A family dinner. I think she was surprised to talk to me. But she invited us both. I said we might be able to make it."

"Did you want to go?"

"I don't care. Whatever you want."

He looked at his watch, muttered, "Shoot," and stood. "You can stay and finish that. I'm going to take the subway over —"

"I can drive you over and wait. I picked up your car. They changed the oil and did the maintenance you wanted. I used one of the checks you signed."

"Thanks, but it could be awhile. I'll call you after I turn this stuff in, let you know about dinner."

She dropped him in front of NC-1, and he waved as she pulled out.

"Great, you're back," said Westerhouse when he stuck his head into the project manager's office. "Got a potato you need to get hot on right away. We just got a heads-up, one of the things the committee's going to look at Monday is our change costs and subcontractor data."

Dan stared at Westerhouse. Last year, when he reported in, his boss had impressed him as heavy, if not overweight. Seeing him after a couple of weeks away, now he realized he looked gaunt, almost frail. "Sir, are you all right? You've lost a lot of weight. Is something wrong?"

"Just stopped eating as much. Can you get on up there? I want you to go help make some sense out of what you set up with Vimy and FMC and those guys."

"Sure, sir, but I have to get this midtest report put together for Colonel Evans."

"Part of living in a multiple-crisis environment. Bad news: The new deputy SecDef's saying he's going to shift ten billion dollars from the Navy to the Army."

"*What?* Can he do that?"

"Not alone, but he's got a lot of friends on the Hill. He plays golf every weekend with the Army Chief of Staff. The kicker is, he's a former pilot, and he's locked in with Dwayne Harrow."

"The congressman who called these hearings."

"Right. And *he* interlocks with Jack Wagner, who gets the carriers built in Virginia, and 'Flyboy' Koelpels, the congressman from Grumman. But right now, we got to put out this fire with the Defense contracting guys or they're going to have another dagger to dirk us with. Call me at seventeen hundred and we'll figure when to get together with Bucky Evans for the preappearance run-through."

"Yessir."

"Oh, and Lucille's got some registered mail for you. Don't have any more personal stuff sent here; that's not what our mail system's for."

It was a sealed box, insured. He'd purposely given the jeweler his military address so it wouldn't get delivered to the apartment. He took a second in the corridor to unfold the tissue paper. A marquise-cut diamond glittered up. Not huge, but blue-white. A white-gold mounting — he'd noticed Kerry didn't wear yellow gold.

From the door, Westerhouse said, "Are you going up to Financial?"

"Yes, sir, on my way." He folded it hastily and buttoned his pocket over it, then ran lightly up the fire stairs.

The financial office was filled with hastily drafted civilians and officers. They wanted a breakout of engineering, general, and administrative costs; the costs of materials, sustaining engineering, and sustaining tooling; a breakdown of all the above in terms of total labor cost, and a single dollar figure in constant fiscal-year dollars over the life of the production run, representing all subcontracted and vendor costs. At seventeen hundred, he called home. He told Kerry, "Look,

I'm sorry, but there's this big sweat party going on. I'm gonna be here for a couple more hours."

"How late are you going to be? We have that invitation from your classmate. That's for nine, if you'll still be downtown."

He didn't want to go out to dinner; all he wanted to do was go home and lock the door and get her clothes off, fast. But it was the second time she'd brought it up. "Where is it, again?"

"Chinatown."

"Chinatown —"

"The Red Line, Gallery Place. Do you want the name of the restaurant?"

"Not right now. I'm still gonna try to get home. Then you can show me how much you missed me."

"I think you'll be satisfied with the demonstration."

"Oh. Yeah! Look, the sooner I get this done, the sooner I'll be there, so let me hang up now, okay?"

"Okay. Love you."

"Love you, too."

He finally got loose, but then he had to let two trains go by; the Orange Line was packed solid as one of the Cedar Deli's master subs. By the time he got to the apartment, it was eight, and she was already dressed, so he limited himself to a kiss and changed quickly, sneaking the ring into his blazer.

Being downtown after dark was always a scary proposition, but tonight there were lots of people out. They parked on H. The air was bracing and the sky burned yellow-orange under the overcast. He took her arm and felt her shivering. "Want my jacket?"

"I'm okay. Is Canada this cold?"

"Are you kidding? They've got four feet of snow in Cold Lake." He told her about the test and the base till she said, "There it is," and they crossed the street and went down the steps, into the basement entrance of the Pearl of China.

"Dan! You are here." Mei kissed his cheek, shook hands with Kerry, and led them back. A separate room with a low patched ceiling was filled with women with babies, smiling old ladies, not one but two tablefuls of clamoring, indulged children. The central figure was a smiling little old man, to whom Dan was introduced with great fanfare, but he didn't quite catch his name, or what relation he was to Mei.

Next up was a middle-aged businessman in a dark suit, wearing metal-on-plastic Yuri Andropov glasses. He had black surprised-looking eyebrows. Mei said, "Dan, I would like you to meet my uncle Xinhu."

They shook hands heartily. Dan thought he and Mei didn't look much alike. Maybe "uncle" wasn't an exact translation. But his En-

263

glish was excellent, and Dan introduced Kerry, and it wasn't long before they were family. One of the old ladies kept talking to Kerry, smiling and nodding. She kept putting food on her plate and patting her tummy. Only Dan and Kerry actually had their own plates. The others helped themselves from the dishes, passing them around and dipping in with their chopsticks, though each had his or her own bowl of rice. Dan's first bite made sweat break out on his forehead. It was savage Szechwan. He glanced to his elbow, where Mei had placed a martini for him. He gulped it before he remembered he was off the hard stuff.

Uncle Xinhu rose for remarks, and everyone clapped and murmured admiringly when he sat down. The little old man smiled so steadily, Dan wondered if he was functional. Then came the toasts. The room grew warm, then hot. He caught Kerry's eye as he upended his cup.

"Your wife is very beautiful."

He twisted his head; Xinhu was bending over his shoulder. He started to say Kerry wasn't his wife, then thought, surprised, Hell, I dated his niece. Does he think . . . He said, "Thanks."

"Would you come with me? Mei has a story she wants to tell your wife."

"Story? What kind of story?"

"An old Chinese tale about a tiny carp who

thought he could leap over a great dam. Come on, we will be back in a few minutes."

It didn't compute, but he gave way to the demands of hospitality and followed Xinhu down a narrow stained passage with sunflowered wallpaper peeling off the plaster. They went up a shadowy flight of lacquered steps, so old that they were worn away in the center, to a dim upper place where men sat in booths. Golden carvings gleamed faintly from glass-fronted cabinets. His host spoke to a bowing waiter as they slid into an alcove.

"Do you have any children, Dan?"

He said he had a daughter. Xinhu said, "How wonderful. The revolution changed a great deal about our own ancient culture. But one thing that remains more precious than any other is the family."

Dan agreed families were important. The waiter brought out fresh martinis. Xinhu lifted his. "Cheers."

"Cheers." Kerry couldn't see him now, so he drank it swiftly. When he went back downstairs, they'd make their excuses and leave. In an hour, he'd be in bed with her. . . . Xinhu said, "Mei tells me she enjoyed very much going out with you."

"Yeah, it was fun. No more, sir, thanks. Actually, we need to leave pretty soon. Thanks for dinner."

"In a moment. Mei tells me you are very intellectual in the Szerenci class. She tells me you are in the Navy?"

"That's right."

"I was in Shanghai when the first U.S. Navy ship arrived to visit it since 1949, when the bandit Nationalists fled. Everyone was very happy to have the U.S. Navy return. Have you ever been to China?"

"Uh, no. I'd like to see it sometime, though. The Great Wall and all."

"Why not? There are American military missions there now. Building a common front against our mutual enemy. Many U.S. government agencies and commercial companies are helping China strengthen herself. Have you heard of that?"

"Sure. Engines for your new destroyers. Lightweight torpedoes. Things like that."

"And where do you work, Dan?"

"In Crystal City."

"Oh, yes. Mei mentioned to me, that you gave a report on your office. This is very interesting, this idea of the cruise missile. I wonder if you would be willing to assist us in understanding it."

Dan was trying to penetrate the gloom to see what the carvings were when he caught what Xinhu had said. "*Assist* you? What do you mean?"

"We would not want anything that was classified, of course. I am not asking about anything like that! But things that are permitted to you to give out. Articles, the public-relations photographs, what companies are building the various parts. A telephone book would be very helpful."

"I don't understand. If you want a phone book —"

"I'm sorry, I do not mean the Washington book. Of course I have that, and as an attaché I also have the Defense Department telephone book. But there is also one for the office where you work. Isn't there?"

A blade edge of wariness tested his alcoholic bubble. He looked toward the bar, avoiding the stocky man's eyes as he tried to focus in the martini dim. He wasn't up to doing partial integrals, but it didn't take much extension of the trend lines of the last few remarks to see what Xinhu was aiming at.

Mei's uncle? He doubted that now. Whoever he was, he obviously thought Dan and Mei had gotten it on. That was what he meant by the references to "family," the fulsome compliments for Kerry and questions about children. Had Mei told him they'd done the deed? Xinhu seemed to think so; he thought Dan and Kerry were married; thought, therefore, he had something on him. He fingered his glass, wishing he hadn't drunk quite so much. "Uh, why would you need something like that?"

"I would like to know more about the people in your office. Could you tell me about some of them? Is there anyone who owes money? Or who disagrees with policy?"

"Uh, I don't really know. Nobody comes to mind."

"Are there any Chinese? Americans of course, but of Chinese extraction?"

A face came to mind: a sergeant in the Advanced Systems Group he'd dealt with when he was running the Combined Federal Campaign. But instead of mentioning him, he said, "I don't recall any. Why?"

Xinhu sketched some uninterpretable figure or sign with his finger. Dan wondered if it was an ideogram, and if it was, what it meant.

He said, purely out of the blue and being drunk, "This phone book thing. It sounds like what you're talking about is the *Employee Handbook*. It's got the director's bio, and the wiring diagram for the organization, and in the back there's a list of office numbers."

"How many pages are they?"

"How many? Oh, they're not very big."

"Could you photocopy one for me?"

"I don't know."

"It could help your family."

Dan felt a sudden chill, and it wasn't the icy gin. "Help my family?" he repeated.

"That's right. You could send your parents extra money, for example. I would be happy to pay you for the copies, and for your time."

Dan wondered what kind of picture the man had of American life. He said, "I'd have to think about that."

"I would also like you to meet a friend of mine. He is named Li. Not here, but somewhere else. To discuss other aspects of cooperation. Can I call you?"

"Whatever. Hey, thanks for the drinks, but . . . can we get back to the others?"

"Certainly," said Xinhu. He searched his pockets and held out something. A card? It was so dark in the room, Dan just put it into his pocket, and as he did so, his fingers brushed the little flat box. She wasn't his wife yet, but it might happen.

"You are smiling. Did I make a funny remark?"

"No, I'm just happy." He stood, almost fell, then steadied himself on the table. As he followed Xinhu down the staircase, he felt it rolling around him, as if they were at sea in a storm. It actually made him homesick. If you missed your home, it was homesickness. If you missed the sea, it wasn't seasickness, though. Funny language, English.

Kerry greeted him with a strained smile. He kissed Mei, shook the geezer's hand, saying their good-byes. A child was bawling; another slumped, asleep.

When he hit the cold air outside, he all at once felt really, really drunk. He said, "Hey, would you mind driving?"

"I was about to ask you for the keys."

When they got back to the apartment, she

disappeared into the bathroom. He stood in the bedroom, waiting. It seemed like a long time.

Finally, he went into the kitchen and opened the upper cabinet. There it was, his fallback bottle. He tipped it up, then capped it and slid it back and closed the cupboard gently so that it wouldn't bang. She came in a moment later, as he was drinking orange juice out of the carton. He stayed bent into the fridge. "Nice party, huh?"

"They were nice. . . . Where did you go? There in the middle?"

"Her uncle wanted to talk."

"What about?"

"I'm still not sure." He wanted to think about it when he wasn't shit-faced, but it had seemed an awful lot like an intelligence approach. If it was, he ought to report it. But if he did, that could get Mei in trouble.

"That Chinese girl —"

"Mei?"

"I saw the way she looked at you. Is she an old girlfriend?"

"I took her out a couple of times. But it didn't go anywhere. Just a classmate is the most accurate claff— *class*ification. Are you ready for bed?"

"In a minute. I still have to change." She left the kitchen again. After a moment, he glanced out, made sure the coast was clear, and pulled the bottle out for another long swallow.

Bottle lifted, he stared up at the ceiling as the liquor scorched his throat.

The next morning, he woke not only with a paralyzing headache but also with the sense something was dreadfully wrong. When he got his eyes open, he was alone in bed. He was naked. He forced himself up and staggered to the closet. His hands shook as he fumbled with the ties of his bathrobe.

She sat by the sliding windows in the living room, sipping tea and reading the "Lifestyle" section. He eased himself down across from her, trying not to hurl. "Hi."

"Hi. Do you remember what happened last night?"

"Last night. The dinner?"

"After that."

He waited for her to tell him. She flipped a page and said, not looking at him, "You drank a lot, apparently. I didn't see you do it, but you were so drunk, you couldn't make love. You tried, but eventually you went to sleep. I woke up later, and I heard water running. At first, I couldn't figure it out. Then I saw you standing in the corner."

He closed his eyes. Red motes illuminated a pain-filled darkness. "I don't remember that."

"Go look."

"I didn't mean that. . . . I'll go clean it up."

There didn't seem to be much else to say,

and she just kept reading, so he staggered into the bedroom and found the patch of soggy carpet. Could he really have . . . Yeah, he had. Whizzed in the closet. Actually, on his running shoes.

The scary thing was that he didn't remember it.

It took awhile to clean up; he had to sit on the bed and say calming things to his stomach between fetching paper towels. When he was done, he took three aspirin, then went into the shower and scrubbed from head to toe under scalding water.

When he came out, he felt like a too-light photocopy of himself. He pulled on sweatpants and a T-shirt and went back out.

She was sitting in the same place, staring out the window, with her chin on her hand. He said, "I'm never going to drink again. Liquor, wine — I'm on the wagon for good. You'll never see me in that condition again."

"Dan, I hate to say this, but we already had this conversation. Remember? After you got so stinking drunk in Annapolis that I had to wash the vomit off your face."

"I didn't promise not to drink then. I said I'd cut out hard liquor."

"A promise that you then went ahead and broke. Both at the restaurant last night and after we got home. From the bottle in the kitchen. Right?"

He didn't say anything. She waited, then

added, "Do you understand what I'm saying? Do you really?"

"This time's different. I give you my word."

She just kept looking out into the daylight, as if she could hear him but wasn't listening. He waited, hands in his lap, dumb as a dog under a blow. Finally, she said, "I believe you mean that. What I don't know is whether you can keep that promise. I've seen so many people at the house, and on the street, who can't stop. Drugs, or alcohol. They *want* to — but they can't."

"I don't think it's the same. Comparing me with them."

"Just because you aren't homeless at the moment? Dan, they had jobs once. They had families. I don't think you understand how much danger you're in."

He couldn't believe she was comparing him with street drunks, with addicts, with the winos who lay in the doorways of abandoned buildings and stood stunned or mumbling by every subway entrance. He hadn't meant to start drinking at the dinner.

Then he saw what she meant. He'd resolved never to get drunk in front of her again. But after that first drink, he'd wanted more and more. Stopping had never occurred to him. Only hiding it. All he could say was, "Well, this time, I'm serious."

She didn't answer, and after studying her, he went back into the bedroom and found his

273

blazer lying on the floor. He had a bad moment when he couldn't locate it, but then the corner touched his palm. He came out, holding it behind his back. "Here. This is for you."

She looked at the blue velvet box.

"Go ahead, take it."

She opened it. Finally, she said, "Is that a diamond?"

"Uh-huh. Not a big one, but it's good quality. That's a marquise cut."

Stop babbling, he told himself. He couldn't breathe, waiting for some response. But he couldn't tell if she was thrilled, or taken aback, or if she felt anything at all. "Try it on. I had to guess at the size."

She put it on her ring finger, but only for a moment. Her lips compressed. Then she took it off and slid it onto her index finger.

"Too big? I can have them fix that. Look, say something. Do you like it?"

"I don't know, Dan. It's lovely, but . . . Yesterday, I would have been excited. But this morning, I don't know. Are you sure you want to offer me this? This is an engagement ring, right?"

"Am I sure? Yeah, I'm sure. I want you to marry me."

"You're not just doing it to ask forgiveness, or to make me forget last night?"

He thought about that; then he made himself tell the truth. Tell her the damn truth, if he could just hew to that . . . "A little. But I had it made specially for you. I ordered it when we were in Annapolis. Remember when I asked you to wait in the car? That's when I picked it out. I want you to forgive me, and I want you to marry me. And I'll never drink again."

She sat silently, twisting it around her finger. He felt detached, light-headed, as he waited to hear what she would say next. Finally, she murmured, "I won't wear it."

"You won't."

"No. But I'll keep it. And we'll talk about it again in six months. All right?"

He nodded, closing his eyes. He'd been afraid she was not only going to refuse it but leave him, pack up and go back to the house and Carl. "So, what's the plan today? We could do a museum or —"

"Wait. Not so fast." She reached to cup his face. "I want you to remember that promise. Because I remember the ones I make."

"All right." He had to blink back sudden tears, looking into a face transparent with love and doubt. "I'll remember it. I make mistakes. I don't always know the right thing to do. But I don't make promises I don't keep. And I love you."

Their lips met in a kiss that made him weep. And a little later, she whispered, "Since you're feeling better, let's go into the bedroom. And you can finish what you started last night."

## 16

Captain Westerhouse called him in on Sunday. They worked into the evening, recasting the testimony to respond to an article that had just appeared in *Aerospace Daily*. The story had reviewed the budget shortfalls, Tomahawk's uninspiring test record, and Niles's "desperate" attempt to get the program moving again by threats, firings, and demotions. It concluded with a blunt assessment of what was likely to happen after the upcoming hearing: the supplemental defeated, the missile defunded, the program terminated. Dan's skin crawled as he read it. It was by — surprise — M. W. Tallinger. He couldn't imagine how the guy got this stuff. He called Kerry at seven and said he wouldn't be home. At midnight, he went into the ladies' room, taped a MAN SLEEPING sign on the door, and crashed on the couch.

Monday, appearance day, dawned with him back at the transparencies. Evans and Westerhouse had come in early, and they thought of things that needed changing. He broke only once, to run upstairs to Shirley Toya's office. He said hastily, leaning in, "Hey, can I talk to you a second? In private? We're leaving for the Hill in a couple minutes, but

I wanted to tell you about something funny that happened Friday night."

He'd thought this through over the weekend, and had decided to get it over with. If it meant Mei would catch hell, well, she shouldn't hang around guys like that. He told Shirley about the class, about dating Mei, and that she was employed at the embassy. He told her about the dinner, and everything he could recall of what Uncle Xinhu had said. Though the card he'd given Dan carried another name, Zhang Zurong. Toya had started making notes, but when Dan said, "He says he's from the Chinese embassy, a military attaché," she stopped writing.

She seemed doubtful as she examined the card. "He gave you this?"

"That's right."

"Actually, attachés are supposed to do this sort of thing. And he's right — we're putting a lot of effort into helping the Chinese."

"Well, I'm supposed to report recruitment attempts, right?"

"That's right. And thank you."

"Wait a minute. Are you going to pass this on? To those guys from the FBI, or the NIS?"

"I haven't decided yet. If he contacts you again —"

Burdette, at the door. "Dan? We got to finish the rest of those graphs, get the progress reviews ready."

"Look, I've got to go. We'll talk later, okay?"

She nodded.

He was kept running back and forth from the PR office — where the guy was who made the transparencies — right up till they were getting into the cars to go. Even then, some of the slides were still being worked; the PR director said he'd take them over to the hearing as soon as they were done.

An hour before the scheduled start, he followed Niles, Evans, and the senior staff up the steps into the Rayburn Building for the Procurement and Military Nuclear Systems Subcommittee hearings. He carried two file cases of documents, references, extra transparencies. Two Air Force sergeants were humping projectors, screen, handouts, and a complete Litton LN-35 inertial navigation unit in an aluminum shipping case as a show-and-tell. Dan wished he could have gotten home for a clean shirt. But he'd shined his shoes with the kit he kept in his desk, and brushed his blues. He wasn't going to testify anyway; all he had to do was sit behind the admirals and hand them whatever they needed during the questioning. He helped set up at a long table with microphones, then collapsed into a chair in back. Then Evans asked him to go down the hall and see if he could locate some coffee.

From the *Hearings before a Subcommittee of the Committee on Armed Services*, Government Printing Office, Washington, D.C.

House of Representatives,
Committee on Armed Services,
Procurement and Military
Nuclear Systems Subcommittee,
*Washington, D.C., Monday, January 16.*

The Subcommittee met, pursuant to notice, at 10:15 A.M., in room 2337, Rayburn Office Building. Hon. Vesey M. Osborn (chairman of the subcommittee), presiding.

MRS. ROMANICK. Our chairman is not yet here, but he is on his way. I think we should get started. I will read his statement:

Today, the subcommittee's hearings will consider supplemental funding of Navy strategic systems.

As the members are aware, the Procurement Subcommittee is responsible for authorizing the procurement of the Navy's Trident ballistic missile, maintenance of Poseidon ballistic missiles, and development and procurement of antiship and land-attack cruise missiles for either strategic or tactical purposes.

There has been much discussion of the Tomahawk missile now under development. This unproved missile may become an issue in the full committee this year. So that the members should have some familiarity with it before that stage, I have asked Navy witnesses to address the Tomahawk program in detail this morning.

Our first witness will be Vice Admiral Charles L. Willis, Jr., USN, Chief of Naval Materiel.

MRS. ROMANICK. Admiral Willis, before proceeding, will you please introduce those witnesses who are accompanying you?

ADMIRAL WILLIS. Thank you very much for the introduction. I have looked forward to the privilege of testifying before this committee once more. I would like to introduce Rear Admiral Barry N. Niles, director of our Joint Cruise Missile Project. I will open with a statement, after which we will be happy to respond to your questions.

MR. OSBORN. I am informed by staff that the testimony you are giving is classified, so we will now go into closed session. Before we proceed, we will make sure that the room is secure.

ADMIRAL WILLIS. As you know, I am here to represent the Tomahawk portion of a possible supplemental budget request. In addition, I will address those items for which your subcommittee has expressed a desire to receive information.

Dan slipped transparencies on and off the projector as Willis went through the prepared statement. The vice admiral called Tomahawk the next breakthrough in naval warfare. He pointed out the missile's antiship and land-attack capabilities, its ability to arm both submarines and surface ships, and its survivability against present and projected enemy defenses. He outlined the need for a supplemental to cover shortfalls and to procure long-lead items for the next fiscal year's buy. The vice admiral spoke calmly, with occasional touches of dry humor. Dan recognized the words he'd sweated over night after night, but it sounded as if Willis was doing it off the top of his head. He paused in his remarks while they showed the film, the in-flight and terminal-homing footage supplied by Convair. Finally, he closed, then asked for questions.

MR. OSBORN. Where do we stand in terms of the testing of this missile? My understanding is that you are still having problems with it — it didn't perform well, so why should we put procurement money into it if it isn't working?

ADMIRAL WILLIS. It has performed in its tests, sir, and I will defer to Admiral Niles, the program manager, for the specifics. Admiral Niles.

MR. OSBORN. Before you begin, Admiral, let me welcome you to the committee. I do believe this is the first time we have had a — we have had you appear before the committee. Welcome, and we will try not to make it too hot for you here on your first appearance.

ADMIRAL NILES. I thank you, sir.
    Mr. Chairman, the initial operational test-flight series on the antiship version was completed with three out of four flights being hits. We found several anomalies we will correct before we go into procurement. In the land-attack version, we have a total of —

MR. WOODRUFF. That doesn't sound as if you have an operational capability. We had trouble with our torpedoes during World War II. Two or three out of four didn't work. Now you say you've got three out of four. A 75-percent failure rate, is that what you consider good? Why should we get into this thing and start building it and spend $200 million dollars or whatever and then you'll say, well, geez, we had a little anomaly there and we'll have to spend fifty, sixty million to go back and tear it apart. It looks to me as if we're headed into the barrel again on this program. We are seeing some shocking overruns on the submarines, too.

MRS. ROMANICK. Mr. Woodruff, I believe what the admiral was trying to get across was that they had experienced a success rate of three out of four, not a failure rate of three out of four. The actual failure rate would be 25.

MR. WOODRUFF. All right, that is a much better rate.

MR. KOELPELS. But Mr. Woodruff has a good point — that we need to demonstrate a dependable system before we invest procurement dollars. And I would ask in addition, were these tests flown in an environment that simulates a combat environment — with enemy fire and so forth?

ADMIRAL NILES. Let me address those two issues separately, if I may.
The anomalies we need to resolve are

in the software for the weapons control system and the transition-to-flight regime for this missile. We are currently participating in a series of Air Force tests in Canada. I have with me one of my staffers who witnessed the tests. The missile was recovered after an 1100-mile flight and the accuracy was spectacular.

Including the contractor's test and evaluation flights, we now have over seventy flights of one variety or another on this airframe, including numerous tests in a simulated combat environment. It is a mature missile, and it is reasonable to go into limited production. Lieutenant Commander Lenson is handing now to the committee a summary record of the tests, the reasons for each failure, and the modifications made to prevent further failures in that mode.

Dan got up and handed them the copies. He'd almost tuned out. He'd been wondering what he was going to do with the rest of his life. The merchant marine was shrinking, but there might still be opportunities. . . . He'd heard of guys getting mates' licenses based on their conning experience.

But merchant guys spent a lot of time at sea, too. Did he really want to leave his wife behind again? It hadn't turned out so hot with Susan.

MR. KOELPELS. Admiral Willis. Did I understand you to say in your testimony that the missiles we buy this fiscal year will not be delivered until two years after that?

ADMIRAL WILLIS. That is correct, sir.

MR. KOELPELS. You mean we will have to wait till then before we have a single operational Tomahawk on a ship?

ADMIRAL NILES. No, sir. We have enough in the pipeline to support the first submarine and battleship platforms. From that time on, the numbers grow at a rate consistent with the number of ships configured to launch.

MR. KOELPELS. Exactly how many are we talking about?

ADMIRAL NILES. (Deleted).

MR. KOELPELS. You have around five hundred ships and how many missiles?

ADMIRAL WILLIS. (Deleted). That is only the initial capability. The number builds up rapidly from there on.

MR. KOELPELS. That's certainly encouraging, only (deleted) submarines with this weapon that is supposed to be the substitute for our carrier attack aircraft. What if one of them springs a leak? That cuts your capability in (deleted). Can you tell me what the Tomahawk is supposed to do that carrier-based aircraft can't?

ADMIRAL NILES. A carrier is a potent weapon, but also a very expensive one. That means that we can afford only very few — fifteen, in the current budget — a relatively small number compared to the number of trouble points the Navy is tasked to monitor on a year-round basis.

Tomahawk carries the potential of making each destroyer and cruiser in the fleet a threat to enemy ships and land targets, the way the carriers are a threat to them today.

Dan's thoughts once again drifted to Kerry. What if she *didn't* marry him? She still had his ring, but she hadn't worn it. He hadn't had a drink since Friday night, but he was starting to wonder how long he could keep it up. What if he had just one beer? Would she leave him over that?

MR. WOODRUFF. I would like you to address the nuclear issue. Presumably, the President is the only one who can authorize the use of a nuclear warhead. Now you fellows have the Lance; you have the Polaris; you want the Tomahawk now. It took two or three days to get hold of the White House back when the *Pueblo* was captured. We may have an even worse time trying to determine whether we should fire one of these weapons so that we can hit a ship that was far away and we were not sure we could hit it with a conventional weapon.

ADMIRAL NILES. To clarify that, sir, all the antiship Tomahawks are installed with conventional warheads.

MR. WOODRUFF. I thought I read somewhere you said they had half and half?

ADMIRAL NILES. The land-attack version does have both warheads.

MR. KOELPELS. I would like to echo my colleague's concern. All the evidence I have heard before this committee is that there is very strong nuclear superiority on the part of the Russians.

MR. OSBORN. What do you use for targeting?

ADMIRAL NILES. There is a variety of

over-the-horizon systems. Some of this can be better explained with a transparency. . . .

(Pause)

First, the antiship targeting. Our airplane and overhead surveillance data is brought together in a system that was called "Outlaw Shark" in its experimental days.

For the land attack, the Tomahawk navigates inertially, with periodic waypoint checks by terrain-contour matching. At the end, you can use scene-matching technology to get accuracies of (deleted) or better. Let's skip that view graph. . . . I'm looking for mission planning. Here we are.

This is the screen from a prototype display, showing how the routes are laid out. This also shows defenses in the area, the missiles and antiaircraft and so forth. This is where the human being gets into the flying of the missile. He can vary the route here till he gets one that is satisfactory to him. This is fed into a disc storage. The disc is delivered to the ship, wherever it happens to be. In the future, the planning could take place in a carrier's combat information center.

MR. KOELPELS. So you are assuming that there will be a carrier nearby. Then why not just have manned aircraft fly the mission?

ADMIRAL NILES. As I stated, sir, there will be a continued requirement for carriers. We cannot fight without control of the air. The mission update could be done on a carrier, or it could be done ashore. Our first mission-planning capability is entering operation shortly in Norfolk, Virginia.

MR. OSBORN. If there are no further questions, I will adjourn until one-thirty this afternoon.

When the chairman stepped down, Dan stood with the rest, but he was astonished at the whole procedure. He'd expected a solemn atmosphere, serious questions, moments of drama. Or, failing that, a boring but thorough grilling. But the federal court downtown had been more solemn; hell, traffic court in Charleston had been more impressive when he'd gone in to argue a ticket.

To begin with, when they started, there hadn't been one actual representative in the room. When Romanick had asked Willis to start by presenting his statement, Dan had scribbled a note and showed it to one of the financial people. It read, "Who's she?" He got a whispered response: "She's the senior subcommittee staffer."

The chairman, Osborn, had strolled in in the middle of Willis's statement. The admiral had stopped, but Osborn had flipped his hand, gesturing him to continue. The chairman had talked to Romanick and another staffer in a barely lowered voice as Admiral Willis read. Later, Woodruff had ambled in, carrying a paper cup of coffee, and Koelpels hadn't shown up till the session was well under way. Dan had come armed with twelve copies of every handout, to cover the ten congressmen on the subcommittee and leave a couple for the staffers. But only five had ever shown their faces in the room; two had sidled in unobtrusively, sat for a few minutes, then left again. Only Osborn, Koelpels, and Woodruff had asked any questions, and Osborn had spent much of the time, even when the witnesses were answering, talking to Romanick. Koelpels had arrived with a sheet of paper in his hand, and he had spent part of the time making calls on a phone in the corner. Once or twice, he'd laughed so loudly that whoever was testifying paused, uncertain whether to continue. The only one who had paid attention throughout the proceedings was the stenographer who sat recording the testimony. Occasionally, before Osborn had asked a question, Dan had seen a staffer pass a slip of paper to him.

He couldn't decide whether to laugh or weep. If he'd only known, out on watch at night, that this was how national policy was made. If he'd understood back when he took *Reynolds Ryan* to sea with her boilers shot, with rust in her fuel, undermanned, how it had all began back here, with politicians who cared so little, they didn't even bother to show up for hearings.

Now it was lunchtime. Niles, Willis, and the other principals filed out, leaving the documents and references on their table. Evans said, looking at the enlisted people, "We're going to need someone to stay in the room with this stuff. Sergeant? Thanks."

"If you want to eat in the building, there's a cafeteria." The senior staffer gave them directions and said, "You don't need to be back before two for the afternoon session." She gave them a faint smile, and headed off after Osborn.

He and Westerhouse and Evans and Burdette were at one of the round tables in the basement when Dan said, "I didn't realize they were this . . . informal."

"Go to the big authorization hearings, the full committee, it's a little better. But not much," Evans said. The Air Force colonel seemed preoccupied; he pushed his salad around on his plate, then pushed it back and sat with his arms folded, looking away from them.

Dan asked Westerhouse, "How do you think it's going so far, sir?"

"I think we're going to catch some harder pitches this afternoon. The heavy hitter wasn't

291

even here this morning."

"Harrow, you mean?"

"Right, Congressman Harrow. But so far, we're looking okay."

"When do they vote?"

"They report their findings to the committee, and the vote takes place there. We'll never see it."

Westerhouse explained the appropriation process. Dan hadn't realized it was so complex. Several civilians set trays down near them as they ate. Then they talked about this and that. He tuned back in a little later when Burdette said, "But what about that stuff Koelpels was asking about? The idea we're behind in nuclear weapons?"

"We're not. Not according to warhead count."

"But how do we know how many they have? No, don't tell me. They submit the annual warhead report, and we bump that against NATO's."

"I think we've got plenty," said Dan, remembering Szerenci's analysis of deterrence. "Actually, we probably only need a couple of hundred. If we need any — which I'm not sure we do."

One of the civilians said politely, "You don't think we need nuclear weapons, Commander?"

"There are good arguments we don't. If we ever use them, it's a disaster. If we don't, it's a waste." He shrugged. "So I wonder sometimes: Why are we still pouring money down that rat hole."

Evans cleared his throat, frowning. He seemed about to say something when Captain Westerhouse got up. He hadn't eaten much, barely touched his bean soup. He said casually, "Dan, you done? We need to get back and relieve the good sergeant."

"Yes, sir."

Westerhouse didn't say anything till they were back in the hearing room. He told the sarge he could go eat. Then he turned to Dan, the two of them alone now in the echoing high-ceilinged chamber. "I just heard a couple things from you I don't understand. Would you like to offer me an explanation?"

"You mean about the nuclear issue?"

"That's right."

"I just don't think we need 'em, sir. The Navy doesn't, as far as I can see. It doesn't increase our security; it escalates the —"

"I understand you were with a group of people who disrupted an international arms exhibition last month. Is that right?"

Dan found himself at a loss. Certainly it was true, but how did Westerhouse know? "Uh, who told you that, sir?"

"That's immaterial. Were you?"

"I wasn't 'with' them, sir. In the sense of participating in what they were doing."

"But you were there. And you knew them."

He agreed that he had. Westerhouse looked at him for a few seconds, then said, not unkindly, "Sit down, Dan."

He did, and watched the captain's hand pass over his thinning hair. Saw the dark patches under his eyes. And something told him that what he was going to hear next was important, at least to the man across from him.

"Dan, I'm afraid I'm not going to be with the program much longer."

"What do you mean, sir?"

"I'm not doing well. It's metastasized."

"Excuse me, sir?"

"I guess I haven't kept you up-to-date on all this. I have myeloma. Cancer of the bone marrow. The docs at Bethesda found it when I went in for some back problems. I did some chemo and radiation last year. Felt better, for a while. But now they've found several more tumors."

Dan stared into the flat, fatigued eyes, and for a moment didn't know what to say. He fumbled out, "That's horrible. I didn't know, sir. I mean, I thought you looked tired, that's all. But you must be in . . . in pain, too."

"I don't like to advertise things like that. Daresay most men don't." Westerhouse looked away, down the empty room. "They offered me medical retirement. But to be frank, there wasn't anything more important I could think of I wanted to do.

"But the point I want to get to is not my health. The point is to give you some advice, get you back on course before you get too far off to steer back.

"Now, I don't know how deeply you're involved with these people. And it may not be my business, whom you associate with on your off time. But you're here to do a job. If you've got a problem with working on a nuclear-capable missile, you can either salute and keep your doubts to yourself or you can resign. Do you understand what you've just been told?"

"Yes, sir, but there's a third alternative."

"What's that?"

"That you take me off working on the nuclear Tomahawk."

Westerhouse looked as angry as Dan had ever seen him, but his voice stayed level. "Wrong. We don't make choices on what we do or don't work on. We execute the orders we're given. The single exception would be unlawful orders, and we are not talking about those. We're sitting on the Hill right now. These are the people who make those decisions."

"Sir, you've seen how they conduct hearings. Do they look like they know enough to make a decision? And you're saying our orders aren't unlawful. We're a party to treaties outlawing weapons of mass destruction."

"Commander, we're not here to discuss the

295

political system, or international law. Your friends are your business, but your performance is mine. You took off running on the ABLs, getting the missile on the battleships, but now . . . Let's go to the bottom line. You can either go to work, and by that, I mean keep on busting your ass to get this system operational, just like the rest of us, or turn in your letter. I am not going to listen to any more disloyal and disgruntled talk! No, that's enough! I'm chopping this discussion off now."

They stood, falling silent as the admirals filed back in. A little while later, Mrs. Romanick entered, and after her the stenographer, and the afternoon session began.

The subcommittee met at 2:15 P.M. in executive session, Hon. Vesey Osborn (chairman of the subcommittee) presiding.

MR. OSBORN. At the request of recently arrived members of the committee, we are extending this hearing in order to look into the Tomahawk program a little more thoroughly. However, I need to underscore that we are getting to a point where we have a tight schedule. We have to reconsider the Department of Energy bill and complete markup of HR 2970 by the finish of business on Friday. Now, to begin. I know that you gentlemen have the impression we don't generally look very closely at the documents you hand in to us, but as it happens, we have examined Admirals Willis's and Niles's statements this morning. Here is my first question. On page 8 you stated that the inventory objective was (deleted) missiles. Where does a number like that come from?

ADMIRAL WILLIS. It's the output of a model. It includes the interplay of various weapons, surface, air, and submarine forces, all in threat-oriented scenarios. What I want to know is the probability that each vessel in a task group will have the rounds he will need to play the scenario. When you crank through all that, a number pops out.

MR. MULHOLLAND. We are talking about an increase in the size of the Navy, an increase in the number of combatant ships to 600; has that been taken into consideration?

ADMIRAL WILLIS. Yes. I think Admiral Niles's team has brought a slide that relates to the — yes. Now, this is what the model kicks out and says I want to have at a given year in the future, say five years out.

Mrs. Romanick. We are seeing escalation on the costs; we are seeing escalation on the inventory of missiles; we are seeing escalation on the number of launchers. Are we going to have the ships' capabilities increasing proportionally?

Admiral Niles. Speaking as someone who in time of war might find himself in command of a group of ships armed with Tomahawk, I can say that these would be much more capable ships in a tactical engagement.

Mr. Mulholland. And you are going to make the schedule on these ships?

Admiral Willis. I can't speak for submarines. But in the surface ships, I have looked at the risks in terms of vertical launch systems, which we are developing for the out years, and backfit of armored-box launchers, which will give us the most immediate capability. The first battleship will be ready this coming summer.

Mr. Osborn. Mr. Harrow? I understand you had some questions you wanted to ask.

Mr. Harrow. I do.
First, I have a financial question. As our

senior staffer has pointed out, we are faced with rapidly escalating costs on this program, unbudgeted costs, and this is a prime reason we are conducting this hearing. These overruns are worrisome to all of us up here. We must live within our budget. Now, I understand that — this didn't happen on your watch, Admiral — but I understand that it was known that money for production had run out year before last, and that rather than stop production and come back and ask us for more money, new contracts were let. The end result being that we will pay a charge of roughly fifteen million for scrapping the old contracts, and that we will end up with fewer missiles than authorized. I understand that we are also being asked to consider an additional Tomahawk support-equipment request for $176 million. This provides 9 surface weapon-control systems and 18 submarine system modifications. In addition, it provides for the backfit of one vertical-launch system in the DD-963-class ship and for two in the SSN-688-class submarine. My question is, is it your intention to actually produce these specified weapons and systems, or are we going to see a repeat of our previous overruns?

ADMIRAL WILLIS. I will take that, if you

don't mind. But first, let me deny the implication, if that is what I heard, that there has been any wrongdoing or concealment governing the use of appropriations.

Willis went through a mind-numbing exegesis of developmental funding and from which pots of money it had come. Dan quickly lost track. From the glazed eyes, none of the congressmen were following, either. But Harrow just made a note, face impassive.

MR. HARROW. My next question is more, you might call it a philosophical question.

This program seems to me, and to many informed defense experts, to be a duplication of two ongoing defense programs. On the strategic side, it duplicates the Boeing AGM-86B, developed for launch from B-52s and B-1s, which have recently deployed out of Griffiss and other Air Force bases. Deep strike is and always has been primarily an Air Force mission. Second, as I understand Mr. Koelpels pointed out this morning, it duplicates our very robust and successful Navy air attack arm, a flexible and responsive medium-range strike force that I have been privileged to support over the years. Now, let us leave aside the question, on which I have personal feelings, of whether an unmanned aircraft is going to display the same resourcefulness and skill in carrying out its mission as our Navy and Air Force and, I might add, our Marine Corps aviators have demonstrated over the years. Leaving that aside, I still have to say that Tomahawk seems to me to straddle the two missions and, I have to say, doesn't give very much promise of doing either any better than what we have on the shelf right now.

Given the redundancy of this program, it seems to me that we have areas of the defense posture that demand more of our immediate attention. The Army attack helicopter program, for example, which could well do with additional funding.

ADMIRAL NILES. We stated the rationale for this system in this subcommittee earlier today. It provides for a distributed offensive, which allows us to carry the battle to the enemy —

MR. HARROW. Yes, I know what you said this morning, Admiral. I have your statement here in front of me. And what you describe is a system in technical trouble. You said — let's see — you called them "anomalies we need to resolve . . . in the software for the weapons control system and the transition-to-flight regime."

Let us be more specific. Your software for the weapons control system for the surface ship installation is written in assembly language, and each change has a ripple effect, and now it's a year behind schedule. You had twenty-nine sets of the thrust-vector-tab control systems delivered wired backward, due to the quality-control inspector being dyslexic. And this little difficulty in the "transition-to-flight regime" can be better described as a consistent and inexplicable tendency for the missile to crash without warning.

Dan couldn't believe what he was hearing. It was as if the congressman had been reading the minutes of the progress conferences. Then he saw Niles looking back toward him, and he re-collected himself. He pulled the tabbed rebuttals and passed them forward.

Niles studied them for a second after Harrow was done speaking, then responded to each point the congressman had raised. He pointed out that the thrust-tab problem had been detected and corrected, that the other problems were being worked on.

ADMIRAL NILES. In fact, this is the main purpose of a developmental program: to stress a new system, expose glitches, and fix them. To be frank, if we did not see any problems in the development phase,

I would question whether we were testing a system to the limits of its capability.

MR. HARROW. I see. Well, now, looking back over the line of reasoning we have developed here, it seems that we have established three points. First, that this program duplicates not one but two ongoing and very successful programs, one Navy and one Air Force. Second, that it is over budget and behind schedule, and that we are being asked to bail it out without any very clear idea when it will come on-line. And three, that the program is by all accounts, including that of some very astute analysts in the aerospace field, in very deep trouble indeed, technically.

Now, given all that, I have to wonder whether we should be wise and parsimonious public servants and avoid making major investments for the time being. In other words, extend this program's developmental time frame in order to make absolutely sure we indeed have a dependable weapon that fulfills an actual need. I don't want to be a stumbling block, but after due consideration, I do not believe we should commit ourselves to advance procurement funding at this time.

MR. MULHOLLAND. I would take issue with that. My point being that we tend to do this sort of thing too often, allocate just enough to keep new programs alive, but not enough to actually increase the fighting ability of our boys at the front lines. I've read somewhere it takes twelve to fourteen years to get a new weapon from the initial idea to something you can use in the field. We need to short-circuit this development folderol and get the pipeline going. None of the anomalies the admiral mentioned has anything to do with the actual missile. It flies. The engine runs. It hits things. I think those other are minor problems that are within the area of postdelivery tweaking. What we need to do now is to get off the couch and start buying these things and get the cost down. Admiral, what are our cost figures?

ADMIRAL NILES. As you pointed out, the per-unit cost drops as the buy increases. For example, this year we are talking about a $2.7 million per-unit buy. As we increase the total buy, the average cost of the missile declines to around $2 million.

MRS. ROMANICK. Is there a potential for a multiyear buy?

ADMIRAL NILES. Possibly. Let me make a statement here about the buy-size issue. The members' questions are on target, but they are matters we have excogitated on, as well. We have tried to strike a balance between early procurement and completed testing. There is also a relationship between extending our developmental time frame and increasing our unit costs. My personal opinion, as someone who lives with this, is that the buy Admiral Willis has outlined is the balanced figure and that we can't go too far wrong with it.

MR. HARROW. And the point that we are raising is that it may be wiser to slip our schedule for one or two years, since we have the mission covered by other elements of our defense establishment.

Dan sat with his fingers tented, following the duel. It didn't sound like an acrimonious debate. There weren't any raised voices. But Harrow was carrying out a savage and deeply informed attack. Mulholland was defending, but, on the other hand, he wanted to increase procurement funding, boosting the buy before they had a reliable missile. While Niles was trying to fend off from both sides of an increasingly narrow channel.

He was pondering this when he saw Harrow lean over toward where Mulholland sat. The Pennsylvanian glanced up. Harrow dropped a piece of paper in front of him. Mulholland frowned over it for a moment. Then he sat back and nodded, poker-faced, and Harrow returned his attention to the floor.

MR. OSBORN. I don't like to cut off what seems like fruitful debate, but as chairman, I have to point out that we must move on very soon. Mr. Mulholland, did you have a rejoinder?

MR. MULHOLLAND. I believe we have all stated our positions on this matter.

Neither Koelpels nor Woodruff seemed to have any more remarks, and the senior staffer turned the discussion to Nunn Amendment reports and DSARC milestones. Meanwhile, two more representatives had come in. One was seated on the dais, scribbling on one piece of paper after another. The other was talking to a chubby young man in glasses. After a moment, Dan recognized Andy DeSilva.

Evans passed him a note for Niles. Dan hesitated, then got up and went forward. Admiral Willis was explaining how under certain circumstances Nunn Amendment calculations would show a cost increase even though the cost per missile was decreasing. He placed the note in front of the admiral, then retreated to his seat, feeling again, as he had every day since he had come on shore duty, how junior a lieutenant commander was in the scheme of things here. The revelation-slash-ass-chewing by Westerhouse had been disturbing, too. He hadn't had any idea his boss was . . . terminal.

He sat with his chin in his hand, staring at the fungoid faces that parroted questions passed by their staffers. He'd thought admirals were God made visible, yet here they were being harassed like schoolboys summoned to account for a prank. Subjected to stupid questions by politicians who knew nothing and cared less, dependent on the machinations of sleazoids and contributors. Westerhouse thought this was important. So important, he was literally dying to put Tomahawk in the fleet. He had to admire that kind of dedication. But was it true for Dan Lenson? Was there nothing better he had to do with his one unique and precious stay on earth?

MR. OSBORN. Thank you, Admiral. If there are no more other questions, I believe we can now move on. You will be back later, will you not?

ADMIRAL WILLIS. Yes, sir, we will be back tomorrow afternoon to revisit the Poseidon and Trident strategic systems.

MR. OSBORN. Thank you very much.

Dan and the sergeants crimped themselves

into the back of the sedan. Evans and Westerhouse rode up front. Nobody said much. Until Westerhouse asked Evans, "So how do you
think we did?"

The deputy just shrugged. "We'll find out
when they vote."

"That Harrow's sure got a hard-on for us.
He made some yardage, too."

"That's why they call him 'the congressman
from Boeing.' "

Evans shrugged again. They rode the rest
of the way back to Crystal City in silence.

# 17

The next day, he came in early, to find three message slips already on his desk. Number one was from the site manager at Kearney Mesa. Number two was from Long Beach, about *New Jersey*, no doubt. And number three was from Carol, asking him to come up to the admiral's office at his earliest convenience. Instead of going right up, he looked through his desk and found Sandy Cottrell's new card. A colorful logo, an address in Falls Church, out near the Beltway. She answered on the first ring. "Kinetic Solutions, Legislative Affairs, Ms. Cottrell."

"Hi. Sandy? This is Dan."

"Who's this?"

"Dan Lenson, from Eddie's class."

"Oh. . . . How *are* you, Dan? Still standing firm?" She sounded spacey, slurred, even though it was only — he glanced at the wall clock — 0710.

"Uh, okay. How's the new job? You're out at that new start-up Dr. Szerenci was talking about, right?"

"Right. Here in my nice new pussy pink office, and already I have second thoughts."

"What is it, think tank? Policy?"

"Oh, the usual shit. But this is even sleazier than I expected."

"Uh-huh. Well, look, you still got your Rolodex from the Hill, right? I called to see if you could find something out for me."

She asked him what. He said, "I told you about the hearing? Armed Services, subcommittee on military nuclear systems. I wondered . . . you know the staffers . . . maybe DeSilva — do you think you could get me, uh, some kind of readout on how they think it went? I mean, whether we're going to get our funding?"

"Well, listen to this. You're learning."

"Learning?"

"To play the game. Isn't this what we're all playing? A game? This can't be for real." She laughed, kind of nuttily, like Goldie Hawn.

"Sandy, are you sure you're okay? Maybe you need to get some kind of help."

"Yeah, I need help all right. . . . I'll see what I can find out. Give me your number again." He gave her his JCM extension.

Time to see the admiral. He took a moment before he went up to transfer a couple of sheets of paper from his briefcase to a blue correspondence folder.

When he stepped off the elevator, he touched his ribbons, ran a hand down his buttons, checked his shoes. He felt detached, unable to believe the moment had arrived. He thought, Every habit I've got is Navy. Practically every thought I have is Navy. Can I really go through with this?

It seemed like a long walk across the carpet, skirting the low coffee table with its pristine new copies of *Armed Forces Journal*, *Military Technology*, and *International Defense Review*. Past the leather couch. Carol pointed him on into the inner office. He took a last deep breath, then went in.

The admiral was sitting at his desk in his shirtsleeves, reading a report. His blouse hung from an oak stand. Past and below him spread the fields and railroad yards that were slowly sprouting more office complexes. One wall was covered with photographs of ships and unit plaques. Dan centered himself before the desk and came to attention. "Lieutenant Commander Lenson, sir."

Niles's eyes came up slowly. "Carry on, Lenson. Fireball?"

"No thank you, sir."

"Sit down." Niles reached out to the intercom. "Carol, give us twenty minutes." The secretary said, "yes, sir," and Dan heard the door close.

Niles looked back at whatever he'd been reading. Dan let himself down into the chair, realizing this was the first time he'd ever been alone with the man. He remembered when he'd first met Niles, a captain then, in a concrete-block admin building at Charleston Naval Base. He'd faced him again after the incident off Cuba, in *Barrett*'s wardroom. Niles had chaired the investigation. He suddenly realized it must have been Niles who'd put him in for the Silver Star.

Now the report was laid aside with a grunt. Once more, the little eyes with the sleepy, freckled lids perused him; again the mustache turned down above grim lips. It was as if Niles, too, was remembering.

The admiral rumbled, "You've been doing a lot of work for the deputy."

"For Colonel Evans? Yes, sir."

"What you get assigned seems to get done. Those were good briefing papers for the hearing, too."

"Yes, sir."

"But now Dale tells me you've been criticizing the program. I'm getting that from other sources, too. What the hell's going on?"

"I said something. Yes, sir."

"In front of congressional people, staffers."

Now Dan saw the problem. He remembered the civilians sitting with them, in the Rayburn Building's basement. Finally, he said, "Sir, that was bad judgment and I apologize for that. For giving a personal opinion when I was in uniform. But the fact is, there have been some changes going on in my life. I don't know how to describe it."

"You don't like what's going on at the hearings?"

"That's not the biggest issue, but no, sir, that's not exactly inspiring, either."

Niles selected a red sphere from the container and unwrapped it. He held it close to his eye as if examining it for imperfections. Then popped it into his mouth and said around it, "I don't like it myself. In fact, when I left yesterday, I had to take down my pants and kiss my ass just to get my self-respect back.

"You know, they say every weapons program has two phases: too early to tell and too late to stop. Every program takes hits from Congress. But we've got our mafia out there, too. This missile's going to fly. I promised that when I took over."

"Well, sir —"

"I know it's not that inspiring looking at American government in action. But ask yourself: How sharp a lens do you want them to be supervising us through?"

Dan thought that through. "I'm having trouble getting my arms around that statement, sir. Are you saying it's better for us if Congress doesn't know what they're doing?"

"Well, not exactly. But those are the people we work for, and if we had it any other way I know of, we wouldn't like it any better, and probably a lot less. Hear what I'm saying?"

"Well, sir, I wasn't actually talking about the hearings."

Niles's forehead turned slightly darker. "So what exactly is the problem?"

"Sir, I'm just . . . undergoing a change in attitude on participating in the development of weapons."

"You didn't seem to have any problem handling weapons when you took out those gunboats and aircraft on *Barrett*. And faced down that son of a bitch Harper with a forty-five."

"He had the forty-five, sir; I had the riot gun. But I guess my thinking has evolved since then."

Niles grunted. "Go on."

"Well . . . we're so focused on violence. Every ethical system says it's wrong to kill, and here we are prepping for it night and day and on weekends." He felt silly even as he said it. What else was the military for? Words that had felt simple and right in the bare dining room at the Dorothy Day House sounded naïve here. Niles blinked in sleepy incredulity, but Dan kept on. "We're the best-armed country in the world. Most of our R and D money goes to weapons development. And we wonder why the Japanese and the Europeans are ripping us up on imports. The cities are going to hell; we're running this tremendous deficit — when do we say enough?"

Niles sat back, sucking the candy. After a pause, he said, "We're facing a country that spends fifty billion dollars more a year on weapons than we do. They just invaded Afghanistan. They outnumber us, they outspend us, and they hate our guts. How do they fit into your picture?"

"I'm not sure. But we've got to look like

just as big a threat. We've got armies in Europe, carriers off their coasts; we've got more warheads pointed at them than they have pointed at us. I've been on one of their ships. They're not supermen. The damn bulkheads were made out of wood. They're probably as scared of us as we are of them."

"They're the ones with massive armored forces threatening Europe. They're the ones pointing SS-twenties down our throat. If working on offensive weapons is what's bothering you, Tomahawk should go down smooth. It's obviously not first-strike."

"Tomahawk's deep-strike, power-projection. If there is such a thing as a purely defensive system, that missile's not it."

When Niles locked his hands behind his head, his chest looked even more massive. "Whether or not that's true — and I don't think it is — you're not talking to our mission here. Let's let State psychoanalyze the Russians. We're the ones the country trusts to develop the weapons to keep them off our backs. One, for deterrence, so we don't have to fight that war. Two, so that if we have to, we'll win."

"Can anyone win a nuclear war, sir?"

"I don't know, but I want to be damn sure the other side figures they're going to lose at least as much as we will. And they're not the only bad guys, in case you haven't been reading the papers. It's a dangerous world and we're a fat, tempting target."

Dan sat forward. He'd been trying to put what he felt into some logically consistent statement. Now Niles was leading him to what he'd been groping for. "Yes, sir, but — that's what bothers me. There's all kinds of arguments you can make to justify building whatever you want. But if we've got them, the way I read history, sooner or later they'll be used."

Niles started to answer, but Dan saw with lightning suddenness how it all fit together. "Just a minute, sir. What I'm saying is, we can't build our arguments on threat, or economics, or even politics. Because those are all *feedback* systems. We build; they build. They strike; we strike back. The institutions can't change. If we had real peace, they'd evaporate, and no institution ever liquidated itself. If we didn't have the Communists anymore, we'd go find somebody else to hate and fear.

"The only way we can escape is individually. If I choose not to resist evil with violence" — Niles's eyelids elevated a millimeter — "that breaks the loop. We are all, each, *individually*, responsible for the way things are. Only if we opt out *individually* will it ever stop."

He stopped, feeling dizzy. Then he leaned back and waited for the shock front to hit.

Instead, Niles just nodded. Then said, "A lot of people tried turning the other cheek with the Nazis. It wasn't a successful strategy.

But I hear what you're saying. It's about as good a way as I've ever heard of dicking yourself, careerwise. Short of sending a Polaroid of you and your dog to the selection board."

"Sir, they told us both at the Academy that sometimes doing the right thing means you accept adverse outcomes. I'm thinking more and more that the right thing for me is to get out of weapons development."

"And use?"

"Yes, sir, that's the logical next question, isn't it? If I'm going back to being an operator, how is that different from developing the hardware?"

"No, it's horseshit," Niles rumbled. "I think you're getting confused by C rays."

"Sir?"

"I think you're under the influence of this girlfriend Bucky Evans tells me you're seeing. This peace protester, or whatever she is."

"You can leave her out of it, sir. These are my own thoughts."

"All right, you lifted your safeties. Now you got a decision to make. Because all I have to say is the same thing Dale tells me he told you. If those are the lines you're thinking along, you don't belong in the military. You figuring on the church? A preacher, a rabbi, a priest?"

"I don't think I've got a religious calling, sir."

"Well, then, you already know you can either change your attitude, and we'll close-hold this conversation between us, or you can put in your letter." The eyelids drooped; the fingertips met. "Have you got any leave on the books?"

"I'm due back in Cold Lake for the second half of the tests, sir."

"Somebody else can cover that."

"Sir, I don't think the shop's got anybody else with the background. I signed up for it and I'll finish the job." Dan took a deep breath. It was here, the moment he'd thought would never come.

Getting up, he laid the folder he'd brought in with him precisely on the centerline of Niles's desk. "Captain Westerhouse presented me with that choice yesterday, and I thought it over last night. And I typed this up."

Niles looked at the folder. "This what I think it is?"

"Yes, sir."

"This is stupid. I need you here. You love the Navy. Don't you?"

That was true, so he said simply, "Yes, sir, I do."

"If I open this, I have to forward it. You know what I think? I think your head's so full of pussy, you can't think straight."

Dan said tightly, "Sir, I don't think that's an appropriate thing for you to say. I believe you owe me an apology for that."

Niles thought about it. Finally, he grunted. "Sorry. Your life's your own. I just hate to see a good officer put himself in the compactor." He waited a second more, but when Dan said nothing, he reached for the folder. He lifted it, his eyes still holding Dan's.

Dan had a moment of uncertainty, of something not far from terror. Was Niles right? He was tossing away everything he'd sacrificed for, suffered for. Maybe he should reconsider. . . . Shit, his emotions were all over the screen.

Niles held it suspended for a moment more. Then, when Dan still said nothing, he opened the folder. He glanced at the letter, then tossed it onto the desk. It slid along the slick surface, almost to the edge, and teetered there. For a moment, Dan thought it would slip off to the floor, but then it decided to stay.

"You know these aren't granted automatically. Especially now, when we're short of trained ship drivers. It could hang fire for a while."

"Yes, sir, I know that. 'At the pleasure of the President.'"

"So you could hold on to it, make sure you don't have any second thoughts."

"I'm not pulling it, sir. I want out."

Niles swiveled his chair away from him. He picked up the report again, the one he'd been reading when Dan came in. Lenson stood there uncertainly. Finally, he said, "Am I dismissed, Admiral?"

"Get the fuck out of here," Niles said.

He worked for a couple of hours with steadily decreasing enthusiasm before Sakai came over to show him a drawing. He gazed at it. "What the hell's that?"

"Part of the booster subassembly. The part that catapults it free after the pyrotechnic cord cutter shears the bolts that hold it on. See these little detents here?" He pointed to six little ears that ringed the portion of the booster that fit around the stern of the missile airframe.

Dan said he saw them. Sakai said, "These here could be the source of our hang-up problem. Under certain circumstances, what if they jammed? Like a screw top on a pickle jar when you get it cross-threaded."

"You think that might be it?"

"I don't know. Trouble is, both times it did that, the missile took a header into the water. The divers found the missile once, but not the booster. The other time, they found it, but it was so banged up, you couldn't tell what happened."

"You want to request another redesign?"

"Can't. I don't know the failure mode, whether it jams forward, aft, from torque, or what. Just thought I'd show it to you."

Sakai went back to his desk. Dan sat with

320

his head in his hands, pretending to read, but actually worrying.

If he really resigned . . . Shit, he *had*. What was this *if* business? But what if it came back approved next month? Where would he go? The merchant marine idea was stupid. The other possibility was to use his engineering experience. The natural place to go would be the defense industry. Convair or FMC or IBM Government Systems Division. But what sense did it make resigning from weapons development to take up weapons development.

Finally, he decided that when you put his résumé — which he had better start working on — together with the job market, he got commercial software development. He understood computers. He could manage a team. It sounded boring, but, on the other hand, he'd be making a lot more money.

The phone rang. Burdette yelled, "For you."

Great, now what. . . . It was Ms. Toya. "Hi, Shirley. What you need?"

"Remember what you told me about yesterday morning? Before the hearing?"

He strained his brain for a second before remembering: the approach by Mr. Zhang Zurong. "Yeah. What about it?"

"Certain people found it very interesting. So interesting, they're in my office right now. Can you come up and see them?"

Two familiar faces looked up from the settee beside Mrs. Toya's desk. The NIS guy, Pat Bepko. The older agent, from the FBI, Attucks. He hesitated, then sat down with them. Toya said, "This is between you and them, Dan," and excused herself, closing the door.

"Smoke? Coffee?" said Bepko. Dan said no, that he didn't smoke and didn't need coffee. He was getting tenser by the second.

Bepko kicked off. He said he'd taken the call from Toya; had done a little research; had finally called Attucks. "He thought it might be worth looking at while it's a hot offer. So, if you've got a few minutes. . . ."

Dan said he did, and Attucks pulled a briefcase off the carpet and unsnapped it.

The FBI agent said, "First, let me make sure we have this straight. Shirley says you were the subject of what seemed to you like a recruitment attempt, backed by a — was it a romantic involvement?"

"Not exactly. There was a girl, but no romance." He explained what he thought was going on, told them that Mei might have given her uncle the impression they'd been intimate, mistakenly or otherwise.

"Well, that may or may not be relevant downstream. It might be helpful to maintain the idea you care for the girl. Or do you?"

"I like her, but I'm engaged to somebody else. At least I think I am. Look, what I'm hearing — Shirley didn't seem to think this was worth getting excited about. She said it was the kind of thing attachés were supposed to do."

"On the contrary," said Attucks. "Let me show you a couple of things we've developed. Since we last talked, I mean."

The last, and actually the only, time they'd talked had been before he left for Canada, at the interview where Attucks and Bepko had told them somebody had left the hull plug out of the Tomahawk program. That had been a waker-upper. But now he had a lot of other things on his mind. He propped his hand under his chin as Attucks extracted a photo from the briefcase. He handed it to Bepko, and the NIS agent slid it over in front of him.

It made him sit up in his chair. A round, heavy-eyebrowed face. No glasses, but it was definitely "Uncle Xinhu." Only he was in uniform. A high-collared, red-tabbed uniform.

"This looks like an official photograph."

"It is. This is Col. Zhang Zurong, the defense attaché of the People's Republic of China."

"His card didn't say anything about him being a colonel. And he used a different name at the party."

"Probably his nickname. They don't use first names to be casual, the way we do. The first name you hear is the family name, by the way. But he's military all right. Korean War veteran. He graduated from a Soviet staff college before the split between the Communist powers. We believe he's on detached duty from the Military Intelligence Department of the People's Liberation Army General Staff Department. We call it the Second Department. It would correspond to the U.S. Defense Intelligence Agency, or the Soviet MVD."

"He's a Chinese spy?"

"He's definitely got the connections. Zhang's one of the new breed. Speaks good English. He's doing graduate work at Johns Hopkins School for Advanced International Studies here in Washington.

"We suspect his assignment in the United States is twofold. First, Shirley's right — he does the kinds of things an attaché does no matter whether he's Brazilian or French or whatever: gathering open-source data, making contacts, picking up whatever he can about host-country military capabilities. But we think his covert, and probably higher-priority, mission is to acquire advanced technology that can be adapted for use by the Chinese military."

Dan studied the picture. Yeah, he'd called it, drunk as he'd been. "So he was actually pitching me."

"Believe me, this doesn't happen on the spur of the moment." Attucks explained that the recruitment process had three phases:

spotting, assessment, and, finally, the approach. "He didn't see you at that party and decide to hit on you then and there. They researched you thoroughly before they made their move. Your motivators, your weaknesses. Now, they first spotted you probably based on your access to specific data. That's backed up by — Pat?"

"He has a clean clearance," said Bepko.

"It's backed up by some intercept material from back in November, the data we tracked back to JCM. So you apparently were the source." Attucks raised his hand. "Save it! We know about your presentation in class. You're in the clear, okay? You've done everything exactly right: act noncommittal, remember the details, and report it immediately. But apparently the girl passed her class notes to Zhang, and now, somehow, they have the idea they can get a handle on you. Anything been said about your friend being pregnant?"

He goggled. "She can't be. We never —"

"Don't get excited. All I'm saying is, it'd be consistent with the way they've operated before. What was he asking for?"

"Phone books. Personnel information. Oh, and he wanted me to meet a friend of his."

"Who? Where?"

"Somebody named Li. That's when he gave me his card."

Attucks nodded. He and Bepko exchanged glances; some message was passed, but he didn't catch what. Then Attucks passed over another photo: black and white, grainy. It showed a stubby-bodied airframe with swept-back wings, on the rail of a truck-mounted launcher.

"A Styx?"

"Very good. Actually, it's a Silkworm. The Chinese variant."

Attucks said, "We're starting too late in the story. First, let me tell you a couple of anecdotes.

"The first took place two years ago. Two Chinese officers, from the consulate in Chicago, were arrested attempting to purchase blueprints and seeker heads for Sidewinder missiles. They made contact with a naturalized citizen who worked for the company that builds the seekers. They met with him on several occasions and discussed what they needed, how much they were willing to pay, and how to manipulate end-user certificates and shipping documentation to forward the missile heads to the People's Republic via Hong Kong. Customs was able to penetrate the conspiracy and arrest both the Chinese and the employee. Just in time — because when they searched his home, he'd already copied most of the blueprints. Who did the consular officials work for? A guy who was at the time third secretary to the PRC mission to the United Nations in New York. A guy named Zhang Zurong.

"The second concerns a U.S. embassy employee in Peking. She was a State Department communications officer. She got involved in a relationship with a male Chinese national. We don't know whether the relationship was preexisting, and the Second Department discovered it and decided to exploit it, or if they arranged the entire thing. But they attempted to use it to blackmail the young woman into spying. Fortunately, she reported the recruitment effort to embassy security, and she was recalled."

Attucks cocked his head. "Now, bearing those cases in mind, we have your call come in. And we ask ourselves, Is there a smarter way to proceed than just telling this young officer he's done the right thing by reporting this contact, and letting Zhang run on until he finds somebody he can develop as an agent in place?"

Dan said, "And you think now he wants Tomahawk?"

"Not exactly," said Attucks. "Pat?"

Bepko took back the Silkworm photo and laid out a list. Dan studied it. It showed the ranges and guidance systems of ten East Bloc missile systems. The right-hand column was in U.S. dollars. It was headed "Quoted price."

"Recently the Chinese have stepped up their attempts to sell military hardware to foreign countries — South Africa, Libya, North Korea, Pakistan, Iraq. The biggest handicap they have is that their gear isn't that advanced. It's inexpensive, but it's just not comparable to current NATO equipment, and it lags behind the Soviet export stuff, too.

"To get significant sales, they need to upgrade their technology. We think the Second Department is getting directly tasked by the People's Liberation Army with information objectives in support of their weapons-export program. We suspect that may have at least partially motivated the attempt on Sidewinder, along with the PLA Air Force's own desire for the missile. But this effort, the one that zeroed in on you when you made that presentation in the presence of your girlfriend —"

"She's not my girlfriend."

"Of your classmate, then. Our interpretation is that this effort is export-driven. Correct me if I'm wrong, but what's really special about Tomahawk isn't the missile. It isn't the engine. Is it?"

"That's what helps make it so small." But Attucks didn't go on, and Dan completed the thought on his own. "They want the guidance system," he said.

"That's our conclusion, too. Equipment that can navigate it a thousand miles, no matter what the weather, and fly it through the front door of a hangar.

"Look at Silkworm again: a dependable, big, relatively long-range cruise missile. They've got hundreds of them, if not thousands. But both Silkworm and Styx are inaccurate as hell. And so stupid, they're easy to decoy or jam away from a live target.

"But what if they could put a terrain-matching guidance in the nose? Even if they used a relatively heavy analog scene-matching correlator for the final approach — hell, the damn missile could carry it — it would end-around the ballistic missile nonproliferation regime. It'd give countries like North Korea and Iraq a means of nuclear delivery, or precision nonnuclear delivery, close to the best we have."

"I get the idea," said Dan.

"And we think you should give it to him," Bepko said.

He started to say, "Well, sure," but he didn't see a smile. "Are you serious?"

"Only half," said Attucks. He ran a hand over his suit. "Okay if I smoke?" Dan shrugged. The FBI man lit a Marlboro. Bepko lit up, too.

Attucks said, "Can you stand being exposed to a little bit of bureaucratic politics?"

"I'm developing a tolerance."

"The problem we're facing is threefold. We have thousands of Chinese students, resident aliens, and immigrants in this country. Most of them are clean. But there's a steadily increasing effort by the PRC intelligence agencies. We've sent that message up the chain, but nobody in the administration seems to

329

take it seriously. Somebody, maybe the trade people, blocks it at some point. It's almost an annoyance when you go up to them and say that here we have people doing so and so, which is a clear violation of law and sovereignty. We don't have the language capabilities, we don't have the organizational focus, and most people still think of them as friendly, or at least harmless.

"So we need to send a signal. One, to the Chinese: We are not a soft target. Two, to the upper levels in our own government: We have a real problem here.

"We'd like to use Colonel Zhang to send that signal. Customs elicited his involvement in the Sidewinder case, but we weren't able to tie him to it convincingly enough to get the UN to take action. This time, we want him and anyone else who's spying out of the embassy. We want you to go back and say, 'I've thought about it, and I could use some cash. Here's your phone book; what else can I get you?' My instinct is he'll go straight for TERCOM."

"And then?"

"Then you give it to him," said Bepko.

"No way," said Dan.

"Or something that looks like it," said Attucks. "We can put together a package that looks convincing. So convincing that we hope they'll launch a reverse-engineering effort. But that effort will actually lead them down a dead end."

"You're not going to feed them some Rube Goldberg approach. They'll see right through it."

"Well, we've got our people looking into it. . . . But if it turns out you're right, then we cut our losses and arrest the guy at the turnover. But to bottom-line it, we'd like you to go back to Zhang. I'll be straight up: We can't pay you anything. There might even be some risk. The one thing that would have to motivate you would be an old-fashioned value known as patriotism."

"So you're actually asking me to be like a double agent."

"Your government would very much appreciate your help on this," said Attucks quietly.

"Well, there's something you ought to know."

He told them about his resignation letter, the possibility he might be moving to California or Seattle. He concluded, "I don't know how long it'll take to process. Probably not long. And I'll be out. So, I wish you luck, but maybe we better not plan on my being part of this."

The NIS agent said, "Jesus, that's a fork in the toaster all right. Are you telling me there's some kind of loyalty issue here?"

"Loyalty?" He felt angry. "You can still be loyal to the United States and not want to work on weapons. Can't you?" Bepko looked doubtful, so he kept talking. "How about this.

He asked me at one point if there were any ethnic Chinese in the program. I didn't tell him this, but there's one, a techie over in the Advanced Systems shop. I forget his name — Hung, or Yung, something like that. Air Force."

"The trouble is, then we got to dangle him out there." Attucks mused over it. "But if you're saying count you out —"

"That's what I'm saying, yeah."

"Then that settles it, I guess. We go to plan B. And you'll keep this all under your hat?"

Dan said he would, then got up. Attucks and Bepko got up, too. They shook hands. "Good luck on your new career," Bepko said. Dan gave them a wave and headed out the door.

He was going over the preparations for *New Jersey*'s sailing date when Cottrell called back. She told him that according to DeSilva, the subcommittee was going to recommend nonapproval of the supplemental. Mulholland had changed his vote. There was no way to tell what the Senate was going to do, but as far as the House was concerned, the way things were looking right now, they couldn't expect to go to full procurement next fiscal year. And it was perfectly possible, if that slipped, Tomahawk might die on the vine. "He said to tell you he's sorry," she said. "Something about a bouncing ball. Better luck next time."

He sat back after hanging up, rubbing his face. Feeling, oh, he didn't know what. Only that he felt something.

Then he leaned forward again and went back to work.

# 18

His return to Cold Lake for the second half of Primal Thunder was less dramatic than the first arrival. No crowded, Spartan C-130 interior. Instead, he touched down in a little commuter plane, commercial air out of Edmonton. Decker was waiting in a Hummer. Dan threw his bag into the back of the utility vehicle. "Thanks for coming for me."

The security officer squinted up. "It wasn't for you. We got mail, too. See you dressed heavier this time."

"I'm learning."

"How's D.C., Commander? Sweater weather?"

"A little colder than that."

"Well, we got about a foot more snow since you left. And looking for a blizzard on the way."

"A blizzard? Isn't it cold enough?"

"It ain't cold that makes the storms fun around here," Decker told him. "Or at least not just the cold. Congress gonna keep us alive?"

"We didn't look good in the hearing. A lot depends on these tests."

"Well, we're doing our part. I'll tell you, the boys are getting fed up with this weather, the isolation — all of it. Had to break up a fight yesterday." Decker started up. They stopped at the canteen in hangar number one to pick up sandwiches and hot coffee, then headed out onto the snow-covered two-lane road that led north.

Six hours later, battered and bone-tired, he climbed out into the dark. There hadn't been much chance for discussion with the Hummer in low gear most of the way. He got his chance to drive after a couple of hours, and it had been fun all right. The last thirty kilometers were in the dark, on unpaved roads, with unintentional cross-country excursions. Decker had to get out and shoot compass bearings twice. It was the first time Dan had been in the utility vehicles, and he doubted the old Jeeps would have made it over some of the terrain — especially under deep snow — that the Hummer had negotiated.

The mess tent was warmed with a hissing Coleman and lit with strung bulbs. A generator set hammered not far off in the woods. The perimeter had been pulled in; all the vehicles and service areas were huddled closer together. The crew looked up as he and Decker came in, shaking snow off their parkas. Yeah, not many happy faces. "Mail call," said Decker, tossing the bag on a table. He sat down where Dan was already muzzle-deep in a mug of hot cocoa.

Manhurin was out making the evening tour,

but Sparky brought him up-to-date. The time since Dan had last been there had been taken up with security drills and a site shift, to test their ability to do a hop-skip relocation under battle conditions. Sakai had used the break to get into the software with the contractor rep.

Launches would resume tomorrow. The schedule called for one shot a day, to allow for aircraft repositioning and chase team turn-around. Two would be daylight, and two at night. The Canadians were deploying anti-aircraft radars across the flight path to see what kind of detection rate they got. The final conference would be at 0800, launch around 1000 tomorrow. Lenson nodded, making a note. "What about the protesters?"

"Something funny happened three days ago. They disappeared."

"Left town? Folded their tents and took off?"

"Oh, the tent's still there. Decker says there're more people at the gate than ever, they got reinforcements. But the original ones, they vanished. Made a couple of threats to a reporter from the Edmonton paper, then dropped off the scope."

"What kind of threats?"

"Oh, the same stuff as before. How they were going to make it impossible to continue the cruise testing. What's happening back at Crystal City?"

Someone in an exposure mask came in

while Dan was summarizing the testimony. He saw it was Manhurin when the major joined them. But he kept talking; this was something the flight commander needed to hear. "Bottom line, we've got to get good results on this series. If we don't, they're probably going to fold the program. Maybe not your chunk of it, Steve — the allies would scream too loudly — but the Navy buy could get postponed, or even zeroed."

"Wonderful. So it isn't really a test, is it? Now it's got to be a demonstration of success."

"I guess so. Though I'm not really sure how to read what I was hearing up there." He told them about the casual atmosphere, the obvious incapacity or lack of interest of the committee members. "It looks like they're basically finger puppets. They do what their staffs tell them. The only thing that makes them sit up and bark is if they sense some way of getting a buck or a job into their home district. Anyway, enough about that. What's on our plate?"

The flight commander passed him a schedule. Dan ran his eye down it. "So you've already started setup and checkout."

"Uh-huh. That'll run all night. Oh, and I got to tell you, Sparky here's been a big help. Showed us a way to speed up data output that'll cut five minutes off our download time."

"That's what I brought him for."

"We'll do a murder board before the launch. Navy's invited. Of course, it depends on the storm."

"Who decides go/no go?"

"That's fuzzy, to tell the truth. I suppose I could, or at least I could scrub our launch. But the Canadians are officially in charge, since it's their turf."

"When do they make the call?"

"It's not like that — we're gonna fly unless they tell us otherwise."

"Can the weather hurt us? Affect missile performance?"

Manhurin shrugged. "The engine's supposed to run in low-level, subzero, heavy-precip conditions. The guidance system's supposed to recognize a hill whether it's bare or covered in six feet of snow. And everything's designed to cold-soak and still fire. But that's what we're here to find out."

Dan remembered Niles's directive to wring the missile out. He said, "So if it doesn't work, it helps us testwise, but hurts us fundingwise."

"Well, this is a pretty robust system, like I told you before. Sparky, you back that statement up?"

"There's no such thing as bug-free software."

"Thanks for nothing. . . . Anyway, the weak link out here's probably the chase guys, the CF-eighteens they fly to escort the missile.

They have to be visual flight rules, so the weather's a major factor there. Anyway, I'm gonna turn in."

"Yeah, I better crash, too."

Again, Dan lay in the cold darkness. Soon he'd be out of this whole military thing. No more saluting. No more orders. But life was a succession of changes. Each took courage. Courage and faith. He'd made a leap when he went to the Academy. Until now, he'd never looked back.

He was going to have to start working on his faith.

"Sir? Magic telephone."

He woke with a start. He was still fully dressed; it was ice-cold in the tent, and despite the stoves going full blast a coating of ice shone on the inside of the canvas. So that when the messenger said he was wanted on the secure phone, all he had to do was pull his parka from over him and put it on, then jam his feet into his mukluks. He followed the messenger out into a bitter snow-whirling night.

Halfway to the LCC, he realized he'd forgotten his mask. He stumbled the last few yards, his gloves sealed over his cheeks. With this wind, the chill factor had to be minus sixty, minus seventy.

Geddes was there, on watch, or coordinating the preparations for the morning. He said,

"Here he is. Over." Then he covered the mouthpiece. "For the JCM liaison."

Dan took the red handset, waited for the beep of the covered satcom. He spoke slowly and as distinctly as he could, given the fact his hand was covering his numbed nose. "Lieutenant Commander Lenson. Over."

The voice came in crackly but loud. "Commander, this is Admiral Willis's chief of staff. The admiral's been getting some questions about the tests. He wants to know if they're going to be canceled."

"Sir, I don't have much of a handle on that from here. I'm out in the field with the flight. Over."

*Crackle. Beep.* "What are the conditions up there?"

"What's it look like tomorrow?" he asked Geddes. The crew commander shoved him a message; he read from it into the handset. "Minus thirty degrees. Possible fifty-knot winds. Heavy snow."

"Jesus. Can we postpone? At least till the weather clears?"

"Sir, in the first place, that's not our decision. And in the second place, I don't think it would be wise. We're up here to wring this system out in northern European-type winter weather. The flight crew's showing the strain. They're great guys, but the living conditions are pretty basic. Plus, we're getting rumors the Canadians are thinking about pulling out

340

of the agreement. Right now, we're go. But if we postpone, we may not end up with a test series at all."

"We can move it back to Dugway."

"It was originally scheduled for Utah, sir," Dan told him. "But it was moved up here for good reasons. Sir, please tell the vice admiral that if he's asking for my opinion as the guy on the ground, we ought to go for it. The guys have spent days peaking and tweaking. If we shift back to the States, it'll look like we ducked a tough one. That might not play too well in the media."

The chief of staff sounded only half-convinced, but he said he'd relay that. He signed off. Dan told Geddes, "Last minute cold feet upstairs."

"We've been listening to the Canadian test freq. They're going soft, too."

"They must be used to this weather."

"I'm not sure that's it. They're wondering where the activists are."

"Oh yeah?"

"They think they might try to penetrate the launch area," Geddes told him. "Gene's got the security force on alert. The trouble is, weather like this, the PEWS — the ground radars — they don't work for crap. They could waltz right through the perimeter."

"I don't think they'd hurt anyone."

"They don't have to. All they have to do is cut a fiber-optic cable, or ding up a launcher.

We just don't need more publicity."

Dan thought they were getting worked up over a fairly insignificant threat. He and Decker had had to shoot bearings to find the site, and they knew where it was. How were a few demonstrators going to locate it in four thousand square miles of damn-near-roadless wilderness? But he just nodded, looked at his watch, and said, "Well, I'm gonna try to get my head down for a couple more hours."

"Commander Lenson? Captain Geddes wants you."

"Shit, again? What time is it?"

"Oh-three hundred. Come on, sir, I'll take you over there. Don't forget your mask."

Outside the tent, the Arctic wind sheared effortlessly through parka, gloves, even his heavy boots, leaving him shuddering. The steps slammed into his shins just as the messenger said, "Step up here."

"Thanks a whole shitload," he muttered.

"Commander. Hi. Sorry to get you up again, but we got a conversation going on the test net you might want to get in on. They got good weather out of the States, but it's closed down so hard up here, they don't think they're going to be able to get the chase planes off."

"Can we get a chase bird out of some other base?"

"No. It's got to have the tone generator, and that's down at Cold Lake."

"Shit. . . . Okay, show me what to do."

Geddes installed him at the fold-down Teletype keyboard. Dan read the conversation as far as it had gone. The last message read:

ALCMLAUNCHHASBEENSCRUBBEDDUE TO BAD WEATHER OVER TRACKING STATIONS IN THE US. GLCM LAUNCHES SKED FOR ALTERNATE TIME WINDOWS IN N-S CORRIDOR WILL ALSO POSTPONE TILL STORM FRONT PASSES. HARRUP, SCMTT

"Hey, this is bullshit. They're shutting us down. You better get Steve up here. And the Canadian — Thompson."

As Geddes dispatched the messenger, Dan asked him, "Who's sending this?" The deputy said SCMTT was combined Canadian–U.S. test team command. Harrup was the U.S. rep from SAC.

"Oh yeah, I met him. Hey."

"What?"

"A light dawns. . . . It wouldn't look real good for the air-launched guys if they couldn't shoot and we could. Would it? Can I send on this thing?"

"Sure. Go ahead and type in what you want. Just remember this is an uncovered circuit." But he was already hunting and pecking.

GLCM FLIGHT E IS READY TO LAUNCH ON SCHEDULE. DO NOT UNDERSTAND NATURE OF PROBLEM REQUIRING SCRUB — LCDR D LENSON USN JCM REP IN FIELD. PRIMROSE

NATURE OF PROBLEM IS THAT POSITIVE CONTROL IS REQUIRED FOR ALL CRUISE FLIGHTS OVER CANADIAN TERRITORY. CANADIAN-US TEST PROTOCOLS REQUIRE TWO CHASE PLANES WITH VFR HANDOFF. SCMTT

IS THIS REALISTIC REQUIREMENT CONSIDERING UNPOPULATED NATURE OF TEST CORRIDOR? DUGWAY

"Jeez, who else we got listening to this?" Dan asked Manhurin, who had just arrived and was reading over his shoulder. The flight commander said NORAD, SAC, Primrose, Dugway, CFB Edmonton, Bagotville, the AWACs bird, Cold Lake, Tinker, and Blytheville, Arkansas.

CONTRARY TO WHAT USAF SEEMS TO THINK, THERE ARE NATIVE POPULATIONS IN THE OVERFLIGHT AREA. EDMONTON

Dan typed:

UNDERSTAND THAT, BUT WE'VE BEEN

344

FLYING TOMAHAWK OVER AREAS OF
CALIFORNIA AND NEW MEXICO THAT ARE
FAR MORE HEAVILY POPULATED THAN
THE NORTHWEST TERRITORIES. ARE ANY
CHASE AIRCRAFT AVAILABLE DOWN-
RANGE? JCM PRIMROSE

TWO F-15S ARE ASSIGNED FOR SEG-
MENTS A AND B OUT OF ALASKA. NORAD

THIS SEEMS ADEQUATE. THE RISK OF
IMPACTING ON TOP OF ANYTHING IN
SPARSELY POPULATED AREA IS LOW.
USAF FLIGHT ONE OF THE 868TH HAS
COME A LONG WAY TO TEST THIS BIRD
IN ADVERSE CONDITIONS. JCM

IS IT JCM'S OFFICIAL RECOMMENDA-
TION THAT THE TEST CONTINUE AS
SCHEDULED REGARDLESS OF AVAILABIL-
ITY OF FULL CHASE TEAM? SCMTT

He thought that one over, hands above the
keys. Harrup was asking for his balls on the
bartop. If by some horrendous mischance the
missile did come through the snow-covered
roof of some local's house, there'd be no question who was responsible. For a moment, he
wondered if he should play it safe. Then he
thought, Shit, my letter's in. He turned to
Manhurin, who was still at his shoulder, then
swung around to Thompson, the Canadian

liaison, who was listening, too. "You guys buy what I'm saying? Or should I leave you out of it?"

"Shit, yeah. Let the fat lady sing."

"I'm gonna steal that one. K.T.?"

The Canadian hesitated, then shrugged. With a delicious sense of liberation, Dan typed:

JCM ACCEPTS LACK OF CHASE OVER PART OF FLIGHT PATH IN THE INTEREST OF A REALISTIC TEST UNDER WORST-CASE CONDITIONS. FLIGHT COMMANDER AND CF LIAISON ON SITE CONCUR. LET THE FAT LADY SING.

The print head remained motionless. "Come on, you twits, take the dare," he muttered. Then it blurred into motion, chattering its way across the paper.

AT REQUEST OF JCM REP ON SITE, AND UNLESS OBJECTED TO BY NORAD AND NATIONAL DEFENCE HQ OTTAWA NOW BEING CONTACTED, GLCM207 WILL LAUNCH ON SCHEDULE 1030Z. SCMTT

"REVEILLE. Breakfast in ten."

He grunted, turned over, then remembered the launch this morning. And if it went wrong, his name would be pasted all over it. He got up and pulled his gear on again.

Outside, it was still dark and the wind made

it hard to stand. Someone had strung lines during the night, rope stretched on sticks between the tents and the other points in the dispersal area. Like the lines they'd rigged on *Ryan* when she'd fought an Arctic storm. Christ, why had he butted in last night; he didn't want to stand before another military court. . . . He tried to shove his misgivings aside as he followed other bent shadows to the mess tent. No MREs today, but eggs and toast and coffee. He ate fast, eager to get over to the LCC. But when he was outside again, halfway there, he reversed his direction and fought his way back along the line through the dark to the secondary control trailer, the one Steve Manhurin used as a command post.

The major was sitting in front of the console. Dan stripped off his parka, noticing the test director, the launch crew, the maintenance guys, and the contractor reps. The air was clammy, both cold and humid, as if the van had been submerged a long time. A fax machine beeped, and he saw it was a weather map emerging. Yeah, the blizzard was coming right over them.

"Where are we, Steve?" he asked the Air Force officer's back.

"Looking at our launch window opening at ten-ten. We already got the execute message."

"How's it look?"

"There was more discussion on scrubbing. I laid it on the line. Afraid I had to use your name in vain. Just between us, how much authority you got up there?"

"At JCM?"

"Yeah."

"Enough to decide what pictures go on my desk," said Dan. "But this is what my boss wants — to wring the system out. I think if it comes down to push and shove, he'll back me."

"Anyway, they bought it. We just better not fall out of the sky on somebody's dog team." Manhurin told Geddes, "Okay, take it away."

The crew commander started through the checklist, person by person, asking if anything could go wrong. One of the techs expressed concern over a section of fiber-optic cable that had apparently been gnawed on by something at some point during the road march, but when pressed, he said it had tested okay, that all he was doing was surfacing the issue. They discussed whether the extreme cold would affect the elastomer seals and O-rings on the missiles. They came to no clear conclusion, but Dan added it as a point of concern in his wheelbook.

When it was Decker's turn, the security officer said, "We got only one possible show-stopper. That's these two, three peaceniks loose in the woods. My guys are good, but we don't have wire, or any physical barrier, and the visibility's steadily going down."

Manhurin said quietly, "You're in counter-terrorist deployment, right?"

"Right. And I'll defend us, Steve. Make no mistake about that."

"Then that's about all we can do, I guess. All right, missileers. Make or break time, and just to make it interesting, we got some major winter weather incoming. If we can launch in this, and get a guide to a hit, we're going to look golden. If we don't, the winged wonders will eat our lunch. Let's go out there and make it happen."

Dawn broke as they went to their stations. Dan stood watching the tops of the aspens poking the gray sky. Still snowing. Then the cold grew too intense to stand, so he waded to the test van. The techs there treated him with a mixture of standoffishness and compassion. Of course, they'd listened in on the exchange at 0300. Well, soon he'd know if he was a hero or a leper.

At T minus five, with alignment and target download complete, he went outside again. He'd intended to watch the final checklist in the primary LCC, but now thought, I've seen countdowns before. So he just stood leaning into the wind, watching the shadowy form of the TEL off between the trees. The falling snow wavered between him and it. The launcher was erected, the single steel rod looking spindly and fragile under the bulk of the lifted container. The camo netting flapped wildly in the icy wind.

Decker seized his elbow. The security officer yelled into his ear, "You're inside the safety range. Get back, unless you want perforated."

Dan nodded and followed him away between the trees till they reached a little tumbledown bunker with half its roof fallen in. Beside it lay the remains of a slit trench. He wondered what they'd tested here before, and how long ago. . . . A knot of observers and off-duty guys stood huddled against the flaking concrete, in the lee of the wind. The exposure masks made it tough to tell who they were, but he could make out Sparky's dark eyes, and Thompson's parka had a rocker that read CANADA. Decker handed him a little package: earplugs. He crimped the yellow foam and worked them under his hood. Now the world went silent. The trees were whipping violently, streamers of snow leaping and writhing along the ground where the forest opened. Yet all took place in peace, save for the thudding of his heart.

He was glancing at his watch for about the tenth time, wondering if it had stopped in the cold, when they came out of the woods.

They came as low-bent shadows, crouching and rising as their ski poles rose and dipped. Like gray-white ghosts, slicing between the trees, in a cupped line.

He stared in disbelief. Then Decker was yelling into the radio, "Perimeter penetration. Perimeter penetration, one four zero! Pull in, close-in defense!" Breaking into a run, Decker drew his sidearm. Dan ran after him clumsily in the heavy suit and boots.

The line converged, sweeping inward around them as they stumbled out onto the field. Now, closer, he could see that their upper bodies were masked by white smocks or capes. Behind them more white-parkaed figures came into view out of the woods. The security force was moving fast on snowshoes, but not as fast as those they pursued could travel on the long cross-country skis.

Then blowing snow erased his vision, and he ran blindly, cursing, afraid every moment that the booster would fire. Decker was a few yards ahead, and Dan jerked the earplugs from his ears and yelled, "Cancel the firing! Hold the launch!" But either the security chief didn't hear him or didn't want to stop. Then he saw why.

Pointed at the sky, it must have been hard to miss. It loomed over the trees, above the white flurries that blew close along the ground.

The sweeping sickle of intruders was converging not on them but on the launcher.

He panted, trying to speed up, but he was losing his breath. It was rough going, through the deep snow.

Decker halted. He had his sidearm cocked, angled up. He squinted into the tree line, talking into the radio. Dan caught up to him, sucking wind. He followed the troops with his eyes, then blinked. They were dropping to one knee, raising their weapons.

Decker said into the radio, "Lock and load, boys. Lock and load." As his own weapon came down, steadied.

Dan yelled, "No!" and chopped the pistol out of the other man's hand. It spun away and vanished, swallowed by the snow. Dan looked back over his shoulder. Sakai was right behind him, and Thompson and the others who'd huddled by the bunker were coming up, strung out across the snow.

"Form a barrier," he yelled as he swept his arm in front of the launcher, understanding as he did it that they were fouling the range, too, that now Decker's troops couldn't fire.

The skiers reached them before they were formed up. They came fast, folded low. Snow spurted from their poles. The only point in favor of the defenders was that the TEL was on a rise and the skiers lost momentum as they swept up it.

One cannonballed toward him, and he went to a lacrosse crouch, wishing he had a stick. His eyes locked with those of the oncoming figure — or would have if eyes had been visible. But all he met were dark-tinted ski goggles and a faceless balaclava. The skier head-faked, but Dan watched the skis instead and dove out in a body check.

They collided, hard. The other man left the skis and traveled a few feet through the air. Dan and Sakai were on top of him before he stopped rolling. Dan grabbed the mask and stripped it up and off in one brusque yank.

Shining blond hair, snapping blue eyes, and the collar of an Indian-figured sweater. It was one of the women who'd stood vigil at the gate. "Murderer," she snarled. "How many children are you going to fry with this missile?"

"Wait a minute. You got it all wrong here."

"Let go of me, you son of a bitch." She twisted free and sat up. He started to get up, too, and released her arm.

Before he could react, she was up on all fours, knocking them both down, then scrambling past. He caught her boot and held it as she tried to kick his face in and nearly succeeded. Sparky piled on a second time, to the accompaniment of muffled punches and grunts. When she lay motionless again, all three were breathing hard. Dan sat up again, warier this time when she rolled over.

Her hand came out suddenly from under the parka, and he gasped at the slap of warm liquid in his face.

The Ziploc fell to the snow and lay there, leaking the last droplets. He looked down at himself, at the thick red running down his parka.

"That's what belongs on your uniform," she said. "Fucking Nazi. You take money to kill —"

Without thinking, he grabbed a handful of snow and rubbed it hard into her face. Then he rocked back on his heels, shocked at the rage that had suddenly made him wish he'd just let them go, let Decker shoot them down.

"Nonviolent, huh?" Sakai said beside him. "Yeah . . . sure glad we didn't get one of the violent ones."

Dan said roughly, "You got her now, Sparky?"

"I think so."

"She's bigger than you. You sure?" But another airman joined them just then. Dan turned away from her accusing stare and jogged over to where the others lay and sat.

There were three of them, sitting in a battered group on the snow, and the security force was leading another out from the woods. Dan recognized Murdoch. He squatted there, his cheek bruised, his arms twisted behind him.

Manhurin trotted across the field. The major stood staring down at the captives while he got a recap of the action. "Who's the leader?" he said.

"We don't have a leader," a woman said defiantly. "We're all equal here."

"This one," Dan said, pointing to Murdoch.

Manhurin asked him, "Are there any more of you people in the woods?" When the protester didn't answer, he said to Decker, "Gene, pull in tight and reinforce. This could be a diversion."

The security force commander spoke to a trooper; the man trotted off, rifle at port arms. Then he said to Murdoch, "The major asked you a question."

The thin man said nothing, and Decker backhanded him. The crack of the blow seemed loud even against the howl of the wind. Dan looked at Manhurin, who stood with eyes narrowed. He understood. He wanted to hit somebody, too. But instead he said, "Steve."

The flight commander blinked, seemed to recover himself. "Don't do that again, Gene. Hear me? Prisoner of war rules."

Decker looked around, and suddenly Dan realized how alone they were, how empty the forest around them was. "We ought to take them for a walk," Decker said in a low voice. "Search them, make sure they don't have explosives or weapons, and then take them for a walk. Nobody'd miss these creeps."

Manhurin took his arm and led him a few meters away. When they came back, the security commander's face was flushed, lips pressed tightly together. Dan caught the major's last sentence to him: "Not that I give a shit, Gene, but we don't need martyrs on our

355

hands. Understand?" Decker looked away.

Manhurin looked at Dan's chest next. "Is that yours?"

"What?"

"The blood."

"Oh, no, one of them threw it on me. When she saw we weren't going to let her get to the launcher."

"We'll get you a clean set."

One of the guards stepped away from the prisoners, carrying a cartridge box full of wallets, keys, and change. Manhurin peered in, rummaging around. Then his face changed. He held up a ragged sheet of paper, stared at it, and then motioned Dan in to share it.

They looked down at a map of the Primrose test site, a secon- or third-generation photocopy, speckled and aslant, but obviously from the same source, if not from the same page, as the briefing package that had been distributed back at Crystal City. Two points were marked on it in pencil. One was the flight's initial location, where they'd been for the first set of firings. The other was their hop-skip relocation position, where they were now.

The radio crackled. "Sir, we're still on hold back here. Still got a green missile, but we're closing in on the end of the window. Do you want to scrub?"

Manhurin snatched it. "No. Resume launch sequence. Clear the fly-out vector." To Decker, who had just come back, he said,

"Put these people in the bunker. Double-guard them. And if any of them gets hurt —"

"I wouldn't dream of touching a hair on their saintly heads." Decker sneered. He jerked Murdoch to his feet, and shoved him toward the slit trench. "Move, you Commie piece of shit."

Dan trailed them, guards and guarded, back to the bunker. Two of the protesters limped. The guards shoved them with rifles. He didn't object. The radio crackled, warning everyone in the open to take cover. He stood by the bunker door, glancing at his watch again, then turned to look back toward the launcher.

Just at that moment, as he turned, the booster ignited. Simultaneous with the roar, a white blast of smoke and flying snow bloomed, hearted with an intense orange flare. Fragments of blown-through canister and kicked-up rock and frozen mud whipped through the trees.

He held his breath, shielding his eyes, trying to see. Counting one thousand, two thousand from the first shattering blast of sound, sound that continued, piercingly painful from only a few hundred feet away. It vibrated in his chest, the way a balloon held in your hands hums when you speak.

A flaming sword emerged from the rolling cloud of smoke and snow and flame above the trees. Heat touched his upturned eyeballs.

Fly, fly, fly! The missile rose on a roaring column of yellow flame, bright and building on a pillar of white. There was pitchup. . . . He squinted up, frowning.

The missile, still boosting, lifted its nose. It was still gaining altitude, but it was pitching up hard. Pitching up *radically* . . . flying almost straight up now.

A groan came from around him. His throat closed as he urged it, Come back, come back. Where's the fucking guidance? he thought.

Then, to his horror, it nosed back over.

The group scattered, some diving for the black mouth of the bunker, joining the captives inside, others going flat on the snow. He stood rooted, unable to look away from an all-up missile fueled for an eleven-hundred-mile flight coming back toward him. It wasn't that he didn't want to run. He just couldn't decide which way to go. But as he stared helplessly, the missile steadied. It swung back and regained the vertical.

Still climbing, it vanished into the overcast. The radiance glowed from within it for a few seconds, then slowly vanished.

An ear-ringing silence descended on the woods. Smoke blew downwind. Then his knees started to shake, and he squatted in the snow to disguise their weakness.

"That was exciting," he said to Sparky. The engineer just shook his head.

When they'd recovered enough to make fee-

358

ble jokes, he went over to the test van to see what they had for initial download. The tech said they didn't get instant readouts, but it looked like a transient guidance glitch. Missile attitude had showed ninety degrees at one point, straight up, but then it had recovered and reexecuted pitch-down before heading off. "Downrange?" Dan said hopefully.

"Yeah, but not far. It got a minute out and started to lose altitude. Minute and a half, signal termination."

"What, you lost it?"

"We didn't lose anything that was there to lose, sir," said the tech. "In words of one syllable or less, it crashed, ninety-eight point seven seconds out of the can."

Fucking great, he thought. He was turning away when Decker put his head in. "Everybody to the mess tent," he said. He caught Dan's eye. "Sorry about flying off the handle back there, Commander. With the prisoners. I was just passing a joke."

But Dan thought he didn't look sorry at all.

"Okay," Manhurin said. "First off, our uninvited guests. I called Cold Lake to report their presence and request extraction as soon as this weather lifts. Gene, I want them out of that bunker and into a tent with heat. See that they have food, water, and medical attention."

Decker said he'd take care of it. Looking at

Dan, the flight commander said, "And take care of the Navy, here, too. I don't want him walking around in that."

A sergeant brought him a new parka and Dan handed over the bloody one. There was still a stain on the pants, but he decided it wasn't enough to bother changing right now.

A warrant officer Dan didn't know kicked off the postmortem. "Quick look, there's not much you can say. A pitch-up overcorrection early in the boost phase. Radical g forces. After that, we were basically watching a brain-dead airframe fly on booster power and aero-dynamics."

"Guidance?"

The Convair contractor rep said, "I don't think the guidance system was at fault here. Or at least it was fighting to recover. I don't go with 'brain-dead,' either. Near the end of the boost firing, we were seeing recovery. The missile was actually back fairly close to tran-sition-to-flight profile at that point."

"They should be able to take quite a few g's," Dan said. "They were designed for sub-marines."

"Submarines pull a lot of g's?" the warrant said incredulously.

"No, but they get depth-charged. The mis-sile's been qualified under MIL-S-nine-oh-one-C, underwater shock equivalent to depth charging."

Manhurin said, "Okay, so then why didn't

it tail-deploy, scoop-deploy, engine-start?"

The warrant spread his hands. "Maybe it did. But we aren't going to know until we get a look at it. And right now, I don't think we're going to."

Dan had been thinking during this exchange. It sounded like the same failure mode Point Mugu had reported. The "anomalies" they suspected were due to booster-separation failure. But since the Navy firings took place over deep water, the spent boosters went into the drink and they'd never been able to find them. So they'd had to redesign blind.

Now they had the same type of failure, only over land. Dan asked him, "What do you mean, we're not going to get a look at it?"

"We had ninety-eight seconds fly-out. That's thirty-some boost, actually closer to thirty-four seconds, according to telemetry. That puts the missile three, four miles out at separation. If it's anywhere near the envelope, it's traveling about six hundred feet a second. From there, ballistics takes over." Manhurin jabbed numbers into a pocket calculator. "A wild-ass guess, but you're probably looking at an impact point ten, twelve miles out. More, if the wings deployed."

"Can we see a map?" Dan said at last.

Decker had the best, a Canadian contour map marked "Medley River," showing the quadrant northwest of Primrose Lake in tones of green and white, with pale purple lakes and streams. They gathered around it. Dan noticed the grass-tuft symbols that meant marsh.

Decker said, "Here we are. I guess if we'd of had a transponder active, you'd have told us, right?"

The test technician: "Right. That's why I called it as a crash rather than as a chuter."

Manhurin asked, "You're sure the recovery package didn't deploy?"

"Not a hundred percent, but if all the telemetry stops at once, that's usually a hard-impact scenario."

"So we don't have a beacon. What was the last vector?"

"Two niner two. True."

Dan walked his fingers out. The last one landed on something called the Shaver River, east of an unnamed lake that was no longer or smaller than scores of others. The map showed nothing else out there, no road, only a faint dotted line, which, when you looked closely, the legend said was a trail, cut line, or portage.

"What about it?" he asked Thompson. "Can we get some personnel up there, do a search?"

"In this? Forget it. It can close down anytime to zero vis, and I mean zero. This is the kind of storm coming where people get lost and die between the house and the barn."

He figured the Canadian was indulging in a little exaggeration. So far, the visibility hadn't been that bad. "Well, we've got compasses. Here's what I'm thinking, K.T. —"

"Forget it," said Manhurin. "I'm as eager to find that bird as you are, but I'm not going to risk my people out there. We're technicians, not Arctic-trained Special Forces. Let's wait till the storm's over and we can get a helo up. Take our infiltrators back, turn them over to the Mounties, then go looking for it."

"By then, it'll be covered with snow. It'll be years before somebody falls over it. If we get out there right now, we might even see smoke."

"Not with my men."

"Well, I'm going to take a look," Dan said.

"Forget it," said Manhurin, biting it off. "K.T.'s told us this is nothing to fool around with. You're not going; nobody's going anywhere till this lifts."

"Can we have a word?"

There wasn't much privacy at the far end of the tent, so Dan kept his voice down. "Look, you're not in my chain of command, Steve. So don't give me these flat negatives. I respect your refusal to risk your men. But we need that missile back. This could bust our transition-to-flight problem."

"Is it worth dying over?"

"I don't plan to die over it. If I can get to that southern ridgeline, I'll be able to get a look out over the river valley. Maybe almost as good as from the air. That was a fully fueled missile. If it went down hard, like your guy says, I'm counting on smoke. If I see any, I'll shoot a couple of lines of bearing and come back. Then we can go get it when things clear up." He put his hand on the major's shoulder. "All I need's a Hummer and a compass, and that map."

"You're not going alone." Manhurin raised his voice. "Gene! Who we got who's good in the woods?"

"Sullivan's my best. Orienteering. Expert shot. Climbs mountains in his spare time."

"See if he wants to volunteer to go out with the commander." Manhurin turned away, and Dan didn't see any friendliness in his eyes anymore.

He had a moment of doubt in the Hummer, getting ready to move out as soon as Sullivan came back from the barracks tents. The snow had closed down more already. It was hard to see the LCC fifty yards away. He wondered how much worse it was going to get. Sullivan, a wiry, red-faced southerner, seemed unperturbed, though. He'd put together a couple of packs of gear in case things went sour. They lay in the back of the Hummer, along with Decker's contributions: portable radios, flashlights, spare batteries, a heater and fuel, an armload of MREs.

Deep down, he didn't really think they were going to find anything. But at least he'd be able to say he'd looked.

Sakai leaned in. "I'm going, too."

"No, Sparky. No point risking three guys where two can do the job. Probably a wild-goose chase anyway."

"Then why you going?"

"Just on the off chance." Dan gave him instructions, told him to go over the software again and see if there was anything that could cause a pitch-up overcorrect. "I don't know if they're going to launch tomorrow, but if they do, scrub down that part of the code first."

Sakai hesitated, then nodded and stepped back. Sullivan came out of the snow carrying two sleeping bags and what looked like a mountain tent, all packed into sausage-tight green nylon bags. He tossed them in back and got in. "Me drive, you navigate," he said. "How's that sound?"

"Like a plan." Dan traced a route. "First thing, we gotta go back toward Primrose, then hang a left at the lake. Cross over into Saskatchewan, then come back along this dotted line above the river."

"You know that might not be roadable."

"Well, then we'll know," Dan told him.

Thompson tapped on the curtain. Dan unzipped it. The Canadian said, "Watch out for browns."

"Browns?"

"Brown bears. Grizzlies. We still have a few

up here. Don't go in any caves. Are you taking a —"

"Got an M sixteen," said Sullivan.

Dan asked, "Aren't they supposed to be hibernating? Are they out in the winter?"

"Sometimes, the males. If they start mauling you, play dead."

"I'll bear that in mind. No pun intended. Anything else I should watch out for?"

"Look, you heard my recommendation. You may think you're ready for what can happen out there. You're not."

"Okay," said Dan. "Look, we'll be in touch by radio. We've got heaters and food. If it really closes down, we'll hole up till it blows over."

Sakai stood back, as did Thompson and Manhurin, and Dan refastened the curtain and put the heater on full. He just hoped they didn't have to come back in an hour, tails between their legs.

Sullivan put the Hummer in gear. "Off we go," he said, turning on the headlights. As the faces moved past, Dan gave them a wave, then bent to peer ahead into the storm.

# 19

They made poor time at first, and he wondered if they might not have to slink back after all. The snow came down so hard, they couldn't see the trees edging the road till they were almost in them. But it thinned as they ground on, and they made the pavement down by Primrose Lake in an hour. Which was not so great, considering it was only seven miles from the launch site. But he was happy to see a road again. Not that you actually *could;* it was just an unmarked ribbon of snow.

He checked his watch, noting turn time and speed. He figured he was going to do most of this trip by dead reckoning. "Don't drive out over the lake," he told Sullivan.

"Hey, sir, you want the wheel?"

Instead of answering, he reapplied himself to the map. As far as he could see, whatever it was — timber trail, old fur route — that dotted line was the only way in. They weren't going to do any cross-country work, not over terrain like this, with the storm almost on them.

The diesel growled. The tires droned. Occasional bursts of snow appeared from ahead, as if being generated at a point eight feet in front of the windshield. The heater blasted

367

hot air like the breath of hell. He loosened his parka and worked his toes in his boots.

An hour later, he said, "Okay, it's got to be around here someplace soon. Look for markers."

It took awhile, some backtracking and false starts, but at last they found an opening in the woods. When they swung off the pavement, the Hummer rocked and banged, lurching from side to side. Whatever was beneath them, it didn't seem to be a road. Maybe a portage, along the river to their left. He thought of grizzled fur traders carrying a canoe.

Maybe a mile on, Sullivan coasted to a stop. The Hummer shuddered as the wind buffeted it. "What's the matter?" Dan asked him.

"I don't know where the fuck I'm going. That's what's the matter."

No question, the kid wasn't overburdened with awe of field-grade officers. "The map shows a trail here, Airman Sullivan."

"You see any trail markers, blazes, anything? I don't. If there's a trail here, it's a foot trail. We're not gonna mush this sucker up it."

"We need to go west. A long way west. This is the only route the map shows."

The airman said, pointing, "Well, how about we swing down there and drive on the river?"

"Are you serious?"

"Sure. Shit, it's got to be frozen solid."

Dan looked at the map again. There wasn't any indication how deep it was, but it didn't look huge. More like a creek. Considering the topography, it was probably shallow. And considering the temperature for the last few weeks, he had to agree it was likely the ice would hold them. On the other hand, if he was wrong and they went into the water in this weather, it wouldn't be worth unbuckling their seat belts.

"All right," he muttered at last. "Try it. But take it slow, okay?"

Things got rough on the way down. Dust rose from the floor mats as the frame jolted and banged, the shocks bottoming out. But at least they were moving. Black vertical lines of aspens stretched up on either side of the curving bed of the buried stream. Gradually, the lowering gray sky stopped snowing and a shifting silver light glowed down over everything. He leaned into the windshield, peering out.

Northern Canada. Jolting and whining, they were fighting their way up a shallow gorge, floored by the smooth white featurelessness that in summer might be bars, pools, even rapids. Trying to average the wildly lurching speedometer, he figured they were making about six miles an hour. He didn't like being on the valley floor. They weren't going to see much down here. But according to his reckoning, they still had ten or eleven miles to go till they reached the impact area.

That wouldn't leave a hell of a lot of daylight for the trip back.

The Hummer slammed viciously over some invisible rock shelf, jamming him against the seat belt. Sullivan muttered, hunched over the wheel as the crooked fingers of a dead snag poked black above snowdrifts.

They crept deeper into an abandoned land.

Around three, he said, "Look, we got to get up on one or the other of these valley sides. Get some elevation. We can't see anything down here, and we're gonna be near the impact area pretty soon."

He expected a flareback from the airman, but Sullivan just nodded and looked off to the right. "How about up there?"

He looked up. The snow had started again, not as heavy as before, just a gauzy curtain drawn all around them, moving as they moved, as if nothing existed beyond it and everything past and future was illusion. He couldn't see any treetops beyond the crest. The trouble was going to be getting there. He checked the topo to make sure he wasn't missing anything. When he ran his finger up to where he estimated they were, he noticed a ladderlike symbol. He had to check the back of the map to find it meant "cutting or embankment." It didn't say what for, or how old

370

it was, or how wide. But it was all they were going to get.

"Bingo, nice eye," he told the airman. "Let's run right up that."

"Sure, we'll run right up it. And break an axle. I don't want to have to walk out of here."

"Look, I can do without the sarcasm. If we can't make it, say so. But I don't need this attitude. It's starting to grate, okay?"

The airman rolled his eyes.

Jolting and growling in low gear, they made it to the top at last. He told Sullivan to stop there, see if he could find something to get his bearings on.

He peered through the windshield at a forsaken land. They could see back down to the valley, but the gray prickle of treetops told them nothing. There weren't any trees or bushes up here. Or anything, for that matter. He figured there was marsh down somewhere below the four or five feet of snow beneath them. He was amazed they'd gotten this far. Probably best not to push their luck. But even as he thought this, Sullivan put them back in gear.

The airman worked them gradually toward the closest thing to a rise in sight. When they got to it, Dan told him that was good; they'd stop here and get out for a look around. As far as he could tell, they were at the southern edge of where the missile *might* have come down. Now he understood how hopeless his

371

idea of finding it had been. The sun was dropping. A quick survey and then they'd head back.

Mask time, hood time, woolen inner gloves, outer mitten shells. When he got himself put back together, he unbuttoned the flaps and thrust his legs out, spilling the accumulated heat instantly into the bitter wind. "Don't turn the engine off," he called back.

The wind was even stronger, even more shocking here in the open than it had been among the trees back at Primrose. Facing into it, he literally couldn't breathe. He cinched his hood tighter as he waited for the binocular objectives to chill. When he could see through them, he clambered awkwardly up on the hood. Hunkering against the wind, he slid the field of view slowly around the horizon. Steam streamed from the exhaust, whirling away.

"Let me take a look," Sullivan yelled. Dan jumped down and handed the glasses over, clapping his mittens over the eyeholes in the exposure mask. Shit, it was *cold*. Maybe the driver was right. Tough as the Hummer was, machines broke. Then they'd really be in a fix.

"See anything?"

"No."

"Let's head north a little bit more, then head back."

"You want to drive on this stuff?"

"This is open. It looks drivable."

"There any holes under it?"

"I don't see any on the map. Just marsh symbols."

"I hope they made this map right," Sullivan said. They got back in, and he put it back in gear. The blunt nose of the vehicle thrust itself through the snow like an amtrac thrusting itself through the sea on the way in to a hostile beach. From time to time, they stalled, wheels whining as they spun free in the snow, but each time, Sullivan backed and filled until they were moving again.

Dan watched the odometer. If they were anywhere near where he thought they were, they had to be within two or three miles of the missile. But it could be lying down in one of these gullies and they'd never see it. This wasn't so bad. Why the hell couldn't they fly choppers in this? It wasn't even snowing that hard.

They didn't notice the distant speck of color till much later, actually when they were headed south again, on their way back toward the river. He'd bumped their time out against their time in and figured they might reach pavement again before dark. They were lurching along a low ridge, with treetops nestled below them along the slope, as if huddled for shelter against the blasting wind. Then Sullivan said, "What's that?"

"What?"

"Something orange, down there. You got to wait between these flurries."

"Stop. I'll take a look with the glasses."

It took awhile. The drifting curtains of white, and the failing light made it hard to see. But at last he made out what the airman was pointing at. It was orange, or at least reddish, but he couldn't tell what it was. It might be the parachute, but then again, it might not.

He chewed his lip. The trouble was, they couldn't get down to it from here. The ridge slope was short, but too steep to take a vehicle down without risking a roll. They were lucky they hadn't gotten stuck already.

"What you think, sir?"

"I can't tell."

"What color's the chute?"

Dan was embarrassed to admit he didn't know. Sullivan didn't, either; the security detail didn't deal with the missile itself that much. They had a short argument, which Dan cut short by getting out of the Hummer and using the glasses again, trying to make up his mind what to do.

Sullivan said sullenly from inside, "Sir, with all due respect, you're nucking futs if you go down there."

"You tell me a better way to check it out?"

"Call in the coordinates. Check it out later."

"I keep telling you, I don't know where we

374

are along this river line. If that's it, and we don't mark it somehow, we've lost it. Also, I got to pump bilges."

Sullivan grumbled but finally got out. He reached back and pulled out a pack, then another. "I don't think we need those," Dan said.

"We leave the car, we're taking them. Take your prick-ten, too." He held out the portable radio.

"Why don't you stay here?"

"Nuh-uh. Just tell me the plan if we get separated."

"Look around independently, I guess. But not long. Fifteen minutes, no more. Then rendezvous back here. You taking that, too?"

The airman slung the rifle. "Sure as shit am. You heard Thompson."

They argued again about whether to leave the engine running. Sullivan insisted they had to, it might not start again if it chilled down. Dan gave in this time. He didn't want to tyrannize the guy. But he had Sullivan back the Hummer around till it faced downhill, pointing the lights down into the ravine. "Let's both take bearings," he said. They came up with 012 and 013 to the distant dot.

A few minutes later, they were sliding down the bank, grabbing at the stunted pines to brake themselves. Dan took it slowly. He didn't want to twist an ankle out here. Behind

375

him, Sullivan ghosted through the woods in his camo smock, M16 slung. Well, if it made him feel better. Himself, he didn't believe any bear would be stupid enough to be out in this.

What did that say about them?

When they emerged at the bottom of the cut, he'd lost whatever it was they'd seen. Rises and trees blocked the line of sight, and the air seemed to have thickened. The wind was picking up, peeling up the flaky layers of new snow, sending them whistling along the ground in a milling milkiness. Beneath what he'd taken for ground, his boots plunged through a frangible crust into a whole separate depth of soft powder. With every step, he had to lift his boot back out waist-high. It was exhausting and he had to rest every few meters and peer ahead. His eyeballs felt as if they were freezing into hard round marbles behind the mask. Then Sullivan would yell, "Zero two zero, the hump to the right of the crooked tree up there," and they'd flounder off again.

All this time, he had to whiz. Even the thought of hauling it out here made him shiver. But finally, he couldn't put it off. He bent over in the lee of some stunted bushes and stripped off his mitten shell. Get *this* over with quick. . . . Shielding himself with his woollen inner glove, he nursed out a hasty yellow stream. The urine snapped as it hit air, turning to ice before it reached the snow.

When he looked up, Sullivan was nowhere in sight. He buttoned hastily, pulled his parka down, and floundered around the bushes after him.

The rising wind drove frigid ice needles into his eyes. Dark coming on, too. Bent nearly double, he tried to discern the airman's tracks. It was no use; the surface was a boil of motion. Head down, he plodded ahead. The snow kept giving way under him, making him lurch and stagger beneath the plunging, crackling trees.

"Sullivan," he yelled. Then cupped his gloves around his mouth. "Sullivan!"

A yell came back, faint against the wind. He thought it came from out ahead, and plowed toward it.

The wind roared in his ears and flung handfuls of snow into his eyes. His breath was labored under the mask; he was sucking in air far below freezing. One boot caught a branch or stone beneath the snow and he pitched forward, full length, and came to a gentle rest.

Rest . . . forget it! He levered himself upright again, but now he couldn't see at all. The whole world was white around him, a milling maelstrom. He could tell only one direction: down, and that only because his feet were rooted beneath a surface half snow and half air.

Cupping his hands again, he howled as hard as he could into the unhearing wind.

When he finally accepted that Sullivan was gone, he went to his knees in the snow and tried to calm down. Tried to think. He wasn't lost. He had a back bearing to the Hummer. He remembered how the slope went. Even in the storm, he should be able to guide in on the headlights once he got close.

The wisest thing was probably to start back now. Forget the missile. Just head back.

On the other hand, he'd told Sullivan they'd look independently if they got separated. What if he'd already found it, was there waiting for him?

He was sure now the documentation on the recovery package had mentioned the color orange. The dorsal stripe was orange, so it made sense the chute would be the same high-vis color. He hadn't come all the way out here to turn back fifty meters short. If he could recover it, they could find out what had gone kerflooey — not just with this round but with a lot of others, too.

Or was he just being stubborn, maybe even fatally stubborn? Because cringing beneath a Canadian blizzard, alone, already half-frozen, he was beginning to suspect Thompson was right and he'd been far too casual about this. If he made the wrong decision, he could die out here. They could *both* die out here.

Finally, reminding himself he still had the radio, he chain-hoisted himself to his feet again. Corrected to the left — he had the feeling Sullivan had been leading them too far east — and floundered on. He wished he had snowshoes. Then he could walk on top of this stuff instead of practically tunneling through it.

He could have been wading now through milk instead of air. "Whiteout," they'd called it in the Arctic Sea. The trees were gray ghosts, invisible four feet away. He slogged grimly on, checking the compass every few steps. Any darker and he'd need the flashlight to read it. He thought again about the radio, and suddenly realized he should be able to get Sullivan on it. He felt for it in his parka pocket.

Empty.

With a sick feeling, he remembered sprawling facedown in the snow, lying there, then getting up reluctantly. That was when it must have fallen out. And where was that? He turned slowly, looking back into an impenetrable white furnace.

He was trekking slowly along beneath dwarfed long-needle pines. They cut the snow, or maybe the storm had lifted its skirts again. But on and off for some time now, he'd heard something that didn't belong. A sound within, but not of, the forest. A *crack* . . . *rustle* . . . *crack* through the continuous heavy roar of the wind. It sounded like a slack jib flogging itself apart in a squall.

*Crack . . . flap.* There it was again. Not far away, and somewhere above him. He oriented and waded a few more steps in the growing dark, then slammed his shin hard and fell over onto it, half-buried in the snow.

The missile lay nose-down, one stubby, crumpled wing sticking up, the other either sheared off or buried deep. He grinned under the mask. Shit, here it was, and a good thing he hadn't waited. Without the bright nylon that fought desperately in the trees, there would be no way to see it. And it wouldn't be there much longer. Already several chute cords danced madly among the branches, torn free from the canopy.

He'd told the bastards he'd find it, and he had.

Squatting, he bulldozed snow and broken needles off with his mittens, uncovering it to the nose. He plunged his arm in to the shoulder and felt underneath it, like a dairy farmer checking a cow's udder. The air scoop was deployed, locked down.

Interesting. He worked his way toward the tail, giving it a quick checkout before he headed back. His thumb slammed into the sharp edge of a fin. If his hand hadn't been numb, that might have hurt. Tail assembly, bent and damaged. . . . He slid all the way aft and plunged his gloves into the liquid made of snow and air and darkness.

Aha. No booster.

T207 had tried to transition to flight. Scoop out, wings out, tailfin deployed. Maybe she'd even tried to start her engine.

But she hadn't flown. Struggling against whatever had gone wrong, the dying missile — could a mechanism feel anguish, despair? — had glided down helplessly from the sky, until the guidance system resigned itself and popped the chute.

All that, he understood.

But then what was that pitch-back on take-off? And why had the missile, obviously in the transition envelope — because otherwise it wouldn't have popped wings and scoop — failed at last to make that final metamorphosis from rocket to bird?

Were the two failure events separate? Sequential? Or were they related in some other, more subtle way?

Do the detective work later, he told himself. Get back now, before it's too dark to see. You know where it is close enough they can get the recovery guys out here two, three days from now, when this blows over.

He went back to the main fuselage, looking for a convenient part to detach. Nothing offered, so he grabbed the damaged wing. He put his weight on the torn section at the edge. It gave, and he bent it back and forth a few times till finally the stress-weakened, cold-weakened aluminum tip snapped off in his

381

hand. He stuffed it into the pack. Just in case it occurred to somebody to doubt he'd really found it. Yeah, he could see that son of a bitch Decker sniggering now.

When he straightened, he noticed the sky had grown black above the stubby, wind-bent treetops. The elation of discovery flicked away. If he dicked up getting back, if he couldn't find the Hummer, he'd freeze out here.

The storm closed down again then, so hard that he cowered against the missile. The wind slashed and gusted, tearing at his parka. The chute thundered above his head like a runaway mainsail during a Cape Horn passage.

And sometime in there, crouched against the hard length of inert metal, with the parachute ripping itself apart over his head, the trees bowing and creaking, and the writhing sky close and lightless, he understood he wasn't going to get back to the flight tonight. He wasn't going to get back to the road. He wasn't even going to get back to the Hummer. Not in the dark, not in the storm that stood up now and lashed the cowering, ice-shrouded trees till they squeaked and cried like the timbers of a schooner in a storm. The wind screamed through their branches with a pitch he'd heard only once before, in the heart of a hurricane. He couldn't see anything now, couldn't see the compass or even — hell, he couldn't even see the *flashlight* when he held

382

it out, the snow was that thick. Shit, shit. . . . What had happened to Sullivan? He both feared and hoped that the airman had done the smart thing, turned back when they lost each other, gone back to the vehicle before the storm and the night really clamped down.

Whatever he'd done, Dan couldn't help him now. Nor could Sullivan help him.

He was on his own.

He understood then, from the dead feeling in his feet, the wooden numbness of his hands and face, that what he was most likely to do out here tonight was die. Ahead of him stretched sixteen hours of darkness. Darkness and cold beyond anything he'd ever expected to face, alone and unprotected. A survival situation he wasn't trained for, equipped for, ready for at all.

He shook himself out of the drowsy contemplation of danger. Before all, he had to get out of this wind. Ducking, he dug clumsily beneath the long cylinder of the fuselage. He burrowed blindly, head turtle-tucked, smashing his way through the crust with his fists and scooping out the powder beneath with both hands. He panted as he dug, and the fear warmed him. But he knew it was a dangerous warmth, and one that would soon pass.

This could very well be the last night of his life.

He shook himself awake in the dark, realizing he'd nodded off. But he couldn't, not here. If he fell asleep, he'd never wake up.

He opened his eyes and strained them around, flicking the flashlight on for just a moment to check the integrity of his defenses.

He lay curled like a dog, shuddering in a snow-walled hole no bigger than his folded body. Above him was the smooth polish of the missile's outer skin. A ragged scratch in the paint showed where it had hit one of the trees on the way down. Part of the dorsal stripe showed at the edge.

The rest of the hole was snow, just snow. Powdery and dry, it had collapsed around him even as he dug, so that now he lay less in shelter than at the bottom of a shallow grave. Above him he looked up and out into the merciless darkness of the storm.

Blizzard. Now he understood what it meant, listening to the ceaseless roar, the tormented creak and sway of the trees. The slap and crack of the chute had stopped hours ago. It was gone, ripped into shreds by the unimaginable fury of the wind. At sea, a storm like this would raise waves thirty feet high, put an unwary destroyer on her beam ends.

But at sea, he wouldn't be alone, abandoned, buried alive, without hope of heat or rescue. Digging had warmed him, for a little while. But he was losing what little heat he had. No matter how his muscles tensed and shuddered, it was seeping away, leaking away into the frigid emptiness above him.

Blinking sleepily, fighting the encroaching lassitude, he dug slowly into the pack and came up with a granola bar. He gnawed it slowly in the dark. It was frozen hard as concrete, and he had to suck on it for a long time before the crystalline ice released sweetness. It tasted strange. Like gasoline. When he checked his watch, the luminous hands told him it was only 1905.

Fourteen more hours till the light returned.

He'd thought at first he might make it through huddled in his hole, balled like a sleeping bear. Dry snow was supposed to be a good insulator. And he was shuddering, putting out heat. The trouble was that he couldn't keep the air his body warmed at such an exorbitant price. The dark wind, tearing past the open top of his hole, seized it instantly, replacing it with more minus-forty air. The missile was a partial roof, but only partial.

He could feel himself freezing to death, and it wasn't as pleasant, easy and comfortable as they said. It was painful and frightening, and as he lay wadded within his parka, he understood he couldn't stay like this much longer. If he did, if and when they found the missile at last, they'd find him curled beneath it, eyes glassy and frozen like two party cubes.

He should have started back even though it was dark. But hell, he might have gotten just as lost by now anyway. If he had to be lost, it was better to be lost with the missile. Wasn't it?

Or did it matter? What did he expect, a posthumous decoration? This was pure stupidity. And that's exactly what they'd think, whoever dug him out and lugged him, curled like a frozen shrimp, toward the helo or snowmobile or whatever they'd use to get him out of there.

Assuming they found him and the missile at all. They could be here till spring. By then, he'd be nothing but a mass of blackfly maggots. . . . Nice thought, Dan.

He had to get some wood, twigs, or he wasn't going to make it. There was a lighter in his pack. All he needed was something to burn.

He shook off the dreams and battered his fists against his face. It was like hammering wood with iron.

He lunged stiffly out of the hole and clawed his way up into the wind, into a roaring blackness that instantly knocked him down, smothered him, buried him. He strained with open mouth behind the mask, and finally, jackknifed into the snow, mittens crimped like icy copper around his lips, succeeded in inhaling a lungful of searing air. His throat closed. . . . Couldn't breathe. . . . He jerked the mask to one side and found that although his whole face was hard and numb now, he could get a little air from a pocket beneath the mask. If he breathed out into the pocket, the air he got back was warmed just enough not to freeze his throat.

He couldn't reach the trees. Couldn't get wood to burn. He couldn't even stand upright.

He crawled back toward where he thought the missile lay, and when his groping hands found nothing but powder and air, he experienced a moment of as pure and complete a terror as he'd ever felt in his life. A sudden panic strength thrust him forward, boots kicking in the snow, and his head slammed into something hard. If he hadn't had the hood on, he'd have knocked himself out. But as he sank and scrabbled back beneath his inadequate shelter, he felt a drag on his right arm. He pushed the mask up as he regained his hole, and put his lips to it, about the only part of his body that retained any feeling at all.

Somehow, crawling around out there, he'd caught and grasped a pine branch. Buried in the snow, probably, torn off the trees either by the wind or by the descent of the chute-lowered missile.

Then the sleepiness became too much to bear. Knowing he might not wake again, he still couldn't stop himself from sliding down into the dark.

It started like it always did. A normal watch. But then, with that ever new knife-twist in the gut, he realized he'd made a mistake.

He stood frozen on *Ryan*'s bridge wing, staring at what had a moment before been empty night. Something seventy feet high had created itself there, running lights burning steady, bow wave sparkling against black. Behind him a cry of "Stand by for collision!" was followed by the electric clang of the alarm.

As the carrier's bow tore into them, the destroyer heeled, knocking him onto the gratings. A long, terrifying loud shriek of tearing steel succeeded the blow. The lights, penumbraed by a fine falling mist, slid by high above. A scream of rending metal and a roar of escaping steam struggled against the drone of a horn.

He scrambled up and was propelled into the pilothouse by the slant of the deck. The boatswain was shouting into the 1MC, but nothing was audible above the din. The light on the chart table flickered and went out. The captain was clinging to his chair, staring out to starboard.

Dan fetched up against the helm and clung to it, looking out. The lights were still moving by above them, like a train on a high trestle. Then they were gone. An explosion came from aft, rattling the windows.

"Abandon ship," the boatswain was yelling into the mike. But it was dead.

He went out to the wing again. The carrier loomed abeam, a black cliff higher than their mast top. A choking smell reeked the air. Flames were shooting up, making crackling, rapid bangs, all along the Asroc deck.

When he turned back, the skipper was looking aft. "Abandon ship, sir?" Dan shouted above the rising roar of fire.

"She never responded to the emergency bell," the captain said. His face was bleak in the growing firelight.

"She's cut in two aft, Captain."

"All right. Do it. Get the order around by word of mouth. Let's get as many off as we can."

He found himself on the main deck. Men shoved past him. Naked from the waist up, a sailor threw his legs over the lines and dropped, running in the air. "Abandon ship," Dan shouted, fighting his way past.

The flames were licking swiftly forward. Their tips fluttered in the wind like pennants. They danced on the surface of the deck, and he thought for a moment the metal itself was burning. The smoke was choking, thick with the smell of fuel. Where in the hell was all the fuel coming from?

On the fo'c'sle, a knot of sailors were dumping life jackets out of a locker. He grabbed one and began strapping it on. His hands shook so, it took several tries to get the straps through the D-rings. Could this be dream, nightmare? No, he knew these men. That screaming was real.

"Better get in the water," he told them. "If she goes down sudden she may suck us under. Jump in and swim clear."

"Aye aye, sir."

He threw his legs over the lifeline and looked down.

The sea was black, highlighted by fire. More men, black cutouts against the brilliance, were leaping now. The fire-sound was enormous but bizarrely cheerful, like a bonfire at a picnic.

He kicked away and plunged feetfirst into the black sea.

The impact burst breath from him. Icy water filled his mouth. Then the life jacket brought him up with a rush. He swam as hard as he could for fifty strokes, then turned and looked back.

USS *Reynolds Ryan*'s bow rose, its deck sloping back toward him. From the forward stack aft, a pyramid of white flame ran down along the sides. The fire and fuel stench was heavy, choking.

He became conscious now of the men around him. Some were moaning, but most were quiet, tossed up and down by the four-foot seas. A sailor called out, "Think she'll float, Mr. Lenson?"

"Not much longer," Dan shouted back.

God, the sea was cold. He kicked his feet, but the numbness didn't retreat. He was still looking at the sailor, trying to recall who he

390

was, when beyond him he noticed the lights of a ship. Good, get in here and pick us up, he thought.

When he rose again, it was almost on top of them. In the firelight, he saw it was the carrier. Fans of light reached out, probing the black sea. Then a wave broke over his head and he sputtered, clawing away salt water that burned like cold acid.

The carrier struck the old destroyer again just aft of the stack, shoving it down to a crunching scream of buckling plates and tearing ribs. The larger ship's side lit in a smear of flame, scattering in gouts of yellow that flared up again into white as it hit the water.

A sheet of burning fuel swept toward him, leaping and guttering along the crests as it ignited first blue and then glaring yellow and then incandescent white. He screamed as it seared his shoulder and arm before he finished ripping the life jacket off.

As the sea closed over him, the beat of the carrier's screws filled his head. He frog-kicked desperately through the icy dark and came up into a stink of kerosene and smoke that seared his lungs.

He was in a shimmering tunnel of flame. The reek of fuel filled his brain, and all around him men were screaming. . . . They were dying. . . . And it was all *his fault*. . . .

His eyes came open and he stared into the

darkness, remembering that helpless terror in the water. Remembering the doomed *Ryan* drifting, burning, then torn apart again by *Kennedy*'s incredible, incomprehensible second pass through the wreckage. Remembering above all that petroleum reek as the carrier's broken fuel lines spewed tons of jet fuel, which was instantly ignited by broken power lines, hot burners, and a hundred other sources of ignition that offered in a ship torn in half by the massive splitting wedge of a carrier's bow.

And with a relief so great that even now, buried in the snow, he felt liberated and redeemed, he remembered that it *hadn't* been his fault.

The relief faded, replaced by fear again. He shifted uneasily. The numbness had reached his knees. The stink of fuel lingered from the dream. Strange how smells persisted in memory, especially that one. When he was filling the car up at a gas station, his gut would suddenly tighten. And out of nowhere, he'd be back in the black sea, the Atlantic night. . . .

He closed his eyes, then opened them again. He stared into the dark.

Suddenly, the flashlight was on in one mitten, and with the other he burrowed with frantic haste, digging till a white wall fell away and the spot of dimming light showed him stains and strings of a purplish gluey mass. It looked like grape jelly, oozing down into the snow from above. He cocked his head like a wondering dog, then understood.

The jelly was RJ-4. From a full fuel load, enough to power the little engine over a thousand miles. Gallons and gallons of it, leaking out of the cracked airframe and cold-thickened to the sticky consistency of napalm.

His hands were clumsy. He kept dropping the lighter. It didn't want to work. Shoot, hadn't he read a story about this? About a guy trying to light a fire and knowing that if he couldn't, he'd die? And in the end, he'd died anyway. He looked at the lighter again, then shook it and turned it upside down. He held the flashlight to it till the colored plastic glowed.

The clear fluid inside was frozen solid.

He thrust it into his mouth, ignoring the instant pain as his tongue froze to the metal cap, and searched through his pack for something to burn the fuel in. He came up with the scrap of wing metal. He worked for a few minutes, bending and crimping it against the fuselage, then wedged the makeshift cup into the side of the snow cave. Then he pulled it out again and stuffed pine needles under it. If this worked, the metal was going to get ultrahot. He didn't need it melting itself down into the snow and disappearing. With shaking hands, he scraped a tablespoonful of the sticky stuff out of its snow matrix with a twig clamped between his wrists and arranged it in a heap. He took the lighter out of his mouth, prayed, and tried it.

The fuel sagged under the sickled yellow flame. Then, without preliminary smoke, a blue radiance played over its surface. It grew and built until a four-inch-high white flame danced in the draft. The heat reached through the eyeholes. He pulled the mask off and let it bathe his face, his numb, cracked lips, till they unbent into a smile.

He tended the little fire all that night with the total and utter dedication of a vestal. Once the stringy, cold fuel clung to his fingers, and he lit them by mistake. But that was a simple matter of plunging his hand into the snow. Everything was simple, now that he had a fire. All he had to do was tease out another lump of congealed fuel occasionally and drop it onto his makeshift lamp. That, and stay awake.

And think.

For the first time in months, he had time really to think. So he did.

All that endless night, curled around the high-energy flicker, he thought his life over. Face-to-face with death, he reviewed his standoffish, suspicious relationship with Kerry. He could do better than that. He could love now, without so much thought for himself, concern for himself, fear for himself.

Toward morning, he was confident enough even to go to sleep for short bursts, once he had the plate heaped with fresh fuel.

Once again that night, he had a dream — not of *Ryan* this time, but of hovering somehow above his motionless sleeping body. He looked down at the pine-screened opening, at the flame-light whipping in the relentless wind. He felt no terror anymore, no loneliness. Only a vast compassion for the being that in some mysterious way was a broken-off piece of himself. Creature half of darkness, half of light. Half of hope and half of desperate and eternal fear, feeling and creeping its way over an immense and shadowy plain. So much could be forgiven, once you understood.

He wondered how he could tell it that: that everything, in the end, was going to be all right.

The storm didn't slacken till the afternoon of the next day. That was when he crawled outside at last and built a bigger fire. He heaped pine branches onto it till a greasy, viscous smoke shouldered upward through the trees. And it wasn't long after that till he heard the thud and flutter of helicopter blades. He staggered about, scuffing desperately at the snow, and at last stared upward, arms spread wide, welcoming the hovering descent of life.

# 20

A week later, he stared down at Washington once again through the window of the plane. Seemed like he was spending half his life bouncing from one end of the country to another. He winced and removed his fingers from his nose. They kept drifting there, despite his intent to keep them away.

The chopper had taken him back to Cold Lake for a checkout in the base infirmary. Frostbite was nothing to screw around with. No permanent damage, the doc said, but he had black blisters on his fingers and his nose. He was having trouble with his feet, too. But barring the blisters and peeling, and a lengthy time of sensitivity after that, he should recover full function.

The Huey had gotten to him in time because Sullivan, exercising his own judgment, had made his way back to the Hummer as soon as they got separated. He'd waited there all night long with the engine running and the lights on, in contact with Primrose by the vehicle radio. Toward morning, he'd had to refuel from the jerrican, but basically he'd spent the night safe and warm. The chopper had dropped him a bladder of fuel, and he'd arrived back about the time Dan was reaching Cold Lake by air.

He pulled his fingers away from his nose again. Damn, it was sensitive all right. He'd had to wear a glove liner stuffed under his mask whenever he went outside for the rest of the tests. Which had gone gratifyingly well. Riding in the seat pocket forward of his knees were the quick-look results for the completed Primal Thunder series. The final three missiles had launched and flown smoothly. Final box score: eight launches, seven successes, one failure, although one missile had impacted out on the edge of the target area; it had been snowing heavily at Toktoyaktuk at the time. But that still gave them an 87 percent success rate, which materially boosted the average. He hoped he could do as well in the next series, the Navy antiship-missile tests.

The flap about the demonstrators had ended with a whimper rather than the bang they'd probably hoped for. They stayed in a comfortable tent all through the blizzard, eating MREs and drinking hot cocoa. Then left meekly, heloed back to Grand Centre, where, as far as he knew, the Canadians would decide whether to charge them with trespassing. As for the map, he'd faxed it back to JCM, pointing out his suspicion that it had come from the briefing package, but without any explanation as to how the protesters had gotten it. Because, although he'd puzzled over it, he actually couldn't think of any.

He was looking forward to telling all this to

Kerry. He'd called from the infirmary, but his lips had been so cracked and sore, he'd kept it short. The one jolt had been her telling him all the defendants in the sabotage case had been found guilty. Sentencing would be in a few days. He did manage, though, to tell her he loved her, and that his offer still stood — to wait for her till she was free again.

So that remained to be faced. He took out his wheelbook. Other things going on. . . . Standing up the team for the antiship tests. . . . New Jersey's installation and checkout should be complete. . . . All in all, when the word came through, he could turn things over in good shape to whoever was going to relieve him.

"Drink, sir? Last call."

He shook his head. He was keeping his promise.

Nursing that glow, he leaned back. In only a couple of hours, he'd be with her.

He looked for her as he came out of the gate but didn't see her. Probably she was down at the soup kitchen. He took the Metro to Crystal City and hobbled through the mall.

"I'm back," he said, thrusting his head into Westerhouse's office. "D'jou get my message? Seven good shots out of eight. And we've got a lead on where number five failed. Still taking it apart, but it's definitely hardware."

"Ah . . . your nose?"

"Frostbite. Looks ugly, but it'll heal." He rattled on about the tests, then noticed his boss wasn't listening. "Something the matter, sir?"

"Just a minute." The captain picked up the phone. Dan noticed, with a pang, how heavy it seemed in his hand; how clearly, now that he knew, pain could be read in the sagging cheeks. "Mr. Lenson just reported in. Yes, sir . . . just now. Okay, be right up."

"What happened, sir? My resignation come through?"

"The admiral wants to talk to you."

They rode up side by side in the elevator. He wiped his hands on his trousers. Since the frost nip, they tended to sweat easily.

"Did you get the secure fax I sent, sir? About the map we found on the infiltrators?"

"Yes. Yes, I did."

"Did you pass it to Shirley?"

"Yes, I did," Westerhouse said. He looked at the panel. "Okay . . . here we are. No, you first."

Niles was standing when they entered the inner office. His hands were locked behind him, making him look more than ever like a gloomy, and dangerous, bear.

"Dale. Dan. Sit down, please."

"Thank you, sir." He and Westerhouse sank into the upholstered chairs normally re-served for visiting VIPs. No question, he was here for his official farewell. It was a solemn moment, and he felt a nervous mixture of regret and eagerness.

Niles sat heavily, moving like Marlon Brando as the Don. He slipped a piece of paper from his desk and stared down at it.

The admiral said, "This is a difficult thing to tell you. I don't know any other way than just to say it. I'm afraid your fiancée is dead."

Dan sat there, unable to move or to think. Finally, he made a little noise — not a chuckle, but an expulsion of breath. "Sir? What are you saying? I talked to her just a couple of days ago."

"She was found on the C and O towpath, day before yesterday. Here's the clipping from the *Post*. I'm sorry we had to give it to you this way. It wasn't brought to our attention till yesterday, and by then you were en route. I decided to wait till you arrived and tell you face-to-face. I'm sorry."

Westerhouse added something, but Dan didn't hear the words. He took the clipping and held it in the tips of his bandaged fingers, staring at words that didn't Velcro into sentences. The headline read ACTIVIST FOUND SLAIN ON POTOMAC BIKING TRAIL.

Niles sat down next to him. But he didn't say anything.

Dan said, "We brought back an eighty-seven percent success rate."

The director cleared his throat and glanced

at Westerhouse. "Did you? That's good."

Then suddenly, he was sucking in great whoops of air. It lasted only for a couple of seconds, though. They were watching him. . . . Had to get out of here. . . . She'd be waiting at the apartment. He felt confused, sleepy, as if he was freezing again. He shrugged off the admiral's hand, struggling up from the chair. "Sir, permission to go ashore?"

"Go home, Dan," Niles said, and his little eyes weren't hostile for once. Just sad. "Dale, I don't want him driving."

"I'll send Vic Burdette, sir."

"Okay. Thanks for the report, the good work out there. . . . We don't need you back here till Monday, Dan. We'll talk some more then."

"Aye aye, sir." Thank God for rote responses. He couldn't actually force a thought through his mind. He came to attention, about-faced, and left.

He endured the ride home in a confused stupor, alternating with flashes of disbelief. He didn't respond when Burdette said something comforting. Just got out of the car and carried his luggage into the lobby.

He knew the apartment was empty the moment he unlocked the door. He put the card that had been taped to it on the coffee table and went through each room in turn: living room, kitchen, bedroom.

Her blue dress, the one she'd worn to the party, hung in the closet, safe forever inside a sheath of plastic. Her scuffed shoes lay by the bed, where, apparently, she'd left them when she changed. It struck him again how little she'd owned.

The zombie body that carried him around inside it picked up the phone and dialed the number on the card.

He found himself talking to a hurried-sounding detective named Joe Ogen. Ogen said, "You're Lenson. Okay — yeah — boy-friend number two."

"Number two?"

"Her driver's license address took us to a guy named Heineken."

"Haneghen."

"Right, up in Northwest. He gave us her parents' number. That wasn't an easy call to make. How about you? You taking this all right?"

"So far."

"Haneghen gave me your name, said you were Navy, said she'd been living with you the last couple months. But after I left the note at your place, we found out you were up in Canada, and confirmed that with your boss. So right at the moment, I'm not sure whether you need to come in."

"Of course I'll come in. When?"

"Well, let's go over a couple things now, over the phone. . . . She had a bike, right?"

the cop asked him.

"That was mine."

"What kind was it?"

"A Motobecane. Grand Touring. Silver. . . . How did this happen? Can't you tell me a little more than what was in the *Post*?"

"We don't know a lot more than that. We're thinking right now the original motive was robbery, and that there were multiple assailants. We found her wallet thirty yards up the trail. It was empty. That's not a good place to be after dark."

"You said 'the original motive.' What does that mean?"

"I mean that after they got her off the bike there — and apparently nobody was around — they got her off into the weeds."

Dan said numbly, "And then killed her."

"Uh-huh. With a knife, it looks like. Though actually it could have been anything, piece of glass, so forth."

"Have you got any . . . leads?" Shit, he thought, I sound like a TV show.

"Give me your number there again. I'll give you a call tomorrow, okay?"

"Wait a minute. Where are you? I've got to talk to you about this."

"Whoa, not today. Just had another shooting, over at Foggy Bottom. Give you a call. Got to go."

He sat on the bed, marveling at how little he felt. It was like frostbite. He knew he was injured. He knew when he thawed out that it would be painful. But just at the moment, he didn't feel anything. The room looked as if she'd just stepped out. There were her things, still lying on the bed — her bra, her purse.

A black-bound book, edged in red. The cover was limp leather and he thought at first it was a Bible. But when he picked it up, he found it was a diary.

He gave the doorway a glance, as if she might surprise him in the reading. June, then August . . . dissatisfaction with Haneghen. . . . October . . . a brief mention of meeting him.

Then, with a sudden stillness of his heart, he was reading the last words, judging from the pen thrust between the pages, that she had ever written. He could hear her saying them.

*He says he's going to leave the service. I never asked it of him. I told him I loved him, the way he was. And it's true.*

*The one thing I'm not sure of is his drinking. When he drinks, it's terrifying, like he's someone else . . . not violent, but out of control. If he can't stop, I can't stay with him. I'm not going to place myself in that position.*

*But if he can, I'm going to marry him. I will marry him, and when I come out of prison, I will stay with him forever.*

Holding it on his lap, he drew a shuddering breath.

After a time, he got up and went into the kitchen. Opened the cupboard where he'd kept the scotch. To find a note propped in front of it.

*Please don't. Not till you talk to me. I'll help, whatever it takes to get your mind off it. Okay? Remember, I love you!*

He stared at it, then closed his eyes. The shuddering began again, deep in his diaphragm.

Suddenly, he jerked the bottle out of the cupboard, lifted it high, and smashed it apart on the counter with every ounce of his strength. Glass and liquor exploded, stinging his hand. But he didn't care. He didn't care at all.

Like a cloud sliding over his heart, he shuddered to the first icy breeze of an all-consuming storm.

# IV

# THE TEST

## 21

The District of Columbia Municipal Center was north of the Mall, a sandstone block with Art Deco stainless panels and Egyptian capitals. The steps at the entrance were thronged with loungers, jugglers, scowling matrons towing whining kids. Seeing his uniform, a man with whiskey breath and melted eyes stopped him to tell him about Anzio. Dan tried to be polite, but found a dollar bill worked faster. A desk cop in the lobby said Homicide was on the third floor.

When the elevator doors opened, he confronted two dozen grim-looking men, smoking and leaning against stained pink marble wainscoting as high as their heads. A sign read THIS WAY TO LINEUP. He went the other way, down a corridor of locked doors, and found 3032. This, too, was locked, though phones were ringing inside. He knocked and waited, his breath a pale plume. The building seemed to be unheated.

No one answered. He was knocking again when two bulky-chested black men in short jackets strolled wearily down the corridor toward him. "What you got goin'?" said one. "Want to take a ride?"

"See what I got goin' with cold cases first." They reached around him and punched a code into the lock. He grabbed the closing door.

Homicide Branch had green walls and a pink tile floor and no partitions among the thirty littered desks. Phones jangled. Radios blared. Portable heaters whined. Someone was yelling frenzied obscenities at the far end of the long, narrow room.

Behind him, one of the cops said, "You havin' problems?"

"Looking for a Sergeant Ogen."

"Right through to there. Four desks down."

Ogen was about six four. He had suspenders, a crew cut, and an impassive stare. He wore a large revolver in a shoulder holster. When Dan introduced himself, he didn't offer to shake hands, just pointed to a chair beside his desk. Hardly able to hear himself through the pandemonium, Dan said, "Is there someplace quieter?"

"What?"

"I said, there someplace quiet we can talk?"

"Just a minute," said Ogen, and he went back to his study of the binder he'd been looking at when Dan came in.

At last, he closed it and sighed, then got up and led him to the far end of the room. On the way, Dan noted a blown-up wall poster of Dick Tracy talking on his wrist radio; a chart with colored tape showing trend lines, all headed up; and a map of the District divided into seven parts. Red pushpins dotted it, each bearing a twisted wire pennant with a date. There were a lot of pins.

The room ended in four smaller spaces the size of junior officer's staterooms. Ogen opened a heavy door and motioned him into one.

Inside, the walls and ceiling were completely covered with dirty acoustic tile, the white kind, with small black holes. A fake-walnut table squatted between gray steel swivel chairs. When he sat in one, it sagged backward. He wondered how many murderers had sat in this broken chair, this squalid room. With the door closed, it was quiet now, so quiet that he could hear his lungs pumping air in and out, his heart pumping blood.

Ogen said, "The patrol officers who found the body were out of second district, George-town. Idaho Avenue, if you know that area. There's not much that'd interest you on the PD-two fifty-one."

"What's a PD-two fifty-one?"

"Incident report. I went down to do the death report and take pictures and so on. We've been working it since then." He examined Dan's uniform. "What are you?"

"Navy officer. Why are you investigating this? I mean, why the District police? Isn't the canal federal property?"

"Yeah, it's a national park, but we have jurisdiction till it gets into Virginia. You can

411

call the park police if you want. But I'm afraid you're gonna be stuck with the Municipal CID on this one."

"I didn't mean that."

After a moment, Ogen said, "Good." He seemed neither hostile nor polite, but he was definitely listening to everything Dan said — so closely that it wasn't a conversation, but something else. The detective creaked his chair around and put a form on the table between them. "This is a one nineteen, a background statement. I need to ask you about her habits and so forth."

"Go ahead."

"Okay, Miss Kerry R. Donavan. Your relationship to her?"

"Fiancé."

"Give her a ring?"

"Yeah."

"Set a date?"

"No. Was the ring —"

Ogen consulted a list. "We didn't recover one. She lived with you, correct?"

"That's right."

"How long?"

"Three, four months."

"Did she use drugs?"

"No."

"Sexual habits?"

"What do you — oh. Normal. I mean, heterosexual. Look, you said you talked to Haneghen. Didn't he tell you any of this?"

"I'm talking to you now. Where did she work?"

"At a charity organization. Ninth and G. I think the House runs it."

"Yeah, the House. Who were her friends there?"

He named those he'd met at the Day House and at the kitchen. Ogen listened expressionlessly. "Peace activists?" he said at last.

"Right."

"That would explain the felony trespass on her record."

Dan said that was correct, and that she'd been awaiting sentencing for another trespass charge and one of sabotage. Ogen scrutinized his hands while he explained. When he was done, the detective said, "What are you doing hanging around these people, Lieutenant?"

"Lieutenant commander. I was in love with her. They were her friends."

"Now, she used to live with Haneghen, right? At this commune, or whatever it is?"

He said that was right.

Ogen said, "Did you have the impression this ex-friend resented you takin' her away from him?"

"No. He was always . . . well, not exactly pleasant, but he seemed to accept it."

"But maybe deep down he didn't?"

"I don't think you're going to get very far with Carl Haneghen as a suspect," Dan told him.

"We had a judge kill an eighteen-month-old last year. His secretary-girlfriend left her with him. She wouldn't stop crying. So he threw her against the wall. You'd be surprised at the kind of people who commit murder."

"I don't think it would be Carl," he said again. "And anyway, you said it was probably more than one person."

"I don't recall saying that."

"That's what you said on the phone. Who do you think killed her?"

"That's what we're trying to find out. But you're right, from the scene and the way we found her it was probably multiple assailants. Let's go over this again. You were in Canada. Did you talk to her on the phone while you were there?"

"Yes."

"Everything normal? No mention of threats or scenes or anything out of the ordinary? Think back."

"All she said was that she missed me, and she told me about some minor things that happened down at the kitchen."

"Any mention of anyone giving her trouble, possible admirers, stalkers?"

"No."

"So then she goes down to the towpath. She's riding your bicycle. Your place is how far from the canal?"

"Mile and a half. All downhill."

414

"She go there often? That a normal thing for her?"

He remembered a raucous October night, moonlight on a black domino. . . . "We met near there. We went there to run. She was getting into biking. Yeah, it was normal."

"Anybody else ride with you?"

"Her other friends aren't into exercise."

"So you know that area?"

"I've run it forty, fifty times."

"Isn't it cold to be out running, biking?"

"You generate a lot of heat."

"The patrol guys figured it happened at dusk. Would she be going down there then, or coming back?"

"Most likely coming back."

"Did she often go out after dark?"

"She said once — not long after we met — that she wasn't going to let fear run her life." Dan straightened again, feeling the horror grip him so hard, he felt faint. He wanted to get it over with and leave. He said, "Do you want me to identify the body now?"

"Her parents did that. They came yesterday and took it back north."

"She's gone?"

Ogen nodded, still watching him.

Dan sat with his hands clenched together. The cold air was damp and close, and carried still somehow, some presence or vibration of all the evil that had crouched and lied in this cubicle. "Do you have any idea at all who

415

might have done it? I asked you that when we talked on the phone, but —"

"Like I said, we're working on it."

"You and who else?"

"Just me, so far."

"How many other cases are you working?"

"We had two hundred and thirty homicides last year. Over fifty so far this year. Divide that by fifteen detectives. But we're working it."

"Have there been any other murders down there?"

"There are murders everywhere," said Ogen. "You saw the map. Right now, there's a war on over coke and PCP territories. If you want my instant take on it, you were my first suspect, then her friend Haneghen. But now I figure it's either some sleazebag that fell in lust with her on the breadline, or else there're some loosely organized gangs that work the back streets in Georgetown at night. One of them might have found their way down to the towpath. I'm going to call pawnshops, bike shops, see if anybody's seen a silver Motobecane."

"What you're telling me is that you don't have any idea who killed her, and you don't think you're going to find out."

"A lot depends on luck. Sometimes somebody'll decide to open his mouth. We'll keep the case open till we solve it. But the question in my mind right this second is, how are you doing with this?"

"Not too well. What do you expect me to say?"

"It's tough coming to terms with a murder."

"I don't intend to come to terms with it," Dan told him.

Ogen reexamined his face. "What's that mean?"

"I plan to find out who did it."

"With or without us?"

"Either way."

"You're not trained for this, Mr. Lenson. Get it off your chest if you want. But after that, why don't you go dive in a submarine, or whatever your job is, and let us handle this."

He knew it was unfair, that this detached, inscrutable man was his defense against chaos, but he was too angry to think it through. All he saw was a disorganized, dirty office, a too-small staff overwhelmed with a tidal wave of crime. He didn't think calling pawnshops was going to find Kerry's murderer. He stood up. "I'm going to be calling you every day. She's not gonna be one of these cold cases. Find out who killed her!"

"Thanks for the direction, Lieutenant. And for coming in," said Ogen. At the door, they didn't shake hands.

He started the car, then snapped the key to off instead of putting it into gear. His thighs shook. He felt like throwing up. Drive like this and he'd run somebody down. He wanted to kill, but not at random. Could anybody have been more innocent than Kerry? Could anyone have loved her neighbor more?

At last, he got enough control to turn the engine on again and pull out. He drove aimlessly, drifting westward through noonday traffic. In front of the White House, barricades cut the flow to one lane. Trucks were parked along the wrought-iron fence. Police waved him on as drivers craned their necks. Only when he found himself on the Whitehurst did he understand where he was headed. He came back to himself then and gripped the wheel and took the roundabout exit onto M. He found a parking spot under the loom of Georgetown University's stone towers, locked up, and headed downhill.

The wind was cold, but there were people out hiking and jogging, older couples bundled, young guys striding along in running suits and earbands. A woman on a bicycle, but not her, not her . . . He pushed himself into a walk along the frozen canal. Gravel and then frozen mud and then gravel again crunched under his shoes. He glanced down, to find their glossy surface filmed with snow and ocher dust.

He kept looking downhill, into the trees and brush that fell away down to the roof of the Canoe Club and from there down to the river.

Once he saw a scrap of yellow, and slid down the bank to it. But it wasn't a police tape. Just an old candy wrapper, bleached pale with time and exposure.

At last, he came to the mile marker, a wooden obelisk beside the trail. He stood looking around, shivering as the wind nosed its way under his reefer and nipped at his ears.

A willow across the canal stood dark and sere, branches frozen into the immovable surface. The sky was close and almost black. Somewhere here . . . She'd gotten tired, ridden out to the four- or five-mile mark, then stopped to rest before heading back. And meanwhile, it had grown late, or maybe she'd had trouble with the bike. The chain tended to desprocket. He'd been meaning to look at it, but he'd kept putting it off.

No. No, goddamn it! He pulled his cap off, wiped his eyes on his sleeve, screwed it back on against the insistent wind. He couldn't make it his fault. He insisted on making himself accountable for things that weren't his fault and sometimes not even his business. But someone else had done this. She'd screamed to this unfeeling sky, suffered, and died.

Innocent.

And doomed, like all innocence. Like his was dying now.

Everything was going to be all right? What a puerile, childish faith.

Looking around one last time, he turned back toward the bridge, walking into the on-coming wind, air, welcoming its icy sting on his exquisitely tender frostbitten cheeks.

When he got to the Dorothy Day House, dusk was falling. The windows glowed. He stood looking at the porch swing. It seemed like a long time ago, but it had only been last fall.

He went up the creaking stairs and knocked, listening to children shrieking inside. After a while, the porch light flashed on and Ken Zinkowski peered out. He seemed not to recognize Dan at first. Then he unhooked the outer door. The warmth felt good on his face. He hung his cap and coat and followed Ken's limp down the hall and into the common room.

It was dinnertime, and he knew some of the faces around the big table, and others were new. There were as many kids as ever, the smaller ones howling and food-smeared. Stone-faced women held newborns to opened blouses. A grizzled man in a wheelchair gave Dan a salute, a blanket where his legs should have been. The same oldster he'd noticed on his first visit stared with rapt patience into space.

He found Haneghen organizing mis-matched bowls into rows on the porcelain-topped kitchen table. A Mexican woman was slamming out tortillas on a flour-dusted slab. The ex-priest gave him a sad smile and asked if he was staying to dinner.

"If it's all right. Thanks."

"Ken had a talk with the guy he works for at the Safeway. They're going to let him take the damaged produce. Some of it's bruised, but it's all fairly fresh. All we have to do is go by Tuesdays and Fridays and pick it up."

"That should help. Something different from beans and rice."

"Well, that's what's cheap," Haneghen said. He began ladling tomato soup into bowls, and Dan started carrying them out.

He found a seat between the vet and one of the women. The vet said he'd been in the Happy Valley with the 101st. He'd lost his legs not to a mine but to diabetes. He lived on the street, had a habit, would probably go back to it; but he had to have a fixed address while he was getting treated for tuberculosis. The woman was a war refugee from Guatemala, living here till she could pick up welfare benefits. A heavy-shouldered woman with a Brooklyn accent asked Dan who he was and why he was with them. She reached across the table to flick a finger off his uniform.

Deborah said, "Leave him alone. He's a friend of ours."

When the food was on the table, they joined hands. Haneghen said the Lord's Prayer. Some joined him in English, others in soft

Spanish. They sat, and hands reached out for serving plates. Then Haneghen cleared his throat.

"Before we eat. We have a guest here — in fact, we have several guests. Welcome to our table. But I want to remember somebody who's not here."

A child screamed from upstairs; the old man whispered unendingly to himself as Haneghen took a tortilla from the stack, paused, then tore it apart with his fingers. Taking a piece for himself, he passed one half to his left, the other to his right. He said softly, "This is in memory of those who sacrifice themselves in the name of God."

Next he took a pitcher of juice and said, "This is for those who work in the name of peace, and love for their neighbor."

When it reached him, Dan tore a piece from the hot tortilla and laid it on his plate. Then he put his hand over his eyes for a while, till he was able to eat.

He was saying his good nights when Haneghen came out. "Can we talk for a second before you go?"

"Sure."

"On the porch?"

An errant wind drove dead leaves past like cat's claws scratching down the cracked, empty pavement. Dan caught the distant crackle of shots. It was still going on, the war that was being fought every night on the streets of every city in America.

"I'm going to be leaving soon," Haneghen said. "And somehow I don't think you're going to be coming around very often anymore. So maybe we should say good-bye now."

"Relatives? Change of scene?"

"Lewisburg, Pennsylvania." In the light from within, he could just make out Haneghen's grin. "Minimum security, but it's still a penitentiary."

Dan didn't know what to say. His first impulse was to congratulate him, since it seemed to be something he'd wanted. Or had at least invited, over and over. Instead, he muttered, "How long did they give you?"

"Eight years. I have previous offenses."

"Eight years . . ."

"She was spared that, Dan. At least."

"We discussed it. I told her I'd wait."

"Did you? I thought you might. I knew she was moving away from us, toward something else." He looked out over the darkened grounds of the old soldiers' home, and they both listened to a siren rise slowly and then fall. "But I'm not worried about her. Whatever happens after this life, she's going to be one of the . . . I hesitate to use the word *elect*, that sounds so theological. . . . Anyway, I'm not worried about her. I'm worried about you."

Dan didn't answer. Haneghen said gently,

"How *about* you? What are you feeling about this?"

"I feel like killing whoever killed her. That's how I feel."

"Would it change anything?"

"It would feel right."

"You know what might be a better response? Praying for whoever did it."

"What? Fuck that. Fuck *them*."

"Revenge doesn't change a thing. She'd be the first to tell you that."

He clenched the porch railing, so angry that he had to hold it tightly to keep from striking the pale face next to him.

"Thinking about it?"

"Yeah, I'm thinking. I've heard that before. It appealed to me."

"I thought it did."

"But I'm starting to see where it's selective or something — that some hearts will change and others won't, or can't. . . . Whoever killed her, did it make any difference to him what she believed, how good she was? It didn't make any difference! Did it?"

"Sometimes it does."

"But only if the other person's already halfway, if there's already some enlightenment, or faith, or compassion. If there isn't, all you're doing is delivering the innocent up to evil."

"That's not our judgment to make."

"What if they catch them? What do you

think should happen?"

"What do *you* think should happen?"

"Me? I think they ought to be tortured, then killed. We don't need them around."

"That's another judgment we don't have any right to make," Haneghen told him. "Have you sat with a condemned man in the last hour of his life? I have. He's no different from us. We can't give life. Therefore, we have no right to take it."

Dan stood looking out over the city. Bitterer words than he'd ever spoken came to his lips, quivered there like bubbles, then subsided. He took a deep breath, then another.

He said, "I don't think we can agree, Carl. But I appreciate you making the . . . offering for her. In there."

"We both loved her, Dan." Something moved in the darkness, and he found himself holding Haneghen's hand.

When he got to Lee Highway, the place he remembered seeing there was still open. A White Tower burger joint was next to it, and a bar. Men stood under the neon arguing and drinking from brown paper bags. He looked at the sign for a moment — NATIONAL PAWN, INSTANT CASH FOR ANY ARTICLE OF VALUE — then pushed the door open.

The clerk at the counter tried to sell him a revolver. He said they were safer, easier to clean, and less complicated to use under stress. Dan said he was used to automatics. He eyed the big Colts and Berettas, but suspected a full-size gun would bulge even under winter clothes. Finally, he settled on a smaller, lighter one, a 9-mm automatic. He had to sign a form saying he wasn't a felon or a drug addict. With a box of hollow-points and the tax, it came to $196.

# 22

When he reported back in, Vic and Sparky were already at their desks. They said, "Hi." He muttered something and sat down, not returning their uneasy glances.

His desktop was covered to a depth of several inches, and his inbox had obviously toppled over and been restacked. One huge box crouched on top of everything. Except that perched on top of *it* was an envelope with his name in a feminine hand.

The card was signed by everybody in the office. Some he didn't know well, and some were people he didn't really get along with. But their signatures were there, too, each with a word of condolence. He tossed it in the drawer.

"Sparky. Sparky!"

"Yeah!"

"What is all this shit? What's this box?"

"Uh, I was going to start on that if you didn't come in today. It's the prelim drafts of the tech manuals for handling, quality assurance, and inspection. Twenty-one volumes. They want our comments by the end of the month."

"How's it look on *New Jersey*? We gonna have her ready for deployment?"

"That depends on how you define 'ready.' "

"Okay, talk to me." He leaned back, trying to forget for a few seconds that he'd lost everything that mattered in the world.

The advanced analysis class was much smaller than the introductory one had been. He took a seat in back, making sure everyone saw him. He called to Cottrell, "Hey, Sandy?"

"What?"

"Thanks for the call back on the subcommittee thing. Hey, where's Mei?"

She looked away coldly. "I don't know. I haven't seen her for two or three weeks now."

A clearing of the throat, and Szerenci came in, looking testy. Seeing Dan, he said, "Ah, back from Canada. Did it fly?"

"Seven out of eight."

"Expect a much lower P-sub-S on a battlefield. How's your pacifist friend?"

He dropped his eyes and didn't answer. Szerenci shrugged off his coat and searched for the chalk. "Okay, let's get started."

He launched into a lecture on guerrilla warfare. Dan's hand noted each point without hearing it. He was remembering when Kerry had told Szerenci off at his party. How oldmaidish he'd been, flinching when Evans had called her "dangerous," worrying every time he saw an activist and a military type in speaking distance. But, at the same time, how proud he'd been of her. His hand started to shake and he had to take a couple of deep breaths.

"Now for some numbers. There have been between a hundred and twenty-five and a hundred and fifty wars since the end of World War Two. About two-thirds of those qualify as unconventional wars. Beyond that, or below that on the spectrum of violence, lies the area of even less conventional resistance, which we call 'terrorism.'

"Unless, of course, our guys are doing it. Then they're 'freedom fighters.' But usually it's aimed against us. Why? It's the penalty of power: that when resistance is impossible by conventional armed force, it's transformed into terrorism.

"Example. You all heard this weekend about the bombing of a shopping mall at an Army base in Germany. Twenty-eight deaths. We're not sure yet who's responsible. But, assuming we can find out, what can we do about it? What sort of counterstrike can we make without doing exactly what they want us to, injuring innocent people, turning world opinion against us? Do we have to put Americans on the ground, nose-to-nose, with a body count to match? There are those who think *that's* going to be the face of war in the next century."

Dan took notes automatically. He wasn't thinking about terrorism. He was still seeing her smile, and still remembering her face.

Later that night, he stood at the top of the

steps that led down to the towpath, the gun heavy under his jacket. Around him, the copper-colored lights of the Key Bridge lit every detail of crumbling concrete, drifted trash, naked treetops.

He'd left Szerenci's class at the break, while they still had an hour to go, strolling away as if to the Coke machine. He figured at least half of the class would be willing to say he'd been there the whole period.

He'd never done anything like this before. Just carrying a concealed weapon in the District of Columbia was a major offense. Not that that kept the criminals from doing it. . . . Above him, the stars were gone, blotted out. To the north, the overcast sky pulsated with saffron light. Behind him, the skyscrapers of Rosslyn glittered like a miniature Manhattan.

But down there on the path, beside the canal, was only one vast pool of darkness.

He unzipped his jacket experimentally. His glove caught in it and he fumbled, jammed it. Crap, that wasn't going to work. He'd better just jerk his jacket up with his left hand and go for the gun with his right.

He stood above the blackness as he'd once stood suspended above the screaming, lightless chaos of an Arctic sea. His heart pounded. His kidneys hurt.

Before he could talk himself out of it, he went quickly down, steps scraping in the enclosed stairway, and emerged onto the tow-path.

Down here, the hill and the mass of the trees, bare of leaves but still dense, absorbing light, covered him and everything around him with impenetrable shadow. Fighting the impulse to turn and run, he stepped out. He was wearing his shipboard steel-toes, jeans, and a flannel shirt, as well as a sweater and then a padded jacket over that. A dark blue wool watch cap was pulled down over his ears. He had gloves on, but they weren't heavy enough. His hands were tingling. His face and nose hurt. He ignored this. He stood in the center of the path, swiveling his head from side to side, and slowly the darkness became transparent and lighter shadows seemed to move toward him through the gloom.

The towpath was deserted. Its slaty gray curved away alongside the utter black of the icy canal. The wind was a faint cold breath in his face.

Once again, he debated turning back. In some basic and fatal sense, he stood at the brink of traducing everything he'd once believed.

What would she say? What would she think, seeing him here?

Then he thought, It doesn't matter what she'd think. This is what I have to do, in order to live with her memory.

Looking over his shoulder, he started down

the path. His boots crunched on frozen gravel. Too fast, too fast. He forced himself into a saunter. He kept turning around, feeling as if his back was naked.

He couldn't help wondering if she *did* see him somehow. The wind in the treetops reminded him of that Halloween. Of the time when — what had those drunken idiots been talking about on the bridge? — when spirits came. Could it be possible, that they lived on? Judged, or punished . . . but still an individual, still recognizably you? He'd believed that once, with all the simple faith of a childish heart. In that case, he might see her again. In some future life . . .

But looking at it coldly, he had to conclude this was probably all there was. One of Szerenci's catchphrases: "Free yourself of all illusion." The simplest explanation, and therefore the most likely to be correct: that the cold equations of matter and the void described all that existed. That his own encounter with the dead had been just that, illusion, spun of morphine and stress. One life, seventy or eighty years, then oblivion.

And never, never would he ever meet her or anyone remotely resembling her again.

He was wiping cold tears from his eyes when his neck prickled.

Above him the city was a glowing jewel. The bridge was a floating arch of salmon-colored light. But behind him was only darkness.

His straining ears caught only the faraway descending roar of an airliner. He floated his gaze above the black emptiness, using his peripheral vision. Still nothing, but . . . He slid as quietly as he could off the path, blundering into a crackle of brush, and crouched. He slid the gun out and held it, cocked and locked, thumb on the safety.

Nothing happened. No one came down the path. He waited till his thighs ached, till the cold crept through his boot soles and chilled the steel inserts and, within them, his toes.

Finally, he straightened and went on again, glancing back every few seconds to make sure he wasn't being followed.

He went all the way to the second milepost, lingered there, then walked back. In all that time, he saw no one. He stood by the steps for a few more minutes, shivering, and then climbed them and walked slowly back across the bridge to the car.

Halfway home, he pulled off the road into a lighted lot. He didn't think about it; his hand turned the wheel, his foot tapped the brake, and he was there. He was opening the car door when he realized where he was and what he was doing.

It was a liquor store, and crystallized in his mind was the image of a bottle of Cutty. He could smell it. He could taste it on his tongue. A couple of glasses, straight, no ice, and it wouldn't hurt anymore. . . . He sat staring at the glittering glass and colored labels that filled the window. Any of them would do. As long as it wasn't the one she'd left the note on.

*Please don't. Not till you talk to me. . . .*

He rubbed his forehead, found it slick with sweat.

Look, you know you're going to get drunk sooner or later. One of these nights. So why put yourself through this? You might as well get it over with.

Or was that him thinking? Because there were two people inside his head. One wanted to blot out his regret and rage with the only thing he'd ever found that made him feel as good as everybody else. The other wanted just as desperately not to.

He got out, but before he reached the store, stopped again. Remembering her hands on his face, the night he'd gotten shitfaced in Annapolis. The way she'd reasoned with him after his blackout. And for one despairing moment, he prayed, *Kerry, help me.*

A moment later, his shaking hands groped for the key. Somehow, he backed out of the lot and out onto Lee Highway again. For a moment, he grinned with wolflike glee. But then the smile faded.

With a sinking heart, he knew he wasn't going to be able to do it again.

# 23

He spent the next morning getting things set up for the upcoming operational evaluation aboard *Merrill*. TASMEX I, on the Pacific Coast test range, would be the first operational — meaning, it would be done by fleet personnel rather than contractors — firings of the all-up antiship round.

At eleven o'clock, he picked up the phone and tapped in numbers he knew by heart. Said, "Detective Ogen, please."

He listened to the background noise of the squadroom as he waited, shoving a pen around on a scratch pad, drawing sharks with bared teeth, lashing tails. Finally, the slow voice said, "Ogen here."

"Dan Lenson. Any progress on Miss Donavan's murder?"

"You know, the more time I spend on the phone, the less time I can be out working the street."

"That would make sense, except that every time I call, you're right there in the office."

"You call in the morning, Lieutenant. Late afternoon, evening's when your sleazebags come out to play. That makes my day twelve hours long. Why don't you get off my desk and let me work the case?"

"How many murders have you had since hers?"

"Six. And no, none of them were on the C and O."

"You're telling me she's just another in a —"

"No, I'm telling you I'm working it. And that's all I'm gonna say."

Dan slammed the phone down. Breathing hard, he looked around the office. Burdette and Sakai had their heads down. He got up and went down the corridor, into the head, and washed his hands ferociously, slamming the paper towel into the wastebasket. Knowing even as he did it that he was acting all the angrier because he felt so totally helpless.

At 1120, Lucille put her head in. "Commander? Captain Foster's here. Captain Westerhouse says stand by in the outer office, they'll start the meeting in a few minutes."

He tried to organize his thoughts as he pulled files out of his desk. "Sparky, CO of *New Jersey*'s in the admiral's office. Can you come along?"

But when they got there, Niles's door was closed. Westerhouse was on the sofa, reading that morning's *Early Bird*, the Pentagon-generated world-news summary. The headline read DIA CONFIRMS LIBYAN TIES TO TERROR BOMBING. Carol smiled at them, not interrupting the steady clicking of her keyboard.

The door opened a few minutes later. Niles

436

leaned out. "Come on in, Dale . . . Mr. Lenson . . . Mr. Sakai. You all know Bill Foster." They settled in the office, Dan and Sakai leaning against the window. It looked like rain.

Niles rumbled, "The captain was just telling me about the commissioning."

Foster gave them a quick recap: how President Reagan had arrived by chopper, given a fifteen-minute speech, then formally put her in commission. "He was like a kid, touring the ship. I never saw anybody over ten that happy before."

Niles said, "Bill tells me we're not going to make his sailing date." He didn't sound as enraged as he could have been.

Westerhouse nodded. "Yes, sir, due to the delay on the software. We reported that some time ago."

"But the ABLs and the other equipment are aboard."

"Right, sir, Dan's people got that produced and installed faster than I expected."

Niles said, "Tell me again when we're delivering software."

Dan wondered why, since he'd covered this all in his reports. Finally, he decided it was just to make sure there were no misunderstandings. So he gave a summary brief. He finished, "As a backup, we're working on a lash-up alternate programming set. All I can say is, we'll get it to the ship as soon as

437

humanly possible."

Foster said, "There's been a lot of heat on everybody. I think we've done pretty well."

Niles grunted. "What's your predeployment schedule look like?"

"Structural firing of the sixteen-inch guns. Harpoon firing. Then refresher training, a week in Long Beach to catch our breath; then we'll shove off for the Med."

"We'll have you operational before then," Dan said. Niles tilted back and laced his hands behind his head. A moment later, he came back upright, groped for an Atomic Fireball, and leaned back again.

When the admiral relaxed, so did everyone else. Foster started packing a corncob pipe. "You know . . . I'm already seeing how this is going to be the start of a whole new mindset for surface guys. I came up through destroyers, cruisers. Started out on *Willis Lee*. *Des Moines*. On the *John R. Craig* off Vietnam. I had *Ault* during the Syrian incursion."

Dan sat up. "You were skippering *Ault*, sir? I was the guy directing your gunfire that day."

"Is that right? I remember your voice. Sounded like it wasn't exactly a unanimous decision. . . . Have to compare notes sometime.

"Anyway, I came up through the classic surface pipeline, and tactically we'd think offensively — seize the initiative, strike first, manage the battle in our favor — but our basic mind-set's always been defensive. Defend the carrier. Defend the convoy. Defend ourselves. We left the offensive to the aviators.

"But having Harpoon and now Tomahawk on board — it's going to be like the days when Preble could stand off Tripoli and everybody knew, tick this guy off and he'll blow away your palace."

After a few more pleasantries, Niles and Foster left for lunch with Admiral Willis.

Dan got a dog from the cart and was eating it at his desk when the phone rang. "JCM, Lieutenant Commander Lenson, this is a nonsecure line," he said, holding the phone with a cocked head.

"Dan? Steve here."

"Oh. How are you doing?" It was Manhurin. "Where are you calling from?"

"We're back at Provo. How's the frostbite?"

"Getting better. What you got? There're a million things on my desk." He pulled the scratch pad over.

"It's about T two-oh-seven. The bird you slept with. Here's what we found out. We originally figured it was either the booster not separating or the tailfin shrouds hitting something on the way back after they opened. Well, when you found your missile, there wasn't any booster with it. So that cut the booster nonseparating theory to hell. Then we took a close look at the tail."

439

"That chewed-up area?"

"Yeah. You noticed it, too. The top and starboard fins are gnawed to the point where they finally gave way. Looks like a big beaver got hold of them. Here's what we figure happened. You know you got two cables between the missile and the booster. They come out of the right side, through an access plate, and go back into the booster."

"Right." He reached out for a pub as the Air Force officer talked. He stopped at a diagram of the pyrotechnic separation system headed "Cable cutter at tail cone."

"Well, the booster's bolted to the airframe during launch. When it burns out, there's a ring of shaped-charge explosive that runs around it."

"Right, to blow away the booster and clear the exhaust port. We checked all that out."

"Yeah, but that still leaves the cable. There's a separate cutter for that, inside the tail cone door. It's not explosive. It's pneumatic, actuated by the pressure cartridge that runs the valves and the thrusters. Follow so far?"

His mind jumped ahead. "So what you're getting at is, it doesn't cut clean."

"Right, a half-assed blade strike, or none at all. That's a big cable. It's got a slew of wires in it; it carries the power to run the thrust vector tabs."

"But if it doesn't cut, it'll still tear out of the booster as it blows free."

"Right, only there's a steel bracket that helps the cable bend down as it runs into the booster. It tears out at the roots, but it's still got that bracket hanging on at the end of about a foot of cable. And it flails and flails in that five-hundred-mile-an-hour airstream till it shreds the tailfins. The guidance keeps trimming to correct, but eventually it loses so much control surface, it falls out of the sky. Kerblooey."

He swung his chair, visualizing it. "What's the cutter look like?"

"We opened that port up and, bingo, it's got a big crack in the housing. Factory's taking it apart."

"So it's not thrust tabs, not the booster; it's some sloppy-acting cable cutter? Why'd it take us so long to figure this out?"

"My guess is that sometimes the blade works, sometimes not. It might mean you're getting low pressure off the cartridge. Or grit, corrosion . . . anything that keeps that piston from sliding. But why it took so long . . . well, when it crashed before, when the airframe hit the ground, the cable must have sheared away then. The only way we could have found out what was really going on would have been if we had a soft recovery of a failed bird. Like the one you brought back."

"It's consistent with the pattern of short flights. When's the report due out?"

"Next week."

"Let me have what you got now in rough. We got Block I missiles going to the fleet right now."

Manhurin agreed to overnight-express him their preliminary notes, then hung up. Dan sat back. Maybe that night in the snowstorm hadn't been a complete waste.

At 1700, the bar on the Hill was filled with pols and staff members, reporters and lobbyists, jackets off, ties loosened. Ceiling fans beat hopelessly at cigar smoke. He found a booth where he could watch the door. At twenty after, Sandy Cottrell dusted rain off her hat and shook her hair out. She looked around, saw his lifted hand, and threaded her way toward him. Faces turned, and she called back greetings, but not as obstreperously as she usually did. She looked drawn and somehow subdued as she slid in opposite him. "Sorry I'm late. A lot's been happening in my life."

"How's the new job working out? Kinematics, was that it? You sounded unhappy with it."

"I was. It's Kinetic Solutions, and the job is past tense."

"Gee, I'm sorry to hear that."

"Don't be. I left voluntarily. I'm a free agent at the moment. Rog wants me back, but I'm holding off on that, too. Till I get a couple of things straightened out."

The waiter stopped at their table. She ordered a Perrier and twist. Dan asked for a draft. When he left, she said, "I don't understand why you called. You didn't seem very interested the last time we got together. Though my recollection may be a bit fuzzy."

"It's not exactly a date," Dan said. He sucked a breath, then hurled himself in. "Do you remember my Christmas party? The girl who was there?" She nodded, and he went on to tell her about the engagement and then about Kerry's murder. She lost the suspicious look halfway through. "So I'm sorry if I was rude to you at the reception. We were going to get married. And now she's dead."

Their drinks came. He actually had his hands on the cool curved glass when he remembered. Said to the waiter, "What's this?"

"What you ordered, sir. Miller draft?"

He almost said, "Oh. Okay," especially since Cottrell was squinting at him again. And he wanted a beer; he *needed* a beer. But he made himself say, "My mistake. I'll pay for it, but could you take it away and bring me a coffee instead? Thanks."

The waiter said sure, as if people did that every day, and left. Dan told her, "Sorry, I'm still . . . confused, I guess. Anyway, that's where my life is at the moment." He leaned back, wishing he'd never have to tell the story again. And at the same time, he felt inexplicably lighter just seeing the sym-

443

pathy in Cottrell's eyes.

"Jesus, I'm sorry. And the cops have no idea who killed her?"

"I'm not saying it's their fault, but — Christ, they had two hundred and thirty murders in this city last year. There're only about a dozen detectives. They're not going to find him."

A suit leaned over the table. "Sandy, hi, you gonna help us out on the Bialas hearing?"

"Oh, I'm on personal time now, all right? Call me at Rog's office next week; we'll talk then." He left and Cottrell frowned. "Trial Lawyers Association. . . . Anyway . . . Look, I understand now. That's awful. But why did you want to see me?"

"Well, I don't have too many close friends here. I know we didn't . . . hit it off, and all that, and I'm sorry. I like you, but . . . Anyway, the point I'm sort of groping around for is that you're the closest thing to a woman friend I've got."

"Okay, and?"

He glanced around, making sure the lobbyists and staffers were intent on their own concerns, their own deals. "I want you to help me find out who killed her."

"You mean, like to have Roger call Marion Barry? Put pressure on to get more resources committed —"

"No. I want something else. Something personal."

Her eyes narrowed again. "Something *per-*

*sonal.* What? Or is this just a ploy for a little stopgap bedtime companionship?"

Lowering his voice, he told her, "No, Sandy. I want you to help me set a trap."

# 24

Friday night — 6:00 P.M., which in March meant that night was falling.

He stood at the top of the steps once more, looking down again on the place that obsessed him now even in his dreams. Beneath him, the canal lay like a walled-in road under the stone battlements of Georgetown University. To his right were the complex of bridges and viaducts that channeled traffic from Arlington and downtown D.C. into the trendy shopping areas around M. A few brightly colored patches bobbed in the failing light: hikers, bikers, and joggers. They were leaving now, streaming up past him, abandoning the park to darkness.

Beside him, Cottrell said, "How about giving me a hand with this?"

Shaking off reverie, he hoisted her bike to his shoulder and carried it down the steps. It was light, some kind of titanium-framed wonder. Beneath the viaduct, the shadows were dark as the interior of a submerged wreck. The wind smelled like fear.

Cottrell had seemed subdued when he'd met up with her in the lot of the Rosslyn Marriott. Her normally flaming cheeks were like wax. She was dressed in a blue nylon windbreaker and stretch biking pants and high-tops. Her blond frizz was stuffed under a beret. Now she shivered, looking around. "Was this where it happened?"

"Out west, along the path. Got your whistle?"

"Right here. When?"

"They're not sure. Probably not much later than this."

"Great." She shivered again and started searching through her pockets. "Not yet, damn it. I need a butt before I do this."

He paced around, eager to get started, yet at the same time dreading it. He'd imagined this again and again lying through the nights. Imagined hearing Sandy's whistle . . . running to catch up to her. Then afterward . . . driving across the Chesapeake Bay Bridge, the gun spinning away and down into the blue.

But in between, what he actually *did* — he hadn't imagined that, only a confused blur of blood and shouting.

An early cricket sawed in the underbrush. The red star of her cigarette glowed. Then, cursing, she suddenly slapped at her side.

"What's wrong?"

"Got to quit this dirty habit. I just burned a fucking hole in this brand-new jacket, can you believe that?"

"I'm sorry. I'll get you another one."

"Forget it. You know, I'm not sure why I'm doing this. Is it for thrills? I don't feel thrilled."

447

"You did it because I asked you to. And I appreciate it."

"Sandy's on-call bait service. Making the world safe for little girls to go walking in the dark. Don't lag back, now. I don't want to blow this fucking whistle and not have anything happen."

"I'll be behind you. And look —"

"What?"

"Once it starts, if anything starts, haul ass and don't look back. I don't want you to get involved."

"Seems to me I'm about as involved as I can get."

"I mean — never mind. But if you hear shooting, don't come back."

"Don't worry about that. I'll be breaking the sound barrier." She swung herself up, almost toppled, then regained control and wobbled off into the dusk. He waited, letting her get a head start. Then started after her at a brisk walk.

The dark came down liked a black blade not long after they left the bridge. It fell over the path and over the trees, over the canal and the tangled underbrush and scrub that fell away on his left, down toward the river. When the canal ran straight, he could see the pale blue patch that was her back. She was going slowly, sticking to the right-hand side, away from the downslope. But then they'd come to a curve, and he couldn't see her anymore. Then he'd walk faster, fighting the urge to run. His mouth tasted as if he was sucking pennies. The gun was as hard and dangerous-feeling against his ribs as if it was pointed at himself.

Not for the first time, he wondered if this was smart. Ogen had warned him to stick to what he knew.

But it was the only way he could think of that had even the slightest chance of finding whoever had murdered Kerry.

And that wasn't all he wanted to do. He had to admit that, striding along, sweeping his attention from side to side, pricking each shadow with an adrenaline-sharpened stare.

Once he found him, he intended to kill him.

The trouble was, along with the fear, along with the hate, he felt shame. After all the talks with Carl, after Kerry's example, after seeing them stand up against violence — what was he doing? Forging another link in the chain of murder. Not just willing to kill, *eager* to.

But then, as if his brain were some antiquated mechanical computer, it made an almost-audible *kachunk* and called up another template. He wasn't perpetuating violence. He was establishing deterrence. If the police and the courts could no longer mete out justice, what was the alternative? Purely and only a return to the most primitive and most basic system of justice: revenge.

But if he killed those who killed, would the killing ever end?

But if no one punished those who did evil, wouldn't evil rule the world?

Halting for a moment, he listened to the gurgle of black water, the receding crackle of gravel beneath racing tires. His whole body felt heavy, massive, dense as the lead in the bullets he carried.

Which was the right way to view the world?

*Was* there a right way to view the world?

Or was it as Szerenci taught — that the universe was simply raw material, to be re-interpreted and refashioned moment by moment by every individual?

Red lights sparkled far off, above the black scrawl of a budding tree. He stared, then blinked, pushing himself into motion again. For a moment, the far-off lights had seemed to move; and his tired brain had taken him, for a second, back to sea.

Abruptly, he wished for the familiar hermetic world of a destroyer's bridge. As dark as this, but in a different way. Instead of the pale curve of the towpath, the broad curve of the wake, glowing and whirling with pale green fire. Instead of the whine of traffic the roar of the blowers, the gyro drone, the endless chant of the engines humming through the steel hull. Instead of distant streetlights, the slowly moving red and green and white lights of ships. Far at first, then riding with slow majesty closer and closer. Till through raised binoculars they jumped close, other selves moving across the empty deep . . .

At sea, you ran the bridge team from night orders. Directions so simmered thick over centuries of experience, there was no contingency they couldn't cover, from mutiny to meteors.

But there weren't any night orders to tell you how to live. There wasn't any captain. Or if there was, he didn't answer when you hit the buzzer and put your ear to the voice tube. To hear only the hollow sigh of an empty seashell, and the frantic pounding of your pulse.

He stood alone under a wheeling universe of stars. And remembered another night, long ago, and a story Al Evlin had told him on the midwatch. About the holy man who had two disciples who complained they never got enough to eat.

Evlin said the prophet had given them each a chicken. He said, "Go and kill them where nobody can see." The first man went behind a house and killed the chicken. The second man walked around for two days, carrying the chicken, and then came back. The holy man said, "Why didn't you kill it?" And the man said, "Wherever I go, the chicken sees."

He'd blinked, there on the doomed *Ryan*'s bridge, and wondered, Who was the chicken?

He still didn't know.

451

★ ★ ★

Sometime later, he came to a straightaway and saw a figure ahead, not on a bike, but standing at the edge of the canal. It was so dark, he wasn't sure it was her till he was only a few steps away. He took his hand off the pistol. "Sandy! You all right?"

"Yeah. Just resting."

"You sound winded."

"Fucking cigarettes. But I still gotta have 'em." A flame flared. He looked away instantly, but afterimages still pulsated like luminescent jellyfish.

She said hoarsely, "Think this is doing any good?"

"I don't know. I haven't seen anybody yet."

"I don't think anybody comes here after dark."

"Maybe not."

"And if there's never anybody on the fucking trail at night, why would the guys you want come down here? Ever thought of that?"

He didn't answer. She inhaled again, making the cigarette tip glow, and he saw her eyes, squinted closed, ember-lit. Then he heard the *phut-hiss* as the butt hit the water. "Saddling up."

She disappeared again into the gloom. Too late, he thought of telling her to put her light on. Attract some attention, plus, she wouldn't steer herself into the canal. As if she could hear him, he saw the cone of white light come on, narrow, not all that bright, but just enough to light the path ahead.

He checked his watch when they reached the turnaround point at the old wooden locks. Eight o'clock. They sat on the lock, feet dangling. "Man," she said, "I'm wheezing. That's the next thing, cutting these out. Every one I smoke, I think, That's the last one. Then I want another. . . . You ever smoke?"

"No, I never did."

"Pretty soon, I'll be Ms. Clean Living. Probably weigh two hundred pounds."

"What do you mean? You quit drinking?"

"Actually, booze wasn't my drug of choice. I was putting half my salary up my nose. But I've been off everything for two months now. I'll be picking up my red chip next."

"What's a red chip?"

"AA talk for being clean for ninety days. I'm in Alcoholics Anonymous."

"Is that right? Does it work?"

"If you work it."

He didn't know what that meant; it sounded flip. But before he realized it, he was telling her about his own battle to stay sober. He told her how he kept going to the cupboard to read Kerry's note. "Like she's still talking to me. But I don't know how long I can keep it up."

"Do you really drink that much?"

"Not every day, but when I get started, I can't stop."

"That sounds like it all right. Ever been to a meeting? There are people there who've been sober for years."

"You mean who stopped drinking? I don't need to stop. I just wish I could cut down."

"Well, you might want to hear what some of them say. Where's your office? Crystal City? I'll find out where the nearest meeting is and call you."

"What's the latest with you and Szerenci?" he asked her.

"That's kind of on hold for now. But if I can get through this, I don't know — I've got a lot of stuff to work through — we might get married. Not too far down the line."

"Really? I didn't get the impression you were into monogamy."

"That's a nice thing to say to somebody who's hanging her ass out here for you."

"I'm sorry. I guess it was kind of —"

"That's okay. I know what you mean. I'm trying to let go of that shit, too."

They sat silently for a time. At last, she said, kicking the wood with a *thunk* that made him flinch, "Look, lemme ask you this. What if nobody shows up tonight? If I just troll myself back and forth here and nothing happens?"

"We try again next week."

"For how long?"

"Till something happens."

"I'm not spending my Friday nights here for the rest of my life, Dan."

"Then I'll ask somebody else."

"I hate to tell you this, but I don't think anybody else is going to do this for you. In fact, halfway down that path, I decided this is my last time."

He didn't answer, and she prodded, "Did you hear me? I'm not doing this again. It's too dangerous. We should leave it to the cops."

"I heard you. So, are you ready to head back?"

He was exhausted. He wanted just to keep sitting there — or, better, to lie back on the cold ground and flake out for about an hour — but he forced himself to his feet again. The whir of the bike receded into the dark, and he set out again, past thinking whether or not it was right.

They were almost back to their starting point, the viaduct leading over the canal to Georgetown, when he noticed she'd stopped again.

His eyes were better adapted now to the city light that came back from the sky. Brighter than the stars, but different, the metallic unwholesome radiance yielded from the torment of heavy atoms: copper, sodium, beryllium. He could see by it, just enough to sense the black shape that was her on her bike.

Then he saw she wasn't alone. Other shapes surrounded her. He thought for a moment they were trash cans or mileposts, something inanimate.

Then he heard the voices.

He broke into a sprint, instantly reproaching himself. He'd lagged back. . . . Should have kept closer to her. . . . He prayed desperately for nothing to happen before he got there. His boots pounded on the gravel so loudly, he couldn't believe they didn't hear him. He started to yell, then let the sound die in his throat.

Surprise was the key to winning a fight. Surprise, speed, and ordnance on target.

He pulled up his jacket and yanked the Colt out. He ran fifty more yards, then slid off the gravel path and into the dry, dead, whispering grass that bounded the precipitous void that was the brush-lined ravine.

"I don't have anything you want." Cottrell was trying to reason with them. "I don't have any money. Let me go!"

"You best have something we want, bitch."

The voice was young but utterly cold. It made the hairs rise on the back of his neck. All his fatigue and sleepiness had vanished. The night enfolded them, but it was as if he could see everything, hear everything, as if the gain on his senses had been turned up a hundred times. The gun felt slippery and he realized he was bearing down on the trigger. He took his finger off it and placed his boots gently through the dead grass. He was lower than they were. Another few yards and he'd be between them and the ravine.

"You want the bike? Go ahead. Take it."

"We doin' just that, bitch." Coughs and laughter from the dark. "Yeah . . . what else you got there? Got you a wallet? Cigarettes?"

It was just as if he were there, God help him . . . and the frightened voice wasn't Sandy's; it was Kerry's. . . .

A muffled cry, and a voice muttered, "Nothin' here, Peterbilt. She don't got shi'."

"Nothin' but what between her legs, man."

Cottrell screamed suddenly, a full-throated, incredibly loud sound that rang off the stone walls across the canal. His name was part of it. Then it was cut off, and somebody laughed, low and gay. "He ain' here. What you gon' do now, honey?" someone crooned.

He stopped, knee-high in dry brush. He sucked air, trying to slow his runaway breathing. A scraping sound moved toward him. Her shoes, on the pathway. So he had that right — they were dragging her into the ravine. But what he hadn't anticipated was being unable to tell which shape was her and which was them.

He shouted out as loudly and harshly as he could. "Let go of her. Get back!"

The shadows stopped. "Who the fuck is that?"

457

"Hold on to her, man. Who the fuck's that, man? Where he come from?"

Suddenly, he felt cold. The gun steadied in his hands. His breathing slowed. Movement and sound slowed. It was the fire curtain coming down, the separation of observing self from the body. An impenetrable barrier between his emotions and the one who watched from within his heart. . . . He felt calm now, icy-calm.

"I'm here, Sandy," he said.

He had the 9-mm straight out now, two-handed, pointing it at the only figure he could make out as standing off to the side. The safety came off with a snap.

"Who the fu' is that?"

"I've got a gun. Let her go."

"Didn't you got that thirty-two, LeCool? He say he got a gun."

"He ain't got no gun."

"Told you we shouldn't of come down here."

They sounded younger than he'd expected. "Let her go!" he yelled, and pulled the trigger, swinging the muzzle aside at the last instant before it went off.

The muzzle flash showed him three frozen figures, and a fourth, crouched, arm twisted behind her. "Shee-it," someone said. "He really *do* got a gun."

Then one of the shadows was running toward him. He jerked around, tightening his grip, and almost fired before she screamed,

"It's me. It's me, Dan. *Shoot them!*"

They stood rooted. He rasped out, "Don't move. Sandy, go get the cops."

"What's going on, man? Who are you?"

"You killed somebody here. Another woman. Sandy, *go* —"

"Just a minute, I'm catching my fucking breath."

"No, no, no. We never been down here before. We from Woodley Park."

"We never killed nobody, man. We's robbers, but we ain't —"

"We leaving. Get away from this crazy man."

"Stay where you are. Stay where you are!"

"Dan! Are you letting them get away? *Dan!*"

He was still holding the gun on them, but he heard a jingle of metal, the scrape of shoes. He yelled again for them to stop, but the stealthy retreat did not cease. He could kill them all if he fired now. If he fired *now* —

They'd tried to rob Sandy, been dragging her toward the ravine.

But they were *kids*.

But they were old enough to be criminals. Maybe even old enough, in a pack like this, to kill.

His finger tightened. He sucked a breath, aligning the black mass of the pistol's slide on the one he figured was nearest.

Murmurs. The scrape and crunch of gravel, faint, furtive.

They wheeled suddenly, and he heard their striding steps, light and long. But before they faded, a taunting voice floated above the still, dark water. "We come back, motherfucker. Come back with guns. We find you here, we shoot you daid."

"Shit," Cottrell muttered. Her voice shook, and when he looked toward her, he saw she was sitting on the path. He suddenly became aware he had to piss. The muscles of his arm were cramping. He brought it down along his leg. The hammer slipped as he was trying to lower it, and he came within a wet hair of shooting himself in the foot. "Christ," he muttered, his voice as shaky as hers.

"What the hell do you think you're doing?"

"Putting this on safe." He wobbled over to her on his noodly legs and squatted on cold gravel.

"Jesus, Dan. *Jesus.* What the hell took you so long?"

"I was trying to get between you and the ravine."

"I thought you were gone. And then, when you shot, you missed them."

"That was a warning shot. I didn't know if it was them."

"If it was *who?* They took my bike. They took my purse. And you heard those . . . those little assholes. They were getting ready to —"

"They didn't hurt you, Sandy. We stopped anything bad from happening."

She nearly screamed, "What do you mean, *nothing happened?* Those little monsters were squeezing my tits. They were dragging me down there to rape me. Is that *nothing?*"

"I know. Okay, listen, I know." He couldn't tell her what was going on; he couldn't tell himself. Just that a hurricane was whirling in his chest. If they'd hurt her, he could have shot them. If they'd attacked . . . but he hadn't done a thing. He'd let them get away.

He understood with a sinking heart then that it was hopeless. He'd never find Kerry's killers, and neither would the police. It might have been the twisted hardly more than children he'd faced tonight. Or their older brothers, or someone entirely different . . . black or white. . . .

What he understood now was that evil existed. He'd stood face-to-face with it that night. Heard it in human voices. Deprived? Abused? He'd grown up with hunger and beatings. He didn't buy that as an excuse.

It existed, and she'd been defenseless when it found her.

Cottrell was still spitting curses. "Okay, call me stupid, but I don't get it. I put my ass on the line to lure those animals down here. I thought you meant what you said."

"I did. I was about to start shooting when they let go of you. I just didn't know if they were the ones who killed her."

"No, tell the fucking truth. What happened

461

was, you just wimped out when it came time to actually *do* something. You just fucking wimped out."

He blew out, feeling incredibly fatigued. He checked the gun again, then shoved it back under his belt. "Whatever you say. Let's get out of here, okay?"

"Great, shithead, but count me out if you think I'm ever going to trust you again." She wrenched at the bike, pulling it upright, then thrust it violently at him. She stalked away, erect and unspeaking. After a second or two, he followed.

She reached the stairs a few paces ahead of him and started up. He was pushing her bike. One of the wheels must have gotten bent. It squeaked as it went around.

He was hoisting it, getting ready to follow her up, when a voice said from under the bridge, "Don' move."

He froze, cycle balanced awkwardly on his shoulder, as a man in a black nylon jacket stepped halfway out from the darkness. Something gleamed in his hand. He couldn't tell what it was, gun or knife. His own weapon was out of reach, shoved deep into his pants.

"My frien' got killed, too."

"What?"

"Another gang. She got killed. Don't move. You know, us didn't mean to hurt that other girl you talkin' about. She your wife, right?"

"What are you talking about?" He felt

weird, as if he were floating. He had to remind himself he was in danger. He shifted his feet, getting the bike ready to throw. Knock him off balance, if he was lucky, long enough to go for his own gun. . . . The other took another step out from the shadows and became not a man but a small boy, no more than eleven, shaking with fear.

"Us didn't mean to kill her. Reeney said they was only supposed just to rough her up, then give her . . . this. This you, right? I heard her yelling for you. Is you him?"

In what felt like a trance, he took the extended envelope.

"Only some of the older guys, you know, they doing that angel dust, and it got out of hand. So that was what it was. I wouldn't do nothing like that. . . . I told you about my frien'."

Then he was gone, the black cap melting back into the darkness.

Sandy came slowly back down the steps, toward the fading scuffle of footsteps. She said, "What did *he* want? Was that one of them?"

"I think so." Dan stared at the envelope. Then shook himself, hoisted the bike again, and carried it up to the street. The river spread below them, the bridge flaming with light, the city flaming and sparkling away into the distance. It was so bright, it hurt his eyes. He propped the bike against the bridge railing and took out the soiled, crumpled envelope.

It was still sealed. It had his name on it. He shook his head, uncomprehending, and tore it open.

All that was inside was an anonymous scrap of white paper. Carefully penciled block lettering read: "Family is the most valuable thing there is."

Cottrell said, "Look, I'm sorry I blew up at you down there. I was scared."

"I was scared, too."

"You didn't wimp out. Maybe you did the right thing."

"Maybe," he said. "I don't know, Sandy. Sometimes it's real hard to tell."

He stayed alert all the way back to the car, but they didn't see anyone else.

# 25

"It was the same thing Colonel Zhang said in the restaurant," he said the next morning, in Attucks's office.

Across from him, the agent leaned on one arm, forefinger extending alongside his right eye. Pat Bepko sat to the side, equally intent. They had both remained motionless through his story. Their initial attitude had been skeptical. "So now you want to cooperate" had been Bepko's words when he'd phoned to ask for a meeting.

Now he was explaining why. Attucks's office was in the huge moated FBI building on Ninth and E. Dan had been talking for nearly half an hour. Now he fell silent and waited for their reaction.

Neither spoke for a time. Bepko smoked reflectively. Attucks looked out the window, down at the city.

"The note?" the FBI man said at last. Dan passed it over. He examined the paper, the envelope, and the printing, then shook his head. "Could have come from any dime store in the District."

"It sounds to me like they put these guys up to scare her. Or scare me, through her. Frighten her, rough her up, then give her the letter, addressed to me. I read it and get the

465

point: give them what they want, or she gets hurt."

"Only it didn't happen quite that way," said Bepko softly.

"Obviously discovering that makes a difference in how I feel about cooperating with you."

Contemplative silence again. At last, Attucks rose and took a turn around the room. "Obviously. But the question that occurs to me is: They haven't contacted you since then? Since your fiancée's death?"

"No."

"They know it went wrong. So they know they no longer have that handle on you. Why should you come back, offer to help them?"

He took a deep breath. "I've thought about that. First, they probably don't suspect I know they were linked to it. Assuming I don't, and I have loyalty problems, or money problems, or both — which you said they'd probably already found out about — wouldn't it make sense for me to have second thoughts? And look them up again?"

They considered this. "It might be credible," said Bepko. "Sort of a belated walk-in."

"It could also be risky," said Attucks. "Using an urban gang for threats, enforcement — that's new, a disturbing development. Could get dangerous fast, if you slip up. Or even if you don't, if they begin to suspect you for some other reason. Does that put you off?"

466

"No," said Dan. "As long as we can nail whoever put that gang out on that trail that night, looking for her. And that reminds me." He went over what the boy had said again, finishing with "And he mentioned a name. Something like Reeney. And I thought, There's a guy in D.C. Homicide named Joe Ogen who seems to know the gang scene. Or says he does. Maybe he could make something out of that."

"A slim lead, but we'll pass it on," said Attucks, making a note.

"About helping us. Am I hearing that's your sole motivation? Revenge?" Bepko squinted at him doubtfully.

"Pretty much. Yeah. Why? Isn't that enough?"

"Suppose we say yes? Are you prepared to follow orders?"

"Sure. Though I still have things I want to get finished up around the office here before I leave, too."

Bepko said, "All you need to do is the foreplay, get Zhang hot. Then we'll go in and fuck him."

"Okay. But I'll need a letter."

Attucks looked blank. "Letter?"

"Yeah, stating what you want me to do, and that it's being done on behalf of the FBI and NIS. I don't want the Navy coming back and charging me with spying, and you guys hold up your hands and say, 'Who? Never heard of the guy.' Call it paranoia."

"I call it covering your one-and-only ass, and it makes sense to me," said Bepko.

"With a hand-carried copy to Admiral Niles. And he signs off on it."

"Done. Maybe I should say now that we'll cover any incidental expenses you incur — say like he wants to meet you for dinner at 1787 and you get stuck with the tab. Though they'll usually pick up anything like that."

"Save the receipt," said Bepko.

"But *don't* make a big deal of it," said Attucks. "That could tip him off you're expecting to be reimbursed. Enough about restaurants. Your side of the deal: Give Zhang a call. Tell him you got what he wanted — a unit phone book, was that it? That's a common way to start — and set up a meet."

"One piece of advice," Bepko said. "Don't act too eager. Reluctance, suspicion, and a touch of cupidity play a lot more believably."

"When do you want me to make the contact?"

"You're sure you want to go through with this? No more playing coy?"

"I told you. I'm on board now."

"Then there's no time like the present." Attucks pulled a file folder off his desk. He put Zhang's card, the embassy card Dan had turned in through Toya, in front of him; then shoved his phone across.

After a moment, Dan picked it up. He

tapped in the number and took a couple of deep breaths while it rang.

The woman who answered said Mr. Zhang was not in town. He was in Mexico City, observing a hemisphere security conference. Before he had time to register disappointment, she suggested he speak with the assistant air attaché, Lt. Col. Li Chenbin. Dan said all right. Hadn't it been somebody called "Li" Zhang wanted him to meet?

Bepko and Attucks watched silently. He looked away from them, rubbing his mouth.

A new voice came on the line. It spoke in Chinese, then quickly switched to a fast, colloquial English. When Dan introduced himself, the man said yes, he'd heard Dan's name before. "How can I be of service to you, Mr. Lenson?"

"Well, I have something Mr. Zhang — Mr. Xinhu — which is his name?"

"Zhang is his last name. Mr. Zhang is correct."

"I have something he was interested in. A phone book. For the Joint Cruise Missiles Office." Bepko had advised him not to act eager. But he had to keep his real emotions from showing, and that was hard. "He said it was worth something to him."

The other man didn't react for a moment. Then he said, "Well, I'm due at the airport soon, as it happens. Headed for Europe."

"When will you be back?"

"Not for a week or so, and things are busy after that. Where will you be the week of the eighth?"

He ran down his itinerary. Li kept raising objections: He would not be available; it was not a good time; he would be on travel. Finally, Dan said, "Well, I guess we can't work this out. Sorry I bothered you, and thanks for your time." Bepko and Attucks exchanged startled glances.

The voice on the other end said, "Wait. Let me make sure we have your number. . . . It's in Arlington, right?"

"That's right. I live on Cleveland Street." He gave him the number at his apartment. "Don't call me at the office, all right?"

"No, I wouldn't do that. You travel a great deal in your position, don't you?"

"I sure do."

"Where?"

"Well — Florida, Texas, the West Coast —"

"Perhaps we can set something up. It might not be right away, though."

When Dan hung up, he blew out. "I don't think he wants to see me."

"He's suspicious. Which I'd be, in his shoes."

"Or else he's got something else working, some other way into the project," Attucks said. Bepko looked dismayed.

Feeling somehow as if he'd failed, Dan said. "So what do I do now?"

"Just wait," said Bepko. "You're in play now. He may come back. He may not. Welcome to the glamorous world of counterespionage. Eighty percent of our time in this business amounts to variations on standing around with our thumb up our collective ass. So stay in touch, and thanks for coming in."

Dan stood. They waited, Attucks slowly tapping a pencil against his phone. He searched for some parting comment, but didn't find anything inspiring to say. So finally he just picked up his cap and left.

# 26

Some weeks later, he sat belted in as the plane crayoned white circles above Southern California. The crowded interior stank of sweat and alcohol. Another half hour, the pilot had promised, and that had been forty minutes ago. He caught the sweet smell of whiskey as the drink cart rattled nearer. Another round of complimentary beverages. He loosened his tie even more, wondering what had gotten into him to travel in blues.

In spite of himself, he eyed the cart as it paused beside him. The cute little bottles that tinkled so lightly, that glowed amber and clear and gold and ruby. . . . He leaned back, closed his eyes, and reached deep inside. And when the flight attendant asked him what she could get him, he said all he wanted was an orange juice.

He was amazed. So far, it was working. It wasn't *easy,* but it was working.

Sandy had called him after their night on the towpath. She asked if he wanted to go to an AA meeting with her. She knew of one not far from his apartment. "You sounded serious about wanting to do something. Are you?"

"I'm serious, I think."

"Can you do it alone?"

He thought about the racks of beer at the

7-Eleven, about drink menus at restaurants, about wetting-down parties, hail and fare-wells, tailgate parties. . . . "No, I can't."

"That's called being honest. Then if you can't alone — and you really want to — you better come with me."

They met in the basement of a church in Ballston. It wasn't what he'd thought it would be like. A speaker talked about how he'd done it. Dan could relate to everything he said. And they weren't selling anything, as far as he could see. Just the chance of getting some shit off his back, stuff he'd been carrying around for years. So he went back the next week. And found another meeting, in Crystal City, a lunchtime brown-bag one that met in a conference room at Crystal Plaza.

He hadn't done much else but that since the incident on the towpath. The only thing he had left to do was work late and go to AA meetings. It was that or go crazy.

It had taken a couple of weeks, but at last the assistant air attaché had called back. They'd gone around for a while about where to meet. At last, they'd settled on San Diego. Li said he'd be in Silicon Valley at a conference, that he could fly down for a day. Only he didn't say exactly where they'd meet. Instead, he gave him a number to call when he arrived in California.

Spycraft, Dan figured.

And after that, he'd be getting under way

with *Merrill*. Still sealed into the aircraft, beginning its thirtieth circle in the holding pattern, he yearned for it. Sakai and Burdette had gone on ahead to get things set up. At sea, damn it, maybe he could shake some of this depression. Quit thinking about everything he'd lost . . .

"You in the Navy?"

The middle-aged civilian next to him hadn't said a word the whole flight from Cincinnati.

"Yeah."

"My neighbor's son's on the *Thomas Edison*. Ever heard of it?"

"A missile boat?"

"No, a submarine."

Dan said right, a missile submarine. The civilian said, "What're you going to do about this guy Khaddafi?"

"What about him? I haven't been keeping up with the news."

"All this terrorism he's sponsoring. Why don't we go in and bomb that crazy fuck?"

"They decide things like that a lot higher than me, mister."

"This is your pilot speaking. Sorry to have to tell you this, but there's going to be a slight additional delay before we actually get into the landing pipeline . . ."

San Diego was sunny, as always. When they came off the freeway, he scanned the forest of masts and upperworks for *New Jersey*'s immense cruise-liner funnels. Then remembered: She was in the Med now, centerpiece of the new battle group.

At the foot of the pier, a petty officer in a helmet liner held up a palm from a sentry box. Dan pulled his AWOL bag and his hanging gear out of the trunk and paid the cabbie. Then saw the line of phone booths, many occupied by sailors in dungarees. He hesitated, then stacked his bags. He folded the door closed on hot, sticky air.

He'd gone over this again and again in his mind, but it took less than a minute. A Chinese-accented voice answered, Lieutenant Colonel Li Chenbin's. He cleared his throat and said, "I'm calling about the uh . . . air conditioner you have for sale."

"Meet me at Balboa Park. At the organ pavilion. Eight P.M."

He repeated it and depressed the switch. He checked for the dial tone, then dropped another quarter and dialed a second number. He said into the receiver, "I'm here. I made the call. Balboa Park. At the organ pavilion. Twenty hundred."

Bepko's voice: "Got it. See you there."

Heading down the pier, just like so many times before . . . sweating under blue wool . . . The familiar smells of fuel and steam surrounded him. Beneath the gray cliff of USS *Peleliu*, one of the new helicopter assault ships, vans were loading up with marines. Passing sailors in whites saluted. He nodded back, hands occupied.

There she was, outboard another *Spru*-can. He set the luggage down on the stained concrete and propped his shoe against a bollard.

San Diego Bay was placid today, translucent beneath a softening sheen of oil near the piers, like Vaseline smeared over a camera lens. Beyond it lay the Silver Strand, the line of peninsula leading to North Island and Coronado, and past that, distant and blue as Gibraltar, Point Loma, like a great ship headed out to sea.

"Excuse me, sir. Commander Lenson, sir?" a young seaman, expression earnest.

Dan returned his salute. "Afternoon. Yeah, I'm Lenson."

"Office of the deck sent me down, sir. Captain said to take you to his cabin soon as you showed up."

He followed up the laddered brow onto the fantail. The feel of hollow steel beneath his feet and the familiar whoosh of blowers told him that even though he wasn't, in a strange way he was home again.

He prebriefed the skipper, "Duke" Cannady, the executive officer, and the missile officer in the commanding officer's in-port cabin, over coffee and yellow sheet cake. Sakai and Burdette were there, too, and the fire

476

control chief, and civilian tech reps from the test range and Convair. The stateroom was just big enough, with extra chairs brought in.

Cannady began by apologizing for bunking the rider team in chief's berthing. Dan said that was fine, that he didn't want to move people out of their staterooms. Then he started the presentation.

During the next five days, they would be conducting the first operational evaluation of the missile/ship team. Up to now, the Tomahawk shoots had been run by contractors. TASMEX would be run by the ship's crew, the way things would work in combat. The first five missiles would be instrumented shots. The final OPEVAL would be fired with a live warhead. It would be run as close to an actual antiship engagement as possible, with the missile impacting on a target hulk off San Nicolas Island.

Cannady listened intently, fingering a sharp chin. When Dan wrapped it up, the skipper said, "Okay, that all sounds straightforward. Larry, call away the guys for the presail conference. Mess decks, I suppose." As the exec went to the phone, Cannady continued. "Let me ask you something before we go down there, Dan."

"Shoot, sir."

"When we were working for Admiral Kristofferson, we had to triple-check where every byte went, optimize the thread count on every screw. Now it seems like under Barry Niles it's more of a 'throttle-forward, get it out there at any cost' situation. Is that an accurate perception? And does it mean we've got a contingency coming up where we might need this weapon?"

"Sir, here's my readout on that. The program's at risk. We're in a cost overrun status. If Congress doesn't cover it, we're going to be shut down. I understand where Admiral Kristofferson was coming from. But looking at the political realities, I understand now where Admiral Niles is coming from, too."

The ship's officers looked at him with unease and, yes, suspicion. Maybe it was the word "political"? After a moment, Cannady said, "Well, okay . . . but if we actually have to use these things, and they don't work, we're all going to look pretty stupid."

"Yessir, but there can't be too many bugs left to fix." He brought them up-to-date on the redesign of the cable cutter.

"That's not going to modify the ones they've got deployed," the missile officer said. "So what you're saying is, we've got birds in the fleet now that are going to fail."

"True, but the only ones out there now are on the subs and *New Jersey*. Every load-out after that will have the new cutter, and they'll get the updated birds as they come out of Mechanicsburg in the thirty-month recertification cycle."

Cannady got up. He said to the XO, "Make sure we top off fresh water tonight. We've got a lot of extra people aboard." To Dan, he said, "Glad to have you aboard. Shall we go down to the mess decks?"

After the brief, he went down to berthing. A paper towel taped to a stripped coffin rack read LENSON. He hunted up the compartment petty officer and got sheets, a tan bunk cover, and a towel. He made up his bunk, stowed his gear, then took a quick shower and changed into slacks, a polo shirt, and running shoes. He checked his watch. Still only a little after six. He strolled forward, climbed a ladder, and emerged onto the forecastle.

Sakai was there, looking at the box launchers. One was open, the other closed. Dan looked up at the open one, examining the star crimps of the fly-through covers. The weapons were behind them, sealed away in their nitrogen-filled climate-controlled cocoons.

"Hey. Headed into town?"

"Just for a little while."

"I'm going back to the equipment room, observe from back there. Then I'm gonna turn in. We'll be hitting it pretty hard next couple days."

"Okay, Sparky. See you tomorrow."

He lingered as the first star appeared over Mount Laguna. A stream of rippling light outlined the Coronado bridge. Beyond it glittered the Embarcadero. A ketch ghosted by, sidelight glowing ruby as it made for Coronado Keys.

The ship's exec came out. They stood watching the technicians run through a couple of last-minute tests.

"Going steaming tonight?" the XO asked him.

"Just to look around. How long's it gonna take me to get to Balboa Park?"

"Not long. Ten, fifteen minutes. There's usually a cab down by fleet landing. Interstate Five, Pershing exit, that'll put you on the east side of the park."

"What time are we getting under way?"

"Zero-seven hundred. Liberty expires at zero-six."

The tests ended. The FTs coiled up cables and left the forecastle to the evening. Out of nowhere, the exec said, "I heard the last XO board, selection rate was seventy percent, with all the new hulls commissioning."

"Is that right?" Seventy percent was high. Then he remembered. He wouldn't be around.

The other groused that the ramp-up in ship numbers wasn't all good news. Money was going to defense contractors, but the sailors weren't seeing much of it. Between low pay and double-digit inflation, most of his married E-2s and E-3s were on food stamps. "What ship type you favor? You're a destroyer man, right?"

"Yeah. I did my department-head tour on *Barrett*."

"Wait a minute . . . *Barrett*. Something I heard at the club one night . . . about her shooting down a MiG in the Windward Passage."

"I heard that story, too," Dan told him. "Anyway, if I was to be an XO, I'd want a small boy. A *Forrest Sherman*, or a *Knox*, or a *Perry*-class. How about you? Any idea where you're going?"

The exec said no, that he wanted a command, of course, but that his wife wanted him to put in for shore duty instead.

"You got kids?" Dan asked him, thinking about Nan, thinking it was about time to give her another call, see what her plans were for the summer.

"Two boys, six and six months. How about you?"

"One, a daughter. She's with my ex-wife."

A shadow crossed the other officer's eyes. "We been having problems, too."

"She wants out?"

"It's not that bad yet. But she makes it obvious she's not happy."

Dan glanced at him. What was he telling him this for? Then he understood. The exec didn't want to talk about it with anybody from the ship. "Well, at least you know something's wrong. I didn't realize that till it was too late."

The 1MC chose that moment to strike four

bells, then announce "*Merrill*, departing." "Don't stay out too late," said the exec as he headed for the quarterdeck. A minute later, a final bong quivered in the still air.

Dan stood there for a few more minutes, looking out over the bay. Then glanced at his watch and headed aft.

# 27

He'd photocopied his JCMP *Employee's Handbook* in Washington and had put the flimsy damp pages into a government brown envelope. He got them out of the side pocket of his B-4, then headed for the brow.

He left the ship at 1820, and by 1845 was getting out of the taxi at the east side of the park. Enough time to stroll around. He picked up a brochure, then followed the map in it down a pedestrian mall lined with Spanish Colonial buildings and palm trees, heading toward a massively ornate tower at the west end. It looked vaguely familiar, though he'd never been here before. Then turned south, realizing he'd passed what was marked on the map as the Spreckles Pavilion.

He spotted Bepko on a bench. The NIS agent was in running pants, running shoes, a photographer's vest. A camera hung around his neck. He squinted back as their eyes met, then heaved himself up and strolled away.

Message received. Dan sheered off, too, and ambled on, wondering how many of the others who moved with him through the spring-smelling air were also not what they seemed. The park was a popular place. He caught Spanish, Italian, Japanese. Jewelry jangled as women in saris sailed by. It was a great location for a meet, or whatever they called it when a spy met his contact. Maybe he should read some Graham Greene, figure out what the hell he was doing. Or maybe not. Being too smooth might make the Chinese suspicious.

Sprinklers began to whisper. Marigolds and poppies folded themselves silently. The flower-laden air was almost too sweet. Jasmine crept along the ground and climbed fences — shiny green leaves, tiny white flowers in the shape of stars. Scores of tourists wandered about taking pictures of one another and gaping at the buildings.

The pavilion turned out to be an amphitheater, bigger than he'd expected. He strolled back and forth for about forty minutes in front of the arched building that housed the immense organ, till a small, neatly dressed Asian fell in next to him. He carried a shopping bag that read SUNNY'S SURPLUS.

"Commander Lenson?"

"That's me."

They shook hands. "Li Chenbin. You can call me Xiaotu." He pronounced it "Shoe-too."

It was hard to tell how old the attaché was. He had a small mustache without any gray in it, pouchy eyes, and he was wearing sunglasses despite the late hour. Dan noted a striped rep tie under a light coat. His hat was chocolate-colored. His brown oxfords were good quality but scuffed. All in all, a face and an outfit you could find on any city street.

"Is that it?"

"Yeah. This is it." Dan started to look around for Bepko, but caught himself in time. He gave Li the envelope. The attaché doubled it casually and slipped it into the shopping bag.

They walked on, Dan following Li's lead past cottage displays and beds of brilliant poppies. In front of the Museum of Art, he cleared his throat. "Uncle Xinhu — Mr. Zhang — said he'd pay for this. The phone list, I mean."

"Oh, yes. Certainly. But we should discuss some other things first."

"What kind of things?" He was nervous; he'd never talked to a Red Chinese spymaster before. It didn't help that the guy's English was so perfect.

Li turned suddenly down a walkway between the art museum and a botanical building. Dan wiped his hands on his slacks, wondering if being visibly nervous was a plus or not. A gaggle of kids passed, chattering and shrieking.

They came to a concession stand, a low building with a flat roof and stucco walls. Kids congregated in front of the counter, pushing one another and shrieking. Li asked him if he was hungry. Dan said he could eat something. The attaché got them corn dogs, and thick fries, and cans of Slice. They sat at a tile-topped table under a red umbrella. Lights ignited above them, driving the gathering shadows beneath the table. With a mouth half-full of corn dog, Li said, "What's your attitude toward China, Dan?"

"My attitude? Friendly, I guess. I know we're helping your military program."

"Why did you get this material for us?"

"I have child support, other expenses."

"That's right; I remember now. Your daughter lives in Utah, doesn't she? With your ex?"

He nodded, keeping his expression bland. A lion, or some large cat, roared from the darkness beyond where they sat. The zoo must be over there, past the mass of trees. Li was letting him know he knew about Nan. That he even knew where she lived. He would pay for this, too.

"Have you got change for a five?"

"Uh — wait a minute. Yeah, if you can take some quarters."

He put the bills beside Li's fries. It was so smoothly done that he was putting the bill into his wallet when he noticed it wasn't a five; it was a five hundred.

"That's for the list. Would you be willing to get some other materials for us?"

"Uh, that depends. What kind?"

Li smiled apologetically. "I'm sorry, my boss didn't give me a very clear picture of what you do with the Cruise Missile Project.

What exactly *do* you do?"

"I'm in charge of mating Tomahawk to surface ships. Destroyers, cruisers . . . right now, specifically, battleships."

"Ah, the *Iowa* class. That's a responsible position. . . . What is that singing?"

He became aware of music in the distance. Li put his half-eaten dog down. He got up, and Dan rose, too, and followed him. He went back after a few steps and retrieved his drink.

They passed through a grove of ornamental trees. Their fantastical gnarled boles, like the illustrations for a scary children's story, made tormented shapes against the lights. Li stepped out, setting a marching pace. They walked till they reached an outdoor theater. An opera was in progress. The attaché listened for a time. Then he cleared his throat.

"You must have access to technical documentation, then."

"I see a lot of that. Test results, logic diagrams. Yeah."

"Guidance-system documentation? Actual circuit diagrams?"

Goal, he thought. Attucks had been right. "They're in the CMS vault, but I can check them out when I need them."

"What about software? Tapes, data discs?"

He looked around, wishing he had somebody to help him. He didn't see Bepko anywhere, hadn't since they parted at the pavilion. He wondered if there was a second player from the Chinese side. Too many people here, moving through the scented darkness. . . . He said, "I don't know if I could get my hands on anything like that." Playing reluctant, like they'd advised him to.

Another long silence. He didn't know what these pauses meant. Was Li trying to shake him? Waiting for him to fill the gap with words, and give himself away? Did he have other, weightier matters on his mind? Or was he was just enjoying the evening, the overheard performance?

The singer launched into a dramatic aria. Li took his hat off and examined the hatband. He said, "You said you had access. Is it a matter of clearances?"

"No. No, I've got the clearances. I guess I could get what you want. Some of it, anyway."

"When?"

"Uh, pretty much whenever. But not right away. I have to go to sea tomorrow."

Three young women swept by on in-line skates, bare bronzed limbs flashing beneath the park lighting. Li watched them pass. Then turned suddenly. "Holy Toledo. Did you see the tush on that last one?"

Dan shook his head. "Boy, where did you learn your English?"

"Watching TV, mostly. I watch everything. *Dallas. The Jeffersons.* My favorite is *Charlie's Angels.*"

"Jaclyn, Kate, or Farrah?"

"What?"

"Those are the actresses. They play Kelly, Sabrina, and Jill."

"Kelly, I'm in love with Kelly Garrett." Li began marching again, headed back toward the carillon. Dan hesitated, then followed him. "So, you're going to sea. More flight tests?"

"That's right."

"When will you be back?"

"I'll be back in D.C. in about a week."

"Give me a call when you get back. But never from your office or apartment. Only from pay phones. A different one whenever you call. We won't meet again until you actually have something for me. All right?"

"Wait a minute. So you want whatever I can get on the guidance system, right? Is that all? What about strategic targeting data? If I could get that?"

He figured this would appeal. Targeting data was supposed to be the highest of the high-classification material. But to his surprise, the attaché shrugged. "I'm not too interested in that. What I'd be willing to pay for are guidance diagrams. If you can get software, that might be even more valuable. But please, nothing you wouldn't see in the course of your job. You're not a spy."

Dan almost said, "I'm not?" Instead, he said, "Well . . ."

"I know you've had some problems with

your superiors," Li said softly. "Because of your involvement with the peace movement. But I'm never going to ask you to do anything harmful to the United States. You and I, we're on the same side, man."

Dan stared at him, feeling himself start to tremble. Fighting the sudden terrifying sense this half-smiling man knew everything. He knew about his problems at JCM. He knew about Nan. He knew about the Dorothy Day House. But now Dan knew something, too. It wasn't Zhang who had set Kerry up on the trail. Somehow, it had been this man, with his fluent American slang, his hooded, anonymous face and practiced furtiveness. Maybe not intending for her to be killed, but he'd made it possible. Thirty percent guilty of her murder? Fifty percent? Seventy-five? He sucked air, trying to filter hatred out of his eyes, out of his voice. He said, "Who's on the other side?"

"The Russians, of course."

"Right. But still, I don't expect to do this for free."

Li smiled suddenly, as if he'd had to save up for it. "If you can get us useful stuff on terrain comparison, and digital scene correlation, we could pay ten thousand, maybe even as high as fifteen thousand dollars. That should help with your alimony payments."

Reluctance and cupidity. He gave it a beat, then said, "That's not very much."

"It's what you make in a year."

"No. I make around thirty-five a year. With allowance for quarters."

"Jeez, is that right? My information's dated. Maybe we can do twenty thousand, then. If you come through. We don't withhold taxes, so that'll like double your income. I'd like to make that much! And another thing: I'm repeating myself, but I don't want you to take any risks. Hear me?"

"I hear you."

"I want our acquaintance to last for a long time, Dan. So . . . ciao, okay?"

With a squeeze of the arm, he was gone, marching briskly away into the jasmine-scented dark. Dan realized he'd probably walked over from wherever he was staying, wherever he'd been when he took Dan's call from the pier. He stood looking after him as the coated figure shrank away into the crowds, into the evening dark, the shopping bag swinging like a martial metronome. How sure of himself he was. Attucks was right: Somebody needed to hold a wake-up call on the counterintelligence community. Maybe this would do it, tearing the lid off Li and his boss.

But after that, none of it would be his concern. He'd be out in the real world. Running a software team, or being a systems analyst.

He turned and headed back toward the street, gradually lowering his head as he walked.

# 28

Four days later, he stared through borrowed binoculars at a shrinking speck. Others watched too, crowded elbow-to-elbow along *Merrill's* bridge wing. The chest-vibrating ignition roar and the slow, agonized climb-out had been succeeded by silence. The exhaust column, shining in the afternoon sun, fell away astern as the destroyer hummed on through three-foot seas.

"Aw, hell," someone muttered. He knelt abruptly, the better to point the glasses upward, resting them on the edge of the splinter shield.

Thousands of yards away, the speck slowly fell toward the waiting sea. It seemed to take a long time, drifting down out of the blue. He tried to urge it on through the miles of air, willing it to fly. But it didn't. In the vibrating soundless field of the binoculars, a distant jet of spray burst upward, then subsided, till there was only the saw-toothed horizon again, the waves marching along the distant razor line where sea met sky.

The spell broke. The commanding officer, Cannady, asked him. "Did you see wing deployment?"

"I thought so, Captain. Pretty sure I saw the wings out."

"But no engine start?"

"No." He felt sick, depressed, enraged. Chase planes overhead, telemetry manned, everything ready . . . and one loose wire or line of buggy software dicked everything.

"Take it easy," said the CO, laying a hand on his shoulder. "Your face is white, know that?"

*Merrill's* spacious pilothouse was crowded with the bridge team and phone talkers and, of course, the riders. Cannady swung himself up into his leather chair, an unlit stogie drooping from his mouth. As Dan got to the ladder, he said, "Okay, I guess we'd better get on over there. Call away the whaleboat, see if there's anything left floating around."

One deck down, CIC was black dark and freezing cold. He stood blinking and peering, then felt his way onward as the hull leaned into the turn.

The ship's Tomahawk team were still sitting at their display terminals. The last frame of launch data glowed in front of them. Burdette stood behind them, arms folded, along with a barrel-shaped man in a blue jumpsuit: the Missile Test Center rep. "Any idea what went wrong?" Vic muttered as he came up.

"Looked like an engine nonstart. Boost phase, fine. But then . . . zilch. Never even saw the starter cartridge."

Sakai came up from the equipment room, face closed. He said he'd help the DSs take it down to parade rest, make sure it wasn't software. Dan talked to the missile officer, confirming prelaunch had gone normally. Then he went back to the fantail to watch the search for debris. They found one of the shrouds, but nothing else.

He left the deck abruptly and headed down to the berthing area. It was empty, lights dimmed, curtains swaying on untenanted racks. He grabbed a handhold and swung himself up. Then stared at the underside of the top bunk.

He and the other riders and the crew had been working through the whole transit up from San Diego. The launch software was the new version. He and Sakai had scrubbed it all down. Meanwhile, Burdette and the FTs had scrubbed down the ship-to-missile interface. Everything had checked out fine.

Then they'd fired it, and it had tumbled into the sea.

He lay motionless, fighting the impulse to slam his fist into unyielding steel.

So far in the series, they'd had two go birds and two failures. The first shot had jumped off the foredeck and cruised off into a cloudy sky, chase planes hot on its tail. The pilots reported when it broke from the search pattern and steadied on an approach course, dropping to within fifty feet of the waves. Everyone in CIC listened as they reported the terminal maneuver: an abrupt pull-up five miles out from the target hulk, then a dive-in at a precisely calculated angle. The missile was less than a mile from impact when the pilot took control and pulled it out of the dive, then headed it for the sea recovery area west of San Clemente.

OT-2 had gone even better. This time, the launch team plotted a reverse approach, sending the missile circling the target before pouncing from the rear. The payoff on this maneuver would be in attacking a heavily defended, high-value unit. With six or seven missiles arriving simultaneously from all points of the compass, even an Aegis cruiser would be hard pressed to go through the detect-track-engage cycle fast enough to knock them all down.

He'd thought they were in the clear at last. Till today. This morning, OT-3 had flown out great. It went into the third weave in its search grid, hesitated, then came out of it headed for downtown LA. The chase pilot had given it five seconds, then did a command override. And now OT-4 had just fallen out of the sky.

They had one more chance, tomorrow morning, before the final OPEVAL.

He sat up, dangling his legs over the edge. Asking himself, Well, so what? You're not going to be here. What difference does it make? Even if the whole program gets canceled?

The difference it made was that the surface fleet, *his* friends and shipmates, goddamn it, needed a long-range missile. If Tomahawk couldn't come through, the tailhookers and the Air Force would win. Carriers were great, but they were too valuable to put in the front line. He knew who'd have to go in instead, the next time the balloon went up. The small boys, frigates and destroyers. The all but defenseless amphibious ships. And men he'd served with, men he cared about, would die, unable to hit back at the launching platforms. Missile after missile, incoming, till one got through.

He didn't want to think about that again. Not the flames, the stink of oil, the screams of drowning men.

At dinner that evening, *Merrill's* skipper sat with his chin propped in his hand. The missile officer was flicking a fork. Finally, as the steward cleared dessert, he said, "Sir, I got a problem to surface."

"Batteries released, Jim."

"This is supposed to be an operational test. Meaning my guys do the hands-on stuff, from test to launch. Well, we're not."

Cannady studied his coffee cup. "XO, loan me your stateroom?"

"All yours, sir."

Dan followed them into the exec's cabin. He, the missile officer, and the test rep perched on the settee as Cannady took the desk chair. The skipper said, "Okay, if I read what you're telling me: you're being micro-managed to the point you think it may be affecting the results."

Dan shifted on slick leather. "We're giving technical advice, Captain. That's all."

"Too much assistance can be as bad as too little."

"You've got a brand-new software set there, sir. Not to put your guys down, but Mr. Sakai's a lot more qualified than they are to troubleshoot it."

"Are they too deep in your shorts, Jim?"

The missile officer hesitated, then nodded, eyes hard.

"I don't go along with that, Captain. That somehow because of our helping out, something went wrong that wouldn't have otherwise."

"It's not a critique," Cannady said. "I know it's hard to let go of the baby. But at some point, the developmental community's got to turn Tomahawk over to the fleet. And if a crew as sharp as this can't handle it, we need to get that message up the chain."

Dan held his silence, too angry to trust himself to speak. These guys didn't have the big picture. But on his own deck, the captain was God.

"Okay, that's settled. Jim, these guys are here to help you. If you got a question, ask 'em. But unless they do —" He looked at Dan.

"We stand around holding our doughnuts," he said. "I got it, sir."

Cannady's eyes went flat for a moment. "We're all on the same side," he said, and got up. "Remember that."

The next morning he woke early, but couldn't go back to sleep. So he got up and threw his khakis on. It was still a couple of minutes to reveille when he got to the bridge. The captain was there already, talking the day's events over with the navigator. Dan stood with his back against the surface plot board and watched.

He'd dreamed of sitting in that leather chair. Of command. Another illusion given up. Like the dream of living with Susan and Nan. Of marrying Kerry. . . . To hell with it. . . . That was life, kicking holes in dream after dream till you realized they were nothing more than that. Fantasies.

The JA talker nudged him, and he stepped up beside the skipper. "This one's gonna fly," Cannady told him.

"I sure hope so, sir." He looked down and out through the huge, square, freshly cleaned Plexiglas windows.

*Merrill* rolled gently on an azure sea. Sea swallows wove and dipped along the wave lines. Far to the east, low clouds glowed tentatively scarlet in the direction of land. He examined a xeroxed chart of the test range. They were in area W-61, 120 miles west of San Clemente Island. The pulsating red numerals of the fathometer read 1,500 fathoms.

Gradually, the sun ballooned up. It ruddied the haze gray sides of the ABLs. It set fire to the water, glittering and rolling in the morning light. He made out beneath the surface waves the slow but enormous heave of some far-off storm. Far to the west, a containership moved bulldozer-slow across the horizon, loaded with compact cars and consumer electronics from Taiwan or Hong Kong or Mainland China.

His hands tightened in his pockets. The serenity of early morning dissolved as he wondered if it was Li himself who had targeted the gang on Kerry. The Second Department officer was the best candidate around.

But still his eyes lingered on the sea. And looking out over its ever-changing, ever-constant face, he suddenly knew he wasn't going to be able to leave it. He didn't know what it was he loved about it. He couldn't even call it love, because he hated it, too, had cursed it and feared its power. It was all the more fearsome because it didn't care. It didn't *care*.

The sun blazed across its face, throwing a level beam of heat like some futuristic directed-energy weapon across the bridge. The officer of the deck was a young lieutenant (jg) who stood slumped against the gyro stand, one leg wound around it. Dan envied him suddenly with all his heart.

But then it all went to shit. They were finishing the engagement checks, and he was standing on the starboard wing, when, inside the pilothouse, someone yelled, "High temp alarm in number one ABL." Cannady looked up sharply from his seat, where he'd been going over the morning traffic.

Leaning over the splinter shield, looking down thirty feet, Dan saw something his mind failed to accept at first. The whole starboard launcher was coated with a sheath of yellowish white smoke. It seemed to come from the deck itself, flowing up the sides of the armored coffin, clinging to it, then curving in at the top before rising off and wafting back toward him. He stared, then pulled his head back and yelled into the pilothouse, "White smoke, starboard ABL."

An instant later, echoing from the 1MC: "Fire, fire, fire — class charlie fire in the starboard box launcher, on the fo'c'sle. Repair three provide."

He realized he was in the open, exposed. He got inside and dogged the door. Then he ducked out again and grabbed the lookout, who was staring obliviously out at the Pacific through his binoculars. Thank God, the live warhead was in the other ABL, on the port side, but there was a booster in there, three hundred pounds of solid propellant and oxidizer, and a full load of fuel; if it blew, there'd be fire all over the forecastle, fire and highly toxic combustion products.

Cannady was out of his seat, staring down. The smoke was thicker now, coming up around the access doors at the rear of the box. Dan joined him as he told the officer of the deck to put the wind astern; then he hit the 21MC. "CIC, DC Central: This is the captain speaking. We have smoke from ABL number one. Secure power to both ABLs. Seth, radio that to Point Mugu, and make sure they have our posit." When he clicked off, his eyes met Dan's. "The internal fire protection's automatic, right?"

"Yes, sir. There's a Halon system in there, and a saltwater deluge. Internal temp goes over a hundred and eighty, the Halon triggers. Over two forty, the saltwater system lets go. You might want to pull your topside personnel in."

"Eric, get everybody inside the skin of the ship. Set up to shift the watch to secondary conn. Boatswain! Temperature reading?"

"Two hundred degrees, sir."

"Pass to DC Central: Activate saltwater deluge system in ABL number one. The Halon's either not triggering or it's not putting the fire out."

"Get back," the OOD yelled. "Stay back from those windows. Clear the bridge! Everybody not on watch, off the bridge!"

Cannady stood with his hands in his back pockets. Dan stood beside him; this was his system, after all. In a low voice, the skipper asked him, "Exactly how thick is that outer casing?"

"Not that thick, sir. Maybe two inches. And it's aluminum. It's not going to contain any major explosions."

"We've got a live warhead there to port. Practically spitting distance from it. What should I do about it? Douse it, too?"

Dan thought fast about the live shot in ABL number two. The warhead was 450 pounds of H6, a mix of RDX and trinitrotoluene that came out about twice as powerful as straight TNT. It would do a thorough job on a thin-skinned ship like *Merrill*. He was conscious of Cannady waiting for an answer. The trouble was, if they sprayed it with salt water, there went the OPEVAL, too.

He said finally, "I don't have any real firm guidelines to offer on that, sir."

Cannady nodded. He stayed at the window, looking down.

It seemed like a long time later, but it couldn't have been more than a minute or two before water started spraying out of the launcher. Smoke yellow and thick as snot vomited out, too.

The smoke stopped. The boatswain reported that the temperature was dropping.

Cannady told DC Central to give it another minute, then secure water pressure. He clicked to the damage-control circuit to talk to the team leader.

The number-one man came out in breathing apparatus and battle helmet, accompanied by someone in civvies. Together, they got the access door open. They stood peering inside. Finally, they looked up toward the pilothouse. The one in blue jeans made a thumbs-up sign, and Dan saw it was Sakai. Cannady sighed. "Well, that wasn't as bad as it could have been. With a full load-out of five-inch in the magazines. . . . Okay, secure from GQ."

Dan felt weak. He'd forgotten about the forward magazines, twenty or thirty tons of high-explosive shells and powder charges. Enough to turn the whole front half of the ship into smoke and razor blades. The captain still looked relaxed, but now Dan noticed dark arcs under his armpits.

Cannady mused on, "I'm going to ask you to recommend whether we proceed with the operational launch this afternoon. After we figure out what went wrong here. I'm figuring a short of some kind in the missile interface."

"There's not that much juice in there, sir. Not more than fifteen volts. I'll go down and take a look, but I figure it's the elevation hydraulics."

Cannady said that would make sense, since it had happened as they were starting to elevate. He looked around the bridge, then added, "I'll be back in my cabin, changing my shorts."

After crawling into the blackened, stinking, still-dripping launcher interior, the missile hanging above him, he and Sakai agreed it was probably the elevation circuitry. The interesting thing was that the hold-downs were still set. It looked to him as if the latches had jammed and the motors had burned out trying to elevate while they were still holding it shut. There was an interlock, to keep the clamshell from elevating until the hold-downs released, but obviously it hadn't worked. He wasn't surprised to note that this was a Vimy product, the contractor who'd tried to bribe him.

He couldn't think of any good reason not to fire the OPEVAL as scheduled, and reported that to Cannady. "We've got the range cleared and everybody in place. If you don't, we'll just have to go out and do it again after they fix the fire damage. And it's gonna delay the program." The CO said he was inclined to agree. He went down to talk to Range Control on the radio. Dan looked at his sooty, water-stained khakis, only now realizing how totally wiped out they were.

The noon meal was tense and silent. Afterward, Dan went to CIC; Burdette was in the equipment room; Sakai stood by in the breaker, in case they had a repetition of the latch problem.

The cave was filled with the hum of voices and the whine of cooling fans, the obbligato hiss and chatter of the radio circuits. The black bulkheads receded as if only space lay beyond the amber glow of the plot boards. He moved through it with anxiety and nostalgia. So familiar . . . but he'd never see this again, would return to it only in dream and memory. The watch team supervisor laid a finger on a flickering symbol twelve miles southwest of the ghost shape of San Clemente. A conversation at the air-intercept control station: The chase planes were checking in. The controller assigned them to orbit at angels five — five thousand feet — twenty miles west of the ship.

The general quarters bell went. He felt the familiar shiver as the electronic tones cut off and the 1MC stated: "This is a drill. This is a drill. General quarters. General quarters. All hands man your battle stations." There wasn't the usual scrambling and running. The men simply buckled their helmets on and sat back down at their consoles, pushing their gas-mask packs back so they wouldn't sit on them.

The control officer came over the net, advising them the range was clear.

At the Tomahawk consoles, he found the petty officer struggling to program in the search pattern. He chose the wrong mode, and Dan started to say something; then didn't. He made himself stand back, like Cannady had during the fire, while they went through the documentation and argued about it and then eventually deselected it and entered the right command.

The last minutes ticked down, then the last seconds.

Thunder rattled the deck plates. A fine gray dust sifted down from the overhead, and the fluorescents flickered. The reports came in from the chase planes as once again they screwed themselves to the missile's tail.

They followed it all the way to the hulk. A silence, and then the pilot's voice came from the speaker: "Fireball. Just aft of the stack . . . a little off the centroid. Fragment spray on the water. . . . Black smoke coming up. . . . Solid hit. Definitely a mission kill."

The hulk had been an old destroyer, ex-USS *Higbee*. The pilot kept talking, giving them a blow-by-blow as the old tin can burned vigorously, heeled over, and at last slipped beneath the waves. Dan could visualize it, all too well.

When the congratulations died down, he went below to the equipment room. Both Sakai and Burdette were there, studying the hard-copy printout. "What's the matter?" he asked them.

"Nothing. They done real good," Burdette muttered.

"It's the rest of the figures that don't exactly happy face," Sakai reminded him. "We came out here to shoot six rounds. Out of that, one fizzled, one headed for Hollywood, two flew good, one was a can't count because of the fire, and the last one flew great. Overall, a sixty percent success rate. And that's under ideal conditions — nice weather, fresh missiles, scads of technical help." The engineer gnawed his lip. "Plus, the follow-on to this machine's got to go faster and do some terminal weaves. That hulk wasn't shooting back or maneuvering. It's not gonna be that easy against a *Sovremenny*."

"We can fix that." Dan patted his shoulder, remembering when all Yoshiyuki Sakai had wanted was to get back to his research. "Let's see if we can get together after dinner, rough out the after-action report, okay? Maybe back here, where it'll be quiet."

Shortly after, the ship came around to a southeasterly course, headed back toward San Diego. He was out running, in the third mile and pushing it as hard as he could on the rolling helo deck, when the 1MC announced, "Commander Lenson, call the bridge." He walked into the hangar, sweaty and loose, and punched the aiphone. "Lenson here."

"Junior officer of the deck, sir. Captain'd like to see you, sir. In his cabin."

"I was running. Take me a couple minutes to change."

"Maybe you better just go on up, sir."

He said he was on his way. He jogged through the passageway, then climbed the ladder. He knocked and let himself into Cannady's sea cabin. The air conditioning made his sweaty clothes clammy. "Lieutenant Commander Lenson, sir."

"Hi, Dan. Sorry to interrupt your jog. This just came in." Cannady handed him a message board. "Sit down, take a look, and then we'll discuss it. Wait a minute — I'll throw a towel down there first."

The message was from JCM, classified "Secret." The subject line read: "Modifications to travel arrangements."

1. (S) ON COMPLETION TASMEX, JCM RIDERS MR. Y. SAKAI AND LCDR V. BURDETTE RETURN TO JCM WASHINGTON DC IN ACCORDANCE WITH PREVIOUS ARRANGEMENTS.

2. (S) THIS MESSAGE CONSTITUTES ORDERS FOR LCDR D V LENSON. ON COMPLETION TASMEX AND DEBARK, CONTACT SATO NAVBASE SAN DIEGO TO EXCHANGE CURRENT AIR TICKETS FOR COMMERCIAL AIR TRAVEL TO STUTTGART FEDERAL REPUBLIC OF GERMANY.

3. (S) YOU ARE HEREBY DIRECTED PROCEED AND REPORT TEMDU ASSIGNED TO:

508

CAPT V. L. GRADY USN, US NAVAL FORCES EUROPE, BUILDING 2358, PATCH BARRACKS, VAIHINGEN GERMANY. FOR ADMIN PURPOSES REPORT TO: COMMANDER IN CHIEF US FORCES EUROPE.

4. (S) IT IS CERTIFIED THAT YOU HOLD A TOP SECRET CLEARANCE FROM THIS COMMAND BASED ON NATIONAL AGENCY CHECK COMPLETED 241180 BY DODMAC CENTER.

5. (U) MEMBER AUTHORIZED TO TRAVEL AT OWN EXPENSE SUBJECT TO REIMBURSEMENT.

The rest of the message was accounting data.

"So, you're off for Germany," Cannady observed, lighting his stogie. "Couldn't help seeing that. Can I ask why? Or shouldn't I?"

"You can ask, but I'm afraid I don't know. Any chance of using a covered phone when we get in? I'd like to call the boss, find out what this is all about."

"Sure, soon's we're pierside. Or we can set up a secure voice circuit right now, patch you via Point Mugu."

"Thanks, sir, but pierside should be soon enough. When are we getting in?"

"We always seem to go faster heading home. I'm figuring ten hundred tomorrow."

When they got in, the captain drove him

personally over to squadron headquarters. Dan asked to use the red phone. Eventually, he was talking to Colonel Evans. The deputy said, "Lenson? Hi. How'd the shoot go?"

"Mixed results, sir. But we passed the OPEVAL."

"Good. I assume you're calling in regard to that message you just got directing you to Vaihingen. Here's the background. Admiral Niles saw General Stahl in London."

"Who's General Stahl, sir?"

"Gen. Roland Stahl, U.S. Army, four stars, is Commander in Chief, U.S. Forces, Europe. He and Niles bumped into each other in the rest room after a meeting at the Ministry of Defence. He asked the admiral, 'What have you got in the bag that can help me do a strike?' The admiral said, 'Tomahawk.' Stahl's curious. So you're gonna be our salesman. Admiral Niles wants you to go there, brief him, and sell him on including the BGM-one oh nine in his plans."

"What are his plans?"

Evans cautioned him on security, then said, "There may be a strike coming up in North Africa."

"That's not in Europe."

"The North African littoral's in CINCEUR's area of responsibility."

He was having trouble believing this. "And he wants me to 'sell' this four-star, this General Stahl, on using GLCM?"

"No, no, no. Not GLCM! But that familiarity will help; you're the only guy we've got with joint experience. Right now, Stahl's thinking either F-one elevens out of England or a carrier strike off the *Coral Sea* and *America*. Niles wants to use the land-attack rounds aboard *New Jersey* instead."

Dan felt his skin creep. "Sir, what we've got out there in the Med is a box with missiles in it. We could probably do an antiship strike. But not land attack. We don't have a mission-planning cell, or a targeting infrastructure, or —"

"That's why we're sending you, to whip one together if we need it. Niles already called the Sixth Fleet commander. Report to Vaihingen. Get briefed in. Call me back before you go in to see Stahl."

"Sir, we're not ready for this. If we shoot craps, it'll kill the program."

"I think your orders are clear," said Evans, the western twang for some reason coming through very clearly.

There wasn't really any comeback possible to that, so he didn't try to make one. He hung up and sat there, appalled. Was this how forces got assigned at the CINC level? Flag officers running into one another in the can? They weren't ready for this. *New Jersey's* software was a bastard of the contractor and in-house versions, with more patches than a hobo's pants. "Jesus H. Christ," he muttered, rubbing his face with both hands.

Cannady poked his head in. "Done? I had the chief shoot over, pick up your tickets. Flight leaves at twelve-thirty. We better run."

Still numb as a tooth prepped for extraction, he picked up his luggage and followed the skipper out.

# V

# THE STRIKE

# 29

The flight stopped in Chicago for fuel, then made the long leap to Frankfurt. From there, he caught a Lufthansa hop to Stuttgart. He'd wondered how he was going to get to the compound, but the worry was wasted. The USO desk at the airport told him he had an hour to wait for transport to Patch Barracks. He had coffee and pastry at a shop with menus in German, English, French, and Italian. Then shouldered his carry-on and followed a group of Army enlisted onto a military bus.

The "barracks" turned out to be a huge base on the outskirts of a city. The bus dropped him on a square surrounded by enormous Teutonic-styled gray concrete blocks. Everything was meticulously landscaped, but the place gave him the creeps. Maybe it was just the feeling of foreignness. Not just Germany, but Army in Germany.

Building 2358 was the most unimaginative structure he'd ever seen, a blank-faced three-story puce concrete warehouse. Antennas protruded from the peaked roof. He crossed a courtyard of pink asphalt and cobblestones, enclosed by concrete walls that looked like tank barriers, and headed toward a beige steel door with a plaque that read HQ USEUCOM COMMAND CENTER.

Inside, further passage was blocked by a sergeant in a white helmet liner sitting at a desk. After examining his orders, the soldier picked up a phone. When a female Navy lieutenant showed up, the sergeant signed him in. Dan clipped on a bright yellow ESCORTED badge.

The lieutenant took him down a narrow corridor and then up a concrete and steel stair so tight they had to go single file. The stairwell smelled moldy and ancient. At the top, he followed her down another corridor. The tiles on the overhead were missing, revealing beams coated with asbestos. Finally, she punched a combo lock and held the door.

The NAVEUR office was big enough for a metal desk and two filing cabinets. It opened off another, not much bigger, but with four desks. The lieutenant said Captain Grady was at the morning brief. She got Dan coffee and a copy of *Stars and Stripes*. He cleared his throat and asked, "I know what EUCOM is. European Command. But what's NAVEUR doing here? I thought he was in Naples."

"He is. But he works for General Stahl, so he's got a liaison here, too."

Grady came in at 0845, looking tired. He was about fifty, with startlingly white hair in a widow's peak and round gold-framed John Lennon glasses. He wore submariner's dolphins and a command pin. "Lenson?" he said, looking him up and down. "Okay flight?

Where you bunking?"

"Nowhere yet, sir. Just got off the bus."

Grady yelled into the outer office, telling the lieutenant to call over for a room. Closing the door, he said to Dan, "First time at Patch?"

"Yes, sir."

"This is actually an old panzer facility. Built as Kurmärker Kaserne in '36. We bombed the hell out of it in '45, then moved in. We'll get you installed over at the Q. That's in Craig Village."

"Walking distance, sir?"

"Oh, yeah. Ten minutes. Go back toward the main gate, where you came in, then turn right. Head down Katzenbacherstrasse till you come to the loop." Grady's face twitched. "Wish you'd have gotten in last night. We could have had you sit in on the commander's brief. But I can tell you most of what you need to know. You're set up for ten hundred in the Fishbowl. If everything goes okay, you'll get asked to go along to the planning meeting."

"Ten hundred." Dan started to feel nervous. "Will General Stahl be there?"

"I don't know if you're actually going to see the CINC himself. There's limited personal availability. The DCINC and the COS—"

"Uh, sir, what are those?"

"Deputy commander in chief, and chief of

517

staff. General Auer's the DCINC." He pronounced it "d-sink."

"Okay, got that." He noted it in his wheelbook. "But the word I got was that General Stahl had asked Admiral Niles a question personally."

"Regardless, you'll still have to impress Auer first. He's the wicket keeper around here. . . . Let me bring you up-to-date on what we got going."

Grady slid open a filing cabinet. His face contorted again, and this time Dan saw it was involuntary. The first briefing slide was classified "Top Secret SPECAT." It was captioned "Operation Prime Needle." Looking over his spectacles like a nineteenth-century professor, the captain said, "We've gotten a warning order to plan a strike against Libya."

"Against Libya." North Africa, terrorist bombings, rumors swirling around; it wasn't a surprise, but it was the first time he'd heard it specified as a target. "When?"

"No date yet, but on short notice. There's a diplomatic solution working, sanctions, but I don't know if it's going to result in anything that will satisfy this administration."

Dan turned the pages slowly. The concept of operations was clear from the charts and target lists. The "forces to be committed" area was still blank.

"The rationale's to make Khaddafi close

down his support of terrorists. The target list is the facilities, training camps, and transport airfields they use."

"Are we sure of that, sir? That he's the sponsor?"

"We're pretty sure he's behind the airport massacres, both support and direction; but on the most recent bombing, we intercepted messages from his embassy, reporting first that the operation would be carried out and then that it was a success. It's him all right."

"What are the percentages we're actually going in? We plan and plan, but —"

"I know what you mean, but that's out of our hands. All we have is the directive to build a viable strike." Grady pulled out one slide. "The analysis guys have come up with three major target complexes.

"Number one: the Tripoli area. Three targets there. Murat Sidi Bilal. It's a naval base, but there's a frogman school we think trains terrorists, too. The Bab al-Azizyah Barracks. That's a command center, and Mu'ammar lives there sometimes; we might luck out. And the Tripoli airfield, where he has his strike aircraft based."

"I thought it was illegal to assassinate heads of state."

"You're right. That was a little . . . pleasantry, if you will. If we're directed to go against one of those targets, the most likely means of attack will be F-one elevens. That's the only aircraft the Air Force has that can do a precision night strike. All-weather, night and day, low-level attack."

"Air defenses?"

"Heavy, and tied together with good early warning and command and control."

"Where would these F-one elevens come from?"

"England." Grady went on without acknowledging Dan's look of surprise. "Complex number two: the Benghazi area, on the east of the Gulf of Sidra. Possible targets there: Benghazi barracks, another terrorist command center, an intelligence compound, and the Benina military airfield. Our idea right now is to hit those with A-sixes and -sevens from *Coral Sea* and *America*."

Dan studied the rest of the slides. "How'd the Air Force get plugged into this, anyway? Can't the carriers hit both target sets?"

"Admiral Kidder tried to set it up that way. The Joint Chiefs put them in." Grady hesitated, then added, "Apparently someone thinks the Navy's been hogging the limelight with Kidder's raids across the Line of Death, down in the Gulf of Sidra. The Air Force wants a buildup to forty wings. If we bomb Libya alone, there's gonna be a natural question in Congress —"

"I get it. The budget." A bitter taste, but he knew now this was how it was done. He put his finger down to the south, far from the sea. "What's this? The third target set?"

"That's Sidi Garib. A new fertilizer plant."

"A fertilizer plant?"

"That's what the Libyans say it is. What we find interesting is that special military-only roads have been built across the desert to it, access is restricted, and it has the same level of antiaircraft and surface-to-air missile protection as Khaddafi's home barracks. The consensus is that it's actually a chemical weapons production complex. And not far from completion, either."

"Jesus."

"Right. If he gets nerve gas, we're gonna really have problems. If we do a strike, it would be a golden opportunity to take this out at the same time. We're going to have to do it sometime, and once it starts up, an attack would smear a plume all across the Mideast."

Dan studied the slide. "What's the scale on this thing?"

Grady got up and went to the safe again. This time, he came back with a map that showed everything, down to the watering holes.

"You're right, the trouble is, it's two hundred miles inland. He put it there on purpose. The other two target complexes are on the coast. That means we could hit them both at once. That would work, you'd have horizontal separation. But if they also task us with a

521

mission that deep in the interior —"

"You can't go at the same time, because your planes will have to overfly the coast."

"Right, and you can't hit it later, because the defenses will be at full alert."

"So what's the plan?"

"Right now, the only idea on the table is to route a separate strike element of F-one elevens around to the west. They'd have to overfly Tunisia and cross the western border here" — Grady's pencil point dotted a remote area of desert — "then head east to hit the plant. Downside of that, one, we don't know if the Tunisians will go along. The French and the Spanish have already turned us down on overfly rights, so why should the Tunisians give us permission?

"And two, even if they did, you're looking at a twenty-hour mission. It's six thousand miles round-trip from England to the Libyan coast as is. You extend that, you're going to have exhausted aircrews going against a heavy defense. We went to the Forty-eighth Tactical Fighter Wing on that, to get their opinion. They didn't sound enthusiastic."

Dan studied the map. The area Grady had indicated was marked sand, silt, and gravel. It was absolutely flat except for the hills around Sidi Garib itself. He remembered stories of B-17s that had come down in the Libyan desert and not been found till forty years later. "Plus, if they have to punch out in there,

there's no way we can rescue them."

"That's right. So now you know why you're here. The ten hundred briefing will put you face-to-face with the planners. I'll leave you the warning order and these charts. Anything else you'll need?"

He tried to think. It wasn't entirely out of left field, but to have it looking up from his plate was something else. "Uh, you got anything more detailed on this chemical plant? Overheads, or layout?"

"I can get something from J-Two for you. They'll scream, but I'll get it. Anything else?"

He couldn't think of anything else he needed except about two weeks, but he didn't have that. He had two hours. Finally, he just asked where the coffee was. Grady took him out for a refill, then escorted him back. The captain told him if he needed anything to call the lieutenant. Then he excused himself and closed the door.

Two hours later, he stood on a dais in the Fishbowl, holding his handwritten notes. Behind him were six big situation-display screens. He shuffled his papers on the briefing stand, trying to keep the butterflies down. He took a sip of water and cleared his throat.

At 1010, there was a stir. He lifted his eyes to the balcony, but it was still empty.

The Fishbowl was an enormous room with sallow stucco walls and the same acoustic tile on the ceiling as the interrogation room at D.C. Homicide. It had two levels, not unlike a small opera house, but here the floor was filled with desks and display terminals instead of an audience. The audience that counted here was in the balcony.

Another stir, and a procession of uniforms filed forward from the low-ceilinged J-2 spaces. Three flag officers with stars or gold shoulder boards trailed by staffers. They climbed a spiral staircase to the upper level, disappeared for a few seconds, and then reappeared as heads only, looking down at him.

The briefing spots came on, equatorial-brilliant suns. He gave it another moment, till the three-star, who should be the deputy CINC, turned from a remark to the man next to him. He raised a hand, and Dan took that as the signal to begin.

"Good morning, General Auer, other members of the EUCOM Staff. I'm Lcdr. Dan Lenson of the Joint Cruise Missile Project Office. I'm here in response to a question addressed to Admiral Niles by General Stahl in London two weeks ago. That question was: 'What have we got in the bag that can help me strike Libya?' Admiral Niles asked me to brief you on the BGM-one oh nine Tomahawk land-attack cruise missile."

He'd given this opening brief many times before. The slides flicked smoothly up, showing the missile, its variations, launch platforms, guidance, and typical mission profile. Next came a grease-penciled graphic he'd produced that morning, tallying the TLAMs available in the Med: the load-outs on *New Jersey* and the two submarines. He hoped the silence from above was a sign of attention. He segued from that to the plan he'd generated hunched over Grady's desk.

"The BGM-one oh nine is not intended to replace or obsolete manned aircraft, either Air Force or Navy. It's a force multiplier that can lend a synergistic advantage to the mix. The most appropriate use in the Prime Needle strike scenario is as follows." He crossed the stage and pointed at the chart that came up on the middle screen.

"Tomahawk flies at a lower altitude and has a smaller radar signature than either the F-one eleven or the A-six. However, its warhead weight is limited. For that reason, it should not be used against the principal targets of this raid — camps and training facilities.

"Tomahawk's optimal employment is as the first element across the coast in the defense suppression mission. It should be targeted on the early warning radar sites, on air defense sites such as the SA-five radar site at Sirte and the central air defense bunker outside Tripoli. Destroying these three to five minutes before the first aircraft reports 'feet dry' will give the maximum —"

The first interruption. It came from the

second row, behind the flag officers. The voice was dry, skeptical. "Are you saying it's accurate enough to hit a radar?"

"Yessir."

"We have Shrike and ARM to take out radar sites."

"Yes, sir, but Tomahawk doesn't need a plane to carry it. Also, we don't need a radar output in order to guide in."

He couldn't tell if they bought it or not, so he went on. "My second recommendation is that if we are directed to strike the chemical complex at Sidi Garib, we hit it with TLAM alone. The missile should be highly survivable at night across that terrain. I've done a preliminary run-through with rules of thumb we've developed from attacks at Tonopah. Based on that, we should target between six and ten rounds against the complex."

"Exactly how much explosive are we talking about?"

A question from the front at last, from an Army general. The chief of staff? Dan said, "Each TLAM carries a thousand-pound warhead. Ten of them would be five tons of explosive."

"We can multiply, commander."

Laughter from the back row. "Yes, sir. Sorry, sir," Dan said. *Asshole,* he thought.

"One F-one eleven-F carries twelve five-hundred pound Mark eighty-two Airs."

"Yes, sir, but we can target TLAM more

closely than they can lay iron bombs. We've been hearing about pinpoint bombing for a long time. Now we've got it."

The icy silence from above told him how welcome that remark had been. To hell with it, he was sick of putting spin on things to make people happy. On the other hand, his orders were to sell the system.

Sell a bright and shiny new weapon. . . .

A voice was saying, "How does it stack up against a laser-guided Pave Tack toss?"

"I can't make comparisons with other systems, sir. All I can say is that we have a circular error probable right now of less than fifty feet. With that kind of accuracy, we can target against individual process towers, control centers, and the power plant building. Let me also point out that we won't be risking any pilots. Sidi Garib is heavily defended, and the crews would be hitting it at the end of a very long flight."

A different voice from the rear, a Chuck Yeager drawl: "Can you guarantee a TOT? Time ovah target?"

"We can."

"To how close?"

"To twenty seconds," he told them. "The course computer can adjust speed and flight time. Actually, it's better than scheduling an aircraft strike. Aircraft, you have to leave clearances in space and time between attacks so you don't have collisions. But you want missiles to arrive simultaneously, to saturate the defense."

A different voice said, "What's your PD on the chemical plant?"

"Probability of damage, sir? That's a tough one." He did an off-the-cuff analysis, going from vulnerable dimensions metrics through munitions effects to expected lethality. He concluded, "Some of those numbers are still theoretical. But based on the intel I've seen on the installation, I think we can shut it down for at least two to three years."

Silence from above, then: "What you're sayin' is, all us attack jocks might as well put in for early retiahment," the Yeager voice said.

Chuckles, and he saw Auer turn his head, smiling, and make a remark. But when he faced forward, he was grim again. Dan answered the question: "No sir, this system's only suitable for a mission you can plan ahead of time, against a fixed location. Mobile targets, fast-breaking situations, it's going to be a long time before we can build something like that into a computer."

There were a couple more questions; he thought he handled them well. Now he felt relaxed. He felt as if he could stand up here all day long and take hostile questions.

But finally the deputy CINC stood. The others leapt up. "Thanks for the brief, Commander. You make a good case for your system."

"Yes, sir." Dan went to parade rest, holding the pointer parallel to the deck.

The others made as if to leave, but Auer lingered. "I just wanted to add, no prejudice to you, but we've heard this presentation before."

"About Tomahawk, sir?"

"No. But every few years, someone comes up here and tries to sell us some gee-whiz new standoff system. Unfortunately, every time we bite, we get burned. Effective precision munitions that operate in a battlefield environment have not yet arrived. Maybe they will one day. But even then, they won't be cheap, and the enemy will come up with countermeasures. The only foolproof targeting mechanism is the human eye. It's true — putting live guys over the target means we have to accept the possibility of loss. But the Air Force's job, I'm sure, like the Navy's, is to get the mission done."

Dan remained silent, since this seemed unanswerable except by saying flatly that the general was wrong. He didn't know much about flag officers, but he knew they didn't like to hear that.

Auer went on, "We don't entrust major missions to untried systems. For a couple of reasons. Here's one you don't seem to have considered. What if one of these missiles crashes out there in the desert?"

"I'm not sure I follow you, sir."

529

The general said patiently, "What if one crashes and the Libyans recover it? Then they hand it over to the Soviets, and you have a whole new technology compromised."

He didn't have a ready answer for that, mainly because he was remembering his own recovery of T207 at Primrose. Then he remembered: the operational missile wouldn't land soft. If it crashed, it would plow into the ground at three or four hundred miles an hour, along with a thousand-pound warhead fuzed to detonate at impact. If anybody could reconstruct it after that, they were magicians.

But it was too late now; Auer was coming down the spiral ladder. He stopped at the bottom and added, "Leave a copy of your slides with the J-Three office. Again, thanks for the presentation."

"Well, that was a pretty obvious waste of time," Dan told Grady when he got back to the third floor.

The liaison considered that, rubbing his glasses with a tissue. "I was listening. Down on the floor. I'm not so sure about that."

"You heard him turn me off, sir. And they didn't ask me to the planning meeting."

"He asked for a copy of the brief."

"A pat on the head."

"Maybe. But would you do something for me? Draw me up a description of your attack plan. Make it a point-paper format. As long as you're here, I have some people I'd like you to show it to."

# 30

"Marching in chains through the streets of Tripoli? Is that the scenario we're sweating here?"

"It happened in Hanoi," said another aviator. An O-6, he could have flown in Vietnam. Dan couldn't see his ribbons under the flight jacket. But he seemed receptive, and Dan looked at him, avoiding the hostile faces his own age, as he went on with the briefing.

Gaeta, Italy. He'd flown in in the rear seat of a T-34 at 0600. A pretty little town on the west coast of Italy that was the homeport for Commander, Sixth Fleet, the admiral in charge of all Navy forces in the Mediterranean.

It was three days after his briefing to Auer, and he'd been refining the plan since, interspersed with calls to Crystal City on the secure phone. At Grady's urging, he'd called the planning people in Norfolk, too, alerting them a mission might be coming down. They wanted op orders, tasking messages. He told them he didn't have those yet, but said if they wanted to be ready when the checkered flag came down, they'd better start digging out data now.

Now he stood in the flag plot aboard USS *Cochrane*, a *Charles Addams*-class guided-missile destroyer. The only one who could generate that tasking message was the tactical commander, COMSIXTHFLT. Whose staff officers sat listening now, some frowning, others with their jaws on their fists. This was the strike planning group for Operation Prime Needle. The trouble was, they were fighter jocks, attack pilots. They weren't enthusiastic about handing their jobs to a missile.

But the man who counted sat opposite him. Admiral Kidder's operations chief was diminutive and intellectual-looking, with a Polaris five-patrol pin on the breast of his blues. He didn't speak often, but when he did, the others remained silent after he stopped, as if giving themselves time to make sure they understood exactly what he'd meant before they responded.

He came to the end of his remarks — he'd been speaking all this time, while the rest of it parallel-processed through the back of his skull — and snapped off the projector. The pilots stirred. "Those are my recommendations. Any questions?"

The ops chief sat immobile. The pilots glanced at him, then leaned forward to drill in. Missile dependability, optical and infrared visibility, reattack requirements, penetration percentages against a fully activated, technologically sophisticated air defense. After the face-off at Patch, he was able to field most of them. Through it he watched the older flier.

He didn't ask questions, just let the younger men quiz him. Finally, there was silence again.

The ops chief said, "Captain Friedman?"

The 0-6 cleared his throat. "I was remembering the Thanh Hoa bridge."

"I thought you might be."

"Seven hundred sorties, and all those guys we lost. We kept thinking, if we just had the balls to get in close enough . . . but it wasn't a question of balls."

"Could this be the same sort of situation?"

"There's only one way to find out if something like this is going to work."

"Which mission? Air defense suppression?"

"Absolutely."

"Special missions?" This was shorthand for the chemical plant.

"Probably not. If those targets have absolutely got to be covered, we're better off putting air over them."

"Our Air Force friends seem to be having doubts." The N-3 waited, then added in that low-key way, "Or we could hit them ourselves. Second day, after we carry out the suppression mission."

"The numbers look bad on that, sir."

The ops chief turned to Dan, the first time he'd spoken directly to him. "I believe you should see Admiral Kidder."

"I'm ready to do that, sir."

"Have you reviewed our strike plan?"

"Captain Grady showed it to me at Patch, sir."

"That one's pretty much overtaken by events by now. Neal, how about going over our current thinking with him. Take him up to see the admiral at twelve-forty-five."

Friedman took him deeper into the ship, into the intel spaces. Locks snicked shut behind them.

This was a different world behind the "green door." It belonged to the 1400s, the intelligence specialists. Even Friedman was an intruder, as the jaygee who fell in as their escort made plain. The aviator took him down a passageway and into a small briefing room. When they were settled and green fiberglass mugs of coffee steamed in front of them, Friedman said, "How much you know about the LADC?"

"Not even what it is."

"Libyan Air Defense Command. Grady didn't brief you on this?"

"Some. Not in depth."

He took a slug of coffee as the first slide came up: the by-now-familiar wedge shape of Libya. An irregular border on the west was bounded by Tunisia and Algeria. To the east was Egypt; to the south, a pie slice deep into the Sahara. The spatter of cities and military installations showed that most of the population was clustered along the

Mediterranean coast.

"First off, what we're facing here is the most sophisticated air defense any air force has ever tried to penetrate. Khaddafi takes this seriously. The LADC is damn near as big as his air force and navy combined." Friedman went through the chain of command. "HQ's outside Tripoli, at what used to be Wheelus Air Force Base. The three air defense regions — RADs — are Tripoli, Benghazi, and Tobruk.

"We think each RAD has two SA-two missile brigades, three or four SA-three, two to four SA-six or -eight. Then there're radar companies and antiaircraft batteries. The exception is SA-fives; they protect the airfields and we figure they're under direct control of headquarters at Wheelus. The coverage overlaps. If the brigade structure follows Soviet practice, they've got — well, I won't go down to the number of launchers per battalion, but it's heavy coverage. The numbers add up to over a hundred batteries of SA types and three brigades of Crotales.

"Who's running all of them? Not just Libyans. There are East Germans, Poles, Czechs, and Russians. Some British and French personnel there, too.

"Okay, what are their weak points? We don't have much intelligence, but there's some interesting stuff. This next shot was taken by a Blackbird out of Mildenhall."

Dan peered at the slide. Even he could see

the missiles, laid out on the sand, shadows stark beneath them. "No camouflage?"

"No, but notice anything else funny?"

"No — other than that they're lined up, they look unprotected."

"Right, there's no shade. Soviet missile guidance systems are real sensitive to high temperatures. We did three separate photos over a week, and these guys were sitting there every time we went over. Conclusion one: They have a lot of spare missiles. Conclusion two: They don't take good care of them." Friedman handed the slide back to the jaygee. "Other vulnerabilities: The Libyan pilots don't fly at night. Also, dark of the moon would make it real hard for all those gun batteries to aim visually. Put those together and we've got a night mission. That goes good with our rules of engagement, too: Most of your civilians are going to be off the streets at night, especially around two, three in the morning."

"What are the rules of engagement?"

"Stringent. No plane goes unless all its systems are at a hundred percent. All targets have to be militarily significant. Collateral damage minimized."

'Collateral damage' was the euphemism for noncombatant casualties. Dan said, "Okay. What else?"

"The SA missiles have a limiting envelope of one hundred and fifty meters. If we can get below that their radars can't see us. We'll have EA-Six-B jammers in the air early and F-eighteens and A-sevens to do air defense suppression." Friedman sat back and wiped his hand through his hair. "I wouldn't be honest if I didn't say this one scares me. I flew downtown over Hanoi, and that was bad. This is a much heavier, newer, more capable air defense network. We can lose a lot of guys if we dick up."

"Which is why you thought I could help."

"I sure as hell hope you can. Because when we go up to see the vice admiral, I'm gonna recommend we bet some pilots' lives on your new toy here."

He felt apprehensive about it all morning, which was odd, considering he'd briefed higher-ranking officers than Kidder at Patch. But Vice Admiral Kidder was different. He was Navy, for one thing, and no matter how joint you got, a general just didn't have the impact on his nervous system an admiral did. Kidder also had a reputation for being hard-nosed, demanding, and irascible. First seating in the wardroom was full, so he went down to the mess decks for a bite before the brief.

They were hot and crowded and noisy. Men in dungarees and coveralls stained with paint and grease gave him incurious glances as he dropped his tray on the table; then went back to bitching about the watch bill. He dug into the overcooked, greasy chow. One said, "So Cudjoe, he goes up to this butt-ugly whore and starts giving her shit. And she speaks pretty good English, and she's giving him shit right back. So finally, he says, 'Hey, all I want is a little pussy.' And she says, 'Hell, so do I; *mine's* as big as a bucket.'"

Dan grinned. Sailors. They'd never change.

At 1240, he was standing with Friedman on the bridge wing, looking out over the placid Med toward the distant tan buildings of Gaeta, when an aide touched his arm and said, "Admiral will see you."

Kidder was bullet-headed, with bushy eyebrows and hairy hands. He sprawled in the padded leather chair, his worktable covered with message folders and document files. He didn't greet Dan or say anything welcoming when Friedman said, "Sir, this is the rep from JCM." He just grunted and kept reading. Dan waited, stealing a glance down at the water. It looked inviting. If he got a spare hour, maybe he could borrow fins, a mask, take a quick dip.

Still reading and without looking up, Kidder said, "What's EUCOM think about including Tomahawk in this strike?"

"Hard for me to tell, sir. General Stahl originally asked Admiral Niles to send me out to . . . uh, consult. But General Auer wasn't very enthusiastic when I briefed him."

Kidder leaned back and locked his hands

behind his head. "I've been reading about this thing for a while now. All the crashes. My impression was it's nowhere near ready to deploy."

"It's deployed, sir. You've got them aboard your six eighty-eights and *New Jersey*."

"I also know some of those canisters are empty. Can you take on Sidi Garib?"

"We can do a better job there than aircraft, sir."

"Give me the downside. Tell me why I shouldn't use your new toy."

He swallowed, realizing how cleverly Kidder had turned him into the devil's advocate. But maybe it was good; he could off-load some of his own doubt. "Well, it's fresh out of development. We're gonna get some failures. But we can overtarget to allow for that. One of Auer's staffers was afraid a bird would soft-land and compromise the technology. I think that's unlikely, though."

"How's it compare to air strikes?"

"Well, sir . . . there's less flexibility. You don't have the choice of ordnance, and you can't alter your tactics when you get to the target. And you're not going to get any damage assessment." He hesitated. "Aside from that, I can't think of any other arguments against."

"Arguments for?"

"You don't risk the plane or the pilot, and you get better surprise due to the low radar cross section."

"Collateral damage?"

"No more likely than with air strikes."

"We screw up and hit a hospital, the world press'll have us on a plate."

"You're right, sir. They will." Beside him, Friedman flinched, but he thought, The hell with it. The guy asked me.

"What do you think, Neal?"

"Sir, there's a risk, but we can use something like this. It could deny that son of a bitch the opportunity to parade hostages around."

Dan waited. Kidder fiddled with the papers. Finally, he said, "Work it up for defense suppression, the intel headquarters, and Sidi Garib. But back it up with air wherever you can."

"Aye aye, sir," said Friedman, and Dan followed him out again into the sunlight.

Stifling his desire for a swim, he went back down to the planning cell. He spent that afternoon huddled with the pilots and intel types, taking apart the air-attack plan and sliding in Tomahawk. They grumbled, but Friedman took the most vocal objectors out into the passageway. When they came back, they cooperated.

Midway though the afternoon, the jaygee brought him two folders in numbered orange jackets. One contained photos and technical data on the nerve-gas facility at Sidi Garib.

The other held photos and layout of an office building in downtown Benghazi identified only as "Target 3-C." He put in a couple of hours studying the plant and plotting the vulnerable points. When he turned to the office building, he noticed it was in the middle of a highly populated area. Looking at the damage overlays, it might be better not to target it. He finished the evaluation anyway and included it in the message. By then, it was midnight, and he crashed on a cot in sick bay.

When he woke the next morning and went back down to the cell, it was locked. No one was around.

He found Friedman and the other pilots drinking coffee and telling flying stories in the wardroom. He asked him, "What's up? I went to the strike cell. Nobody was there."

"We got told around four this morning, it's off."

"What's off?"

"The whole op plan. Somebody leaked it, and NBC decided the world had to know. Jim Miklaszewski reported on it. 'Air strikes planned against terrorist camps in Libya.' Then the *Post* and CBS picked it up. Everything's there, all the details — F-one elevens, A-sixes, even which targets we're going to hit. There're some angry people today."

He shoveled a tasteless charge of grits and eggs into a disgruntled stomach. It happened all the time. Everyone got all spun up, worked their tails off, and then at the last minute everything was called off. But it was especially bitter to have it happen because your own side had screwed you. Who could have leaked something like that? Why? All this work, and to have it called off like that. . . . He remembered the office building. "Hey — that Target Three-C. What was that?"

"Libyan Domestic Intelligence. Some nasty things go on in the cellars there."

"Well, it turned out to be right in the middle of a residential area. Any rounds that missed would hit apartment buildings, the streets, houses. You'd get collateral damage from the blast even if you impacted at point of aim."

"Well, doesn't matter now." Friedman pushed his plate back. "What're your plans? Gonna head back?"

"I guess so, if everything's canceled. I better call the office."

"Going to want transport back to Germany?"

"No, I'll probably head right back to the States."

"I can get you down to Sicily. You can hop a P-three back to Jacksonville from there."

Dan said that would probably be okay. He sat there for a while longer, torn between regret and relief. Then he went off to make his call.

543

# 31

He landed at Andrews two days later, after a twelve-hour flight from Sicily via Spain and Florida. Traveling in a P-three was Spartan. Crew seats, no heat, box lunches, no rest rooms. When you absolutely had to whiz, there was a metal tube jutting up out of the floor plates. The whole way across the Atlantic, the big turboprops droned too loudly to talk, even if the others sitting on their luggage had felt like it.

When the hatches cracked open at last, he went down the access ladder feeling as if he'd just been let out of prison. He stopped on oil-stained concrete, raising his arms in a stretch, sucking in the sun-filled air. Then picked his luggage up again and trekked after the space-A passengers toward the terminal.

When he humped it into the office, the familiar faces looked good. As usual after a trip, his desk was covered with mail and routing folders. He parked his luggage and stripped his jacket off. He considered going over to the workout club, showering and changing there. Instead, he sat down and started through the mail.

The second envelope he opened was from the Bureau of Personnel.

AIRMAIL
BUPERS ORDER 005651
LCDR DANIEL V LENSON, USN
JCMPO, ARL VA 22246

REF: (A) BUPERSMAN 3810260
     (B) YOUR RESIGNATION LETTER

ENCL: (1) APPOINTMENT IN US NAVAL
          RESERVE
      (2) DISCHARGE CERTIFICATE

WHEN DIRECTED IN JUNE DETACHED
DUTY; ACCORDANCE REF (A), REPORT
PRESENT CO TEMDU CONNECTION SEPA-
RATION PROCESSING. UPON COMPLETION
AND WHEN DIRECTED DETACHED. BY DI-
RECTION OF THE PRESIDENT, THE SECRE-
TARY OF THE NAVY HAS ACCEPTED YOUR
RESIGNATION OF YOUR PRESENT COM-
MISSION IN THE U.S. NAVAL SERVICE SUB-
MITTED IN REF. (B), TO TAKE EFFECT AT
2400 ON DATE OF DETACHMENT FROM AC-
TIVITY AT WHICH SEPARATED.

YOUR DEDICATED SERVICE TO THE
NAVY AND YOUR COUNTRY IS DEEPLY
APPRECIATED, AND IT IS HOPED THAT
YOU WILL ENJOY EVERY SUCCESS AND
HAPPINESS IN THE FUTURE.

He sat motionless, holding the scalpel that
would in not very many days sever him from

everything he knew and had done since he was seventeen years old.

At last he put it in his drawer and tried to go on, but his eyes wouldn't focus. The trouble was, the Navy had been everything he'd ever wanted. . . .

His phone rang. It was Lucille. "Mr. Lenson? Captain Westerhouse was wondering if you'd gotten back yet."

"I just walked in."

"Could you come up and see him? He has a meeting he has to go to in half an hour; he wanted to see you before he left."

Dan said he'd be right there, then told Sakai where he was going. Sparky nodded absently, eyes welded to the computer screen.

Westerhouse was sitting with his seat tilted back, eyes closed. Dan stopped in the doorway, shocked. Every time he came back from a trip, his boss had looked thinner, more tired, sicker. Now he looked as if he might never wake. What was Niles doing, letting him keep on coming to work? He was dying before their eyes.

His boss stirred, blinked, and edged his chair erect. "Dan . . . good to see you back. C'mon in. Sorry the mission got scrubbed."

"Too many leaks. All over the news."

"Yeah, it's got a lot of people steamed."

"Who leaked it? Anyone know?"

"The usual. 'Informed sources.' "

"Could it be some way of sending a message? Back off the terrorism or we'll hit you for real?"

"I doubt it's that deliberate. Somebody just told the press to show off their access. Anyway, it's off now. We'd lose an awful lot of guys trying to strike an alerted air defense system. I was listening to NPR this morning driving in. The President's rejected the military option. Too many hostages left in Libya, too many Arabs who don't like whatever we do. So we let this asshole kick us in the nuts and get away with it again."

"Well, it wasn't a total loss. I got in some face time with Admiral Kidder. They know they've got the capability now."

"Did you get to *New Jersey*?"

"No. She's off Lebanon."

Westerhouse cleared his throat, looking awkward, and asked how everything else was going. Meaning, Dan supposed, how he was recovering from Kerry's death. He said he was coping, a response Westerhouse probably took the way he meant it, which was that he didn't feel like talking about it. His boss struggled up, throwing a look at his watch. "Well, sounds like you did all you could. Thanks for taking that on."

"You want me to make any more posttrip briefings, sir? Colonel Evans, Admiral Niles?"

"I don't think so. Just do a trip report. Put in what you told me about briefing the flags. Going to the wetting-down tonight?"

Dan said he was going to go straight home after work and get some sleep instead. Westerhouse nodded and left.

He was at his desk when the phone rang. "Lenson," he said.

"Dan."

He searched his mind for the voice. Then remembered. "Special Agent Bepko."

"Yeah. You ready? It's time for Operation Snapdragon."

"What are you talking about?"

"Remember the package Li wanted? The stuff we were talking about? It's ready."

"The guidance documentation?"

"That's right."

"Where did you get it? Is this the real thing you're giving him?"

"You don't need to know that. All you need to do is to pass it to the colonel."

"Look, know what I'm holding in my hand?"

"Your cock?"

"Funny. My detachment orders. The date is June. Hear me? June."

"I heard you the first time. Where you going? Any plans?"

"Actually, nothing concrete. I was thinking computers on the West Coast."

"Well, that's your business. All you have left to do is hand this tar baby to the good Mr. Li. We take him down, and hopefully

Col. Zhang too, you're even Steven for your girlfriend. Then you can ride off into the sunset. If you have to come back and testify, you even get paid, how about that?"

That sounded acceptable, so he said, "So, do you want me to call him? Set up a meeting?"

"Yeah. That's the next step."

"Where? It's probably going to be someplace out of town; he doesn't seem to like to meet in D.C."

"Well, we got a problem with that. I made the one in San Diego, but we don't have unlimited travel money. So make it as close to here as you can. And we need time to scope out the place, get gear installed. We're going to film this; I think I told you that. If he proposes a hotel, find out which room."

"What should I tell him I've got?"

"Don't go into details. Just tell him you have what he wanted." Bepko left the phone, then came back on. "Sheck — Agent Attucks — says to tell you he'll be backing you up."

Dan said to pass his thanks, that he'd go make the call now. But Bepko was saying, "Go make it? What do you mean?"

"He said to always call him from a pay phone."

"No, no. You're working for us, not him. Make the call from your office phone. That way, we'll have it on tape, as evidence."

"That way — wait a minute. Are you telling

549

me you're tapping my phone?"

"Absatively. For your protection, Dan. Call me back as soon as you're done."

He said he would and hung up. He got up and walked to the end of the hall, then back, struggling to get his feelings under control. Trying to become another person, one who didn't know what the man he was about to talk to had done. Finally, he picked the phone up again and dialed Li's number.

The attaché sounded angry he'd called. Dan said, "Well, I have something you want. In fact, I have almost everything you want." He remembered to play greedy. "And I expect to get paid. Twenty grand. That's what you promised."

A pause. At last Li said, "You know how long the average Chinese has to work to make twenty thousand dollars?"

Dan said no money, no diagrams. Li said to wait, that he had to go off the line for a minute. Finally, the attaché came back on. "Tell me again what you have. You said diagrams. Of what?"

He winged it. "Of what? Of the LN-thirty-five. And hard-copy printouts of most of the terrain-comparison software."

"Very good. *Very* good. . . . We can bring some cash. Not the whole twenty grand. But five or six. We'll get you the rest in a week or two."

"Okay, where? I don't want to go too far.

I'm tired. Been traveling a lot. And I want to get rid of this stuff. I don't like having it around."

Li said he'd call back. Dan said no, if the attaché wasn't interested, he was going to start feeding the shredder; said he was having second thoughts anyway. That got a response. Li's voice turned steely. He said no, they wanted the material. Where was it now? Dan said it was in his office, in a personal safe. "And I want to get rid of it. Can we meet tomorrow?"

Li said brusquely that was out of the question. "We set the schedule. You don't," he said sharply. "I told you. We'll call back. That's the best I can do." And he hung up.

He worked for another hour, till 1530, the earliest moment he could go out the door and still feel he'd put in a full day. He went down to the Crystal Underground, picked up his dry cleaning, and bought a *Post*. He read it on the subway, then lugged his gear home through the back streets of Arlington. The air smelled of returning life. The trees were budding. Damn, it was spring already.

When he let himself into his apartment, a fistful of mail in his hand, it was waiting for him. He'd blotted it out on the flights across Europe and the Atlantic, and during the briefings. He'd driven himself so hard during the planning sessions because it did just that. But now he was face-to-face with it again. He sat on the bed, looking at where she'd slept. The afternoon sunlight came through the blinds and rested on the coverlet. Dust drifted through the air like tiny sparkling worlds. When he'd been small, he'd wondered if tiny beings lived on each drifting mote, fought and loved and died just as they did in the world he knew.

He felt empty. As if he'd never feel anything again.

Half an hour later, he got up and went into the kitchen. The pantry held midget pickles and sardines in mustard sauce, neither of which he felt like eating.

Before he remembered, he had opened the cupboard. Her note was still there, but the current of air as he opened the door sent it airborne. It evaded his hand and swooped to the floor.

Soundless tears slipped down his cheeks. The last hand that had touched it had been hers. Now it was dirty, and time would fade it, and eventually he'd throw it away, or lose it. Nothing would remain. . . .

He put it back and closed the cabinet, trying not to think of her, or of how quickly a drink would numb the pain. He went into the living room and stared at a shelf of books. He picked one up and looked at the page. The words made no sense. He put it back and started ripping open the mail.

A form letter. If he had any additional information on the matter recently reported, the District of Columbia Police stood ready to help.

Suddenly, the apartment was too empty to stay in a moment longer. He stripped off his uniform, took a quick shower, and put on slacks and a light jacket.

Outside, the sun was lower, the air cooler, the clouds darker. He wondered whether he should have brought a raincoat. To hell with it. He headed downhill, the evening traffic bumper-to-bumper, inching past him as the sidewalk dropped toward Rosslyn. An occasional biker pumped past, calves bulging. He didn't look up from the sidewalk. As far as he could, he didn't let himself think at all — beyond how nice it would be never to have to think again.

Dusk fell as he reached the bridge. He breasted the still-running tide of students, workers, and shoppers streaming out of the city. Then stopped halfway across and leaned over the rail, looking down.

The river ran heavy and swift and blackish green, foaming around submerged rocks. He watched it for a long time. Pedestrians pushed by on the walkway. He didn't feel them. It was as if filling his eyes with the unceasing motion of the water occupied his brain, too, made it possible not to remember.

When he went on at last, it was night. The air moved over him, cool with coming rain. The lights were flickering on in Georgetown. He walked for block after block, eyes passing unseeing over antiques, rare books, carpets, all the lures of the city. For behind them, a dark bridge arched over a still canal.

Had it only been last October? It seemed like another lifetime and himself another man than the runner who'd followed a penguin and a Red Death across a bridge he could never cross again. To meet eyes that shone through a black mask. Eyes and hair and a smile he'd never see again.

What had he learned?

He stopped at a Vietnamese restaurant and had dinner in a garden out back. The waiter stood silently beneath glowing incandescents as they stirred in the wind. Shadows lurched and swayed as if trees and bushes and buildings were all rolling in some immense sea. He ordered at random, and ate without tasting what he put into his mouth.

What had she left him?

The rain started as he finished his meal. He paid and stood outside in the drifting mist, getting wet but not caring. Cars tore writhing curtains of water off sparkling asphalt. When they were past, the black mirror lay there, reflecting again, a path of gold and ruby light.

He raised his eyes to their source.

He crossed the street, eyes on the gay, inviting colors. It wasn't a fancy place. Just a neighborhood hangout. You could get something to warm yourself when you were wet and cold. . . .

He didn't want to drink. Yet he couldn't live with what was inside his head.

Halfway across, he stopped and stood on the white line as cars sped past him. Mist rolled, clammy on his face, like sea fog. A taxi's horn wailed.

When he went back into the restaurant, the checkout girl looked at him silently. Dan's hands shook as he dropped coins into the pay phone. It rang and rang. The number didn't answer. He called another. A man's voice answered. Dan told him who he was, where he was, what was going on. The voice talked to him. It went on and on as he listened, willless, blank.

"You feeling better now?"

"I don't know. Maybe."

"One day at a time, buddy. That's the only way we can do this. One day at a time. One hour at a time. One minute at a time, if you have to. But it works. Eat something with sugar in it. A lot of sugar. Sometimes that helps."

The waiter looked not at all surprised to see him again. Dan said, "I thought I'd have dessert after all."

He had a flan, smothered with sticky syrup. He ate it slowly. The caramel sweetness seemed to lessen the craving.

When he left again, he didn't look across the street.

The rain came down steadily now. He heard laughter and music. He saw the smiling faces of women through brightly lit windows. He went on, the rain soaking through his jacket.

As the slippery, gritty concrete steps rose behind him, the sounds of cars and voices faded, replaced by the silence of trees and stagnant water. The rain hissed into the surface of the canal, swallowed instantly by everlasting darkness.

Finally, he came to the bridge. He stopped there, sheltered by its black arch. He stood looking down into the lusterless water. The rain aureoled a distant streetlight.

He didn't know what was right anymore. Once he had, or thought he had. Tell the truth, act honorably . . . do his duty . . . but it wasn't as simple as that.

He'd been born into a family and time that believed the United States had saved the world. His father's old uniforms in the closet. Memorial Day parades. Shoot-outs on TV every evening. A childhood spent in dread of a lifted hand, a belt, or a two-by-four. He'd accepted that as a child accepts things. That was how it was, and they'd told him it was right.

From that narrow world, he'd gone to Annapolis, and believed with all the enthusiasm of youth. When he'd stood in Memorial Hall, he'd dreamed of attacking Japanese battleships in a heroic charge that would change the course of history.

Instead, the protective womb of Mother Bancroft had contracted mercilessly, expelling him into the seventies. The country had lost a war. Glory had turned to ashes. Half his division on his first ship had been potheads, and most of the rest alcoholics.

That Navy had passed away, replaced by a growing fleet that anticipated a blue-water battle with the Soviets. In his short career, he'd known war and peace, victory and defeat, buildups and downsizing, public adulation and public contempt.

But he'd always tried to hold fast to one thing. They'd called it honor at the Academy. Now he thought maybe it was something less loaded with pride and self-regard. Maybe just integrity. Or maybe even something as simple as doing what you ought to without thinking of yourself.

Whatever you called it, it meant you made the right choices. But how, *how?* It was easy to decide between right and wrong. But how did you decide between two things you knew in your heart were both right?

He was thinking of Haneghen.

The renegade priest wasn't the kind of hero they built memorials to. His deeds were small:

a futile protest, two or three paragraphs in the newspapers, a second or two of film at eleven. They didn't change anything. But he kept on. Even if it brought prison, fines, separation from those he loved.

He shivered, leaning against the cold stone. Yeah, Haneghen had guts. Along with a simple answer to the immense puzzle and challenge of the world. He said violence was never justified, even in self-defense, or in defense of the helpless.

The trouble was, he couldn't accept that. It sounded good, but — shit, it had *happened*, when Nan and Susan had been hostages in the Med. Yeah, he'd had to kill. And he would again! Abandoning his family wouldn't have been an act of courage. It would have been a crime.

He'd never let anyone helpless be harmed if he had the strength to stop it.

Maybe he just wasn't evolved enough morally to see it. That was possible. But look at it in terms of police, he told himself, sliding to a crouch, hugging his knees. Maybe they weren't always honest. Or efficient. But most did the best they could, and he didn't think a world without police would work. He didn't think a world without the U.S. armed forces would work, either. All it meant was that the people who *didn't* believe in tolerance and peace would rule it.

He was shuddering. The stone he perched

on sucked warmth out of his flesh. He wrapped his arms around himself.

The trouble was, he didn't know if he was being realistic or if he was making the same error that had made the world the hell it was.

He'd asked, and he'd thought, and he'd pondered. And all he had left to grasp was the doubt, and the wonder, and the seeking.

He stared unseeing into the dark water. Only hours later, deep in the night, did he hoist himself stiffly to his feet and find his way home through the rain.

# 32

He kept expecting a call back from Li all the next week. But it didn't come. He'd almost forgotten about it when at 1530 Friday the phone rang. Bepko said, "Just checkin' that you were there. I got a hunch you're gonna get a call from our mutual buddy shortly."

"What, you have him bugged, too?"

"The less you know, the better. Just stick close to your desk." The NIS agent hung up. And sure enough, about twenty minutes later, a soft female voice said, "Dan?"

"Yes?" Then he recognized it. "Mei!"

"Can you be at the central newsstand, National Airport, this evening at seven P.M.?"

"Tonight?"

"That is right. Can you make it tonight? At seven?"

"Well, gee — wait a minute." He thought, then said, "I guess so." It was one subway stop from Crystal City. Or he could walk over in about twenty minutes. "Mei? I didn't know you were working for —"

"Yes?" No mistake, there was a sadness there. "What?"

"Nothing. I'll be there." He set the phone down and took a deep breath, flexed his shoulders.

The phone again. Bepko. "Okay, all right!

That gives us about three hours to get everybody contacted, get into position. Everything go on your end?"

"Not really. Look, where's this stuff I'm supposed to turn over? I don't have anything to give this guy."

"Sheck's on his way over. He'll tell you everything you need to know. Don't worry so much."

"Is he going to be there?"

"Everybody's going to be there. Remember, we wanted to use this to wake people up to what these guys are doing to us? Well, there's going to be lots of cover. Several federal agencies. The local cops, to show them what we do. Be a couple of senior people watching the handoff, too."

"Great, now it's a spectator sport. Just keep them out of sight, all right? This guy's not stupid. In fact, he's damn sharp."

"You'll never see us. Got to go. Just keep your cool. Soon as you hand off, we move in. Cuff him, take him away; it'll all be over but the shouting."

Dan said okay and hung up. He sat for a little while, staring blankly at a page of test results.

Half an hour later, the phone rang again. This time it was Shirley Toya. The security officer told him a gentleman was waiting for him in her office. Dan said he'd be down as soon as he got changed.

★ ★ ★

The "package" was a government-issue manila envelope inside a black plastic portfolio. Attucks pushed it down the counter to Dan. "Welcome to Operation Snapdragon," he said.

"Uh-huh. This it?"

"That's right. What is that, your gym gear? I'd like you to go back up, get back in your uniform."

"It'd be a lot less obvious in civvies."

"Did Mr. Bepko mention there are going to be some important observers?"

"He did."

"It was felt that the impact would be greater if they saw an officer in uniform there, handing over things to a foreign intelligence agent."

"Are you kidding? We're doing this for drama? Man, I'm glad I'm getting out of this circle jerk."

"Easy, Commander."

Dan hefted the portfolio. "Tell me what we got here. What's the classification?"

"The highest classification stamp in there is 'Top Secret.' "

"Okay, let's see it."

"Oh, we sealed it already."

"Then unseal it! Look at this thing — how neat it is. This is something I put together on the sly, sneaking back and forth from the Xerox machine?"

Attucks finally grumbled agreement. They

peeled the flap back. Dan slipped out pages, scrutinizing each.

Finally, he looked up. "What the hell is this? There's nothing here about Tomahawk. This page here looks like some kind of air-conditioning diagram."

"Pretty close. It's the elevator control system, over at the Hoover Building."

"Goddamn it, I told Li I had inertial guidance diagrams, hard-copy stuff on the TER-COM."

"That's too sensitive to hang out there. We've been all over it with Naval Intelligence, and that's the consensus. Anyway, he's not going to go through it there in the airport. In fact, he won't get to open it at all. As soon as it's in his possession, we move in. It doesn't really matter what it is. It's the intent that counts in espionage charges."

"I don't have a good feeling about this. Look, am I going to be armed? I've got a gun at home. I could run over there, get it, come back —"

"You don't need a gun. Counting NIS, Naval Intelligence, FBI, and the Agency, you're going to have almost twenty agents in a hundred-foot circle around you when you step up to that news counter."

"That's a lot of cooks. If this soup gets spoiled —"

"Lay off," said Attucks, and for just a moment, Dan saw contempt. "You're pulling the plug on the Navy. So why don't you just leave it to the counterintelligence professionals. And we'll get your part of it over with as fast and painlessly as we can."

At 6:30 P.M., the arrival area at National was as full of cars and taxis and hurrying, overburdened human beings as Dan had ever seen in a space. Planes pivoted and rolled on the far side of the outflung wings of the terminal.

He was working his way toward the main entrance when he thought he glimpsed a familiar face. He frowned, searching the crowd, but didn't catch it again in the stream of humanity. He nearly ran over three women dragging luggage carts, stumbled, then recovered himself; and there she was. When she saw he'd seen her, she turned instantly away, letting him catch up from behind, as if she didn't want to be seen face-to-face with him. Taxis honked, drivers leaning out.

"Mei. I haven't seen you — you haven't been in class."

She said rapidly, eyes averted, "I know where you're going. Listen. Turn around now. Go back to your office."

"What do you mean?"

"Leave. Just trust me. Go back."

"I have to —" he caught himself. He couldn't tell her about Kerry, about revenge, about the impending sting. She worked for

564

them. "No. I'm going through with it."

"Then listen. There's a man here who knows everything. Do you really need this money? Enough to risk your life?"

"I'm not risking anybody's life. A man who knows everything. You mean Li?"

"No. I don't know his name." She pushed blue-black hair from a lowered face, then shot him one more swift sidelong glance before dropping her eyes again. "I just wanted to say I'm sorry. I didn't want to get you involved in this. It was not why I went out with you."

"It's all right."

"They wanted me to pretend something else — something that would make you more willing to work with them. But I wouldn't."

He felt suddenly cold, felt his legs weaken under him as he understood. And because she hadn't, they'd decided to threaten him in another way. Set a gang waiting for a lone woman on a bicycle. . . . He mumbled, "I understand."

"I won't be coming back to class. I am going back to China."

"You are? You can't finish your —"

"They say I have to go. I have to obey. Someday that will change. But that is the way it is now. So be careful. And can I —"

Before he could respond, he found himself being hugged hard around the neck. Before his hands could come up, she released him. Darting an apprehensive glance around, she signaled to the nearest cab, ducked into it. Then the crowd closed like a curtain and she was gone.

Li was sitting in the row of seats closest to the news counter, looking at a copy of *The Economist*. When their eyes met, he closed it quickly and got up, picking up an umbrella. He was wearing the same light coat as he had in Balboa Park. Unbuttoned, it showed a mustard brown suit that looked as if it had been bought off the rack at a thrift shop.

"Mr. Lenson." The pouchy, tired eyes creased in a quarter smile behind tinted glasses.

"How are you? How's Mr. Zhang?"

"Well. How was your cruise?"

"Okay."

"I don't expect to see you in uniform."

"You took me by surprise. I don't keep civilian clothes at the office."

"There are a lot of servicemen here." Li looked around, a seemingly casual glance that Dan saw was actually a close scrutiny of those around them. He hoped whoever all these observers were, they were hanging back, with a long lens. Binoculars would be even better.

"Do you want this?" he asked the attaché.

Li didn't answer, didn't reach for the portfolio Dan held out.

The little man with the mustache started walking instead. Dan hesitated, then tucked it under his arm and followed. They threaded the crowd down the south wing and into a corridor lined with stores. In front of Olssen's, Li stopped. He put his hands in his coat pockets. "I'm angry with you."

"With me? Why?"

"I told you we don't meet face-to-face like this. It's not safe. And I don't like being jerked around."

"I'm not jerking you around!"

"Telling me to hurry; telling me that if I don't, you'll destroy the material. That's jerking me around."

"I thought you wanted it. That's what you said, wasn't it? I have something you need. And you have something I need."

Li studied him. Again he slid his eyes over the crowd. Finally, he said, "Follow me."

By the Delta ticket counter, a solid line of people waiting to check in screened them from the open area of the terminal as effectively as yards of concrete. Dan switched the envelope from one hand to the other, but Li made no move to take it. Instead, he said, "Now. What did you say you had that was so important?"

"A selection. Some things you might find interesting."

"You mentioned material on TERCOM?"

"That's part of it."

"You seem nervous."

"Hey, I'm betraying my fucking country.

567

They catch me, I go to Leavenworth till I'm eighty. How laid back do you expect me to be?"

Li perused the corridor. He even looked straight up at the ceiling.

He murmured, "Of course, I know you've gone to your security agencies." His pouchy eyes studied Dan without expression.

"What are you talking about? I haven't told anyone."

"Oh, really? You haven't arranged with them to pass faked documents?"

Dan realized suddenly there was no way Attucks could be backing him up here. There were people all around them, immobile in the check-in lines, and Li had been leading the way. They couldn't have agents in every line, yet anyone following them would have been immediately obvious. All the attaché had to do was take his hand out of his coat pocket, shoot or stab him, pick up the package, and stroll off into the crowd.

He forced himself to keep slouching. Li was bluffing, testing him. Dan told him, "Hey, here it is. Take a look at it. That's the real McCoy." But he was hoping desperately that Li wouldn't. Though maybe, if you weren't a missile engineer, what was in there might be enough to fool you, at least for a hurried glance.

"Is there any software there?"

Dan felt sweat rolling down his back. He

should have supervised putting the package together. Now he had to improvise and lie, and hope he wasn't contradicting what he'd said before, which he barely remembered. His mind seemed to be hanging up, like a computer running out of programming. "I told you, some. Hard-copy printouts of new patches."

"Not the complete guidance package?"

"No. Patches are pieces of code that fix areas with bugs."

"I see. Well, we very much would like the complete package. I've discussed this with Colonel Zhang. If you could get the latest version for us, we could pay you up to . . . let's say forty thousand dollars."

"Uh, I'll see. That kind of stuff's not easy to get. Do you want this or not?" He offered it again.

But instead of taking it, the diminutive man in the scruffy coat turned away again. He breasted the incoming current, heading out into the open air through the automatic door. Dan followed him, dodging Pakistanis and barking his shin against a baggage cart. The son of a bitch wasn't making this easy. If he'd just take the damn thing . . . No, he had to take it within range of the cameras, of witnesses. Or it was no good, a failed bust.

Li stood at the curb, hands in his pockets, umbrella tucked under his arm. Dan stepped up beside him. Getting angry, he said, "Do you want this or not?"

"I'm not sure I do." Li didn't look at him directly. He was scanning the line of taxis and limos and cars. Dan staggered as someone jostled him from behind, almost knocking him into the roadway. He clutched at the portfolio. It was covered now with damp marks where his fingers had clutched it. "I'm not sure I trust you entirely."

"The feeling's mutual. Look, let's get this over with." He spotted a trash receptacle a few feet away. "See that shitcan? If you don't want this, that's where it's going. Make up your mind."

The cab in front of them eased out, and another car cut in from the outer lane to take its place. Something large and black, a Caddy or a Lincoln. The driver it cut off leaned on his horn. Someone jostled Dan again.

Then, before he could react or register what was happening, he was being body-blocked from behind, shoved off the curb. He stumbled and flailed his free arm. A hand smashed down on his cap, bending him into an involuntary crouch. A door slammed open, and he was shoved again, propelling him into a gray leather interior. Bodies surged in after him. He kicked, but got a savage blow to his kidney in return. The pain was so sudden and overwhelming that he screamed. It was cut off by the sound of a heavy door slamming.

He lay on the floor, panting, till the pain

ebbed. Then pushed himself to his knees, and looked around.

He was in the passenger compartment of a limousine. The windows were opaque, dark glass. Li sat across from him, hands on his knees. Two other men, much larger than the colonel, sat above Dan in dark suits. One was Chinese and the other was black.

The cabbie's horn sounded again, faintly, from outside. The limo surged into motion, rocking him back, then settled into a smooth cruise.

"What the hell is this?" he said, but not very loudly.

Li said, "Get up, Dan. Take a seat." The two large men sat motionless, watching him. "I'm sorry my sergeant had to hit you. But if you think for a moment, you'll understand. We can't just take whatever you give us and hand over cash. I have the money ready. This isn't a sham. But we have to know if this is the real stuff."

He couldn't think of anything to say. The enclosed space swung from side to side and he felt a surge of acceleration. Moving out of the National approaches onto one of the highways, Glebe, or Arlington Boulevard, or Columbia Pike, but he couldn't tell which. Or which direction they were going.

He was pretty sure Attucks hadn't planned for this.

He was fitting his still-painful back into the

cushioned bench seat when a motor hummed. The partition slid open, and he caught a glimpse of the back of the driver's head, of traffic riding serenely through the gathering dark beyond. Four lanes of it. The partition hummed closed before he could see anything else.

Li reached forward and dusted off his trousers. It was the first time he'd touched Dan. His touch was surprisingly gentle. He said, "Now, let's see what we have."

He took the portfolio at last from Dan's unresisting fingers, produced a penknife, and slit the plastic. He slit the envelope, too, and slid out the documents.

Dan glanced at the door handles. He couldn't tell if they were locked or not. Even if they weren't, he figured by that one glimpse past the driver, and the purr of the engine, they had to be going at least fifty. Go out the door, he'd have about three seconds to tumble and break his bones before the next vehicle behind went over him. Across from him, the large men regarded him silently.

"Can you tell me what this is?" said Li, holding out a page. Dan rubbed his forehead, feeling how wet it was. He said, "I think that's the radar altimeter."

Li tipped down his glasses, regarding him. He kept the page extended for a moment more, then, when Dan added nothing, leaned back and tapped on the partition.

It slid open again, and this time, through the slightly wider opening, Dan saw the side of a young Asian face, male, unfamiliar; beside it, he glimpsed the edge of an arm and shoulder in a pinstriped shirt. Li said something in Chinese and passed the page through, hesitated, then passed the rest of the sheaf after it. The partition slid closed, and again they rode in a taut silence.

"Smoke?" said Li, extending a pack of Camels.

"No thanks."

"That's right, you don't. I ought to quit. One of these days."

Li lit up. Dan visualized lemons, trying to work up some spittle. His mouth was dry as dust. With four people breathing the enclosed air, and now Li puffing away, the atmosphere was suffocating. "Can we get some more air in here? Crack a window or something?"

The black man looked at Li; the attaché nodded. A moment later, cool air hissed. The smoke whirled, thinned, sucked out through invisible vents. Dan dragged his hand across his forehead again. Shit, shit, shit. Why hadn't he listened to Mei? Or to his own judgment, and brought the gun?

The partition slid open. The Asian turned in his seat and began a colloquy with Li. Past him, Dan saw the striped shirt again. A hand came up, holding one of the pages, passing it back to the Chinese. The hand was pale-skinned and freckled. Not Asian. European, Caucasian.

His sight focused on it, glued to it. To it, and to an edge of red-orange suspender and the back of a reddish blond head that moved into his field of view for a moment, then out again.

The partition hummed closed. The attaché set the documents gently on the seat beside him. He sat smoking, apparently lost in thought. Dan sat sweating, awaiting the inevitable.

Finally, Li said, "It's bogus."

"What? No, that's good material."

"Don't take me for an idiot. That man up front's from our missile program. Doctorate from Cal Tech. What you just gave me has nothing to do with Tomahawk, or with any other weapon. It's a farrago of technical-looking crap. So that leaves two possibilities. One: You're a small-time grifter, trying to fish me in and scam me. For the cash. Two: You're working with American counterintelligence. Which is it, Dan? Please level with me. It will get very bad if you don't."

He sat sweating for a moment more. He thought of blaming it on someone else, saying he was just a conduit, that he'd been tricked, too. Then he decided he'd been too dumb for too long. He'd underestimated this man, and his organization, just as Attucks had said they all did. He wasn't going to make up anything else. He simply sat silent, arms crossed, and stared back at Li.

"You aren't answering? Well, perhaps you're right. Perhaps it really doesn't matter which. All right, Mr. Hickey," said Li, and the black man reached forward.

The beating was thorough and professional, leaving him unable to move or speak. He'd tried to fight back, but he hadn't landed a blow. Hickey blocked his punches without expression. Now he lay on the floor, curled like a fetus, tasting blood and only partially conscious.

Later, the car stopped. The voices told him to get up. He tried but couldn't. So the hands gripped his armpits and legs and dragged him out across rough pavement, then thrust him inside another car. He felt cracked vinyl against his cheek, smelled the reek of gasoline and exhaust from a leaking muffler.

When he came to again, he saw a streetlight passing overhead. Then another one, unlit and shattered. Another, lit but flickering.

He dragged himself up, to find himself in the backseat of a large but badly maintained American-made automobile. Strips of headliner hung down. The ashtrays were missing. A litter of fast-food packaging and empty oil cans covered the floor. Hickey sat across the seat from him, a stainless-steel handgun pointed at him. A squat dark man drove without looking back.

"How you doin'?" Hickey said. Dan didn't answer at once. He dragged his hand across his lips and examined the smear of blood.

"Did you kill her?" Dan asked him.

"Who, man?"

"The woman on the trail. Kerry Donavan."

"That was a mistake. We ain't usin' them kids again. Your woman, right? Sorry about that."

He squinted out as they rolled past paintless, sagging houses, massive brick tenements, empty, littered lots, cracked concrete walls, chain-link fences. He didn't know where they were now. Washington, yes, but this was the other face of the futuristic world capital, the dark side of the shining city on a hill: potholed roads, abandoned lots, fear palpable in the deserted streets. There didn't even seem to be any street signs. Eventually, the big sedan's tie-rods creaked as it heaved and dipped over a railroad grade. The driver racked in a knob, and the headlights went out. It rolled slowly through an underpass, swayed into a wide right turn, and rolled at steadily diminishing velocity through a crumbling brick gate. A slow parting of shadows began ahead of them. The tires crackled over shattered glass and loose gravel, more and more deliberately, and at last rocked to a halt.

The window-shattered buildings around them were abandoned and lightless. The only light came from the cupric sky. They sat for a few seconds, the driver, Dan, and the man with the gun, Hickey, watching the last of the shadows drift and stagger out of the court-yard.

"Get out," Hickey said then.

When he got out, he saw cigarette butts, torn bits of foil and paper, and thousands of used matches covering the cracked asphalt. The air was thick with the odor of fresh shit.

He understood now. Blood tasted like cop-per filings in his mouth. They'd find him here in the morning, lying on the pavement deep in the crack district. Another random killing. Another colored pushpin on a map in a dingy office.

"Any point in begging for my life?"

"Don't degrade yourself, man. This is busi-ness. That's all."

"Why are you doing this? Working for them? Don't you know who they are?"

"I know who they are," Hickey said. "And they're gonna be givin' us guns. A whole ship-load a machine guns. So it all gonna work out. . . . You want it in the back of the head? Quick and neat. Turn around if you want it in the back of the head."

He turned slowly, gauging the distance to the open maw of the warehouse — At least fifty yards. The way his legs felt, he wouldn't make more than four or five steps before he fell. But if that was all there was left to do, that was what he'd do. The glitter of broken glass — maybe he could get his hands on a shard.

Or was it time to stop fighting at last, here at the end? Time just to accept?

The click of a hammer going back, the crackle of steps coming around the car.

He lurched into his run, but his legs gave way almost at once. He collapsed, rolling over on the stinking dark ground. His hands searched for something sharp but found nothing.

On his knees, he looked up at the approaching dark figure, its long arm raised, extended at his head. The end, then. And he'd lost. He wasn't thinking of Kerry then, or Nan, or God. He was simply and purely filled with rage, because his hands were empty, because he was dying not just uselessly but helplessly.

The lights came on directly behind Hickey, silhouetting the gun, silhouetting him as he wheeled. Dan cowered, shielding his eyes from the brilliance. The flashing, rotating strobes, repetitive detonations of light that felt as if they were exploding in his brain.

The loudspeaker said, "This is Detective Sergeant Joe Ogen of the D.C. Police. Get out of the car. Drop your weapons and put your hands up."

Ogen brought him a blanket and put him in the backseat of the squad car. The uniformed cops took the others away, leaving the T-Bird sitting in the littered courtyard. The detective leaned in after a time. "You okay, Lieutenant?"

He murmured between bruised lips, "That's about the closest I've ever come."

"We lost you there, after they took off from National. But then I started thinking. Knowin' that your girl got killed by some of the gang bangers. Knowin' somebody called Reeney gave 'em their orders. And knowin' from the street that Rene Hickey was getting guns somewhere. Not just the usual junk, either, but Chinese-made full-auto AK-forty-sevens. This is where he likes to take his competitors when it's shake-out time. So I figured I'd swing by and see if he showed up."

"Good police work."

"It ain't anything intellectual; it's just knowing how these scumbags work. You gonna help us tie him to the Chinese?"

"You bet."

"Good, we might could clear up five or six cases at once. Look, right now there're some other fellas looking for you. So I'm gonna tell 'em I got you and you're still breathing, and see what they want me to do with you."

Dan said that was fine. He sat with his feet on the ground and laid his head back against the seat, breathing slowly and deeply and listening to the slackening rattle of his pulse, fighting the nausea that threatened to turn him inside out like a sea cucumber.

He woke to find Ogen starting the car. He lay back again, trying to marshal his strength. The nausea remained.

When the car slowed, he opened his eyes. The Hoover Building. Ogen drove up a back ramp into it.

Bepko was waiting, looking grim. A wheelchair stood on the concrete in the parking area. Dan fended off his assisting arm, limped for four steps, then gave in. He sank into the chair and gave himself again to semiconsciousness as they rolled him into and out of elevators and through carpeted corridors until at last they were in a large room with recessed lighting and several older men in gray suits. Dan couldn't see them very well. He blinked, shielding his eyes with a trembling hand. Attucks didn't introduce them, just sat down with them. Bepko remained standing beside Dan.

The FBI man kicked off. "Detective Ogen. Good work. Thanks for bringing him back."

Ogen said nothing, and after an awkward pause, Attucks went on. "We've just witnessed the failure of Operation Snapdragon, our maiden effort to identify and trap Chinese agents in the United States. We owe Commander Lenson thanks for his courageous volunteering to act as the link to this spy ring. Unfortunately, this time we were outmaneuvered. Now we've got to decide where to go from here."

He turned to where Dan watched. "Do you have anything to add? Anything you noted, or wish to contribute?"

He mustered his thoughts. "Could I have a drink of water?"

Bepko left his side. Dan took a couple of deep breaths, then stood. Swaying, but standing, he leaned forward and put his hands flat on the table. "You people left me defenseless. Told me I had nothing to worry about. Everything was covered. But if it hadn't been for the D.C. Police, I'd be dead right now."

They watched him, expressionless and lofty as chiseled gods.

He said, "All right, I'm not blameless, either. I wanted to confront him and I did. Unfortunately, I trusted you too much. So there's nothing more to say on that score. But there's something else you need to know.

"There were two Americans helping them."

The gods narrowed their eyes. Bepko came back. Dan sipped the water, then placed the glass on the table. It shook, and a little spilled, making quivering globules that reflected the focused light.

"One's a gang leader. His name is Hickey. Detective Ogen has him in custody. He can be charged with attempted murder. I think there's a good chance he'll cooperate in nailing Li for you.

"The second is white. He was in the car with Li. He helped evaluate the intelligence value of the documents I handed over. His name is Martin Tallinger. I've met him before. I believe he's passing information and advice to the Chinese, and not only that; he's assisting them in recruiting and spying."

The stone faces regarded him. He felt a wave of weakness coming, and swallowed, trying to keep from throwing up. Someone asked if he was absolutely certain the man he had seen was Tallinger. He explained about what he'd been wearing, how he'd recognized him.

"You didn't actually see his face, then? This is a conclusion based on hair color and so forth?"

"I didn't see his face, no. But it's him. He tried to get information from me before; he called me at work and —"

Bepko leaned over. "I think that will do it, Commander."

"Excuse me?"

"It's time to go." The NIS man motioned him to sit. He lowered himself unwillingly.

Outside, he said, "What did we leave for? It was just starting."

"They're starting, but *you're* done. We're gonna go get those cuts dressed, get an X ray on that head. Then I'll take you back to your apartment."

"I'm not leaving now. Not if they're in there discussing this."

"I told you, it doesn't have anything to do with you anymore."

He scowled and fumbled at the wheels on the chair. Bepko's arm shot out, pushing his hands off the brakes. "I said, you're not going back," he said, and Dan saw he wasn't going to talk or argue his way past the guy.

Only when he was hobbling back up the sidewalk to his apartment building did he recall the look in their eyes as he left. That hadn't been detachment. It had been suspicion, as if he'd been dirtied in some way by what he'd done.

# 33

When Dan told him what he wanted, Niles blinked slowly. The admiral didn't answer right away. He swiveled to the window and stared down at power diggers and lines of trucks, ripped-open earth, the renewed bustle of construction after the winter hiatus. At last he murmured, as if to himself, "*You* submitted your resignation. Of your own free will."

"Yes, sir. I did."

"And it was granted."

"Yessir."

"And now you want to withdraw it." Niles shook his massive head slowly. "We don't go about our lives that way. It's not professional. More than that. It's not fair to the rest of us."

Dan straightened, sucking a breath with ribs that still hurt from the beating. He'd figured this wouldn't be easy. That was why it had taken him so long to make up his mind. That, and going through the relevant personnel pubs to see if what he was trying to do could by regulation be done. He'd been nervous just calling Carol to set up the appointment. Now he was on the hot seat, and guess what: It was turning out to be just as humiliating as he'd feared.

Niles rumbled on like a cart over cobblestones, outlining how badly Dan had damaged his career. How this was exactly the kind of thing a promotion board read as instability, wavering, lack of dedication, lack of professionalism. How his Silver Star and his performance at Joint Cruise Missiles had pointed him toward increased responsibilities — until this. Dan sat feeling miserable, but he was determined not to scuttle before he got the word.

"And I have to add, this raises doubts in my mind, too. I know this hasn't been an easy time for you. But a professional doesn't let his personal problems spill over into his performance."

"No, sir."

Niles paused. He slowly unwrapped an Atomic Fireball. Dan noted he didn't get offered one — not a good sign. "You've changed your mind about wanting out. Have you changed your mind about working on nuclear weapons, too?"

"I still can't say I like them, sir. It'd be nice to find a way to get rid of them for good."

"Hunph. But the conventional Navy's good enough for you?"

"It's not that it's 'good enough,' sir. I've just gone through a period of doubt."

"How do you know you've come out of it? Are we going to see another letter from you next year?"

"I don't know, sir." He was trying to be as honest as he could with this man. "But I think that if we're not thinking about what we're doing, we're not doing what we ought to do."

Niles eyed the ceiling. "If you ever get command, Mr. Lenson, you can't put your doubts on display. In fact, you'd better not have any, as far as the men below you can see."

"I'll remember that advice, sir."

"I don't want to sound cynical, but I've noticed that all most people want is just to be told what to do by somebody who acts like he knows. And I'm not just talking about the military side of things, either."

"I'll remember that, too, sir."

Niles grunted again. He sucked at the candy for some time as Dan sat there sweating. From far below, the sounds of machines tearing at the earth penetrated the office.

Finally, the admiral said, "You've done a good job for me here. If you hadn't, you'd have been out the minute you opened your mouth about this issue. They tell me you were a material help on breaking this Chinese thing, too. I know you've been carrying Dale while he's been . . . sick. For a while, I was considering fleeting you up to his job." Niles looked out the window again. "Do you know about his illness?"

"He's discussed it with me, sir. I know he's dying."

"He's a dedicated man. I probably kept him on duty too long. But I can't any longer. His relief'll be here in a couple of weeks. I want

586

you to help break him in, get him oriented."

"Aye aye, sir."

"Anyway, here's my answer to your request. I'll look into it. What it would take to withdraw a letter of resignation."

That was his cue, and he laid the correspondence folder on the admiral's desk. "Sir, I did a little research on that. There isn't really any reg dealing with the situation. The consensus is that if I submit another letter, withdrawing my request, it will be considered. But it has to have the commanding officer's endorsement, recommending I be retained in the service."

Niles nodded, eyes hooded.

"I would appreciate anything you can do, sir," Dan said. Niles nodded coldly again, and Dan took that to mean he was dismissed.

After which he didn't hear anything. He called Carol two days later, asking if the letter had been forwarded. She said that it had. He didn't have any right asking what Niles's endorsement had been, so he didn't. He resigned himself and started getting his files in order for turnover. He told Westerhouse and his own guys what was going on, that he'd be history come June.

He kept going to AA meetings. He couldn't really say how, but it seemed to be working. The craving for a drink came now and then, but he could postpone it. That wasn't the whole program — there were steps to do, meetings, things to work through — but it seemed to be taking hold.

He kept calling Bepko, and Ogen, too. Asking how the investigations were going. Neither was very forthcoming, though Ogen said that Hickey was cooperating. And then one day, Bepko told him both Zhang and Li had suddenly left the country. There wasn't anything the authorities had been able to do to stop or detain them, although neither, of course, would be accredited to a NATO country again.

Dan had asked if Tallinger was being investigated. Bepko said they were working several angles, checking out the analyst and his company, checking out a lot of things; this was turning out to be a real complicated case. "His company?" Dan said. "Yeah," Bepko had said. "Kinetic Solutions, a consulting outfit out on the Beltway."

"I know somebody who used to work there. She didn't seem to like it much, quit right away. Maybe she saw something she didn't like." Bepko had sounded interested, and Dan gave him Sandy's number.

He hadn't gotten anything more out of the NIS agent than that, but he'd reviewed the conversation in his mind several times since.

He thought about starting classes again. With everything that had been going on, he'd had to cancel the spring semester. There were summer classes, but he didn't know whether he'd still be here this summer. He still didn't have any plans for what he'd do, or where he'd go, if they decided not to let him pull his resignation.

A couple of weeks went by. Westerhouse's relief reported aboard and started getting read in. Meanwhile, Dan got sucked into the all-up-round competition. McDonnell Douglas had finished setting up the production line in Florida, and now the Navy had to decide how to split the buy between them and General Dynamics. There were yield-rate analyses to prepare, quality control and reliability projections to do. On top of that, he had the normal plethora of meetings to attend, reports to vet, documents to approve.

He was standing in line at Roy Rogers with Burdette, grabbing a quick lunch before going to a vertical-launch progress review, when Sparky stuck his head in the door. He saw them and pushed through the crowd. "Admiral wants you."

"Who? Vic or me?"

"Both of you."

"Have we got time to grab a sandwich? We're almost to the counter."

Sakai shook his head but didn't say why not.

Niles was standing in his office. "Shut the door," he said. Sakai turned back and closed it as the admiral held out the message.

It was from COMSIXTHFLEET. Dan ran his eyes down it, noting the "Flash" priority.

Prime Needle was being reactivated. He looked at the final date for the attack, then looked again.

"They want us aboard."

"Yes, sir. But this strike date — it's twelve days from today."

"That's right." Niles looked grim. "Where did you leave the planning process? Was Norfolk still working it? Once they called the raid off?"

"I don't think so. Not as far as I know."

"You're going to have to go down there, walk it through personally." Niles looked away. "I don't like to task you with this, since you're practically out the door. But even if we had a relief on board, he wouldn't know what to do. Unless you have a problem with that."

"Sir, I've never not done my duty. And I retracted that resignation."

Niles gave the impression he didn't want to hear any more. He just said, "Your clearances should still be on file at EUCOM and so forth. Where do you need to go first?"

Dan thought fast. The first thing he had to do was check on the mission planning. "Norfolk."

"Who else, with you?"

"Sparky."

"Commander Burdette?"

"Vic's more of a hardware guy. He can hold

590

the office down while we're gone."

"Okay. What's the fastest you can get to Norfolk?"

"Probably best just to drive. If the Beltway's clear."

Sakai said his car was over on Eads Street. The admiral nodded. "Carol will get orders to you en route."

He read the message again, noting the addressees, then asked for a copy to take along.

Twelve days to strike date. He didn't think it was possible. But he owed the Navy that — to give it a try — even if he was on his way out forever.

# 34

Hampton Boulevard was packed, six lanes of traffic streaming out of the biggest naval base in the world as the workday ended. At a fenced compound, a marine glanced at Sakai's bumper decal and waved them through, pivoting his arm in a whip-crack salute as he caught sight of Lenson.

FICLANT — Fleet Intelligence Center, Atlantic — was three windowless stories of red brick. Niles had called ahead, so it wasn't long till they were sitting in an office, listening to a GS-14 civil servant named Bill Powell explain why he couldn't do what they wanted.

"I don't think you want to tell me that," Dan interrupted at last.

Powell shrugged. "You want to go over my head, be my guest. Yeah, I see you waving that tasker. As soon as it slid under the door, I told my guys to dig out the tapes and see where we stopped the effort. But we just aren't going to be able to get you what you want by the time you want it."

"You're the designated support activity."

"That's right, but it's not all we do. Even for this raid. We've got to provide the photo intel and so forth. But talking cruise, our primary responsibility right now is TLAM."

"So what's the problem? That's what we need."

"Our direction is that first priority is TLAM-N. Kola and Siberia, to support the Maritime Strategy."

Dan tried to keep his temper under control. What Powell was telling him was that they were so busy doing programming for nuclear Tomahawk, they didn't have time to work out routes for the conventional version.

"Look, Bill, I know you want to support the fleet as much as any other shore command does. If the hitch is that somebody at CINCLANT gave you a priority and you can't change it without their permission, tell me who. I'll put them in touch with Admiral Kidder's staff and we'll get that priority changed. But the way I read this tasker, I shouldn't have to do that. Emergent operational requirements take precedence."

Powell considered that. Then he picked up the phone and asked somebody named Alix to come to his office.

When she arrived, he introduced her as Alix Honners, in charge of mission development for TLAM. She was a civilian, but she got down to business as fast as if she was wearing a uniform. "What kind of targets are you talking about hitting, Commander?"

"Comm links. Missile batteries. Radar sites. And a chemical factory."

"This way," said Honners, and got up.

Dan, Sparky, and Powell followed her down corridors and through a vault-style door into a windowless room. They signed in.

"This is the SCIF," Powell said.

SCIF meant Special Compartmented Information Facility. Past the access controls, it looked like a combination between a stockbroker's office and a mainframe service facility. Lots of little cubicles, lots of computers, men and women in blues and khakis and a few Army greens and Air Force blues. The air was cold and smelled of ozone.

The Tomahawk Mission Planning Facility was a separate section in back, two rooms of consoles and light tables, scanners and computers. The floor plates were still up, showing newly installed cables and grounding straps. "I don't know just how much you know about the mission-planning system," Honners started.

He decided to play along. "Well, I know it's terrain comparison. You guys make up the flight profile; then the missile flies it."

"Right, but go back to the flight-profile part. This is a very *deliberate* weapon. That means everything the missile does — *everything* — we have to do first, right here," Powell said. "This isn't something, where we sit down at a personal computer and point and click. The system gives the planning officer access to the various data files — terrain-comparison matrix data, weather, target information —

*accurate* maps from satellite measurements, intelligence on air defense, radar coverage zones, et cetera. You can't put them all on one screen yet, but give us a year. We're sort of breadboarding it now; this is Block One hardware kluged together.

"Anyway, as we're getting all that mensurated topography and intel, we're thinking about the specific route. That part of it, you can't automate. We've actually got aviators who sit at the console. They're the ones who get you down under nap of the earth. When we have the approach route nailed down, we start rolling the ball. The system converts that into digital way points the missile can bump the actual terrain contours with as it overflies."

"Where are they?" said Dan, looking around. "The aviators?"

"We'll have them here when we're ready for them." Honners was at a terminal, tapping keys. "Then we get to the DSMAC attack profile. That's where we're not so smart right now."

"Why not?"

"Don't need that fine a terminal guidance for a nuke," Powell said. "Three hundred feet, that's close enough. But if you're handing us a conventional mission. . . . well, suddenly we need images. Photos. The more detailed, the better."

"I sent you a lot of that stuff. Before they

scrubbed the raid the first time. It had impact points. Damage overlays. What happened to that?"

"You weren't listening. You're talking attack planning; I'm talking what the seeker head's got to *see*. We've got to come up with a reference image. That brings our final accuracy down to thirty feet or so."

Honners said, "But there's another problem with that. Smoke, dust, bad weather. No see, no hit. Are these going to be the first strikes in? Or will there be air strikes previous?"

"These are the first weapons in. There shouldn't be any smoke."

"Dust? Rain? Sandstorms?"

"If his weather-guessers tell Admiral Kidder there're going to be storms, he'll postpone the whole operation. Nobody can bomb in a sandstorm."

Dan thought of something else. "What about DMA? They're supposed to give you digitized maps. Can't they help?"

"Not on Libya," said Powell. "Not now. Maybe three years down the road. We're gonna have to do those ourselves."

"North African section," Honners murmured. "We don't have it. . . . But I could get it."

"How fast?"

"That depends." Powell put his hands in his pockets. "You said something about getting this priority. Come through on that, and

596

we'll do your targeting for you."

He left a head-to-head with the commanding officer with a promise that if it was physically possible, FIC would deliver five TLAM-C route profiles. Two would be drawn on the targets near and inside Tripoli, two on the targets near Benghazi, and one on Sidi Garib. If time permitted, they would do an additional route to Sidi Garib, then an additional one on Tripoli.

He wasn't entirely satisfied with this. Using one route for multiple missions would make it easier for guns and surface-to-air missiles to target the follow-ons. But it was a start. Also, he suspected FIC was holding back on being too optimistic, for fear of falling on their face. In that case, he might get more than they first promised, especially if he could turn up the heat a little more.

Back in the lobby, Sakai asked him, "Now what? Back to D.C.?"

"We need to make some secure calls. . . . Let's do it now, while we're here."

Dan checked in with his new boss, at JCM, then placed a priority call to Sixth Fleet on the commanding officer's red phone. He checked his watch while the call was going through the switchboard in Germany. It would be eleven at night in Gaeta. A voice he recognized answered on the first ring. "Sixth Fleet, N-thirty-eight."

"Captain Friedman? Commander Lenson here."

"Roger, go ahead. Over."

He spoke slowly, so the scrambler could keep up. "We got your tasker. I am at FIC getting the missions planned." He brought him up-to-date on the number of routes. He asked Friedman to rate his top ten targets in terms of priority, and to get him as much planning data as he could.

"Can do. Give you a call back in about an hour?"

He keyed, then waited for the beep as the scrambler synced. "Yes, sir, I'll stand by. Also, I think some personal flag-level interest would turn up the heat here. Over."

Friedman said he'd see what he could do, maybe arrange a chief-of-staff to chief-of-staff call. "It's got to be done back-channel, though, because CINCLANT is dual-hatted to NATO. And this is not going to be a NATO strike, because everybody but Maggie Thatcher told us to fuck off. Over."

"Roger. Over."

"This whole thing would carry a lot more weight if we all hit Khaddafi together. Anyway, I'll see what I can do on that issue. Anything else? Over."

Dan said there wasn't, and signed off. He told Sparky, "I'm going to stand by here, wait for a call back. How about some pizza or something?"

The FICLANT commander said, "I heard you talking about the inter-CINC coordination thing. Your best bet might be just to walk down there. CINCLANT headquarters is right down the street. Big gray concrete building. I'll send an escort down with you. Current Ops is the guy you want to see."

Friedman didn't call back till late that night, but when he did, he had latitude and longitude on the launch baskets, complete UTS-coordinate way points, and prioritizations for the top targets. Dan passed those to Powell's people, gargled some coffee, and split a Chanello's with Sparky. The green peppers made it the closest thing he'd had to a balanced meal in days.

Alix Honners came in with a question while they were eating. One of the missions plotted out in a densely inhabited area. Dan said crankily, "They probably built it there for exactly that reason."

She stared at him. "What precisely does that mean, Commander? That we can feel free to kill all the civilians around it?"

He was instantly sorry. "No. You're right. What's the target number?"

"B54."

That didn't tell him anything, but when he looked at the coordinates, he blinked. It was the intelligence building in Benghazi, the one that had been 3-C in Gaeta. "I

599

thought that was scrubbed."

"Well, it's here on the list."

"I'll check on it," he said.

But shortly after that, he got a call from Captain Grady that made him think about something else. They wanted him back in Stuttgart for a command brief the next day. So at 0730 the next morning, Powell dropped him at the Military Air Command terminal at NAS Norfolk and he caught a C-5 to Frankfurt.

"We're here, sir. Sir?"

An official Mercedes and driver had met him at the airport this time. He stretched and grunted — he'd been asleep in the passenger seat — and checked to make sure his briefcase was still attached. Literally. The intel types insisted it be shackled to his wrist, just like in the movies. Sakai had stayed in Norfolk, getting smart on the mission-planning system in case they needed some last-minute expertise.

"Need a hand, sir?"

"No. Just . . . is there anyplace I can shave? Before the briefing?"

The aide, apparently used to such requests, shuttled him into a head, loaned him a disposable Good News, and sent the driver to the PX for new underwear. Dan hoped he was at least fifteen feet from General Stahl, out of smelling range. The aide stood inside the door the whole time he was shaving and changing. Then he took him up the back steps to the grandstand level of the Fishbowl, to join the other briefers for that afternoon.

Gen. Roland Stahl, U.S. Army, had a gray buzz cut on a wide, bony head, making him look like Emperor Vespasian. The other flag and senior officers came to attention as he charged in. Dan, standing in the rear, wished he'd had time to check in with Grady, see how the land lay before he extended his crank onto the railroad tracks. He fingered the still-damp photocopies of his briefing slides. He'd grease-penciled them on his way across the Atlantic.

Stahl took a seat in front. The deputy CINC, General Auer, sat to his right. To his left was an admiral in blues. The chief of staff sat to his left. The rest of the front-row seats the staff left empty.

"Let's get started," said Auer, turning in his seat to give Dan a hostile look.

A colonel in greens and a sweater kicked off. "Good morning, General, Admiral, members of the staff. This will be a quick brief to bring you up to date on COMSIXTH-FLEET's plan for the operation now called Arroyo Gold."

Dan stood at the rear, noting how the strike had evolved. More had changed than the name. It was larger in numbers of aircraft, in numbers of targets. It was a major effort. Stahl took most of it in silence, though occasionally he interrupted with a softly voiced question.

Then it was Dan's turn, too soon, and he stepped up and arranged his notes. This time, he was looking at the audience's backs; they were looking down at the screens and not back at him. He took two deep breaths and pressed the slide button.

"Sir, I'm Lcdr. Dan Lenson, Joint Cruise Missile Project Office. I will brief the Tomahawk segment of the strike. We are currently planning between five and ten missions, with between one and three missiles assigned to each —"

Auer asked sharply, "You don't know how many?" Dan explained the bottleneck at the mission-planning center.

"You're planning this back in Norfolk?"

"Yessir. Right now, that's the only operational mission-planning activity."

A question from Stahl, unfortunately in such a low voice, he didn't catch it. "Sir, could you repeat that, please?"

"I said: Why aren't my people briefing this?"

"Uh, sir, they requested I brief due to my familiarity with the —"

"If we're going to employ this weapon, I want someone knowledgeable on it on my staff."

"This is not yet a fully operational system, General," one of the colonels behind Dan said.

Stahl said sharply, "Why are we using an experimental system?"

Because you asked for it, Dan thought, but he didn't say that aloud. Stahl might have forgotten his remark to Niles. He said, "Admiral Kidder's people asked me to do this brief, sir. I'm also helping set up the mission planning, to grease the skids and make the strike date."

"Go on," said Stahl after a moment. Sweating, Dan bent to the mike. "Second slide, please."

Stahl listened without comment as Dan described how Tomahawk had been integrated into both the Air Force and Navy plans. He asked one question about retargeting, and Dan said it was essentially nonexistent. What the planning activity put out was what the missile would fly. He reached back to his supporting-arms experience in the Med to put the message across in Army terms. "These are like planned artillery fires, General."

"Oh, like planned fires?" Stahl remarked. "I'm starting to get this. All right."

"Yes, sir. Eventually, we'll have a satellite-transmitted update capability, but right now we're limited to canned missions." He waited, then went on to sketch out the routes and then the lay-down. He finished, "There's one target I want to bring to your attention. The intelligence agency building. It's located in the center of downtown Benghazi."

"How many rounds are you targeting against it?"

"Two, sir, currently, but —"

"Two. Is that enough?"

"Sir, that's not the point I want to make. Due to its location, I would like to delete it from the list. Not strike it at all."

A moment of silence and then General Auer said, his voice ringing out, "That's an important target from the psychological operations point of view. I think we should retain it on the target list, sir."

Several other voices murmured, then subsided. "I hear your objection," said Stahl slowly. "But it's apparently something we need to hit."

"Sir, I think that's a mistake," Dan said. "It's in a densely populated area. Fleet Intelligence Center concurs with that recommendation."

He felt the heightening of attention around him. Auer twisted in his seat to examine Dan. So did several other staff officers. Stahl sat without moving. "Go on with your brief, Lieutenant Commander," said the deputy CINC.

Dan hesitated, then said to the motionless green-clad back, "General Stahl?"

"I heard your recommendation. I don't repeat myself, Commander. Retain it on the target list."

"Aye aye, sir. . . . That concludes my brief."

He stepped back from the podium, smelling his own stink, glad to be finished, but also feeling doomed. Stahl had taken the responsibility. That was his job, and he'd stepped up to the plate.

The bottom line was that as much as he thought it was the wrong decision, there wasn't anything more he could do. As the others came to attention, he did, too, watching Stahl's iron profile as he passed them by, paused for a moment at the top of the spiral ladder for a low-voiced comment to his deputy, then disappeared from view.

# 35

He bounced from Andrews to Norfolk on a twin-engine Learjet assigned to the Vice Chief of Naval Operations. Meaning he napped uneasily in what passed for military luxury, a padded seat with a reading light. His body had lost track of time on the way back from Europe, so it had compromised on never being either fully asleep or fully awake. When his eyes came open again, he couldn't remember where he was. Then he saw the sail-dotted expanse of Hampton Roads sliding by below, succeeded by the bristling ranks of pier-nestled ships.

When he got to the Fleet Intelligence Center, Sparky was sitting at the mission-planning console. A Marine Corps major leaned over his shoulder, pointing out the best route to slide in under radars. Dan watched the pip move slowly down a valley east of the Algerian border. Then they looked up.

"Thanks for the shot at it, Major; this is my boss." The marine returned to his seat while Dan folded himself down beside a table between the consoles. It was covered with binders, maps, references, an empty Krispy Kreme box.

"How's the planning going, Sparky?"

Sakai rubbed his eyes. "I called you in Germany. They said you left already."

"I briefed, then got out of there. They still giving you flak over priority?"

"No. No, they pulled everybody off the nuke missions, got new Blackbird imagery; they're going balls-to-the-wall, far as I can see. It's something else. DSMAC. The damn thing's not far from being completely hosed."

That wasn't good news. The conventionally armed missile depended on the scene matcher for the final bore sighting the last mile or two to the target. He asked quietly, "Source or process?"

"Oh, it's process," said Honners, setting down a mug with a Wang logo, a tea bag's string dangling over the lip. Her cheeks looked flabby; unwashed hair hung in her face. "We haven't run it all the way through before. Haven't had to. Unfortunately, the code keeps crashing."

"What about the contractors?"

"First people we called. They're back there trying to get it running."

Sakai said, "We're pouring brainpower on this thing. I think we're going to be able to hand-massage it to the point we get the missions out. But there's a steep learning curve and . . . The point I'm making is, they're gonna have to take some shortcuts to get this thing done in the time frame the Joint Chiefs gave us. That's gonna give us a lower-resolution digital image."

"That could cause us problems with certain targets," said Honners, watching Dan.

Sparky added, "Also, we got another stinky wrinkle: The Air Force wants out."

Dan massaged his face. "What the hell are you talking about?"

"Call from Sixth Fleet last night. Verbal direction from Admiral Kidder, by request of Third Air Force. Delete all Tomahawk coverage of Air Force targets."

"That's crazy. Did they say why?"

"The overt rationale is that this is still an untested system. If we go in before the F-one elevens arrive, and we don't take out the air defense, then it'll be alerted when the manned aircraft go over."

Dan didn't respond right away. You couldn't impose tactics on the guys who had to fly the mission. But he knew the real reason. The same reason the Air Force had dragged at the traces ever since their shotgun marriage to JCM.

He understood, all right. He just hoped no one died because of it.

"You okay?"

"Sorry. Yeah, I'm okay, just tired. . . . There's nothing we can do about that. Have you deleted those missions?"

"Started retargeting soon as that came through. Figured instead of fighting it, we'd use those extra warheads to beef up the Navy half of the strike."

Powell came in. He looked as exhausted as the others. "You heard about DSMAC," were his first words.

"I was just getting that; we're going to see a degradation."

"Right." Powell explained it using the analogy of a gradually grainier photograph. "At a certain level of granularity, you lose the ability to recognize individual faces; at a higher level, you can't tell if you're looking at a person or a mannequin; finally, you can't make sense of the image at all. On certain of these targets, that may not present a problem. Sidi Garib's basically located in flat desert; if nothing else, we can aim using an offset from the image centroid. But the ones with a lot of clutter around them, the missile's going to have trouble figuring out which is which. Especially at night." He hesitated. "No possibility of making this a day mission?"

"Not a chance. The Air Force already pulled out because of the early-warning problem. If we ask for daylight, we're out of business."

They stood around the console, looking down at western Libya. The major rolled the ball slowly, intent on the topo lines and the colored overlay showing radar and weapon coverage. Meter by meter, the pip crept onward.

Dan jerked awake, looked at his watch again. "Okay, so we reorient. . . . When do we have to download to the DTDs? You run any numbers on that, Sparky?"

Sakai pointed to a penciled time line taped to the wall. "I worked backward from H hour. It ain't hard yet, but reading the traffic, I figure it's going to be sometime midnight to early morning on the nineteenth."

"That's good, but set it up in terms of hours for each step. That way, we'll know we're in trouble early enough to do something about it."

"Right," said the engineer patiently. "That's what these numbers are here, along the bottom."

"Good. How do we get it out there?"

Powell said, "I put my travel people on that. Commercial air's the fastest way to get to Rome. Sixth Fleet will need to set up a hop from Rome to Sigonella. Carrier onboard delivery from Sigonella to *America*; helo from *America* to *New Jersey*."

"Great, but don't forget the subs. That's gonna be half our load-out. Maybe helo the disks out to them, have them surface to pick them up." Dan massaged his face again. "I'll call Friedman back. Get them stood up to distribute the mission updates once we get them to the carrier." And ask him a couple of probing questions, he added to himself.

He got Friedman, but the captain said he couldn't talk long. They were getting ready to brief the pilots from *Coral Sea* and *America*. Dan asked him first to confirm that the Air Force was out of the picture as far as Tomahawk was concerned. Friedman confirmed that. "They want no strikes in their half of the theater. Nothing in Tripoli, nothing on Al Azziziyeh. That's a definite."

"Any idea what's behind it, sir?"

"I don't have grounds to speculate."

"Okay, my guys here are shifting those rounds to Benghazi. Have you got an update on your hit list?"

"First priority: The five command and comm centers. Second: the SA-five batteries. Third, the Tall King, Fan Song, and Long Track radar sites."

"If there's any last-minute intel from overflights, sir, we need to have that expedited to Norfolk. Especially imagery."

Friedman said he'd clean it up and put it on the wire. The next question he asked put Dan on the spot. "I'm getting questions from our guys, too. Which targets they can count on you to take out. Also, do we need to schedule backup Shrike and HARM strikes on them. I have to know that within the next five hours. We've got two hundred and ten identified radars in the strike area. We're making final decisions on which ones we jam, which ones we hit, and which ones we're gonna leave to Tomahawk."

Sweating, Dan committed himself formally

to destroy five targets in the Benghazi area and to put at least five missiles on Sidi Garib. Friedman said, "Now let's talk timing. We're planning H at midnight Greenwich, oh-two hundred Tripoli local. We've got to have an absolute guarantee your rounds will cross the coastline between H minus ten and H minus five, and that no, repeat *no*, TLAMs will be in the air after H hour."

"That's an awful narrow window, sir. It's gonna be hard to get salvos off that fast. And is that a firm time on H?"

"Firm as Jell-O. They're running the fly/no fly decision straight out of the White House. That window's all you're going to get. The whole key to success in this gorilla is going to be surprise. We've already lost strategic surprise, thanks to our friends in the press. We've got to achieve tactical surprise or we're going to be folding a lot of flags. It's gonna be one pass, haul ass. A lot of metal trying to occupy the same airspace. I don't want fratricide on your missiles. Guarantee me that, Commander, or I'm going to recommend we drop you from the Navy plan, too."

The fist was out of the pocket. Dan said tightly, "I hear you. No missiles in the air after H hour. Except the ones going south — right? There're not gonna be any U.S. planes down there."

Friedman agreed there wouldn't, and on that note, Dan started to sign off, until he remembered the original reason he'd called. He passed his requirements: dedicated flight from Rome to Sicily, carrier onboard delivery from Sigonella, helos from there to *New Jersey* and the submarines.

When he got back to the mission-planning area, Honners and the pilots were back at it. Slowly etching in miniature the routes that would take tons of ordnance hurtling across ocean and desert. In the back room, Sparky briefed him on how he and the contractors and photo intel people were going to grind out digital images from a system that wasn't supposed to be operational for six months yet. There wasn't much talk back there, just a lot of slack faces, blinking eyes, smoldering cigarettes. Screens and circuit diagrams, fault isolation logic, system manuals. A lot of glancing at the clock.

He looked at it himself. Oh-two hundred Tripoli time? That was less than seventy hours away.

He got himself another cup of coffee, and joined them.

# 36

Two days later, he pushed his way down the aisle of a 747, muttering, "Excuse me" and "Sorry" to annoyed passengers. He wore a polo shirt, chino trousers, and running shoes; he carried his uniform in a hanging bag. Dragging down his right hand was a huge green footlocker. Sakai trailed him, manhandling another.

He checked his tickets, making sure they had the right seats. Four across, all theirs. He took the left-hand one, Sakai the right. The boxes each got their own, snuggled between them. Behind them, Alix and a commander from the sub-launched side of the program escorted two more. Each DTD held all the missions they'd generated, plus the new Track Control Group software. One for each launching unit, and one spare.

He belted his in and collapsed with a sigh. The woman across the aisle glanced up from a paperback, then did a double take. Dan followed her look. The stenciling on the box read ORGAN TRANSPLANT MATERIAL. DO NOT X-RAY.

He reclined his seat and tried to relax as the passengers bustled about, stuffing twice as much baggage into the overhead bins as they were designed to hold.

Honners and the other mission planners had plotted ten routes. Two flight paths to Sidi Garib, and eight to various targets in the Benghazi area. One of them, unfortunately, was still the intelligence agency building.

He shoved that out of his mind — he'd have one more opportunity to get it changed — and closed his eyes, one hand resting on the case. A moment later, he was asleep.

Twelve hours later, he was in Rome. He slung the carry-on over his shoulder and lugged the case down the jetway.

A trio of Italian police troops in tan fatigues waited within the terminal, submachine guns slung. A U.S. Army colonel and two MPs stood with them. "Lenson?" the colonel said. Dan nodded. "Follow us."

"Hold up, more coming."

When they were assembled, the colonel led them through a separate aisle, bypassing customs. A uniformed man asked him something in Italian; he held up a pass; they were waved through.

Outside, the sun glared down. He no longer had any idea what the local time was, nor did he care. All he knew was that they had sixteen hours to H. The troops and MPs escorted them across the tarmac to a high-winged prop plane. AERO SICILIA, the side markings read. Ten minutes' wait for takeoff, and then they were in the air, rocking in updrafts, heading out over the blue Tyrrhenian Sea in a great vulture wheel that turned slowly south.

The carrier onboard delivery flight was a C-2, the ugliest, stubbiest little plane he'd ever seen. Lashed down inside were shipping containers, orange nylon mail sacks, sonobuoy containers. The crew trussed the passengers in so tightly, Dan could only suck shallow breaths. Then they were briefed on how to get out in a crash. They sat facing backward in the padded, cramped passenger compartment for half an hour, baking in the Sicilian sun, waiting for another priority delivery to arrive. At last, the rear ramp came up and locked. The plane accelerated down the runway, the huge blades on the turboprops humming like a runaway elevator, and lifted into the late-afternoon light. When he lifted the padding, he discovered a tiny port, through which he made out the crater of Aetna and, across the strait, the jagged violet mountains of Calabria.

Which fell slowly astern, then sank into the sea. Evening came as the plane droned on across the open Med.

He noticed that Honners, beside him, had beads of sweat sliding down her cheeks from under the protective headgear. She was staring fixedly at the tiny window. He leaned to yell, "You doing all right?"

"I really hate airplanes."

"It shouldn't be too much longer." He actually didn't know how long it would be. The carrier could be anywhere between Cap Bon and Crete. But she nodded, trying for a strained smile, and he patted her hand. She shuddered and leaned back.

An hour later, a crewman squirmed through, making sure they were still belted in, checking the lashings on the cargo. Dan caught sight of a white path on the sea. It ended at the familiar squared-off fantail of a *Spruance*-class destroyer.

"We're over the screen. We'll be setting down pretty soon now," he yelled to Honners. She nodded, eyes still clamped shut.

His ears popped. He was sweating, too, especially when he saw the carrier swing past the window. It looked small from up here. They steadied up, and the engines eased off. His stomach floated, and he gripped the seat frame. . . . Suddenly the engines went to full power. It was so loud, it sounded as if the props were going to tear off the wings and head off on their own.

A sudden giant hand pressed them back into the seats as they hit the wire and dragged to a stop. Too late, he reached out to where one of the DTDs had slipped its lashings and slammed over on its side. Not good. . . . The plane bumped and trundled over the deck. The ramp unlatched with a thud, swung down, and the cool sea wind blew in.

Friedman met them in the lee of the carrier's island. He got the subs' DTDs tagged and headed off. The other commander left with them. As soon as that was done, Dan asked him, "Is there any way I can see the admiral?"

"Admiral Kidder? What for?"

"I owe him a report."

As he followed the tubby flier in a steady climb, he sensed the excitement around him. Usually a carrier felt deserted at night, despite the nearly six thousand men aboard. You could stroll the red-lit passageways for miles and meet only an occasional roving patrol or off-going watch. But tonight, *America*'s flight deck was a carnival of colored lights, a bewildering demo derby of bomb carts and yellow gear as nineteen-year-olds in flight-deck jerseys and Mickey Mouse ear protectors jogged about. The same bustle of preparation was evident within the skin of the ship. It didn't feel grim. If anything, it was lighthearted.

The flag bridge at last, intimate and dimmed. He stood for a moment behind the man sitting there, looking down. Ghost gray fighters and attack aircraft rose slowly into view, then were towed off the elevators and jigsawed into ready positions. Blast deflectors tilted. A helicopter lofted in a strobe-blinking, blade-blurring roar-clatter. Beyond the flight deck was the darkness of the open sea. He was surprised to find the admiral alone. With only hours now to H, he'd expected to find him in flag plot, surrounded by staffies. But here he was, watching evening fall.

Friedman said, "Lieutenant Commander Lenson, sir. The Tomahawk officer." Kidder turned his head. Close up, Dan caught the heavy eyebrows, the bulky body in silhouetted repose against the activity below.

"You left me hanging till the last minute, Lenson."

Dan lowered the case gingerly to the deck. He rubbed his hand; it was cramping from the long climb. "Sir, we cranked these out as fast as humans and computers could get them done."

Kidder eyed it. "Are you saying those are the missions? In there? Neal, we need to get him out to the battleship."

"His helo's coming up, sir."

"They don't really need me out there, sir. The crew's perfectly capable —"

"I want you there."

All he could say to that was, "Aye aye, sir."

"Okay, what's our status? Are we ready to do this?"

He marshaled his thoughts. "Yes sir, as soon as we download mission data. We have ten routes plotted and fifteen targets covered. Most of those in Benghazi are air defense suppression, as you directed."

"Sidi Garib?"

619

"Covered by the submarines. Two routes, three missiles apiece, total six rounds."

"That enough to destroy it?"

"We won't see total destruction, Admiral. We're only talking thirty-six hundred pounds of explosive. We programmed horizontal approach and a twenty-meter airburst. That should give us max effectiveness against medium-hardness industrial structures. But destroying the power plant, the process equipment, the control center, it'll delay completion for years. *And* send the signal we won't permit chemical weapons to be introduced into the Mideast."

Kidder contemplated the intricate sarabande below them, the raked ranks of aircraft. He said in a musing tone, "So this is a historic moment. The first time we're going to use a long-range precision munition. Makes you wonder whether someday all that down there, whether it'll seem as dated as — what? Blackpowder carronades?"

Dan was going to ask him for something in a moment, so he thought before he answered. Finally, he said, "Hard to say, sir."

"Whatever, it'll be nice to have the additional capability — both nuclear and conventional. I suppose this means now I'm going to need a Tomahawk officer on my staff."

"Could be, sir."

"Want the job, Commander? When your tour with JCM is over?"

The offer blindsided him, and he came out with the response too fast. "Actually, sir, I'm trying to get out of the nuclear side of the business."

The instant it was past his teeth, he cursed himself. Kidder's eyebrows contracted like two hostile caterpillars checking each other out. "I guess that's my answer to that question. Okay, anything else?"

"Sir — yes, there is. The LIA building. One of the non-air-defense targets in Benghazi. The three closest structures to it are apartment buildings, and they don't look all that different from the headquarters. We had to accept degradation in our terminal guidance, in order to get the missions programmed in time, and it's not at its best in the dark anyway. To avoid collateral damage, in accordance with the rules of engagement, I strongly recommend we delete it from the attack plan."

"Did you raise that point with General Stahl?"

"Yes, sir, I did."

"What was his response?"

"He said it was . . . psychologically important."

"He directed you to keep it on the hit list?"

"Yes, sir."

"Well, I guess I'll go with his judgment on that."

Friedman was making cut-his-throat motions, meaning, Knock it off. Wrap it up. Let's go. Dan ignored him. He said stubbornly, "I'm not sure he fully understood what I was saying, sir. There's a very real danger, close to a probability, I'd say, of significant collateral damage —"

"He probably did," said Kidder. "I hear what you're saying, too, and I'm not happy about it. I'm the one who put those rules of engagement on the street, by the way. But at some point, you've got to seize the nettle. We've tried to convey our message to Colonel Khaddafi in a diplomatically acceptable way. He doesn't answer the phone. So now we're going to speak another language to the man. Our message tomorrow morning is going to be, Stop supporting terrorism, or we're going to ruin your day for the rest of your life. I believe I'll leave the plan as it is."

Dan stood without speaking, looking out at the horizon.

"Thanks for the effort, getting ready for this. I think that's your chopper they're bringing up on the port-side lift."

*New Jersey* was a hundred miles to the east, the pilot yelled back to him after they lifted off. Sakai was strapped in with him. Honners was getting turned around from *America*, headed back to Hampton Roads.

He pondered Kidder's reply during the long flight. If only he hadn't come out with that remark about nukes. Kidder had meant it as a compliment, asking him to join his staff. He should have thanked him, said he'd consider it. Instead, he'd flung the offer back in the admiral's face.

He didn't care, for himself. But he wasn't thinking of himself.

The pilot leaned back again much later, startling him. He pointed soundlessly down. Dan looked, and saw a shadow.

An immense shadow, blacker than the sea. Around its edges and from the stern swirled and poured a ghostly phosphorescence. The blue-green glow outlined the ship, defining it by the absence of light. He glanced up instinctively for the moon, then remembered: There wouldn't be any tonight.

The battleship was running without lights, and the way she was churning up the sea, she was at flank speed. He glimpsed another shadow miles away: a destroyer or cruiser. Then the helo canted, banking around, and the faintly lit helo deck came into view.

They bored onward. The luminescence unrolled beneath them like a moonlit road, swirling and roiling with that mysterious internal flame. Above it loomed the fantail, huge, bulbous, growing till it seemed broad as a city block. His eyes fastened despite themselves on the locating light above the helo's emergency hatch. If the pilot screwed up, misjudged his sink rate, they'd have about six seconds to get out before they were too far down to escape. Up front, the pilot and co-pilot were flipping through their checklists, discussing wind limits in calm voices.

The dotted white lines and deck-edge lights grew rapidly through the windscreen. Forward of it, an obsidian pyramid emerged from blackness. It was so dark, he could see the stars wavering and shimmering above the stacks. Just as it seemed inevitable they would crash into the uplifted barrels of the aft sixteen-inch turret, the pilot transitioned into a hover. Seconds later, the wheels banged down.

Perry Kyriakou, the missile officer, met them on the windswept deck abaft number three turret. It vibrated beneath their feet, juddering with the thrust and hammer of the huge screws far below. Dan handed him the case, glad to be rid both of the weight and the responsibility. Even when they were empty, his fingers stayed crimped in a painful question mark.

The Tomahawk officer led them forward. The wind was so strong, they had to lean into it. He craned his neck upward, hoping to see the after ABLs, but he couldn't make them out in the darkness.

Inside, the red darken-ship lights were on. Following Kyriakou down the midships passageway, he inhaled the shipsmell of paint and oil, food and damp rubber, the crowd smell of hundreds of men crammed close together without an excess of freshwater. She tilted strangely, rolling a degree or two, stabilizing, then a little more, till she reached the limit and started back. "She does that at high speeds," Kyriakou said when he remarked on it. "How you doing? You look beat."

"It's been a rough couple of weeks."

"Same here. Lebanon and all. Sweat pumps on the line. All we did was stand watches and sleep. And go to GQ for those ghost contacts."

"Well, now you get to shoot back."

"My guys are ready. We've simulated a launch every watch."

"Good. There's a lot riding on this." Then he noticed something different about Kyriakou. "Hey. Those oak leaves?"

"Thanks, yeah . . . I picked it up a few months ago. Not too long after the commissioning."

Dan congratulated him, but he still couldn't get those apartment buildings out of his mind.

"Anyway," Kyriakou went on, "CO wants to see you after you have a chance to wash your face. He's up on the bridge."

"I assume he's on his way to the launch box."

"Yeah, but not a straight shot. We're blowin' south right now. High-speed feint, darkened, emission silent. A Bulgarian intel trawler was bird-dogging us. Captain wants to get well over the horizon from him. All he needs to do is fire off a warning to Tripoli as soon as he sees the booster flashes."

Dan stopped for a second. "Silent? No radar, no TACAN, no radio?"

"Yeah, those guys who flew you out here were good."

"Great." He'd really have been worried if he'd known the guys in the front seat were flying blind.

Kyriakou let them stow personal gear in his stateroom, back by the forward stack. He gave them a couple of minutes in the head, then led them forward through the antiquated narrow passageways — not much changed since the ship had been built in '43 — and past more staterooms, radio rooms, and first-aid compartments and the captain's sea cabin, until they reached the bridge.

Dan found Foster eight levels above the sea, feet propped up in the glassed-in outer bridge. The wide sea was black all around them. The wind whistled through the open doors. The old battleship leaned slowly, in those strange gradations. He remembered how the other ships he'd served in had rolled. This felt different: deliberate, massive. For some reason, he felt nauseated.

"Dan. Good to see you." They shook hands. Foster's voice was soft in the dark. "Did you bring us our missions?"

"Yes, sir. The guys are downloading 'em

now." He turned to Kyriakou. "Oh, Perry, I brought you new track-control software on that drum, too. It's got the train-error thing debugged."

"Bring me up to speed on all this, Dan," Foster said, leaning forward to click on a shaded light. It illuminated the op order and the update messages, with *New Jersey*'s positions and event numbers marked in yellow Hi-Liter. "I don't have to know the minutiae of targeting, but let's go over launch time, number of missiles, salvo spacing. Just to make sure we're all singing from the same score."

The nausea grew, and he felt dizzy. He reached up, supporting himself with one hand from the massive steel shutters that came down during battle. "Aye, sir. The launch order's gonna come in by Anthracite message."

"Anthracite is nuclear. You mean Topaz?"

"Sorry, sir, I'm a little out of it right now. . . . The launch order and time will come in via a Topaz message. The window's supernarrow. You're gonna have to do minimal interval launch. Let's see, which of your launchers are nuke cert?"

"Just the middle deck."

"Then you're set. Just empty out each ABL, then go to the next. How, exactly, did you load? It's been awhile, but I remember you didn't mix and match."

Kyriakou said, "We've got three ABLS full of Cs. The rest are either TASMs or Ns."

"Or empty," said Foster.

"Yes, sir. With the dummy capsules."

Foster got up and went inside the armored conning tower. A flash, then the smell of pipe tobacco. When he came out, he said to Dan, "You'll be helping us out?"

"You don't need me down there, sir. Perry and his crew're perfectly capable of —"

"You were combat systems on *Barrett*."

"Yessir."

"I heard about that. Probably not the whole story, but no doubt more than I should have. And you've bird-dogged this from the get-go. I've all the confidence in the world in my guys. But I'd feel even better if I had you and Sparky looking over their shoulders." Foster trailed the scent of burley the width of the bridge, then said, "I'm gonna go back to the spook room, see if they're picking up anything useful on the coastal radars. Want to come?"

Dan muttered an assent, though more than anything he wanted to lie down. He kept a hand out to steady himself as he followed the skipper aft and down to the little intel compartment. And after a few minutes there, begged off and headed, back to Kyriakou's stateroom, where he fell into the lower bunk. The air was hot as the inside of a toaster oven.

Then, paradoxically, he couldn't sleep. He lay awake, listening to voices speak indistin-

628

guishable words on the far side of the bulk-head. Someone was hammering, far away, but the sound came clearly through steel, conducted to his ear.

Unbidden, resisted, he thought of others sleeping tonight. Innocent men and women. Children. Dark-haired little girls . . . like his own. He remembered how Nan's hair had smelled when he bent to kiss her good night. A smell like shampoo and bubble gum and a hard day of play. They were dreaming now, secure in their beds. In their families' apartments. A few hundred feet from where his warheads were aimed — with their hastily programmed, degraded terminal guidance.

He gripped his face in the dark, horror and shame closing his throat. Telling himself he'd done the best he could. He'd protested to Stahl and then to Kidder. True, he didn't know everything. Terrorist strikes might have been plotted out of that building. There were probably valid reasons for it to be on the target list. But that wasn't the point.

No, that wasn't the point, and it didn't stop the voice in his head that kept telling him he hadn't done enough. He hadn't briefed clearly. He'd been so exhausted. He hadn't said enough about the difficulty of hitting a low-contrast target. Hadn't explained the granularity problem, the degradation they'd had to accept at the price of producing a timely mission at all.

For a few minutes, he thought of going to Foster, having one more try at it. But then he thought, And what's *he* going to do? It was unfair to ask him to overrule a total of nine stars.

Lying in the dark, shuddering, he understood at last that he couldn't off-load the responsibility on Stahl, on Kidder, on anyone else.

He was the only one who understood all the capabilities and faults of the system. He'd helped develop it, had sped it on its way to an early deployment. Without him, it wouldn't be aboard this great ship, preparing now to visit death on unsuspecting civilians.

For whose death, it followed, he and he alone would be responsible.

No, *Christ!* Hadn't he learned anything from the disaster aboard *Ryan*, from Syria, Cuba, Kerry's death, everything that had happened in his life? He wasn't responsible for everything. That was egomania. He was nothing more than a gear in the machine, a link in the chain.

But without the gearwheel, how could the machine run?

Without the link, how could the chain hold?

He lay in the darkness, staring up. Then the moisture sprang into his mouth, and he got up quickly and bent over the stainless-steel sink.

He was back in the bunk, gut purged and

mind drifting, in a strange place where his brain seemed to have given up at last the habit and sickness of thought, when a tap came at the door.

"Mr. Lenson?" a hushed voice whispered from the passageway.

When he cracked the door, it was a face he recognized. A second-class, one of the guys from *New Jersey*'s Tomahawk crew. "Yeah," he muttered, wiping his mouth with the back of his hand.

"Sir, we got us a major glitch. Mr. Kyriakou wondered if you could come down and give it a look."

"A glitch? What's wrong?"

"The RASS. It won't download. We can't get a single byte of data out of it."

"Great." He actually had a moment of relief, till he remembered the pilots depending on the strike to take out radars, missile batteries. Along with the sour aftertaste of stomach acid, he tasted the bitterness of duty. "Yeah — wait a minute. Let me get my shirt on."

He remembered when this compartment had been empty, bare wires dangling from the old incandescent fixtures, bulkheads stripped to bare metal. Now it was inhabited, with the little touches men gave their work spaces. A sticker on one of the AN/SYK-19 control consoles read BATTLESHIP SAILORS DO IT WITH

16-INCHERS. A hand-lettered sign on the wall gave TEN REASONS WHY TOMAHAWKS ARE BETTER THAN F/A-18 PILOTS.

The clock on the bulkhead had a z drawn in Magic Marker on its face. The hands showed 2105.

Less than three hours to H hour. Less than two to launch.

Kyriakou, Sakai, the leading fire control technician, and a couple of the other senior enlisted were in the computer room. He said from behind them, "What's the problem?"

"Great, all the experts are here," said Kyriakou. He had dark half-moons under his eyes.

"I don't know how expert we are, but I'll take a look. Sparky, what have we got?"

"A possible showstopper, boss. The heads are jammed. They're not even going around."

"What stage are we at in the launch sequence?"

"We got the engagement order. The skipper verified it. He and the tactical action officer signed off on it. We went to system warm-up and started to load the missions. Then it froze on us."

"This is a pretty unforgiving system at best, sir," the FT chief muttered. "Like, up in CEC, you're sitting at the terminal, and if somebody reaches over you to change the display before you save the plan, it's gone. Negates the whole launch sequence. Same-same

632

if you hit two touch entry areas at the same time — it crashes. But right now, we can't get to the data you brought at all."

Dan looked at it. The AN/SYK-6A track data storage control center was housed in a standard equipment enclosure, a gray chest-high cabinet. It held the controllers, disk electronics, power supply, and a control panel. The door was hinged open. Two random-access storage sets, essentially big disk drives, were mounted one above the other. The bottom RASS was loaded with the operational program. The upper held the mission data. It was sort of like a personal computer, with the boot disk in the bottom drive and the data disk in the top. The disks, of course, were the DTDs.

He reached for the control panel, then checked his hand; the FTs would already have tried the normal casualty recovery procedures. "You're sure it's the heads?"

"It's locked up solid."

"Are the platters spinning?"

"No."

He stared at it, then closed the access door. He crossed the compartment to the engagement-planning console and stood looking at the screen. One of the men had sound-powered phones on. Dan asked him, "Ask your track control guy to try his touch panel."

"Doesn't respond, sir. The display's frozen."

Sakai said, "It's probably vibration. All that lugging around. Hand-carrying it through customs."

Kyriakou: "We don't have any backup."

"No. I sent the extra disk out to the subs."

The leading FT suggested, "We can try swapping it into the top drive. See if that makes any difference."

"It won't. The heads'll still be locked up," Dan told him.

But he was remembering a trailer in Canada. A freezing wind blustering outside, an Air Force officer explaining a procedure that wasn't in the field manual.

It might work. It might not. But if it did . . . it might be a way to do something else, too.

He felt his legs begin to tremble. It couldn't be coincidence. Coincidence didn't work this way. It was something else. What had Melville said? . . . Something about us being turned round and round in this world like a windlass, and Fate the handspike.

He sat down. His hands trembled on his knees. He curled them into fists, conscious of their eyes on him.

"Got an idea?" said Kyriakou.

"Clear the room."

"What?"

"Clear the room, Perry. This isn't a standard procedure."

They looked doubtful, but he glanced at his

watch to remind them they didn't have time to discuss it. Finally, Kyriakou ordered his men into the passageway. He hesitated at the door, looking back; Dan just sat, arms folded.

When the door was dogged behind them, he looked at Sakai. "You better shove off, too, Sparky."

"What you got in mind?" said the engineer softly.

"Something you don't need to know about."

Sakai sucked a tooth. Finally, he said, "I'll stay."

Dan didn't argue with him. If he was going to do this, he had to do it now, before he thought much more about it. He went over it in his head again, then said, "Help me with that lower DTD."

Sakai caught his breath as Dan pulled the plastic box out, held it a foot above the deck, and let it go. He picked it up on the bounce and slid it back in. "Reboot and see if that did any good."

"Still locked up."

Sweating, Dan pulled it out again. This time, it hit the deck so hard that they both flinched.

"You better take it easy; you're gonna crack the case."

"If we don't get it working, it doesn't matter how pretty the case looks. Try it again."

A moment later, Sakai said, "That did it. It's spinning."

He got on the console and called up the system status display. The screen unlocked and came up. His finger left a hazy dot of moisture on the touch-sensitive entry pad.

The screen blinked, changed, and came up covered with letters and numbers.

Across the top, a line gave him TLAM ENGAGEMENT PLAN. Some of the data elements were blank. Kyriakou's guys still had to enter ship position, initial launch direction, and pre-landfall way points. But the ID number in the upper left told him which mission was which.

"Give me that message board," he told Sakai.

Sparky handed him the board. He watched as Dan scanned down it, found the right mission, and called up that screen.

"That intelligence building?" Sakai asked.

"You're reading my mind."

"It ain't that hard to read."

"This is your last chance to pull out," Dan told the engineer without turning. "You don't want to be part of this. It'll just land you in front of the green table with me."

"I don't think I better, Commander. You ain't exactly a shit-hot programmer in Unix, as I recall."

At the mission screen he hesitated, unsure which way to proceed. Maybe the best thing was just to erase the flight data.

"The hell you trying to do?" Sakai said. "You're gonna dick this up. Believe me. You better let me do this."

Dan hesitated, then got up. Sakai took his seat, did something with the keyboard that he didn't follow.

Suddenly, the screen was filled with lines of computer code. Short, sure fingers skipped lines, then tapped in code. Skipped more lines, then suddenly ripped across the keyboard like a pianist doing a glissando.

"Jeez, look at that. Wonder how that garbage got in here," Sakai said. "Can't use this programming. Throw away two million bucks worth of missile for nothing." He hit several more keys, then went back to the display of the engagement plan.

Minutes later, he got up, still staring at the screen. "You can call 'em back in now," he said. "They still got a lot of work to do, and only about an hour to do it in."

Dan swallowed. His throat didn't work the way it was supposed to. He put his hand on the engineer's shoulder. "Thanks, Sparky."

"I been watching you try to make up your mind."

"I'm sorry you had to get involved."

"You gave me the chance to say no. But one thing I've learned. . . ."

"What's that?"

"You can't eat half of a jelly doughnut."

Dan started to say thanks again, but it seemed so inadequate that finally he just nodded.

When he undogged the door, the others were leaning against bulkheads, squatting on the green tile deck. He stared at their faces, still hardly able to believe he'd done what he'd just done. Wondering if it was the right choice. Then realizing that he'd probably never know.

"Okay, we got it running. Come on in, and let's get this show on the road."

# 37

At five minutes past midnight, the keen of a boatswain's pipe sounded all over the ship. He heard it in the combat evaluation center, where he'd gone after making sure everything was bedded down on the mission programming. The 1950s-vintage 1MC hissed and popped, warming up before it announced in a hollow crackle, "Good morning. This is the captain speaking.

"Sorry to interrupt your sleep, but in five minutes we will be going to general quarters. This will not be for drill. We are making preparations to launch Tomahawks. Our target is Libya, in support of a major air strike going in at oh-two hundred local time.

"We will launch twelve live missiles from the oh three level aft. If you are not involved, stay inside the skin of the ship. We will carry the launching live on channel five, *New Jersey* TV."

Dan drew half a cup of coffee into a paper cup and stirred in powdered creamer. He found a stool and set it down just inside the black curtain that screened the Tomahawk launch and track control station off from the rest of the space. Close enough to see and hear what was going on, far enough away not to be a player. He wasn't one, not anymore.

It was the ship's show now.

After he'd told Kyriakou the system was back on line, the crew had gone to work, building each mission from launch to landfall. Since that route had to avoid ships and islands, it had to be plotted aboard the launching platform, minutes before firing. Only when it made landfall did the missile's TER-COM programming wake. He'd been impressed with how fast the crew worked. What was that old saying — Practice daily with the guns? They'd practiced, and it showed. They had their missions complete and sent up to the launch control group twenty minutes before midnight. Now all that remained to do was to load it into the missile's computer, align it, and they could start the launch sequence.

Piece of cake.

*If* everything worked.

Squatting uneasily, he saw in his mind's eye what was going on all over the ship. Down and aft, armed marines would be standing by in the passageway while Kyriakou and the ship's exec unlocked and deactivated the alarms on the "wizzly box" and FTs inserted the plugs that completed the firing circuits. Other fire control technicians would be standing by at the computers that ran the launchers. Below them, damage-control teams would be buckling on breathing apparatus and checking their fire-fighting gear.

"Engagement plan, sir," said a radioman, thrusting a clipboard at him. Dan ran his finger down the hard copy.

"The original Topaz message?"

"Underneath, sir."

He flipped to it and compared the tasked missions in the engagement order with the ready-to-fire ones line by line. As he'd recommended, Kyriakou had retargeted the rounds earmarked for the intelligence building to a hardened command center outside the city. Captain Foster, the tactical action officer, and the surface-subsurface weapons coordinator had signed off. He initialed it, too.

The general quarters alarm began bonging, and he swallowed the last gulp of acid coffee and crumpled the cup. Despite the fact he actually didn't have anything to do, his heart started to race. He bent to tuck his pant legs into his socks, then exchanged his cap for a battle helmet.

In a way, it was just like all the hundreds of other GQs he'd gone through in his career. But in another, it was different. For the first time, a surface ship was going to strike an enemy nearly four hundred miles away. Submarines, too, would be carrying the war inland.

It was something that for fifty years only carriers had been able to do. If it worked, it would revolutionize naval warfare, and the balance of power at sea.

Looking at the closed-circuit TV monitor above the consoles, he saw figures moving around among the ABLs. Damage control-men, unrolling and laying out fire hoses. In case something went wrong.

Foster pushed through the curtain, waving everyone back down again before they could rise. "Carry on. . . . Perry, we ready to pump these things out? I heard something about a glitch."

"Mr. Lenson took care of it for us, sir. Some supersecret procedure of his."

"Okay. . . . We're on launch course, one-zero-zero at eight knots. Fifty miles to go on this course before we're out of the basket. No crossing contacts. The flight path is clear of aircraft, but be sure and check again before you execute final launch command. If you're ready —"

Kyriakou said he was, and Foster slid his tobacco pouch out. He held up a key. The missile officer took it wordlessly.

"Okay, I'm gonna get out of your hair now. Let me know if any alligators stick their heads up." The captain left, passing through the curtains.

Kyriakou was passing the fire enable key to the chief when metal rang down by their feet. Everyone in the control area stiffened. "Sorry —"

"Look out. Everybody back, goddamn it!"

"Don't kick it between the deck plates."

The chief was on his knees, arms extended, searching. A petty officer was shining a battle lantern into the corners, under the equipment. Almost immediately, the chief stood again, holding the key high. "Got it. Jesus Christ, sir! Back in your seats, goddamn it. Back in your seats."

Kyriakou stepped back, leaving the final preps to the launch controller. He muttered to Dan, "I was shaking the tobacco off it. Slipped out of my fingers. They ought to make that sucker bigger."

Dan's mind drifted, but his ear stayed tuned to the litany of commands and responses. He couldn't hear everything that was going on. Comms were going back and forth with the computer room, damage control central, hydraulic power rooms, the tactical action officer, the bridge. Throat mikes linked the console operators, and sound-powered communicators stood at their elbows. The white-backed binders he'd sweated over for so long sat stacked on the deck, yellow stickies marking emergency procedures: what to do in case of a hang-fire, a misfire, a 28-volt power loss, a booster-not-safe error, a restrained firing.

He hoped they didn't need them. But if they did, he was pretty sure he'd covered all the bases.

Two of the four display terminals were manned; the others were dark, but the seats in front of them were occupied by assistants holding pubs, huddled toward the active screens. Right now, they were deep in the initialization process, loading the complete missions into the missiles' computers.

Yeah, he'd done the best he could. But he just couldn't shake — and maybe he never would — the thought that, just maybe, he was devoting himself to the service of something that was by its very nature morally equivocal. He'd made his decision, that night beside the canal. But that didn't mean he'd never doubt or question it.

Maybe someday there would be a world where men could settle their differences peacefully. Where they could share, and be brothers.

But he just couldn't see how renouncing the ability to strike back could help them all get there.

The only way he could justify it was to make sure, to the best of his ability, that when force was applied, it was as limited, effective, and as just as tactics and technology could make it.

It wasn't a neat solution. It didn't satisfy his soul. It was a compromise.

But in the end, it was the best he could do.

Sometime later, he was recalled by Kyriakou's exhalation of relief. Tuning back in, he recalled the last thing he'd heard. It had been "OFP load complete."

"Going down smooth," the Tomahawk officer muttered. Dan got up and stood behind the console operator, who gave him a glance, then concentrated again.

"Start missile alignment."

"Watch the INS switch-over. WSN-five in manual switch-over mode."

"Hold on. I need to let the screen catch up here."

The 1MC crackled and intoned, "Now set material condition Zebra throughout the ship. I say again, set material condition Zebra throughout the ship. All personnel topside, lay within the skin of the ship."

Dan sat musing. Here he was again, watching the preparations to fire. He remembered the other times. In the Arctic, aboard *Ryan*. In the Med, trying to coerce a cowardly commodore. Aboard *Barrett*, looking across a calm sea from her bridge at the unmistakable silhouette of a *Krivak*-class destroyer. . . .

"TUL fifty seconds," said the phone talker.

"Call Radio. Confirm all whip and fan antennas silent."

"Launcher control remote mode. ABL unlock and elevate."

The monitor showed the marine sentries double-timing off the afterdeck. Now the aft flat lay empty, the long clamshells rising to point into the star-studded sky.

"Check ABL status."

"ABL green. Confirm blast exhaust doors open."

"Alignment complete."

"TUL thirty seconds."

"Vent closure warning. Status of Zebra?"

"Bridge, Tomahawk control. Status of Zebra?"

"Zebra set throughout the ship."

"TUL fifteen seconds."

Kyriakou reached out. He flipped up the cover of the salvo warning switch and held the switch down. The siren would be screeching its lungs out aft, but through the mass of armor between them and it, Dan couldn't hear a sound.

"TUL ten seconds."

"Booster arm command."

Past the shoulder of the men at the console, he saw the final prompt flicker onto the screen. It read RECOMMEND CLOSE VENTS/EXECUTE PLAN ( ).

"Give it Plan One and hit the execute," the missile officer said softly.

Dan got up and stood, almost hugging himself as his vision narrowed to the TV monitor. It was a good picture for a low-light environment. It showed the clamshells pointed upward, the sea rippling past. Even tiny pinpoints of light were visible, low against the horizon.

"Captain, we're ready."

Foster's voice came through the curtain.

"Tomahawk released."

"Shoot," said Kyriakou.

"Salvo firing commence," said the chief. The petty officer reached out, hesitated for a moment, curling his other fingers carefully out of the way; then tapped the screen lightly.

One second, two seconds . . .

A white flash blotted out everything on the monitor. Simultaneously with the loss of picture came an angry roar from aft. It didn't shake the superstructure the way it had on *Merrill*. There was too much steel for that. But they could hear it, a drumming waterfall of noise that gradually increased, then reached a peak.

"Missile in flight," said one of the petty officers. They stared at the screen, which showed nothing but eddying smoke. Then another brilliant glare wiped out the picture again.

He turned and pushed his way through the curtains. Everyone in the larger space, including Foster, had his eyes glued to one or the other of the TV remotes. He undogged the door, went forward, and ran up the ladder to the bridge.

He got there just as the fourth missile went off. Reaching the starboard side of the pilothouse, he was instantly dazzled by the incredible brilliance of the booster ignition.

Four off. He gripped the splinter shield, ignoring the ringing in his ears and the burning writhe of afterimages. He counted seconds, then realized the first ABL was empty. He was on the wrong side. . . . He ran across, almost colliding with the officer of the deck.

The fifth round emitted a blinding flash, emerged from the launcher, and hung in the air off the port side, a hundred meters up. It illuminated the sea beneath it like a star shell, lit the whole side of the ship, made gnomons of the five-inch barrels, casting stark shadows on their slanted shields. He could see the booster firing, but, strangely, he couldn't hear anything. Just like when he'd fired a pistol into the darkness. He raised his fists, urging it into the air. "Fly, you son of a bitch!" he screamed.

The missile began turning to the right. With horror, he realized it wasn't correcting. Its drift was bringing it back over the ship.

Beside him, the officer of the deck and the quartermaster of the watch stood frozen, openmouthed, faces lifted like shepherds to the descent of fiery angels as the missile rolled farther and began to spin.

"Left hard rudder!" Dan yelled, grabbing the man's arm and shaking him. "Come left!"

"Left emergency rudder!" yelled the OOD, coming out of his trance. "Port engines back full. Starboard engines ahead full. Take cover!"

Dan snapped himself out of disbelief. He spun, ducked, and joined the others inside the armored conning tower.

Slowly, almost immovably, the bow swung left. The missile hovered as if fixed in the sky, throwing light through the windows, where it fell in burning squares on the deck. He leaned against the citadel, peering out through a view slit, suddenly and enormously grateful for the shelter of seventeen inches of homogeneous steel. The officer of the deck and the boatswain stood at the armored doors, ready to pull them closed.

Burning in the sky like a nova, the missile drifted to starboard, passing directly over them, two or three hundred yards up. Then its rate of turn increased. It arched off into the night, obliterating the stars, and vanished from sight behind the overhang of the pilothouse.

They pelted out of the citadel. "Where's the escort?" he yelled. The lieutenant pointed, wordless, and Dan spun, to see her riding safely in their wake. He panted, feeling sweat break out all over him. A nonflier. One out of five. How many more —

"All ahead standard. Right hard rudder. Resume one-zero-zero."

"My rudder is right hard, resuming —"

With a flash like the end of the world and a howl like the heart of a typhoon, another two-ton round emerged from the aft ABL, climbed past them, balanced in that tail-heavy attitude that was a holdover from the days when it had been designed to climb not through air but through water. He stared, waiting for it, too, to overcorrect, but instead it gradually gained speed, pitched over, and shrank, climbing, till the fiery marigold eye of the booster winked out. He looked around for binoculars; the petty officer handed him a set. He searched the starry sky but saw no evidence of engine start.

*Flash . . . roar.* Number seven. Number eight followed, climbing slowly out over the sea, then vanishing into the multitude of stars. He clung to the rail, strength ebbing with each successive wave of sound. It was hard to breathe, impossible to think.

With a bone-rattling bellow, missile number nine emerged, back on the starboard side again. Smoke cocooned them, then blew aft. He recrossed the pilothouse on wobbly legs to watch it balance itself on a rippling cone of white flame, fingernailing itself into the sky with that terrifying deliberation.

"Ten," he screamed into a sound beyond all overcoming, unable to hear his own voice. "Eleven."

With the same eardrum-battering bellow, number twelve emerged, performed a heart-stopping correction maneuver, then recovered. It straightened itself out, pointed its blunt nose at the constellation Perseus, and departed into the sky.

He stood mute and motionless, till gradually a sound penetrated the ringing in his ears: a sound from deep in the ship, from behind him in the pilothouse, from below and around him.

The whole crew was cheering, screaming, pounding one another's backs.

Only he stood apart, staring up at where the last missile had disappeared.

The 21MC on the bridge woke. "Bridge, SWC: Salvo firing complete."

"Bridge aye." The officer of the deck snapped the transmit key and looked at Dan. "You okay, sir? Didn't suck any of that smoke?"

"No. No, I'm all right."

"Must be a good feeling . . . to be responsible for that."

He didn't have words to answer. He just nodded once and looked around again at the now-dark sea, at the darkness that surrounded them all, through which they set their course. Then he turned and groped his way below.

"Get that key back to Mr. Kyriakou. Stow and lock the ABLs. Close after doors."

He stood once more behind the curtain. The darkness inside the ship seemed different from that outside: protective, embracing. His ears were still singing, so he didn't hear Foster calling him at first. A petty officer touched his arm, pointing.

Foster sat with legs crossed, fragrant smoke

curling from the corncob. He said, "You were up on the bridge during launch?"

"For about number three on, sir."

"Here's the fire key back, sir."

"Thanks, Perry. . . . We saw one of them fly out — on TV, I mean — but it didn't seem to make transition."

"That was number five, sir. I'm familiar with the failure mode."

"We'll gin up the after-firing report, but if you could press an eyeball to it before it goes out"

"No problem, sir. Happy to."

"Perry says you saved our butts when the RASS jammed. Says he still doesn't know how you did it. There'll be a separate message back, about your indispensability."

"I'm not indispensable, sir."

"Humble, too." Foster grinned, checked his watch, and swung his legs down. "Well, *America* and *Coral Sea* should be just about finished launching the air strike. Now comes the hard part — waiting. Ted, pass 'Secure from general quarters.' Tell the bridge to come up to twenty knots and open the range."

Dan stood there after the captain went forward. He thought of going down to the computer room, checking how things had gone there. Or else of hitting the rack, finding somewhere to lay his head.

Instead of doing either, he went out into

the passageway. Down a ladder, making his way carefully through the eerie ruby glow of darken-ship lighting, then down another.

He felt his way through the darken-ship screens and let himself out into the darkness. Groped his way blindly to the lifeline, and stood there, swaying, buffeted by the sea wind as the battleship left her launch course and increased speed, swinging north to open the range between her and possible retaliation.

Save for the wind, there was no sound — at least at first. Then his ears sorted out other sounds, mingled in the rushing roar that was a great ship plunging through the sea. The crashing hiss as the hull sliced through the waves. A continuous deep sigh, like an ongoing breath, as air was sucked into the intakes far above. No other sound, and on the face of the deep, no other light but the far-off running lights of their escort, moving up now to take position ahead.

Above him, the stars; and among them, far to the south by now, the winged machines that for a little time had wakened from the sleep of inanimate matter, and for a little while thought and knew in their dim way. And after that brief consciousness would plunge downward, to die in a fiery bloom of destruction. Never having known, never having understood the reason for their existence.

Gripping the lifeline, he looked up at the constellations. He'd done it again and again at sea, but each time it was new.

They blazed and shimmered above him, clear and achingly brilliant at the zenith, watery and shimmery closer to the invisible horizon: stars that for thousands of years had guided men over the pathless sea. Here, far from the glow and stain of land, they shone down so close, it seemed that he could reach up and grab a handful.

"I hope I did the right thing," he said to their silent glitter. "If I didn't, I'm sorry. And you know, it isn't as if you gave us what you could call crystal-clear orders."

He looked up into the depths of the universe, and all at once understood something.

He was part of it. He didn't know clearly what part, or what his function was supposed to be. Only that, in some dim way, he belonged.

It wasn't a revelation, or anything like that. It was just a reassurance. And it didn't last. But he knew now it never did. It was only a glimpse, a moment transient as forgetting; a knowledge that faded away even as you realized it was there, shrinking in your grasp to the hard cold pebbles of dead ideas, the withered leaves of lifeless words.

He stood there for a while longer, and then went below.

# VI

# THE AFTERIMAGE

# 38

A week later, he stood in Niles's outer office. Carol was typing. He took a turn around the room, fidgeting. The latest issue of *Time* was on the coffee table. The cover showed an F-111 hurtling through the air. The legend read RAID ON LIBYA. He flipped it open, curious to see how they'd covered the strike.

Most of it was devoted to the Air Force. He could see why. The 48th Tactical Fighter Wing's odyssey from Britain to Libya and back had been the longest combat fighter mission in history. They'd lost one plane over Tripoli, most likely to a surface-to-air missile. Between that and the Navy strikes from *America* and *Coral Sea*, all the terrorist-related targets had been damaged, and much of Libya's air-defense infrastructure destroyed. The dictator himself had appeared only once since then, and he seemed shaken and confused. The article speculated one of the bombs had narrowly missed the tent he slept in. His usual strident advocacy of mass terror had been noticeable by its absence.

But to Dan's surprise, no matter how far he flipped, there was no mention of Tomahawk. No photos, no text. It just wasn't there.

Nor had he heard anything about it on the television news, or in the coverage of the raid in the *Post*.

Not that he couldn't supply the box score from memory. *New Jersey* and the two subs had fired a total of twenty-one missiles, all the TLAM-Cs in the Med. Two had gone haywire at launch. The others had performed as advertised, sliding in under radar coverage to destroy antiaircraft missile sites, command centers, and communications facilities. The incoming strike aircraft had arrived over a confused and largely paralyzed enemy.

Of the six missiles assigned to the chemical-weapons plant at Sidi Garib, five had completed the long overdesert flight and impacted within the confines of the plant. Overhead imagery had shown secondary explosions and fires resulting in an estimated 60 percent damage, setting back any production by at least three years.

According to poststrike assessment, then, the missile had been a raging success. But the only even tangential reference he'd seen in the open press was the allegation by Libyan authorities that some unknown kind of missile or guided bomb had hit a school west of Benghazi. They'd taken media representatives on a guided tour through the wreckage. But they didn't say exactly where the school was, so he couldn't tell whether it was actually a wayward BGM-109, or just a propaganda ploy. Fortunately, since it had been hit at 0155 local time, the school had been empty.

The apartment buildings in downtown Benghazi, though, would have been full of sleeping people. He straightened his back. No matter what happened today, he'd stand by that decision.

"Mr. Lenson," said Carol. Niles's secretary holding out a card. "Did you want to sign this? While you're waiting?"

"What is it?"

"Condolences. To Captain Westerhouse's family."

"Oh. I didn't know. When was it?"

"Day before yesterday. They said it was peaceful."

"Good," he said. "Peaceful is good."

She went back to typing as he added his name to the others. He hesitated, then added, *You can be proud of him. We all were.*

Niles filled the doorway to the inner office. He said to his secretary, "Give us ten minutes." Then he closed the door behind them.

Not a good sign. Dan took his seat, cleared his throat, and waited for his doom to be pronounced.

The admiral settled himself, passed a hand over salt-and-pepper hair. The trop white uniform made his skin look even darker. "Atomic Fireball?" he rumbled.

"Uh . . . yes, sir, thanks." He popped one into his mouth, instantly regretting it. He felt sweat pop out on his forehead, but sat back, trying to relax.

"Let's see. . . . We have several matters to discuss today. The first is your memo to me about your activities in respect of Arroyo Gold."

"Yes, sir. I still think —"

"Don't interrupt me. This explanation of why you altered the targeting orders in defiance of clear guidance from both CINCEUR and Admiral Kidder. The point at issue wasn't that it was in a populated area. The essence of your objection seems to have been the technical question of how well the terminal homing would work under adverse conditions. Instead of arguing it on a personal basis, you should have referred the matter to me."

Explanations and protests bubbled to his lips. He choked them back. Instead, he said in as dry a tone as he could muster, "Yes, sir."

"I have considered what action to take. So far, there have been no official protests from either Stahl or Kidder, though members of their staffs called me. And it may well be they're unwilling to surface an issue that might not . . . look well, should it come to public attention. So we may be able to put that to bed. Other than as it reflects on your own conduct. And that reflection is not a positive one."

He paused, but Dan couldn't think of anything appropriate to say. So he just sat, perspiring and trying to cope with the incendiary candy. Finally, he muttered around it, "We don't seem to be getting any publicity out of this thing."

"If you mean the nonrelease of information on Tomahawk's employment, you are correct. That wasn't my decision. I would have advocated the widest possible dissemination of this new capability. The policy was decided at higher levels.

"The reasoning, as I understand it, is that historically, the mistake commanders have made with regard to a revolutionary weapon is to disclose its existence too early, and to use it before sufficient numbers are available to determine the course of battle. Its psychological impact is lost. The enemy has time to develop countermeasures. The next time we use this missile, it will be in overwhelming numbers. We will paralyze the enemy's air defense, destroy his electric generating grid, and decapitate his command structure. Win the war before ground troops are even committed. Vice Admiral Willis has discussed this with the heads of the appropriate congressional committees. Now that they've seen what we can do, the funds will be there.

"So, for now, our direction is not to showcase its employment in this operation. And in fact, that use is classified and will not be discussed outside official channels."

He nodded slowly. It was disappointing. But it made sense.

"At any rate, to return to the matter at hand. . . . I am also in receipt of a rather . . . fulsomely complimentary message here from Captain Foster, saying that the raid could not have gone in without you, and that during it you also assisted his officer of the deck in saving the ship from possible damage."

Dan waited, not responding to that. And apparently, that was the right thing to do, because Niles leaned back and closed his eyes. Dan studied the freckled lids, wondering what was going on behind them. In a moment or two, he'd know. He had a feeling he wouldn't like it, but at least the waiting would be over.

Niles grunted. "You present me with a difficult decision. The response has come back to your letter withdrawing your resignation."

"Yes, sir?"

"I endorsed it, recommending approval. That, of course, was before this latest defiance of the chain of command."

"It wasn't defiance, sir."

"Shut *up!*" Niles's huge hands slammed down flat on the desk, so hard that they boomed like gunfire. "It was defiance and it was disobedience! Don't call it anything else, because you're damned lucky you're not sitting in front of a green table right now! And you still might, if what I'm trying to satisfy them with is not enough!"

Dan sat motionless, tracking a single drop of sweat as it trickled slowly down from above his ear, down his neck, and under his collar. Finally, he bent his head, tongued out the pale core of the Fireball, and cradled the sticky sphere in his palm. Niles stared at him for some seconds, then subsided gradually back into his seat.

"Your letter was approved."

"The, uh, the one withdrawing my resignation?"

"Correct. But I personally do not think you belong here at JCM. Due to your expressed doubt about nuclear systems, your loose-cannon approach to direction, and also to questions that have been raised about your security clearance."

"What about my security clearance, sir?"

"There seems to be lingering suspicion you may still be involved in some way with the Chinese."

He gaped. " 'Still involved' — sir, I was the one who notified the FBI of the approach!"

"I understand that, and I think they're mistaken on that score. But Caesar's wife must be above suspicion. We are also vulnerable because of the revelations about Colonel Evans."

"Colonel *Evans,* sir? I must have missed those. What revelations are —"

"Of course you missed it — you've been overseas. The investigation's still tearing up the roots that lead out from this Tallinger fellow. He's got a lot of associates, a lot of contacts. Some apparently blameless, such as your professor at George Washington. Others who turned away when they realized what he was doing. Like the Cottrell woman. But others who were not so innocent. Including Scott Evans."

"I'm not sure I understand, sir. Are you saying Colonel Evans was — are you saying *he* was the one passing information to the Chinese?"

"Not exactly. But that was the end result. I don't believe for a moment that Bucky knew that was what was actually happening. He was playing the game for his service. Trying to block our touchdown by leaking adverse data to the press and to Congress via Tallinger and his lobbying association. Even passing certain maps on to those who could use them to embarrass the project, apparently. He didn't do it for himself. He never benefited personally, never took payment or anything like that.

"What he didn't know was that Mr. Tallinger was sharing everything he gave him with Beijing. Unfortunately, that's going to cost him his star."

Dan sat frozen, trying to understand. Trying to visualize the slim, straight fighter pilot as someone who would undercut the project in the interests of his service. "He's not going to be promoted, sir? I thought that was imminent."

"No. He's retiring, and under a cloud. I'm

not condoning what he did. Loyalty pursued too far is as bad as none at all. But it's the way the game is played in this town, unfortunately. Another unfortunate result is that it doesn't look as if Tallinger can be prosecuted."

Dan sat up, astonished again. "What are you telling me, sir? He passed data to the Chinese; he was there when they abducted me; he advised them on what I gave them."

"I'm not entirely clear on the specifics, but apparently the evidence wasn't strong enough actually to go to indictment. Or perhaps there are those who didn't want it to go to indictment. Whatever the reason, a deal was made: his cooperation for immunity, and the dismantling of what seems to have been a very capable and dangerous espionage apparatus."

"Wait a minute. You're saying — what? That he walks away?"

"It's a complex matter. But that's not the point. Let's get back to you. The point is, this is too sensitive a program to signal to the security people that I don't take them, and their concerns, seriously."

"Sir, this is unfair. Whatever I've thought, or done, I've never wavered in my dedication to my country."

Niles cleared his throat. "I hear you, Dan. And I believe you. But the bottom line is this. In view of all the above, I have requested that you be reassigned. Carol has your orders,

transferring you to J-Three as an action officer, effective Monday. Your relief will report
aboard tomorrow. You will give him a complete and thorough briefing, introduce him to
your coworkers, and turn over all your files
and working documents."

Dan sat still as stone, unable to speak. Niles
heaved himself up and went to the window.
He spoke facing away, looking out at the towers of Crystal City, and his voice was different
from how Dan had ever heard it before. It
was soft, almost sad.

"I'm sorry to have to do this. All in all, you
did a good job for me. I will include that in
your detachment fitness report. You've damaged your career, but perhaps not irretriev-
ably."

Silence followed. Till Dan forced himself
to his feet. "Am I dismissed, sir?" he said
tonelessly.

"Perhaps we will meet again, under happier
circumstances. Good luck, Mr. Lenson. That
is all."

He stood in the orange-carpeted corridor,
trying to make sense of it.

On the one hand, he was still in the Navy.

On the other, he'd been fired. He remembered how Munford had sat despairing when
Dan had relieved him. A relief in midterm
meant just one thing. And every selection
board saw it in your record.

And what was this bullshit about his clearance? He was the one who'd alerted them to the attempt to penetrate the program! He should have obeyed his instincts, never gotten near the thing.

Yet he couldn't deny a certain irony to it. The machine that sucked in men and dollars and spat out weapons had ingested him. He'd given it his best, and it had chewed him up and now had vomited him out.

Only one man had walked out unscarred.

Moving like a robot, he went down to his office. Sakai was there, packing up his desk. "Sparky. Where you headed?"

"Back to Dahlgren. This project's operational; I'm done here."

"I guess I'm on my way out, too." He shook the engineer's hand one last time. "It's been good working with you. Thanks — for everything."

"No sweat, man. Have a nice life."

Dan left, not looking back.

Moving like an automaton, he got on the Metro. He rode it unseeing, then got up as the Courthouse exit neared.

Then remained standing. He stayed on past Clarenden and Virginia Square, past Ballston, and got off at Falls Church.

The building was huge and anonymous, set down like a visiting spaceship on what not long before had been rolling farmland. The lobby was pink granite and tinted glass, lofty and shining like some godless cathedral. The list of corporate tenants was engraved in gold.

A carefully coiffed black woman beneath an enormous, vaguely erotic modern painting welcomed him to Kinetic Solutions and asked with whom his business was. He said, "Does Martin Tallinger work here?"

"Dr. Tallinger is one of our principals."

"Is he in?"

She hesitated, examining his uniform. "Can I ask what it's about?"

"Personal matter." He held up his briefcase. "I have something for him."

"Certainly, sir. Second door on the left. Let me announce you."

But he was already striding down the hushed corridor.

Tallinger was sitting with elbows on his desk, head in his hands, staring at a laptop computer with the battery pack taken out. He wasn't wearing the orange suspenders and bow tie, but a rumpled white shirt and a rep tie. He glanced up when Dan came in, looking boyishly annoyed. Then his eyes widened. "What do you want?" he said.

"A personal matter," Dan said. "They told me you aren't going to be prosecuted for being an accessory to Kerry Donavan's death, or for helping Li Chenbin spy on my program. So I thought we'd discuss it man-to-man."

Tallinger cleared his throat. He pushed his

chair back. "How did you get in here?"

"Walked in. Like Bucky Evans probably walked in. Not knowing you were turning everything he gave you over to the Communists. And helping them look for more."

Tallinger smiled faintly, though he still looked alarmed. " 'The Communists.' The Chinese are on our side, Dan. Have been for some time now."

"Is that right? Talk to me. Make me understand."

"Well . . . I suppose you know I was with the government at one point. There's still a linkage there, contacts." Tallinger ran his hands through his hair, adjusted his tie. "I can explain this, you see. Not about your fiancé, of course. But that wasn't my fault. There are important interests to be promoted. China's an enormous market — for U.S. aircraft, arms, computer equipment. Enormous possibilities."

He must have read something in Dan's face then, because he added hurriedly, "But strengthening China serves our national security interest, too — as a counterweight, a force for stability in Asia. Part of that is building trust. You build trust with information. Everything I've done was done with the knowledge of key elements of the administration, as well as other governmental leaders and bodies."

"Building trust with information. Information about missile technology. So they can sell

669

it to Iran, and North Korea?"

"No classified information was passed."

"Don't say it didn't happen. I saw you in the front seat, just before they handed me over to their executioner."

Tallinger spread his hands. "Look, Commander, I hope they convict the man who threatened you. Hickey, wasn't that his name? But you've got my role in this wrong. All I ever did was to represent the interests of my clients. That's our business here at Kinetics — to forge profitable linkages instead of competing interests. Our attorneys have met with special agent Attucks. He tried to make a case. And he couldn't persuade his superiors he had one. I would think that ought to convince you that I've done nothing wrong — nothing that would stand up in court."

Tallinger seemed to have regained his confidence. He smiled up at Dan, his initially apprehensive expression changing second by second into one of triumph.

There was a sound at the door. The receptionist peered in, a wary frown compressing her lips. She was holding two cups of coffee.

He hadn't planned what he was going to do. Hadn't planned any of this. Just gone on from moment to moment. But now, seeing that smile, he sucked the inside of his cheek in and bit down. The pain was incredible as his teeth sheared through the soft flesh. He waited, feeling the salty slickness gather under his tongue as they stared at him.

Then he grabbed the other man's tie and jerked him up over the desk, letting the leash slack for just a moment on the beast that wanted to kill. Computer parts scraped and skittered. Tallinger struggled, but not hard.

His upturned face looked shocked and resigned as Dan spat full into it, spittle and fresh blood mixed.

He rode the Metro back to his apartment. He walked home unseeing though the summer heat, stopping only once, at the 7-Eleven on the corner.

In his apartment, he put the six-pack of beer on the coffee table, went to the bedroom, and took the pistol out of the bureau. He held it for a moment, balancing its solid, deadly weight, then checked the magazine and racked the slide. Loaded. He carried it back into the living room, and laid it, too, on the table in front of the futon. After a second, he got up again, found the phone, and carried it over. Then he sat down, facing the three objects.

He could get drunk.

He could pick up the gun.

Or he could pick up the phone and call his AA sponsor. Was it possible to talk it out, this feeling of doom and waste and grief? He'd fought it since the day Kerry died. It had retreated when he plunged into work with the desperation of one who knows if he ceases to flail, he will sink. But now it was back, cold and choking as an Arctic fog.

Sometimes he didn't want to live.

Outside the window, the day dimmed, turning toward dusk, and the blue deepened until it was violet and then black. Still he sat motionless, staring at the table.

Till he made his choice, and picked up the phone.